William of Archonia
Volume I
REDEMPTION

A novel

By
Jarod Meyer

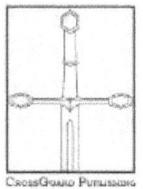

CrossGuard Publishing

CROSS-GUARD PUBLISHING
Iowa

A product of CROSSGUARD PUBLISHING
Cover art: Andrey Vasilchenko
Cover design: Jarod Meyer
Editor: Aaron Bunce
Map Design: Jarod Meyer

TRADE PAPERBACK ISBN: 978-1-7341420-0-6
AMAZON KINDLE EDITION:

3rd Edition. 2019

A NOTE FROM THE AUTHOR

Many people of many different faiths believe that God guides our footsteps, and has a plan for us. Perhaps God's plan for me was to write these books.

I want to remind everyone that this fictitious story was written to entertain and capture the imagination of readers everywhere. This wonderful world is one of the innumerable possibilities that the next life may hold.

It is my goal to have every person that reads these books maintain their unique faiths or creeds. Spread kindness, joy, and live your life unselfishly. I hope you enjoy the story.

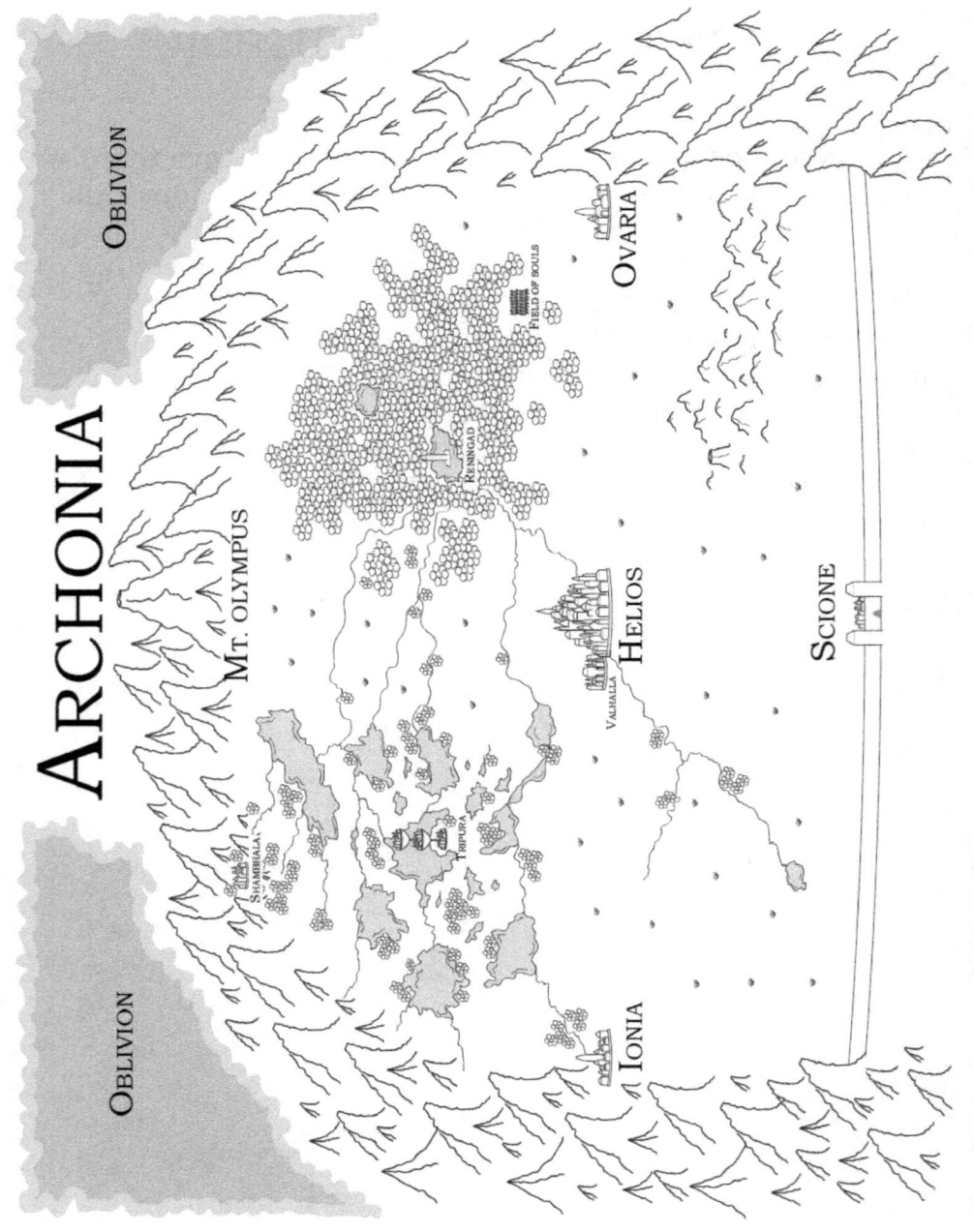

ARCHONIA

OBLIVION

OBLIVION

MT. OLYMPUS

SHAMBHALA

TRIPURA

RENNGAD

FIELD OF SOULS

VALHALLA

HELIOS

OVARIA

IONIA

SCIONE

4

PROLOGUE

Three days and nights marching left William exhausted. His feet throbbed in protest to every step, and his back ached. Not to mention the bug bites and heat rash from tromping through the dense, unyielding jungle. A fat bead of sweat ran down his face, through his eyebrow, and into his eye.

"We stop here for the night," his lieutenant said, before wandering off into the trees.

Probably gotta piss...probably gonna get himself lost, William thought, watching the academy-green officer stagger off. His sergeant took over.

"Bill, you're first watch. No fires, no noise. If you take a shit, I don't want to hear the turd hit the ground. We move out at oh four hundred."

William unstrapped his pack, and plopped down in between the roots of a large tree, the soil squelching under his buttocks, forming a sodden cushion. He stowed his rifle, before rummaging through his pack for an MRE. He pulled one out. It was already open, the stale candy still waiting patiently for him.

The chocolate went down easily, chased by a large drag from his canteen. William stowed the water and dug around in his front pocket for his last cigar. He bit off the end and stuck it in his mouth, shifting from side to side to get settled in.

William chewed on the cigar, the air filling with the lulling buzz of insects. Sweat ran down his neck and back. The heat and humidity pressed down upon him like a blanket. A rat scurried somewhere nearby, rattling leaves and twigs. Martinez, the smallest man in his unit, hummed quietly from somewhere behind him. It was the same song...every time.

Shut up! he thought irritably, turning away and fumbling absently for his zippo. Yeah, that's right. No fire. Damn it.

He didn't actively fall asleep, but at some point his exhaustion-riddled brain slid from consciousness, and the swampy forest faded away around him. Thoughts faded too, sliding into something more basic, more primal even.

The darkness gave way to a light gray, gradually lightening until the world around him was vivid and bright. His hand relaxed and fell to his side, where it brushed against the tassels of long, white grass. His body cast a shadow twice its length in front of him. A cool breeze kissed his face as it moved over the sprawling hills before him, rippling in the bending shoots. He trudged through the untouched fields, no person, or creature within sight. The grass crunched softly under his feet. Some part of William's mind told him that it wasn't real, but every other part of him argued the notion. It felt real, so to him, it was.

The horizon loomed black and ominous, clouds moving swiftly by, ushering in a storm. The air pressure changed, the breeze around him suddenly dying away. He tried to fortify his anxious mind, willing himself forward, accepting the approaching darkness.

It meant something to him, something profound, but he couldn't remember what? Something...everything was at stake, some part of him believed. It compelled him forward, towards the churning, angry clouds.

A flash cut across the sky, his heart beating loudly in his ears. His body tensed as the ground shook, the air splitting from the mighty crack issuing across the plains. He exhaled, letting out the breath he had been holding, and his body relaxed again. Then the sea of white grass began to move violently, a cold, gale force wind rushing over him. William's skin prickled, causing a violent shiver to run through his body.

Two more flashes, but this time he was prepared, and the deafening roar didn't frighten him. The ground rumbled longer and louder this time, reverberating up through his body. The murky clouds bubbled and churned towards him, looming so big they blotted out everything else. He planted his feet, preparing for its violence.

The air rushed over him, covering him in its raw, violent purpose. Somewhere deep inside, buried beneath the disappointment, anger, and regret, a small voice told him that this is what he had been born to do. All the years and battles he fought and won led to this moment.

Lightning flashed right in front of him, momentarily blinding his eyes and sending him recoiling. He covered his face with his arms in response. But no thunder rolled over him, and when he lowered his arms a glistening sword hung in the air before him.

It was a magnificent blade, gleaming brightly in the lightning arcing overhead. It hung invitingly, its hilt leaning just slightly towards him, exhibiting the intricate etchings in the fuller. Without thought, William reached out and clasped the black leather grip firmly, sliding his hand right up to the handguard. The pommel, shaped like wings, lay upon his wrist, each feather perfectly detailed in the blued steel.

The weight of the sword bore down upon his arm, his muscles flexing in response. Just as it did, the sky opened up in a maelstrom of fury, descending upon him in an unforgiving, merciless torrent.

CHAPTER ONE
LIFE

Faith is the idea that there exists something that cannot be seen, touched, smelled, felt, or heard. Humans of all shapes and sizes have placed their hope in this idea for thousands of years. For humans are mortal, and they all must depart from this world in one way or another. For a man named William, there was no such faith. For as long as he could remember, life had not been kind.

Born into this world to an angry father, he was raised without love, and therefore, was doomed to fail. His entire life he had felt disconnected from society, like he didn't belong. No matter how hard he tried, he could never get ahead. He was doomed to be an outcast.

William sat in a wooden chair. The back was broken clean off. He blinked sluggishly, trying to decide whether he should even bother making the long trek to work. As he debated, a train rumbled by somewhere outside his dingy apartment, shaking dust and debris loose from the ceiling.

William struggled to define his living space as an apartment. It was one small room with a grimy, soot covered window, and he was forced to share a filthy little bathroom with five other people. It was a wretched space on the verge of being condemned. His only solace was in the fact that he had a roof over his head.

He coughed and splashed water from an old coffee cup on his unshaven face, which was covered in black soot as well. He hadn't even bothered with a shower the previous night. There was a line at the bathroom, and he wasn't in the mood to wait after his fourteen-hour shift. He was still probably cleaner than the shower.

His thirties had not been kind to him thus far. His long, unkempt hair was showing as much neglect as his apartment.

William looked over at the small, battered clock radio sitting on a chair in the opposite corner. It was blinking 12:00 AM. The faulty power supply to the building had probably made it reset during the night. It made his stomach twist. He'd received warnings from his boss already about being late, and agreed to work more hours to make up the time.

William slowly stood and wiped at the greasy dust on the window until he could see outside. The sun hung just above the horizon, beckoning him out of his dingy apartment.

What's the point? he thought, letting his mind wander back to his paltry bank account.

Despite all of the overtime he worked, he could still barely afford to feed himself. It didn't help that the court was busy garnishing most of his wages. It felt fruitless, but William didn't want to starve, so he mustered up his courage, grabbed his hard hat, and left.

As he went down the dangerously shaky steps to the first floor, he crept softly to avoid attracting the attention of his landlord who had been demanding his last month's rent. He walked carefully, but wasn't looking down when he tripped on a homeless man sleeping in the hallway. He fell to the floor with a crash, and his breath left him. Sucking for air he only found dust and dirt.

William heard the familiar rustling of rapid footsteps. He finally caught his breath and looked up in time to see an abnormally tiny pair of slippers. His landlord was a small man, with greasy, curly hair, and a squat, bulbous nose. He was an extraordinarily ill-tempered person.

"That's two weeks your rent has been due. Not to mention last month's. You're done, Bill. Don't bother coming back, the locks will be changed," the short, sweating man said. He was in a bathrobe and looked, if possible, less hygienic than William did after a full day's work.

William sighed, biting his tongue as he walked past the wretched little man. At least now he was his ex-landlord. There was only one good thing about today. It was the last day of the work week. He would have a free night ahead of him.

He stepped outside, taking in the cool, autumn air. It felt fresh, and clean. He ducked around his building, jumped over a fence, and stepped out onto a lonely dirt road. After a lengthy walk, he found himself at a site far from normal civilization. His current job was working in a coal mine. It was a respectable job in William's mind, and most importantly one which he had held down for over a year.

A burly man with a buzz cut was waiting for him when he arrived at the tool locker.

"You're late, Bill. That's the second time this week," the large man said.

William didn't try to deny it. He nodded resolutely.

"Yeah, Jack, I know. It's that damn building. My alarm clock was out this morning."

Jack Thompson, his work foreman, looked down and shook his head.

"If there is one thing you are, William, it's honest," Jack said.

It was true. More than once he had proven that to his foreman. When some of his fellow coal miners had figured out how to fix their punch cards to benefit themselves, William had not participated and told Jack what had been going on. This of course led to a group of the miners being fired and the rest of them being reprimanded. Naturally, this didn't go over well with his coworkers who had been enjoying the extra bonuses each week.

The men were especially upset because William was at the bottom of the barrel. He was just a general laborer not a trained and educated mining technician.

"Well, honesty is the only reason you still got this job, Bill. Now get your ass down there and haul some earth," Jack finished.

William pulled on his helmet, harness, and grabbed his power hammer, before heading down into the darkness.

He threw himself into his work, jack-hammering the rocks and letting his mind drift. He thought only of money, the meager dinner he would eat later, but more importantly, the large amount of alcohol he would wash it down with.

His sculpted muscles burned as he wielded the jackhammer, pausing only to heft large stones into a cart. His joints ached, the physical toll of his job catching up to him. By the end of the shift his arms and legs were numb. The nice thing about work was that there was a shower he could pay for, if he had the money. William figured he could at least look clean if he was to be seen in public that night.

He stripped down and entered the shower. The hot water hit his face, warm steam engulfing him. He closed his eyes and felt the dirt washing away, taking the stress of the work week with it. He could wash away the dirt and grime, but he could never escape his past. He watched the soot spiral down the drain, losing his battle to keep certain memories at bay.

Images poured into his head, mostly things he didn't want to remember. He saw the children in his elementary school taunting him, and jeering. They laughed as a bully pelted him with garbage. A pretty girl smiled at William as a boy desperately seeking her affection pushed him. William got up and hit him hard, again, and again. The image shifted and he saw the small window in his cell at juvenile hall, where he wept alone for so many nights.

William snapped back out of his daydreams, as the hot water turned suddenly cold. His corded muscles, sore from the week, failed him as he tried to recoil from the water.

"Well, Willy, we might have to tell the boss about you drinking on the job," a tall man said.

William tried to hide his surprise. He hadn't seen them enter.

"Mind your own business, Black," William snorted.

Timothy Black was one of the men who'd gotten away with falsifying his punch card, and not been fired. Of course he'd held a grudge.

Black followed him over to his locker. The door hung wide open. A flask sat tipped over on the shelf, brown liquid dripping out onto the floor. The three men converged on William from all sides.

"Uh oh, I'm going to have to report this, Willy," Black said, barely hiding a sarcastic grin.

William sighed heavily.

Why did I leave my locker open, he thought to himself.

They didn't plant the flask to get him fired. That would have been too easy. They wanted a reason to fight. He didn't really care. He was fed up with their crap anyway. He turned, slipping on an old pair of worn jeans.

"Back off, Black," William growled, his jaw clenched.

Timothy Black's face crinkled up with rage. "You don't get it, do you? Me and my boys here are going to knock your snitchin' teeth out," he said with a sneer.

William wasn't intimidated. His military training kicked in and he flashed back to his days in the Special Forces. He had served his time, and more, for his country. An additional price to pay for the laws he had broken in his youth. Street fighting was not a criminal act. The judge had decided to point William's aggression in a more appropriate direction.

Having joined the military, William quickly excelled. Taking orders was easy; it was depending on your comrades that he had always had trouble with. After his many tours with the Rangers he became Special Forces and eventually was asked to go on black ops missions behind enemy lines. For this he was trained alone. He trained to go on missions alone, and trained to engage multiple enemies at the same time, all alone.

William's favorite military study was hand-to-hand combat. He was not a small man by any means, nor was he the largest man. He used the momentum of incoming attacks against the enemy to catch them off balance, and simple strikes employed in martial arts like Krav Maga to cripple opponents quickly.

His mind immediately sized up the three men standing before him. Black was a brute of a man. He was large and powerful, which also meant slow and clumsy. His two friends were decently sized simply from working in the mine. However, it was easy to see why they followed Black instead of leading him.

A fist swung in, and time seemed to slow. William ducked to the left, avoiding the right cross and heard Timothy's knuckles crunch into the metal locker. He snapped his fist forward, using the practiced movements of a Special Forces soldier, and felt Black's windpipe crunch under his fist.

The goon on his left made a move, but William quickly slapped him in the face with the back of his hand to disorient him. He then blocked a wild haymaker from the man to the right, and kicked the inside of his leg with a quick heel kick. The man's leg gave way and he fell to the ground, screaming wildly. Another jab came from behind as the disoriented man recovered. William deftly snagged the man's fist out of the air, and thrust his elbow upwards against his arm, twisting until the bones broke.

The man dropped to the ground in shock, gasping for air. William refocused his gaze on Black, who was still choking on his own blood.

"Please," Black gagged, holding his hand up in surrender. The other two men were disabled; one screaming and holding his fractured arm, the other a ruined leg.

William walked away as people rushed in to help or gawk. He gathered up what few belongings he had and left. He would not be coming back. Even if he had friends to testify on his behalf, his advanced military training would make him guilty in many people's eyes. To them, he was a loaded weapon just waiting to go off.

It didn't take William long to make his way back to civilization. Walking quickly down a dimly lit street, he squinted at the bright glow from a movie theatre marquee. The sign read "Thor" as it poured light over the rest of the dingy road. He had seen the movie three times already.

The buzz from the sign barely pierced the fog out on the south side. William was familiar with the unnatural phenomenon. It was a polluted mist from the factories of the nearby industrial complex. The humid air clung to his skin and was thick with a toxic stench. William could taste it in the sweat running down his face. He looked down at the colorful water accumulating on the street. It reflected the light from the building's signs on either side of him.

It must have rained while I was down in the mine, he thought absently.

The images came back as if also reflected in the water, all of the sleepless nights spent hoping that his father would be too drunk that night to beat him. He pictured the puddles of his tears on the floor shimmering in the moonlight as he cried alone. His father was an evil man. William was too young to testify in court, but he would forever remember the night his father drank himself belligerent and beat his mother to death. When he sobered up he realized what he had done, and to save his own skin, had jabbed and cut his own body with a knife so he could claim self-defence. William didn't know how it worked, but he had never stopped blaming himself.

He ambled down the street, catching sight of a woman standing on the sidewalk. He was immediately struck by how beautiful she was. Conservatively dressed, in all white clothing, she looked extraordinarily out of place amongst the grime and dilapidation.

The vagabonds passed by, jeering and whistling crudely. As William stepped up onto the sidewalk she turned and approached.

"Hello, my name is Angelica," she said, holding her hand out in a gesture of greeting.

He looked her over. She was just slightly shorter than him, although he tended to slouch. Her hair was long, dark, and perfectly straight, shimmering even in the dark night. Her caramel colored eyes burned with an enthusiasm William had never seen before.

Her smile and enthusiasm annoyed him. "What do you want?" he growled.

She smiled, responding kindly and softly, "I do not know where you are off to tonight, sir, but I was wondering if I could speak to you about Jesus Christ?" Her smile stretched, touching both eyes.

William chuckled and responded, "And why would I want to know more about that son of a bitch?"

Angelica didn't flinch, and smiled again, showing a flash of brilliant, white teeth.

"Because he is the light and through him all things are possible."

"Listen lady," William said impatiently. "Your blessed lord has never shown his face in my life, and I'm sure he's not going to start anytime soon." William pushed past her, a warm shiver moving up his spine.

The woman shouted after him, "He can help you! I can help you!"

These people always showed up down here wanting the lowlifes to see the light. They only did it for their own gratification. If they could help poor people then they felt better about living their own wonderful lives. Williams's life had been devoid of light. And yet, something she said made him pause.

"You can't help me lady," he said, turning slowly, and then turned and walked away.

William continued down the street until he approached his favorite dive. It was the kind of place where the girls were cheap and the liquor was even cheaper. The Dirty Water was an obvious metaphor for the low quality, gut rot beverages they sold. Tom Ryan, the elderly bar owner, greeted him with a smile when pushed through the door.

"What will it be, Billy, my boy?" White hair surrounded his head leaving plenty of space for a shiny bald patch in the center.

"The usual, Tom, and keep it coming."

Two men blocked William's path as he moved to sit. He knew they were from the mine without looking at them .William stared into the closest man's dark brown eyes.

"You're going to pay for what you did today, you piece of shit," the dark-eyed man said, spittle flying from his lips.

"I'm sure I already have," William said, glancing over at Tom. The old man saw the warning signs of a fight and quickly produced a twelve gauge shotgun, which he held tightly to his chest.

"Now boys," Tom said in his familiar Irish accent, "you cut that shite out right now. Everyone is welcome to two things in my bar - a tall drink, and no trouble."

William smiled coyly at the two men, before shoving roughly past them. They were just hollow words anyway. There was too much fear in their eyes. He let it go and sat in his usual spot.

He downed drink after drink, and before he knew it, he was looking at the bottom of a bottle, and everything became blurry. Then the dreams came. The very ones he had tried to drown in liquor every night.

He was a young man, and he was facing another. Sweat dripped down his brow as he gasped, his bare chest

16

heaving. The other boy lunged for him, and William performed a takedown. He heard the crack as the boy's head hit the concrete, and the cheers of the onlookers in the dimly lit alley. Then he felt the sting of his knuckles cracking against the boy's face again and again.

He flashed forward and felt the rush of adrenaline and fear bloom in his heart as bullets whizzed around him. He jumped from cover, returning fire, and saw bullets pepper the body of a boy no older than twelve. The gunfire rattled and cracked around him, but he was frozen, staring at the lifeless corpse of the youth he had just slaughtered. He felt an invisible force hit him hard, followed by a ripping sensation as a hot piece of metal tore through him.

William awoke suddenly, yelling. He felt a dull throb where the bullet pierced his body so many years ago. He looked around in a haze. He was still groggy from drinking. There was nobody left in the bar, except for the bartender who dragged a dirty rag over filthier tables.

"Well there, thought you were going to sleep through the night," Tom said with a chuckle.

"I'm sorry, Tom, I'll get out of your hair," William mumbled.

"It is alright, Billy my boy. Gregory was down here earlier. He told me he threw you out. I figured I could let you stay here one night." Tom walked over and locked the door.

William was a bit delirious. The booze in his blood was preventing his brain from properly communicating with the rest of his body.

"No. No, Tom I got stuff to do," William said, and stumbled towards the door.

"Oh yeah, real important shite, I imagine. Alright, you fool." Tom tried to steady him as he wobbled. "Come Sunday you get your ass to church if you know what's good for you, son."

"Yes. I definitely will," William sputtered. Of course he was lying.

17

William managed to get only a few steps from the bar before tripping and falling to the ground. Hard. The concrete smelled of the sewers, and there was an acrid smell to the air, like the world had been bathed in toxic waste. The liquor wasn't nearly strong enough to drown it all out.

William positioned himself against a brick wall, just out of the street lamps' light. He looked down. His clothes were tattered and he was covered in filth. The street was all but empty. The night was growing old and the underworld of the city was retiring.

After a few deep breaths William got up and took a handful of heavy footsteps away from the wall. He stopped when he realized he didn't know where to go. He had no home, and after assaulting his fellow workers, he likely didn't have a job either. Stuffing his hands into the pockets of his water-soaked jeans, he felt a churning in the pit of his stomach. He wasn't just hungry. There was something else pulling at his insides. Maybe it was anger, or the frustration, or simply a life full of regrets catching up with him. William silently found himself wishing for death. And yet, death would be too easy.

He felt at home in the Army. He thought he found what he was going to do for the rest of his life. Being a soldier gave him focus, but beyond that, status. One moment, on one fateful day, a single bullet changed everything. The military discarded him, and he had been scraping by ever since.

William reflexively thought of the woman in white. Angelica, she said her name was. She had such beautiful eyes. Maybe he could take refuge in her church for the night, then in the morning he could do volunteer work in exchange for food. It would get him by until he could move on, and find a new plan.

Someone screamed nearby, almost knocking William off of his unsteady legs. The shriek was nearly as sobering as the cold concrete he had felt against his face moments earlier. He whirled around, searching for the source of the cry.

It could be anything in this neighborhood, he told himself. He began to walk away, but something tugged at his heart as another scream split the silence. It didn't sound like a pimp beating an unruly prostitute. It sounded like someone wrapped in fear, and pain.

The screams died away as he broke into a stumbling run, moving in what he hoped was the right direction. The screaming resumed just ahead, and grew louder. As he drew nearer, William heard a commotion, accompanied by the catcalling of several men. William rounded the corner of an alleyway and teetered to a stop before a horrific scene. Four men loomed over a prone figure in all white.

William's stomach lurched as he realized I was the woman he had seen earlier. There were dark lines across her face, most likely her own blood. It fell away from her body and pooled onto the street below. For a moment he thought he saw her mouth moving slowly like she was muttering something. The men laughed and spat on her. Then one of them knelt down and began to rip her clothes off.

William had an easy choice before him. Nobody in his life had ever offered to help him. This woman had. He had to help this woman. He had been too young to help his mother when she was in need. He had vowed from that day forward that he would never let anything like that happen again if he could help it.

Hatred and rage pulsed through his veins, seeping into him like a drug. He was outnumbered, and drunk. The four men would likely beat the hell out of him. Maybe even kill him, but perhaps he could give this poor woman enough time to get away.

William burst forward into a sprint. He reached the men in a heartbeat, his foot catching the man kneeling over the woman in the jaw with a crack. The second man recoiled with a grunt, taking William's left fist straight to the face. The man's soft nose gave way to his hardened knuckles.

The third man attempted to grapple William from behind, but some leverage and skill allowed him to toss the man easily to the ground. The pavement caught the creep in much the same way it had William only minutes earlier, and he gasped for air.

Three down and William hadn't even broken a sweat. The fourth man turned to William brandishing a pistol and with no hesitation took aim. William heard a deafening pop and thought he felt warmth begin to spread across his chest, but he didn't care. He was in a combat situation and his mind kept pushing him forward.

He lurched forward, knocking the shooter to the ground, jerking the gun away. Another shot was discharged in the process, and William heard one of the other men cry in pain. His vision started to blur. He whirled around, the gun tight in his hand. He put two bullets in each of the men without a second thought but his arm felt weak. He felt so horribly weak. One of the thugs lifted something and there was another loud pop, and a flash of bright light. William felt his body falling, and then he was on the ground.

Silence filled the alleyway, and William suddenly heard a soft voice whispering. He saw the woman. Angelica. She was speaking to someone. Everything slowly went dark and William could feel his muscles using the last of the oxygenated blood to cling to life, but soon, with a sigh, his last breath left his lungs and everything went dark.

* * *

When William opened his eyes a short while later it wasn't to the pain and cold concrete he remembered. Everything seemed different, though he couldn't immediately put his finger on how. He picked himself up off of the ground and looked around. The four men were lying motionless in the alley.

He turned on the spot, taking in the scene, rubbed his eyes, and looked again. The space between buildings was black and white, as if all the color had been drained away.

Was he in shock? His ears popped and he was a little disoriented, almost like a flash bang had gone off next to him.

Black smoke appeared suddenly, seeping out of the bodies of the four men. William knelt down for a closer look. The smoke forced its way out of their bodies, like it was alive. Stunned, he turned to Angelica who was kneeling above somebody as if she was embracing him. He realized she was weeping.

"It's okay now," William said softly.

Angelica looked up, a shocked look on her face. "How is this possible?" she whispered.

"Honestly, I'm not sure. I was in pretty rough shape when I showed up. I thought I got hit on top of that."

"You did," she said, her voice trembling.

William looked down and patted his chest and stomach. He couldn't find any holes.

"We both must have seen it wrong."

Angelica shook her head and moved aside, exposing the body previously hidden in her shadow. He stared down at the face, and it took him a moment to recognize the features. He was looking at himself. His eyes were dark and lifeless. His body appeared deflated, hollow, and all wrong, like it was missing something. William staggered backwards, his knees suddenly wobbly.

He felt like he was going to be sick, his heart racing uncomfortably. His mind tried to rationalize what he saw, while his military training urged him to take action.

"We have to go," he said, grabbing Angelica's arm.

She trembled and sobbed as he hefted her off the ground. William watched the black smoke resolve into what looked like tall, skinny figures, red dots burning where eyes would be, and knew they needed to leave.

21

"Run, Angelica!"

She didn't move, however. The smoky figures cackled and converged on them with a grace and fluidity he'd never seen before. William forced his fear back and choked down a mouthful of nothing. He leapt forward and with all his might struck the middle figure with a fist. The smoke creature's head split asunder, and a tar-like substance spattered everywhere. The other three shadow creatures screeched and swooped onto William with deathly speed, forcing him to the ground. He felt a sharp pain in his flesh where their skin touched his, and smelled their foul, tainted breath. He struggled to break free, but realized it was no use.

Needle-sharp teeth brushed his neck just as a blinding flash lit the alleyway, driving the wretched smoke creatures away. So bright was the light that it felt like he'd been hit with another grenade. He winced as the creatures writhed in the glow of it.

It was incredibly white and warm. William felt relief, and his breathing slowed. The creatures regained their wits and turned towards the source of the light. William squinted and was able to make out a shadow in the middle. It took the shape of a fifth figure, only this one was tall and broad.

The glow softened and in the midst of the commotion there stood a tall and majestic looking figure. The man had flowing, golden hair and was clad head to toe in ornate gold and silver plate armor. In his hand he held an enormous broadsword that was so large it should have taken two men to hold it. His face was an emotionless mask, and yet William could not deny how terribly beautiful he was.

The creatures converged on the armored man with terrible speed and ferocity. There was a loud snap and an arc of light blinded William yet again. When the light faded, he saw that the creatures were cleaved in half. The beautiful man closed the gap between them in an instant. He lifted Angelica from the ground slowly. She stared into his face in awe and as he spoke his voice filled the air like a chorus of one hundred men.

"Angelica, my name is Gabe. I have come to take you to your new home."

A tear formed in the corner of Angelica's eye.

"Praise God," she said.

He chuckled, and it sounded as if bells were ringing. He stood while Angelica knelt on the ground, her hands raised in worship. William realized how very far away from them he felt, his fists clenched in anxiety. The figure turned slowly, before walking towards William.

"What is your name, brave warrior?"

William looked at Gabe incredulously. He fumbled for the words and only managed, "I'm not a warrior."

Gabe looked at him quizzically. "Did you not save her?" he asked, pointing towards Angelica, who watched the exchange.

"I..." William said, but paused.

The stranger broke the silence. "Will you come with us?" he gestured towards a light growing near Angelica.

"Where?" William asked slowly.

"A new life," Gabe said.

William pondered for what felt like an eternity. This life had held nothing for him. Not love, nor friendship – only sorrow and pain. Gabe extended a hand to William, and he slowly took it. He felt the heat spilling off the armored man as soon as their hands touched, and in the next moment William was consumed in light.

CHAPTER TWO
DEATH

There was a sudden flash of light and William was airborne. His limbs were numb and his throat felt parched. He tried to breathe, but choked, and for a moment, felt as if he was suffocating. He felt his body accelerate, like he was a bullet shot out of a gun. His stomach dropped, and his heart strained to keep pace. It only took a moment, or it could have been an hour, before the chaos around him started to clear.

Then things settled out and were still. He floated, weightless in a white nothingness. He was helpless to move, and couldn't seem to regain all of his senses. William wondered if he would ever feel anything again. Off in the distance he could see the figures of Gabe and Angelica. He tried to call out to them, but no sound came out of his mouth.

Without warning, William started spiraling out of control. It felt like he was falling. He looked down and flinched, as a massive plane of white loomed directly beneath him. It moved towards him suddenly, and he hit hard. William staggered, jarred by the tremendous force and was left breathless.

Getting up slowly, he realized it was no longer nighttime. There was a brilliant light radiating from the sky and warming the air. His eyes finally adjusted, and he looked around, discovering that he was in a field of long, white grass. It looked like a scene straight out of a safari, except there wasn't a single tree in sight. Instead, he saw endless rolling hills covered with white grass, moving almost magically in the wind.

A crystal clear sky spanned above him, a giant yellow sun drifting lazily amidst the cloudless blue. The sun looked much too large, and William discovered that he could stare at it without squinting or having his eyes water.

Far in the distance, he spotted what looked like a small mountain range, and then turning slowly, he set eyes on the most magnificent sight he had ever seen. Jutting above the seemingly endless fields was a massive series of buildings. They were of the most intricate architecture, and every one of them was shining white and gold against the brilliant sunlight. It looked like a mountain of cathedrals interwoven and entwined. Columns and arches reminiscent of Greek architecture could be made out amongst the sprawl of white stone. William's jaw dropped slightly in awe as he stared.

So many emotions welled up inside him, yet he could not look away. He stood frozen and speechless, marveling. He found that he had innumerable questions, but before he could begin to ask them, a voice cut in and snapped him from his thoughts.

"Praise the lord, I am home!" Angelica said.

William turned to where she stood, and caught sight of Gabe.

"Where are we?" William asked.

Gabe smiled, and held a hand out towards the distant city.

"Welcome, young ones. To Archonia," he said, his tone reverential.

"What!?" Angelica gasped.

Gabe's face became more somber. "There is much that you need to understand before setting foot inside the city. We have much to discuss, my young friends, so let us walk," he said, gesturing towards the towering city.

Gabe led the way, his intricately embroidered white cape draped down his back and whipping in the slight breeze.

It was silent for a moment, allowing William to organize his thoughts.

"You're an Angel?" William asked after a moment of deliberation.

"No," Gabe said, simply.

Angelica shrieked in surprise.

"And so... this is not heaven?" William deducted.

"This place has many names," Gabe raised his arms, indicating the world around them. "We that live here do not call it heaven." He paused, considering his words. "Your mortal histories have become distorted and confused by millennia of languages, religions, and translations. Your records are little more than guesses as to what life truly holds."

They walked in silence for a bit, each seemingly lost in their own thoughts.

"Are we dead?" William asked, abruptly.

"There is no such thing as death, only rebirth. Your mortal bodies were a shell. They cocooned your essence, until it was ready to be released," Gabe said casually.

"Released into what, exactly?" William asked.

Gabe stopped walking, turned, and held his hands up as if to indicate himself.

"So what are you, if not an angel?" William shot back.

"You may perceive me as a being of flesh and blood, and yet you also perceive that I share your language. In short, I simply am, as are we all, here in Archonia," Gabe said with a smile.

"Okay, buddy," William snapped, "enough with the riddles."

Gabe chuckled. "I am not trying to upset you, my friends, but these things can be difficult to explain."

William took a moment to consider. "So...back there in the alleyway?"

"Your mortal bodies were destroyed, and your Archonian essence was freed."

"And what exactly is that?" William retorted.

"I am Archonian, and we exist outside the physical parameters of your mortal world," Gabe said.

William couldn't figure out what he meant by that, but before he could ask Angelica burst into tears and ran into the field. Falling to her knees, she sobbed.

Gabe moved towards her, but William held up a hand. Gabe nodded, and let William go instead.

William's stomach clenched as he approached, and realized that her crying unnerved him. It felt as if he was sharing her pain. Angelica knelt in the grass, tears rolling down her cheeks. It made William realize that he had never really comforted a person like this before. He didn't really know what to say.

"Hey," William said, softly touching Angelica on the shoulder as he knelt down next to her.

Tears streamed heavily down her beautiful face, and sparkled like gems in the sunlight, momentarily distracting him.

"What's the matter?" he asked softly.

Angelica shook her head, "we were wrong."

"Wrong about what? You religious types were right about a life after death, right?" William asked, trying to catch her attention. His words didn't seem to console her, so he paused a moment to think.

"Look. This guy Gabe doesn't seem too bad to me," he said.

"But this is not heaven. This is not where I was supposed to go," Angelica moaned.

William looked around. "Everything is gold and white, that guy looks like he came straight out of a movie, and you don't think this is heaven?" William asked, laughing just a bit.

"So they call it something else here. Everyone had their own names for it if I remember right," William continued. "I say we give this guy a chance, before we make too many conclusions."

William used the sleeve of his grungy shirt to wipe the tears from her eyes.

"Hey. Look at me," he said, gently grasping her chin with his fingers. "If this place isn't cool, we can always go check out hell."

Angelica sputtered with a choked laugh. She wiped the rest of her tears away and took William's hand, using it to help her stand. They walked back over to Gabe, who waited patiently.

"Alright, Gabe..." William said, mockingly, "Tell us what this place is all about."

"Fair enough," Gabe said, starting to walk once again. William caught sight of Angelica out of the corner of his eye. She wasn't staring at her feet anymore. Instead, she was looking around at the scenery. Her eyes were still puffy and red from the tears, but William thought that just made her look all the more beautiful.

Archonia appeared to be surrounded by fields of the tall, white grass, but in the distance there were lakes and rivers and plateaus of white stone jutting from the ground. Flocks of strange looking birds flew by, peppering the open sky between them and the approaching city.

"In the beginning, there were nine beings called Archons," Gabe began, drawing William's attention. "People believe the Archons were created to be companions for the creators. The creators realized that these beings were lonely and thus created creatures on a different plane of existence. These new beings were of all shapes and sizes. Massive reptilian beasts and other sorted warm blooded creatures. - They were such beautiful creations. Then something wondrous happened. The creatures evolved and as time passed, some began to take the form of the Archons. People only guess at the truth, but they believe these creatures began to achieve intelligence like the Archons. Eventually, the Archons taught them things and interacted with them."

Thousands of images and ideas flashed through William's mind, and even more questions. He took a breath to ask a question just as bright flashes filled the sky all around them. The tall grass flattened and William was nearly pulled from his feet by a whirlwind of force. William shielded his eyes, and squinting through the gust of air caught sight of twenty or more figures floating in the sky.

Who are they? William wondered.

The mysterious figures floated above them, hovering like large birds without wings. William turned to Gabe just as the new arrivals descended, forming a perfect circle around them. The newcomers were clad in silver armor much like Gabe's, and they carried massive spears. William considered the weapons for a moment. They looked much too large for any normal person to carry.

William stepped in front of Angelica, who cowered in fear, his muscles coiling and tensing in anticipation of a fight.

Gabe placed a hand on William's shoulder, suddenly calming him.

"Greetings, Meredox. How pleasant to see you again, my old friend," Gabe said, his curly golden locks still fluttering in the aftermath of the whirlwind.

Meredox took a step forward. He was shorter than Gabe, and had curly black hair. He didn't appear to be a warrior like the others. He wore a finely tailored outfit of gold and purple velvet beneath highly decorative armor. His face was scrunched up in a very serious grimace as he strutted forth with an annoying confidence. William immediately disliked him.

Stopping just short of their group, Meredox declared, "Gabriel, you are hereby placed under arrest for willfully violating the laws set down by our great Synod. I believe you know of which laws I speak."

Another man in the circle of soldiers smirked and added, "Again."

"Greetings, Brock," Gabe said, turning towards another man in the circle.

Brock was an enormous specimen, easily seven feet tall. His muscles appeared ready to burst from the very skin that held them, and his armor was such that his massive arms could be shown off. He was fair in skin color, and had a bald head. His voice echoed a deep bass. This man smiled while the others looked extraordinarily tense, like they were ready to strike, but were mortally afraid.

"Enough!" Meredox shouted. "Will you surrender?"

"Of course, my friend," Gabe responded politely.

William found Gabe's response strange. He appeared strangely calm for someone who was under the threat of attack.

The soldiers surrounding their group relaxed, and averted their spear tips upwards. Many of them looked relieved. William was not ready to give up so easily.

"What is the charge?" he growled, turning towards Meredox.

"Arrest this scum," Meredox replied quickly, not bothering to address him directly.

William reacted in anger, his fists clenching as he charged at Meredox. He was moving one moment, and the next, he was staggering back, Gabe's massive palm pressing against his chest.

It felt like William had hit a wall. Pain shot through his chest, but he came forward again, trying to push Gabe's arm away, but it wouldn't budge.

"No!" Gabe yelled suddenly.

William thought he was shouting at him at first, but turned as two figures converged on them. William wrenched his hand free just as the closest man swung the butt end of his mighty spear at his head.

* * *

William fell into a strange dream world, where he was swarmed over by memories from his life. He stood over a woman as she wept. A still, prone figure lay in her arms. He looked around and noticed that he was in a village, its buildings ablaze with torrents of flame. People were running and screaming.

William awoke with a start, roaring in reaction to images that were not real. He felt a warm, hard hand on his shoulder again.

"A dream, my friend," Gabe said gently.

"Where are we?" William asked irritably.

They were in a small, dark room made from white stone. There was a window on one wall with metal bars as the only buffer between William and a bright light. The opposite wall opened into a hallway, but was separated by a wall of solid metal.

"Prison," Gabe said casually.

"Why? We haven't done anything." William rubbed his still-throbbing head.

Gabe started out the small, barred window but said nothing. His radiance was breathtaking even when standing still. He was like a model from a magazine. His hair and face seemed to be perfect.

"Where is Angelica?" William asked quickly, looking around the cell and not seeing her anywhere around. Had they hurt her because of his stupidity?

"She is safe," Gabe replied, not looking away from the window.

"She is free. She has done no wrong."

"Neither have we!" William growled, exasperated.

"I am afraid we have. You see, you are not supposed to be in this world. I was not supposed to bring you."

"I don't understand," William responded.

"Things were not always this way. There was a time when all souls were permitted to live in this paradise."

"What happened?" William asked.

31

"It is said that long ago, when the Archons first discovered man, there were two of them that loved man as their own children. But there was another, one who despised them. That Archon's name was Lucifer.

"The devil?" William asked.

Gabe nodded, but continued quietly, "According to your human history, he hated humanity so much that he began to use his power to corrupt them. He taught them to lie, to cheat, and to covet the possessions of his fellow man. The two Archons that loved humanity the most would not stand for this corruption and confronted Lucifer. It was then that he used his power to mortally wound his brother Prometheus. The other Archons could no longer sit idly by, and they swept in, defeating Lucifer swiftly. But they could not destroy him, you see? For they still loved him. So instead, they banished him from Archonia. Lucifer had nowhere to go but the mortal world."

"There he was forced to watch as Prometheus slowly died. Amazingly, with his body broken, Prometheus had but one choice. With his dying breath he reached out to a woman that he had grown fond of during his visits to Earth. He transferred his remaining power to her. Miraculously this woman became pregnant. She bore a son unlike any other human. This baby grew into a man, and eventually as all humans do, he died," Gabe paused, waiting to see if William understood, and continued.

"But it was only his human body that decayed and died. His true essence lived on. He had developed his own Archonian body. This half-Archon had many sons and daughters in his lifetime. They too eventually died and passed into our world as well. Prometheus succeeded where his Archon brethren failed. He made mankind his children.

"Never before could the Archons reproduce, but through humanity a new race was born. It was written that Lucifer could not stand for this, and he began to corrupt these special souls.

"Supposedly, their essence turned black, Lucifer's manipulations twisting them into something unnatural and evil," Gabe continued. "The first of these was a man named Hades. When Hades died, his Archonian essence was released, but it was not like others that had come before him. It was monstrous. The creature had power like the Archons, so naturally more were to follow. The remaining Archons finally saw what Lucifer had done, and they sought him out to deal with him once and for all.

"When they found him, he had amassed an army. The seven remaining Archons used all the power they could muster to destroy the army, but they became overwhelmed and some were destroyed. The others fled, using their power to create a barrier between our realms. Lucifer's demons could not pass and were left to fester in their own lands. Archonia was split in two," Gabe finally finished his explanation.

William was astonished and remained silent for many minutes before softly speaking.

"Those shadowy creatures back in the alley?" he asked.

"Those were the hollow shells of corrupted souls," Gabe answered.

"Human souls?"

"Correct, that through evil, have been corrupted. Or so the histories say," Gabe added, looking out the window.

"So why exactly is it that I am not supposed to be here?" William asked.

Gabe looked back at him, his brows drawn and his face tight with worry.

"There was a time when all Archonian people passed into these lands. Soon however, the darkness of corruption spread. We found that even good souls could be tainted. They passed in our realm, bringing sorrow and pain to this otherwise peaceful world."

"Your people formed a great Synod, made up of the purest and brightest Archonians. It was much like a human government. They decreed that only chosen souls of pure heart could pass into our realm."

"Angelica, her soul is pure. She tried to help me, and I wouldn't listen," William interrupted, before asking, "So what are they going to do with us?"

"I do not know," Gabe sighed. "The penalty for my crimes is banishment."

"You don't seem too concerned," William said.

Gabe didn't respond, and William didn't press the issue. He had a more important question on his mind.

William got up from the stone slab that constituted his bed, and walked slowly over to the window to stand next to Gabe. The metal bars crisscrossing the small portal gleamed brightly in the sunshine.

"What happens to me?" William asked.

"They fear you are a corrupted soul, and will most likely banish you to Dichonia."

"Dichonia?" William asked, before putting two and two together. "Hell?"

Rage sparked within him. He'd never amounted to anything in life, and even now, surrounded by angels, he was still second class. William's anger erupted, and he lashed out, striking the outer wall with all his might. There was a crash, and William staggered back. He stepped forward when the dust cleared, a bright beam of sunlight cascading into the formerly dark space. The stone wall and barred window that had just stood before him crashed to the ground many hundreds of feet below them. He lifted his gaze and took in the endless fields of wind-swept white grass.

"Whoa. How did I do that?" he asked, turning to Gabe.

Gabe smiled. "Do you remember when I said that our world is not based on the same natural laws your world is?"

William nodded. "What did you mean?"

"In this world, you are not bound by the burdens of gravity or weight like your mortal body was. You are only limited by what your mind can comprehend."

This took a second to sink in. "Great! Then we can escape," William said, laughing loudly.

"NO!" Gabe exclaimed with a ferocity that took William by surprise. "Do not cross the threshold of that wall."

"Why not?"

"To be imprisoned in this world is mostly symbolic. Were you to try to escape, it would mean that you are *truly* guilty. They would destroy you without hesitation," Gabe replied.

"How can they destroy me? I'm already dead!"

"Your mortal body has died, and while one's soul may live forever here, their essence can still be destroyed," Gabe explained.

"You said they will banish me to hell anyway. I can't imagine that will be very pleasant. I'm guessing they don't sit around, singing songs and passing out roses down there. At least now I have a chance," William said, thoughtfully looking out at the open landscape.

Gabe wrapped a strong, thick hand around William's arm. "No. You have a better chance if you stay here. I may be able to sway the Synod to let you live."

"And why would you do that for me? Don't you think I'm a corrupted soul as well?"

"You sacrificed yourself to save an innocent, which is no small deed. And after, you did not turn into one of those abominations," Gabe paused. "I made a very similar choice once. So I ask you. Trust me, and stay, my friend," Gabe said very seriously.

William stared at the man for what seemed like hours, going over every possibility, and considering all of the outcomes. He couldn't see a version of this story that didn't end in his death. In the past, he'd always run away from problems. That option seemed like a valid option now.

After all, they would never accept him. He turned away from Gabe and looked out across the endless fields. He had but to run and never look back.

"If I run will they catch me?" William asked, his gaze locked forward.

"I cannot guide you on this matter. You must make this choice on your own," Gabe responded softly.

William looked down, letting his eyes slide over the edge of the wall. The structure they were in had to be at least forty stories high. He didn't even know if he could survive such a fall. And if he did, where he would go? The possibilities flooded his mind, meanwhile a different emotion tugged at his heart.

William had a gut feeling that Gabe would protect him. He turned and considered him. Gabe stood motionless, his crystal clear gaze locked on him. A shiver ran down his spine.

"I will trust you, Gabe."

William took a step back, retreating as men with spears appeared through the gaping hole in the wall. More guards appeared from the hallway, the razor sharp blades of their spears leveled at him.

"Take ease, my friends. He does not yet know his own strength," Gabe said, holding his hands up to shield William.

The guards stopped, their armored bulk filling the space. William winced as a spear tip dug into his side.

CHAPTER THREE
TRIALS

A massive figure appeared beyond the crowd. He loomed above them, so broad in the shoulder he barely fit in the doorway.

"Stand down!"

William watched Brock push through the crowd, before unlocking the cell door.

"I hope you know what you are doing, Gabe. The Synod has convened. They're waiting for you," Brock said.

Gabe grabbed William by the arm and pulled him from the cell, almost yanking him off of his feet.

"I can follow," William snapped, wrenching his arm free.

Gabe didn't respond, he just turned and followed Brock down the hall, his face an unreadable mask. The guards ushered them down a massive hallway, the ceiling spanning at least a hundred feet overhead. They walked for a half an hour, passing through hallways that seemed to go on forever.

Finally, they came to a massive set of double doors, looming at least four stories above him. They were crafted from black onyx, and covered in menacing sculptures. William saw twisted faces and monstrous creatures the likes of which he had never seen. They seemed demonic.

"Do not speak. I will take care of everything," Gabe said, leaning over and whispering into his ear.

William swallowed, but his throat was horribly dry. How many times could he feel mortally threatened in one day? The mammoth doors opened, and a light crashed upon William like a blanket of warmth.

He followed Gabe into the chamber beyond and looked up. The ceiling was so high he could only just make out the intricate murals sprawling across it. Windows sat ten stories high, letting in bright columns of white light. The light fell onto a raised dais in the middle of the chamber. Ten people sat in a semicircle facing him, their chairs large, rigid, and ornate. To their right was a group of people who were perhaps onlookers or witnesses.

The ten people seated upon the dais were dressed in an assortment of the most exquisite regalia William had ever seen and could never have imagined.

William paced forward, his attention drawn down to his feet. Tiny tiles had been perfectly inlaid into the floor to create a sprawling mosaic. The room was completely silent, his footsteps astonishingly loud. They reverberated across the room; a round structure with pillars reaching towards the sky, all perfectly sculpted as if they were part of the earth jutting out of the ground. All of it was silver, gold, and white.

The guards came to a halt, stopping William and Gabe. They stood in the center of the room, and the men surrounding him quickly withdrew. Gabe turned towards the men and women seated on the dais. They sat perfectly still, watching Gabe and William like statues.

This must be the Synod Gabe spoke of, William thought.

The members of the synod were regal, beautiful, and to William, terrifying. They were young and beautiful, blessed with extraordinary features, and looked like giants from where he stood.

Gabe greeted them first with a tone that spoke to years of wisdom. "Great Synod, I thank thee for your audience. I am Gabriel of Archonia, and I come before thee in search of forgiveness," Gabe said in greeting, his tone soft and respectful.

Forgiveness? William wondered.

The Synod sat motionless for several long moments before the man seated fourth from the right, finally spoke. He was wearing robes of dark burgundy, woven with strands of gold and inset with many glimmering jewels. Though he looked young in years, wisdom could be seen in his features.

"You know why you are before us, Gabriel. You have defied us yet again." The man spoke carefully, and with perfect diction. His voice was deep and his words deliberate.

"Yes, your grace. I have indeed defied you," Gabe responded.

This is ridiculous, William thought. *What is Gabe trying to do?* Get himself off the hook and hang William out to dry?

William stepped forward, and was about to speak in his own defense, when Gabe put an arm across his chest. As he did, the guards, crowded around them, brandishing short swords that gleamed fiercely in the white light. Everything happened so fast, William couldn't react, or speak.

A woman spoke, breaking the tense silence.

"So this is the one that you have risked everything for?" she asked.

Gabe nodded solemnly, but did not speak.

She was beyond beautiful, with long red hair that curled slightly as it fell around her shoulders. She wore a robe of green with an assortment of flowers and gemstones. The juxtaposition of something as ever-changing as a flower was astonishingly beautiful next to something as unchanging as a gemstone.

The man to her right, the first of the Synod to speak, cleared his throat. "We have studied his mortal existence, and cannot deny the stain inside of him."

William breathed heavily. He hated this. He couldn't defend himself. He felt helpless, similar to how he had back in his drunken stupor, completely unable to control his own fate.

Gabe quickly responded. "It was obvious to me that there was much more to him than initially believed. I also witnessed his actions at the end of his old life, and when he began anew, and confirmed my suspicions."

The Synod fell silent again, and moved for the first time, as if life had suddenly been poured into them. They looked to each other, debating. A second man spoke. He wore robes of navy blue with golden droplets and an assortment of other things adorned the robe. He had handsome features, and yet, his long, jet black hair fell around his face, giving him an almost sinister look.

"By all means, Gabriel, regale us with this wonderful tale," he said, sarcastically.

"Of course, I would be most obliged in a recount of these wonderful events, but I think perhaps it would be more appropriate for you to hear another's account," Gabe said quickly.

The Synod members exchanged confused glances and murmured quickly.

"And who is this third party, Gabriel?" the woman with red hair asked.

"Her name is Angelica. As the Synod is well aware, I had business in the mortal world. I heard the cries of an Archonian woman, hovering on the threshold of mortal life. She called out to me, and I answered as swiftly as I could. As I arrived I realized that there was nothing I could do to spare her. My only option was to bring her here to start her new life," Gabe paused, eyeing the Synod members each in turn. "For the rest of the account, I defer to Angelica."

The doors to the room flew wide and Angelica swept it, accompanied by Brock.

The huge bald man escorted Angelica forward as if protecting an innocent child. Indeed, Angelica looked quite out of place in this setting. Her appearance had changed, and she now looked even more beautiful, if that was possible. Her long, black hair was perfectly groomed, and she wore garbs of pure white draped all over her, like the chitins of ancient Greece. Her smooth, dark skin shone slightly against the light pouring in through the high windows. William couldn't help staring at her.

Brock bowed low to the Synod, before stepping back next to Gabe.

Gabe whispered, "Thank you, my friend."

Brock smirked.

They smiled and looked forward. The man in the burgundy robe spoke directly to Angelica, his tone now very gracious.

"My dear, do not be frightened of us, as we are your servants. We ten have vowed to uphold the integrity and justice of this world, so that you might live in true harmony."

Though this was a comforting thought, Angelica didn't seem to take it to heart.

"It would give us great honor to hear the tale of your ascension to our world," another Synod member added.

"Yes, of course," Angelica said, quietly.

The room fell silent for a moment, before she continued, "It was Friday night. I was on duty for my church, doing missionary work down by the riverfront. You see, we all took turns trying to save the lost children of God. To convince them to turn away from their sins, and follow the Lord's path."

William was sure that this would evoke some sort of reaction from the Synod, but they sat perfectly statuesque again, as if the life had left them and was replaced by stone.

"It was getting late, and I wasn't having any luck, so I decided to head home. On my way home, I passed a group of men hovering in an alleyway. They surrounded me. I knew what they wanted, so I prayed for help, and the Lord sent me an angel," Angelica said, smiling and looking at the group beside her.

The woman in green spoke first, her voice soft and her tone kind. "It is easy to see why you would think Gabriel to be an angel."

Angelica interrupted, "No, it wasn't him," she said looking at Gabe, "It was him." She turned her gaze to William.

The Synod members looked from one to the other, a rumble growing from the on-looking crowd. William wasn't shocked. He listened quietly as Angelica continued.

"The men hit me and pulled me into the alleyway. I prayed and prayed, hoping the Lord would end my pain, and then I saw him running towards me. He fought the men singlehandedly. He sacrificed himself for me. Everything went black. When I awoke, it was like I was stuck in a nightmare. I saw him lying on the ground, his body broken. I wept for him, asking God for a miracle, and he answered again," she said, smiling widely at William.

It was at this moment that Gabe decided to chime in again.

"This is the truth, my brethren. But the story doth not end there. For brave William would face a new evil. The wretched men lay slain at his feet, but they too would live on, taking on the form of the demon. Four of them there were, and only one of him, but he showed his quality again, striking out at the leader with an iron fist. Split asunder, the evil was reduced to ashen waste, ruined by William's Archonian essence. An essence that I hope and trust you will find pure enough to let live amongst us in our peaceful realm," Gabe finished.

William felt his legs go wobbly, as he was beset from some unexpected emotions. He didn't expect Gabe's words on his behalf to impact him so. The guards surrounding their group suddenly erupted into applause. Several of the Synod members had to stifle smiles of their own.

A small noise cut through the commotion, one that sounded oddly like the clearing of a throat. Everything immediately fell silent. Everyone, even the Synod members, turned to a man seated in the very middle of the group. William hadn't even noticed him. He wore a robe of white with gold trim, and was the first man in this new world that William thought looked older. It could have also been the thoughtful look on his face. It made him look wiser.

He spoke softly, his tone immediately commanding respect. William wondered if it would be this this man who would decide his fate.

"If this was truly the way of things then, Gabriel, your measure of character is impeccable. However, our laws are clear. It would not be balanced to allow some, and not all to enter freely," the man said softly.

His brow showed frustration.

Gabe spoke slowly, "The Synod knows well my opinions on *certain* laws. They also know of my concerns for our future."

"What would you have us do?" a woman in green asked.

"Simple. I would have you find faith in people again. Let more souls cross our borders to live with us. It was Prometheus' wish, one which he sacrificed everything for," Gabe said sadly.

"We have heard you sing this song many times, Gabriel," he said, rolling his eyes.

"And the Synod has disregarded it many times," the man in burgundy interjected.

"You are one of the few who know what happened in those dark times," the woman Synod member finished.

Gabe nearly spat as he retorted, "Of course I was. I sat and watched while my brothers slaughtered one another. I know what is at stake, and I know how important my decision was."

Panic shot through the hall, and Gabriel became terrifying for a moment. The enormous room grew larger, if possible, and stretched, darkening slightly. There was a pause, and Gabe's face calmed. The people in the room fell silent.

Gabe sighed. "I, therefore, ask that I be banished. In my place William will stay, as proof that if given the chance, those on the edge can find redemption."

The room remained quiet. When William had seen the anger in Gabe's face it was frightening. Everyone else seemed to feel the same way, because there was rustling amongst the onlookers again.

"Allow me to serve as the ambassador between worlds. Appoint me the judge of your will. I will see it done. You know this to be true. Let it be my punishment, my burden, for these transgressions. In return, I ask only that this single soul be allowed a chance," Gabe finished.

The man in the middle finally spoke, breaking the silence.

"Then let judgment commence."

A surge of wind coursed through the room, and the light dimmed. A bright ball of bluish light formed in the center of the room. All fell cold and still.

William stood breathless at this display of inherent magic. Since he had been here, he had seen some very extraordinary things like flying men and demons, yet he was still amazed.

"William of Earth, you are hereby judged for all of your evil deeds upon the mortal plane," the man in white said in a deep voice.

The blue light flashed and expanded, and William filled with dread. He saw an image of him sitting alone in his room reflected in the ball of light. He knew what it was – it was the first time he stole something. He was just a boy, sitting in his room playing with a toy that didn't belong to him. There was another flash, and he was a teenager. There was a strange face looking back at him bloody and raw from blows to the face that William had landed. He had to fight to survive on the streets.

William began to shake. This couldn't be happening. They were making him relive the worst moments of his life. All of his sins laid bare for everyone to see.

How can this be possible, he thought?

The ball of light flashed like a video recording in fast forward mode. Many more shameful scenes played out. Terror filled him.

He saw himself standing in a field, rain pouring down. He knew what they were all about to see, and he couldn't bear it.

"No!" William sobbed.

He hadn't realized he was crying. He screamed with a ferocity that shook him, while guards jumped to his side to restrain him. However it was no longer rage that filled him, only despair. He was forced to relive this moment every night in his dreams, but nobody had ever known that this had happened. With the exception of his superiors in the military who had ordered it.

"Sir, those civilians are unarmed," William heard his voice say. It sounded far off.

"They are endangering our operation. I am ordering you to neutralize the threat," another man responded, his voice cold.

A shadowy figure emerged from the bushes. It was him. He approached quickly, and grabbed a girl from behind, and snapped her neck. It was a sickening crunch that he'd heard too many times in his nightmares. The innocent lives he'd taken had now followed him here. He felt his body go limp and he started to gag and heave.

More scenes passed through the light, but it didn't matter anymore. The room was silent, and William knelt now on the cold floor sobbing and choking on tears. Light flooded back into the room, and it felt warm again. William wiped off his eyes and looked around. The crowd stood around him, staring, their faces grim.

"William of Earth. What have you to say for these deeds committed on the mortal plane?" The man in burgundy asked.

A tear slid off William's cheek and hit the floor.

"I am guilty, and will accept my punishment in hell," William said, wiping more tears away.

"Where is the fierce fighter we just saw?" A woman said, stepping forward from the crowd. She was wearing red, decorated with gold, which matched her almost floor-length hair.

"Has he given up?" she asked

"Yes," William said in a tone of finality.

The man in the middle stood slowly. As he did, the rest of the room's attention swayed his direction.

"Your remorse is touching, William. I have never seen a man whose life was so stricken with pain and sorrow. I am truly sorry. Gabriel is correct, my brothers. We have become hardened and cold. We must not forget the compassion Prometheus showed us. My brothers and sisters, we will have much to discuss, but I declare William of Earth to now be William of Archonia," he said slowly.

William looked up. Did he hear that correctly? The man in the middle was now standing next to him. Strange, he'd just been across the room a moment ago.

"William of Archonia, if you truly wish to live with us in our world, then you must still prove your worth. I declare that you shall take the Path of the Sentinel. Learn our ways and laws, and help to protect this world from the evils that you faced on Earth. Do this and I will count you as a brother," the man said in a voice barely above a whisper.

William was bewildered. Not only was he still in shock over the events that had just passed, but he was thoroughly confused by this new chain of events. He didn't know what to say so he simply nodded.

William was certain that the path set before him wouldn't be an easy one. It was a future, however, and that seemed better than the alternative. A brief wave of relief washed over him, but was swept away when a voice issued forth crisply, and defiantly.

"My lords this is most unjust," stated the man William had seen when he first came to this world. He entered the center of the circle, and stood just a few feet from William.

He was no longer wearing his armor. Now he was dressed head to toe in garb that was as elegant as the Synods. William thought that the look suited him far more than armor. His body was leaner than the soldiers standing around. His greasy black hair hung just above his shoulders, and had been tucked behind his ears

For some reason, Meredox seemed to hate him. William couldn't understand why. He had done nothing to him. Hell, he hadn't even known his name until a few hours ago.

The Synod member who was sitting next to the elder in the center stood, looking menacing. William had not noticed it before, but his robes were black, and he wore much silver and red. His dark features accented his angry stare, and he spoke with a booming voice that seemed to shake the walls around him.

"Meredox, you defy the Synod's decision?" he asked.

Meredox seemed to wilt under the Synod member's glare, and lowered his head. "No, my lord. Of course not. I only argue the point of our past. We have tried this before, and as the Synod knows, it did not end well."

"That was many years ago, and it happened differently if you remember, Grand Justicar," the woman in red said.

"I remember it very clearly," Meredox said through clenched teeth.

"This Synod's decision is final, and you should remember your place, Adjudicator," the man in burgundy added.

Meredox bowed low, but the anger on his face could not be mistaken.

47

"Then it is settled. Gabriel of Archonia you are sentenced to ferry souls from the mortal plane in punishment for your transgression. William shall be appointed a guardian companion to help him down his new path," the elder said, after waiting for Meredox's charade to play out.

William looked over at Gabe, who whispered something to Brock. Brock ran forward a moment later, before bowing to the Synod members.

"I will watch over him, great Synod," he said, his voice gruff.

"So be it, Guardian. This Synod is adjourned," the elder declared with hesitation.

CHAPTER FOUR
THE FOUNTAIN

Everyone moved all at once. Brock grabbed William by the arm and jerked him up from his knees. They made their way through the Procession.

"I have to talk to Gabe," William said to Brock, trying to catch sight of Gabe.

"Not possible. He has gone to take care of his part of the deal," Brock said, not stopping.

"What deal?" William demanded.

"He gave you a chance to live here and learn our ways. He gave up his place here for you. Were you not listening?" Brock asked, sighing impatiently.

"But, why? Why would he do such a thing?" William asked.

Brock shrugged his broad shoulders.

"Perhaps he believes you are special, or maybe he was just using you to prove the Synod wrong," Brock said pointedly.

"What do you mean by that?"

"Gabriel thinks that their laws are too rigid, and that many are not given a fair chance to come live amongst us. Just the simple fact that you are here is astounding. A tainted soul has not been within these walls for over a thousand years," Brock said, gesturing to the building around them.

William's stomach lurched.

"You think I am tainted as well?" he asked solemnly.

"Forgive me, friend. It is just a figure of speech. You will soon have to accept the fact however, that your soul is not pure. And the purity of one's soul is the most important thing in this life," Brock said.

They talked and walked, continuing through the vast corridors, before coming to another pair of double doors that dwarfed them. Brock strode forth and pushed open the massive portal. William watched in amazement. They looked like they weighed a ton each.

William was having trouble grasping the physical laws of this world, or lack thereof. Light poured over them as the doors swung open, temporarily blinding William. When his eyes finally adjusted, he took in a sight that left him speechless. Sprawling before them was what looked to be a town square. Buildings made of white stone shot into the sky. William had never seen buildings so ornately made before. The size of them alone would have taken hundreds of men decades or possibly even centuries to construct.

There were people everywhere, dressed in garments of many different styles, each one more exquisite than the last. Groups of people walked around the courtyard, while others flew through the air. An upbeat melody filled the air, coming from a group of men playing strange instruments. Some looked like string instruments and horns he'd seen before, yet they were all different. One man was making the most wonderful sound simply with his voice, though it didn't sound like singing. People laughed and played. They all seemed to be the same age, each one radiant and beautiful.

"These people, they are all the same age?" William asked Brock

"We are all a projection of our soul. No matter what you looked like in the mortal world, you're beauty is limited only by your mind in Archonia," Brock said.

William followed his large companion into the warm light. Turning his head to the sky to bask for a moment in the warmth, he felt that he would never be cold again. This warmth didn't feel hot like a tropical place. More like a warm blanket on a cold night.

He smiled at a group of people passing by, but they recoiled at the sight of him. A wave of panic rushed over him as he realized what he looked like. His long scraggly beard hung from his face while his unkempt hair fell all about. His dirty old clothes were stained with aggregate from his previous life

"Brock, I don't think they like me very much," William said.

"That is because they are judging you by the way you look, young one. Do not despair, they will soon respect you as a soldier of Archonia," Brock replied, smiling and winking at him.

"Well that is a very inspiring sentiment, Brock, but is there any chance I could get cleaned up a little?" William asked.

Brock just chuckled, and said, "Of course, my friend. Follow me."

They set off down a winding street, and began to talk again.

"Was it Gabe that brought you here?" William asked.

Brock nodded. "Yes. He saved me many hundreds of years ago. I once had a home in Germania. It was along the river called Rhine and we worked the fertile land around it. Our ways were simple but peaceful. One warm day that all changed. We were invaded by an army from the south. They wore metal upon their bodies and fought with fierce machines that shot fire. I took the lives of many men, but at long last I was felled. When I thought my life had all bled away I saw Gabe descend from the sky, and hit the ground like a lightning bolt. He grabbed a handful of people out of the field and the next thing I knew, I was here," Brock finished.

William didn't know what to say, so he changed the subject.

"Gabe had a lot of influence at the Synod," he said. "Is he important?"

Brock laughed heartily, and looked down at William.

"I should hope so. He is an Archon, my young brother," Brock said.

William furrowed his brow. "Aren't you an Archon as well?" he asked.

"We all have an Archonian body, that is true, but he was one of the original nine. It was he and his brothers who created us. He is a father to us all. Not only this, he also helped the Synod write the Hosei, which are the many laws we live by. There was a time when the people of Archonia wanted Gabe to be their king. He refused of course. He truly is a great man," Brock said beaming.

Gabe had made no indication that he was better or above anyone else. William immediately gained new respect for Gabe. Not only had he saved his life, but he was practically royalty.

Brock stopped, and grabbed William by the arm.

"Here we are," he said pulling him through an archway.

The archway looked to be sculpted from a single piece of beautiful stone, and was covered with intricate carvings. Figures of ancient peoples bathing and dancing in water were displayed in relief. The archway led them into a large clearing, surrounded by the mountains of looming buildings around. A stair led downward into plush looking green grass. A small tree sat to the right of the clearing, blooming beautifully in large, colorful flowers.

A wide pool of aqua-blue colored liquid lay at the center of the clearing. A small whirlpool spun at the center, noiselessly churning the extraordinarily clear water around it.

William looked between the pool and Brock.

"What is this place?" he asked.

"The Fountain of Cleansing," Brock said, before turning to leave.

"Wait. Where are you going?" William asked quizzically.

"I have some errands to attend to," he said, smiling, his bald head gleaming in the bright sun.

"What am I supposed to do?" William asked in a sudden panic.

"Well, clean yourself up a bit," Brock replied simply.

It was becoming apparent that William was going to have to figure many things out on his own. Brock was a rather poor teacher. He sighed, and looked down.

Next to the fountain, William spotted a plate containing several very odd looking instruments made of silver and gold.

"What are these?" he asked Brock, slowly holding one up to inspect it.

"Grooming equipment. And there are some clothes that should fit you well," The large man said, pointing towards a towel, and a pair of linen garments. They were off-white, and looked very soft.

"I'll be back in an hour or so. I have some business in the marketplace. Do not wander off, little brother," Brock said, leaving nothing but a trail of dust as he disappeared at an incredible speed.

People in this world moved so fast. William had barely blinked and his guardian was gone.

After Brock left, William settled onto the grass and picked up the instruments off the plate. Were they just for him? Or were they always out and available? It was strange. It took him some time, but he managed to shave, using the frightening looking razor. He moved to remove his grimy clothes, but became self-conscious, expecting someone to come through the open archway at any moment."

Finally, William stripped off his old raggedy clothes, and dipped a toe into the water. Strange. It wasn't cold as he'd expected, but very hot. Stranger yet, the toe he had just dipped in looked perfectly clean. The small bit of black grime from his appendage floated in the water, drifting towards the swirling whirlpool in the pool's center. Finally, the circling current caught and sucked it in.

William smiled and waded into the pleasantly hot water. The grime clinging to his body seemed to peel away. Even when he waded back through the black tar-like substance that had come off of him it wouldn't cling back onto his skin. The water was waist-deep, so he decided to swim a little, playfully kicking around for a few minutes just out of pure pleasure.

William felt a slight tingling sensation as he swam in the water. He put his face down so it was just above the steaming surface, and drew in a breath through his nose. It smelled subtly like perfume. He found the scent attractive and wonderfully complex. It wasn't overpowering, but still strong enough to evoke many base emotions. William couldn't help but smile.

He walked out of the pool feeling cleaner than he had in years. He toweled off with the cloth left for him, his skin rejoicing at the silken towel's touch. It was the softest thing that he had ever come into contact with. William couldn't help but laugh.

He chose to shave his head to match his face. It seemed like an appropriate thing to do.

A fresh look for a fresh start, he thought.

He looked at himself in a small hand mirror, admiring his new look.

William slowly donned the clean clothing, and sat down by the fountain. He found that he was in no hurry to leave the small clearing. It was wonderfully peaceful. Brock walked back just a few moments later.

"Perfect timing," William said,

"No. I just wanted to give you some privacy," he replied, looking William over. "Well, the fountain has done a fine job on you, little one."

"Yeah!" William exclaimed, "That water is amazing!"

"Well to be honest, I do not believe that it is actually water," Brock said.

"Really?" William asked with a nervous chuckle

Brock furrowed his brow as if he was trying to remember something. William looked at the strange pool again, a grotesque, squirming feeling rising up inside.

"Well, it does not appear to have done you any harm anyhow. You look like a new man," Brock roared, patting William on the back so hard he nearly keeled forward.

"Woah! Take it easy," William said, regaining his balance.

"My apologies, I forgot you are not used to our strength yet. This is too much for your mind all at once. Well, let us go," Brock stated.

They left the courtyard, passing back through the archway, Brock walking incredibly fast.

"So if that wasn't water, what was it?" William asked.

"The Fountain of Cleansing was created many hundreds of years ago by a very talented Archonian. He saw that everyone who came into our world was very dirty. The stench of the mortal world clung to their bodies, because it was still in their mind. The fountain works because it washes these memories away. The dirt that you saw washed away by the liquid was a reflection of that. Your mind created this when your Archonian essence was formed," Brock said.

William shook his head trying to make sense of it all as they continued down the magnificent looking streets. Large tiles made up the streets, perfectly placed and gleaming in the light. Each tile had its own etching scrolled into its surface. William could barely comprehend the attention to detail, not to mention the time needed for such a task.

His eyes darted around, taking in wondrous new sights. There were people of all sizes, shapes, and colors. They flooded the street with music and laughter. Brock slowed, and smiled back at William, who had become lost in the activities of the city.

Brock walked over to a stand, where a dark-skinned man was displaying odd looking produce. They were small and round, about the size of his palm, and green with white stripes. They looked strangely like a tiny watermelon. Brock waved William over.

"Zunga fruit are delicious. Try one, William," the big man said.

"I don't have any money," William said, chuckling nervously.

"There is no such thing as currency here, friend," Brock responded with a huge grin, before grabbing a zunga fruit from the stand, and taking a large bite.

William's mouth instantly began to water. He cast a glance to the man tending the stand, who gave him a genuine smile and held up one of the unusual fruits.

"Thank you," William said, accepting it and nodding at the merchant. He examined the fruit briefly, before taking a slow bite.

Flavors exploded in William's mouth. It was sweet and juicy, like William had just taken a drink of pure sugar. And yet, the tiniest hint of sour complimented the almost overpowering sweetness, giving it wonderful balance.

"This is amazing!" William exclaimed, turning to Brock. The big man laughed warmly.

William started asking questions as soon as they resumed their walk.

"Why does he even tend the stand if there is no money to collect?"

"He likes to see people enjoying his fruit. It brings him joy. There is also the possibility people might show their appreciation with gifts of their own sometimes," Brock said with a smile.

"It just surprises me. He must work very hard to plant and grow such fruit, and people don't have to pay for it," William said.

"Well I am sure it did take him quite a few tries to get that fruit tree growing properly, but the people here do not need to eat, so it would be rude of him to charge for it," Brock said.

"Wait...we don't need to eat?" William asked incredulously.

"No, little brother. Flavor is just one of the joys of living, and so your mind makes it real here," Brock said.

"What keeps people going then?" William asked.

"I do not want to overwhelm you to quickly, little brother. Our Archonian bodies are not biological therefore they need no sustenance."

"You can't get something from nothing though. What are we made from?" William asked.

"To be honest it is a little beyond my comprehension as well. Suffice it to say that our minds draw energy from a nearly infinite source of power that this world is made up of," Brock said.

A group of children ran by, moving faster than any children he'd ever seen. They were dressed up in funny looking costumes, shouting, and playing.

"Children? Brock, can people have children here?" William asked, shocked.

Brock looked at the kids.

"No, William, they cannot. Your soul cannot reproduce. Those are children from the mortal world who died before their time," Brock said, shaking his head.

"My God. Are they children forever then?" William asked.

"No, my friend, they grow as their minds grow. Some take longer than others, but eventually they reach maturity and stop growing. They become adults, like the rest of us," Brock said, indicating the beautiful people around them.

"What about the children who were never born?" William asked, stopping.

"Well, as soon as a man's seed meets a woman's egg a soul is formed, though it is just energy and has no defining characteristics."

"Dear God!" William breathed loudly.

57

"What is the matter?" Brock asked, stopping to look at William, thoroughly confused.

"There is a...process on Earth, called abortion..." William started to say.

"Rest easy, William. There is an Archonian woman who collects those unborn souls from the mortal world. They are innocent, so they are brought here and raised by loving couples or matrons that wish to raise them. Many of these people you see have never lived a mortal life, and they are much better for it. The physical world is full of sorrow and hatred," he finished, looking at the busy street with a smile.

William shook his head, trying to clear away the darker thoughts "They all look so young. What about the people who died of old age?" William asked.

"Ah. This is because people never forget the way they looked and felt when they were young. The mind or soul reflects what you feel when you are here," Brock said, pointing at a man passing by. He looked more aged than the rest, with a touch of grey hair.

"This world, Brock, it is very much like the heaven described in our religions on Earth," William said.

"Yes, little brother, and each of those religions has some truth to it," Brock replied. "When the nine Archons descended to the mortal world, the tribes of men revered them as gods. They taught them about living and loving and about what comes next, but over time, this knowledge became distorted, and lost," Brock said.

"There was a game we used to play in school," William said smiling. "We would all sit around a table. The first person would tell the one next to them a short story. Then that person would tell the next person and so on, by the time it reached the other end of the table, it was a completely different story."

"That is exactly what has happened throughout the history of man," Brock said, nodding. "The fundamental truths of this life remain, but the story becomes twisted by time, and the minds of men."

"But there are documents on Earth that have been recorded into books," William retorted, "The Holy Bible. The Quran."

"Those stories were written by men, William, and were translated through many different languages," he replied simply.

William thought about it for a moment, and realized the big man was right.

Brock laid a giant hand on his shoulder, and said, "Do not despair, my young brother. Some men were correct. All religions share the same fundamental rules for how we should conduct our lives. Be kind to others, do not be selfish, do not covet or steal, and do not spread lies or anger. Instead, live with joy and happiness."

That makes perfect sense. William thought

"So why don't we go back and teach them again? Can we even go back to Earth?" he asked.

"Would you have continued to live your mortal life knowing of this wonderful place?" Brock asked.

"That's a good point," William said.

"No. The Archons thought exactly as you did, that if mortals knew how to live properly, they would do so. In the end, thousands of lives were lost, simply because they all believed they would come here," Brock said nodding.

"And they didn't?" William asked.

"No. When the Archons first started interacting with humans they did not have immortal souls yet. That was a gift later given to them by the Archon Prometheus. Once the gift was given and the first people started coming here. The Archons knew they could no longer interact with the people unless they were extremely delicate. Otherwise there would be more self-destruction," he finished.

"Self-destruction?" William asked.

"Sacrifices and mass suicides, little brother. Some of the first humans thought that they could achieve immortality by releasing their souls from their Earthly bodies," Brock said solemnly.

"This is a lot to take in," William said, taking a deep breath.

"In time, you will understand everything."

William looked forward, taking note of a group of men and women standing in the middle of the road. They were looking straight at him. Brock put a hand on William's shoulder, anchoring him to the spot.

"We do not want him here, Guardian. His soul is foul," a tan, dark haired, blue-eyed woman said in a dour tone.

This wasn't the first time William had been met with such rejection and hatred. He wasn't taken aback by it, but it still stung a little.

"My friends, please surround your new brother. Welcome him home. The Synod has decreed it," Brock bellowed with a smile.

The crowd didn't move, and another man shouted, "The Synod is wrong! This man is a danger to us all. He belongs in Dichonia."

Some of the others in the crowd murmured in agreement. William was pissed at this point. Brock must have taken notice of this because and he turned, putting a massive palm across his chest. He shook his head, and William was put at ease. Then Brock turned to the crowd again.

"The Archon Gabriel brought him here. Is he also wrong, citizens?" Brock asked.

The crowd murmured, looking at one another, waiting for someone to speak out.

The first woman to speak took a step forward. William noticed that she looked familiar to him for some reason.

"Gabriel would never put us in danger," she said, shaking her head.

"Of that, I can assure you, Lisa," Brock said, addressing her by name.

William realized where he recognized her from the moment Brock mentioned her name. The Mona Lisa. *Could it really be?*" William wondered.

"Gabriel would never bring harm to any of his fellow Archonians. This is why I have trusted his judgment and have not destroyed this filthy soul myself!" Brock shouted, and as he did there was a terrifying force kicked up around the street like an unseen wind. Brock still seemed in control, but he got his point across.

They shuddered and moved away. William, who had seen some very bizarre things today, felt an icy cold shudder go up his spine.

"Now. Disperse! Go about your business and let me take care of this poor soul," Brock said, a smile returning to his face as he turned back to William.

Lisa cast a final hard look at William, before turning around. The others followed suit, either floating into the sky or running at abnormal speeds.

"Brock, how do I make them like me?" William said sadly.

"In the mortal world people treated me this way too."

Brock gave a heavy sigh as they began to walk again. The large man moved slowly this time, allowing William to keep pace.

"Little brother, people will always fear what they do not understand, but that does not mean that they hate you. They simply hate the idea of you. Remember what happened after your judgment? The Synod felt the same way but they did not take the time to get to know you," the large man said earnestly.

"Then why did this happen on Earth? I wasn't so different from people back there," William asked.

The question made William feel naïve. Then again, his father had been a horrible person, so William grew up

61

without a good role model. Now, he was looking to a man that he had just met for advice.

"William," Brock said, placing a huge hand upon his shoulder. "You looked like a loner when you came to Archonia. Is it possible that you have just refused to let people in?"

"I suppose you're right. But what can I do now?" William asked.

"For starters, smile! And tell people about yourself. If someone is unkind to you, treat them how you would wish to be treated. In time, they may do the same."

William felt like a child, his cheeks flushing with embarrassment. He had missed so many fundamental things like this growing up. He'd been too busy simply trying to survive the streets.

He decided to change the subject.

"Brock, who was that woman you referred to as Lisa?"

"Oh yes, Lisa!" Brock bellowed. "She fancies herself a model or some such thing. Some young lad named Leonardo painted a likeness of her on Earth, and apparently it has gained some repute."

William's jaw dropped. It wasn't just some painting. It was probably one of the most famous paintings in human history.

"She had the chap paint her another exactly like it here. She boasts about it often. Personally I think the painting was poorly done. Did you see some of the murals in the Synod chamber? They look almost real," Brock said.

William laughed.

"I did, and now that you mention it, I'd say I have to agree."

What an astounding world, William thought. And silently wondered what other famous figures he would cross paths with.

CHAPTER FIVE
FAMILY

Angelica watched William's frightened face as the large soldier helped him from his knees. She felt pity for him, in much the same way she had when she first met him on Earth.

That poor man, she thought. His entire life had just been laid bare before an entire room of strangers. He'd done some terrible things, much of it out of necessity. And yet, Angelica owed William everything. Had it not been for him, those horrible shadow creatures would have devoured her soul before Gabe could have saved her. She shuddered at the thought and watched as William was led from the hall.

She stood in a crowd of people, yet she felt alone, her thoughts drifting back to recount everything that had happened since her death. After William and Gabe had been taken into custody, she had been escorted into the city by a group of soldiers.

She remembered how one of the soldiers extended an arm, a beam of piercing light flashing out of his hand. The light flexed and expanded, taking the form of a creature. It looked strangely feline, with silver fur and penetrating, blue eyes. Black stripes covered its sleek, muscular body. She thought it looked like a cheetah, even though it was far larger than any cat she had ever seen. The beast caught her gaze, its eyes like ice.

The man who created the beast took a step in her direction, his voice soft and reassuring.

"My lady, have no fear. This gentle beast is of my mind, and will not harm you."

Angelica nodded, unable to speak. The man was strikingly handsome. He had long brown hair, which framed a beautifully structured face. He wore silver armor, the breastplate inlaid with sapphires, and a long flowing purple cape. He stood just slightly taller than her, with green eyes that glowed softly.

"I pray that you ride with me to the city, it will be much faster this way," he said, extending a hand invitingly. She saw a silver band upon his ring finger and became a little disheartened. He must be married. She took it anyway and he lightly hefted her up upon the back of the giant cat.

The soldier's hands were strong. He made her feel like she was weightless. She wasn't surprised by anything right now. She had just seen men flying through the air and one had made a huge beast appear out of thin air. He mounted up on the beast in front of her.

"Hold on to my armor if you feel the need," he said. Then he whispered something into the large cat's ear. Without warning it lurched forward powerfully. Angelica felt like she was on a roller coaster. She shrieked and grabbed onto the thick plates covering her armored companion.

They must have been a hundred miles or more from the city, yet the trip only took a few minutes. Angelica's eyes went wide as they approached. Her heart was already pounding from the speed, but everything seemed to slow down when her gaze locked upon the massive city.

She'd seen the Rocky Mountains while traveling in Colorado, but this city looked like it could have dwarfed them. Its sheer size was unnerving, and made Angelica's knees feel weak. They crossed the threshold of the city, passing through a gargantuan gate, taller than the skyscrapers in her home town. They moved through a large courtyard, and saw a blur of color, and heard a loud humming noise. Her insides churned from the ride, and she couldn't find the focus to make out anything happening around her, so she shut her eyes tight and buried her head into the soldier's back and held on tight.

Angelica's companion didn't seem to notice that she was terrified. She gave a little shriek as the large cat stopped suddenly, smashing her into the soldier's back. He pried her hands loose from his armor, before sliding down the side of the mount. Angelica needed a moment to get her bearings. She took in a deep breath, trying to slow her breathing and her runaway heart. Finally, she looked up and found herself in a small yard filled with lush grasses and flowers. She slid trembling to the ground after a moment, the soldier greeting her with a smile.

"Young One, these matrons will take good care of you. This is where I leave you. Welcome to Archonia," he said, taking her hand and brushing his lips against the top of it softly.

He kicked his heals together forcefully and burst into the sky. The cat that they rode into the city disappeared as it was sucked into the trail of light behind him.

Angelica watched him in wonder, simply stupefied by the fact that he could fly. Someone lightly touched her shoulder, startling her and making her jump a little in surprise. She turned and beheld a group of four young women around her age. They were all beautiful, and she immediately became very self-conscious.

"Welcome, Young One. What is your name?" one of the matrons asked.

"Angelica," she replied shyly.

The group smiled and ushered her towards a strange looking fountain.

Angelica yelped in surprise as the girls began to strip off her clothes.

"Oh hush, child, we need to make you presentable," a matron said.

In just a few moments she was completely naked, clutching an arm over her breasts out of modesty. The Matrons took her to the small pool, where they bathed and groomed her. They scrubbed her body with soft sponges lathered with soapy substances that smelled of fresh fruit and flowers. The dirt and lather was carried away by a strange whirlpool at the fountain's center.

She had bathed herself most of her life, so this was by far the most uncomfortable thing she had ever experienced. She fought the urge to pull away, or cry out, not wanting to be rude. She stood still, her hands covering her breasts, hoping there wasn't an audience watching in the adjacent yard. When she was bathed, they put white flowers in her hair and draped her body with the purest white silk she had ever seen. It was so soft and light she could barely feel it against her skin. She had to check to make sure she wasn't still naked.

Before she knew it, Brock returned, a large toothy grin on his face.

"You look simply splendid, little sister. A true citizen of Archonia," he said, beaming.

"Thank you. Brock wasn't it?" she asked.

"That is my name, young one. I am here because your savior needs your help." He went on to explain that there would be a trial to decide William's fate. She agreed to go.

It is the least I could do for him, she had thought.

Now she felt completely lost, standing alone in the massive chamber as it emptied after the trial.

Will I get to see William again? she wondered.

She looked around, trying to find someone who could tell her what to do next, and locked eyes with one of the women who had helped bathe and dress her. She was dressed exactly like Angelica, with white flowers in her hair, and a flowing white gown. Angelica smiled feebly, trying to hide her fear.

"Hello," she said as the woman approached.

"Baily," the woman responded with a pleasant smile.

"Nice to meet you...err again. I'm Angelica."

"It is quite alright, child. I trust you will meet a great many new faces in the coming days."

"Baily, what do I do now?"

"I know that you feel lost right now, but everything is going to be just fine. I am one of the midwives here in Helios. It is our job to help new souls that pass into our world find their place. One of my sisters was able to track down some of your ancestors while you were in the trial," Baily said, smiling kindly.

Angelica struggled with this news. *Her ancestors? Who could they be?* she wondered.

The woman motioned for her to follow and they exited the chamber together. As they walked, Baily began to talk about the Archonian way of life. There was no currency, and very little possession. There was no need to eat, sleep, or use the restroom, but you could still eat if you so desired. She could enjoy all of the joys of living, with none of the strife. The longer she listened, the more she believed that she had indeed come to the Promised Land.

After a long while they emerged onto the streets of Helios. Angelica watched as hundreds of souls moved about, evidently living their lives in peace and happiness. She listened as Baily continued, and was rewarded with answers to each and every question. She laughed as a funny realization struck her. Baily called herself a midwife. After all, coming into this world was very similar to being born anew. It was a fitting title.

After walking for some time, they came upon a colorful structure. It towered above them, piercing the sky like a hundred palaces had been stacked upon one another.

They entered through a massive door covered in bright carvings. Angelica's eyes bounced from ceiling to wall, taking in every fantastic detail and decoration, until she realized that Baily was no longer talking. She stopped and caught sight of the midwife walking a short distance ahead. Someone else was standing next to her now. The woman was about Angelica's height and had the same flowing dark hair and caramel skin. She wore simple, colorful garbs embroidered in orange and teal. The woman was gorgeous and youthful, with deep brown eyes that Angelica had seen before. Tears swelled up in her eyes as realization struck her.

"Abuela?" she gasped.

"Come here, my child, and give your grandmother a hug," the woman said.

Angelica raced into her arms, tears flooding her eyes. Her grandmother had been the glue which held her family together, and it had been a tragic day when she passed at seventy six. The thought of seeing her again hadn't even crossed Angelica's mind. But now it made perfect sense. How many times had she told herself that she would see her again when God welcomed her to heaven?

The two women embraced, looking more like long lost sisters. Then, without warning, the realization hit her, and the tears let loose like a flood and Angelica started to moan and convulse. She, just like her grandmother, Angelina, had passed away. Her family would be mourning for her right now. Angelina seemed to understand, and patted her comfortingly on the back.

"Oh my sweet child, you were too young, but you must not grieve your death. Our family will do this for you. Take comfort. As surely as you stand before me now, you will see them again," she said.

Angelica calmed quickly in her grandmother's arms, as she always did as a child. Emotion ran deep in her, but the fact that her dear grandmother hadn't shed a tear gave her strength. She must have been expecting her, just not quite yet. Baily mentioned that the soul is immortal, but also that time moved differently in Archonia. Angelica wondered how fast time had moved for her grandmother since her passing five years ago.

Angelica looked around, and realized that Baily was gone. Apparently, now that they had found her family, the midwife's job was done. She held her Grandmother Angelina's hand as they began to walk through intimately sized corridors, wound up spiraling steps, and moved through beautiful indoor gardens. The architecture and plant species were all fairly reminiscent of Central American themes.

"Welcome to the Latin district, child. This is where our family has chosen to make its home," Angelina said.

"How many of our family live here?"

"Well that depends on how far back in our lineage you want to track. The records that I have studied in the Latin district library indicate that we have as many as two thousand relations currently dwelling in Helios alone. Those on our particular family tree number perhaps forty or so," she said, smiling.

It was so peculiar seeing her young face and hearing her voice free from the rasp and soft quaver of age.

"My goodness. Will I get to meet them all? Do I know any of them?" she asked, bombarding her grandmother with questions.

"Of course, Angie, we are having a fiesta tonight in celebration of your coming. And don't worry I will make sure that they don't overwhelm you. They can be a handful," she said, grabbing Angelica's forearm and laughing.

Angelica laughed back and they continued on. She saw hundreds of people passing through the small winding corridors around her. They were all open-aired, and covered in Incan, Mayan, and Aztec inscriptions. In the halls, Spanish and Italian themed paintings and murals filled every available piece of stone. Trees and bushes grew everywhere in this section of the city, making it seem more real and alive than what she had seen so far.

After a brief walk they came to a courtyard with lush, green grass and fountains filled with floating flowers. Children played and the smell of rich spicy food filled the air. After a few moments the people all stopped what they were doing, and turned to stare at her. Her chest grew tight and she took a step back. She looked from face to face, starting to pick out familiar features. They must be her family.

Angelica jumped in surprise, her heart leaping into her throat as the courtyard erupted into cheers and applause. A smile broke across her face and she could feel it flush with warmth. Before she knew it, she was bombarded with hugs and kisses by so many strangers she could hardly keep track. Her grandmother told her who each person was, but there was no way to remember them all.

"This is your great, great aunt Debbie and her grandson, Ricardo. That is your great grandfather's cousin, Emilio and his wife, Daisy," she went on.

Angelica didn't know most of them, but her eyes swelled with tears again when her grandmother introduced her cousin Julia. Her cousin started to cry as well as they embraced. Julia had been very young when she died in a terrible car accident. She was a grown woman now, but Angelica recognized her face. It was the same face that had been in her prayers on so many sleepless nights. After almost a half an hour of introductions and embracing family, she thought that she was finally out of tears.

They ate together as a family, sitting at a long table laden with foods from all over. Angelica talked closely with Julia, filling her cousin in on all she had missed on Earth. Julia likewise told her about Archonia.

"Cousin, I prayed to the creators for years that I would see you again. I was so worried that my family would mourn me too much and not be able to live their lives to the fullest," Julia said.

"Julia, we all mourned for you so very much. I prayed to God that I would see you again. I knew that I would. I guess I just hadn't expected it to be so soon..." she said, trailing off.

"Don't worry, cousin. We will see our families again. We have as many years to be with them as we need."

Julia smiled and wiped yet another tear from Angelica's face.

"Would you like to meet my husband?" she asked excitedly.

Angelica was taken by surprise by this news, but tried hard to not let it show. Julia leapt up, and sped off through the grass. Angelica had never seen anyone move so fast. *She grew up in Archonia. Maybe she learned this speed?*

When Julia returned, she was holding the arm of a tall man clad in silver armor. It was inlaid with gold and encrusted with many gemstones. He wore a long flowing white cape that fell to the ground. His face was long and austere, as if chiseled from stone, and his long flowing black hair fell carelessly about his shoulders.

"Angelica, I would like you to meet my husband, Edmund."

His smile was radiant, and his presence put her at ease.

"He is a soldier?" Angelica asked, her gaze dropping to the very large sword dangling from his hip.

Edmund spoke, his words perfectly pronounced and his voice dignified.

"Not just a soldier, young one. I am a guardian."

"Why does everybody keep calling me that?" Angelica asked.

"Cousin, Edmund is over two hundred years old," Julia said snorting.

The pair shared a smile and Angelica wanted to shrink away. She felt like an alien. An outsider. The prospect of her little cousin being married to someone who was over two hundred years old frightened her. She returned their smile, trying hard to hide her shock.

"And what is a guardian?" Angelica asked politely.

"Guardians are among the strongest and most important militant groups in this world, and of dire importance to the mortal world. We are a battalion that focuses completely on combat, and once a year each member travels on a crusade to the mortal plane to watch over humanity," Julia said, admiring her husband with big doughy eyes.

Angelica smiled and nodded, trying to soak everything in. For the rest of the evening the group sang and danced. Occasionally, someone would hold up their hand and make the most wonderful things appear from pure light. Angelica watched it all quietly, feeling like an infant born into a new world.

After most of the people had gone back to their homes, her grandmother settled down next to her and held her close. They watched the massive sun set over the collage of buildings, casting the city in a beautiful, rose hue. Another tear formed in Angelica's eye as questions started to filter into her thoughts.

The questions flooded in, but she could only manage to ask one.

"Abuela? Is anything from the bible true?"

CHAPTER SIX
TRIBULATIONS

William and Brock walked in silence, simply enjoying the sea of buildings shining brightly overhead. Waves of people flowed around them, their noise like the ebb and flow of whitecaps breaking on a sandy beach.

William tried identifying some of the different styles of architecture. Though his knowledge of this only extended to high school history class, he was sure that he could at least pick out the main themes. Some looked Greek, some Roman, while others appeared Chinese or Japanese. Many had murals or tapestries, decorating their exterior walls.

"Brock, these buildings are larger than anything I've ever seen," William said, breaking the silence.

"Just wait until you see," his large companion said, just as they turned a corner.

Just beyond the square sat the most massive structure he had ever seen. It stretched as far as he could see in either direction, stone blocks the size of a house stacked to create a wall and turrets which dwarfed the sea of buildings around it. The wall wrapped around another mountain of towers, like arms embracing it lovingly. William's mouth dropped open.

"What is this place?" William asked.

A smile broke across Brock's enormous face.

"This is the center of the Archonian military. The ancient Nordic people call it..."

"Valhalla!" William exclaimed, interrupting.

"Correct, and it was so named,"

"Why does Archonia need a military?" William asked.

"Well, little brother, this world wasn't always so peaceful. After the wars of old, the Synod ordered the creation of an army, should our foes ever rise again," Brock said, leading them towards a gate cut expertly out of the outer wall.

"You mean Lucifer," William said, his voice tight.

"Indeed, little brother, I do. But I am not a professor, so I will leave the rest of this tale to your mentors," Brock said.

William followed Brock through the massive gate. If someone told him that giants lived there, William would believe them. There were five portcullises that hung above, the metal so thick that William wondered if explosives could breach it.

Through the gate sat another courtyard. A fountain and sculptures dominated the space, but the main focus was the enormous staircase and the front door. It too was made completely of metal, and adorned with beautiful reliefs of copper and bronze. It was striking, but menacing. William ascended the stair, and nearly tripped over his own feet as he tried to take it all in. He stumbled forward, but caught himself just in time to almost run into a huge figure.

A man loomed above him even more intimidating than Brock. He stood nine feet tall, his muscles bulging through leather armor studded with silver, his arms folded over his chest. He had long white hair that curled slightly as it fell over his face. A scar ran over his ruined left eye, while the other shone brilliant lavender. William could have sworn he saw a flicker of electricity in his piercing gaze. As intimidating as he was, his face was still sharp and attractive.

"How is he so big?" William whispered to Brock.

"I was not as statuesque as I was on Earth either. He has lived here far longer than either of us, and his soul reflects his stature," Brock said with a chuckle.

"Guardian. Thank you for escorting the recruit," the white-haired man said, his voice booming forth.

"Yes, my lord Zeus," Brock said, bowing low and backing away.

William watched him in astonishment. *This couldn't possibly be Zeus, the Greek god of lightning. Could it?*

"I wanted to see it for myself. Gabriel is a fool," Zeus said.

William scowled. Gabriel was the only person that had done anything for him, in either of his lives, save for Angelica. He really didn't know what having a friend was like, but he felt compelled to speak up.

"What's your problem?"

"Be silent, or I will send your tainted soul to Dichonia," Zeus threatened.

"Try it. I'd like to see if your words are as big as you are," William retorted.

"Well, this little soul has no fear. You may make a fine soldier... if nothing else. Very well, Brock, his sentinel training will begin immediately."

With that Zeus turned and disappeared into the shade of the massive hall behind him.

"Bold words, little man," Brock said, slapping him on the back. William raised an eyebrow, and let out his pent up breath.

"Is anyone going to like me here?" he asked.

"I know at least two people here that like you fair enough. Gabe likes you, and therefore, I like you," Brock stated, and ushered him inside.

Brock asked William to wait patiently in the entrance hall. He looked around as the large man walked away. The interior of Valhalla was as equally breathtaking as the outside. It was excessive, really. Massive pillars held up the high ceiling, but he felt a light breeze blow across his shaved head, as if it was open sky above him. Fully armored soldiers zipped by at incredible speeds. Many stopped briefly, if only to stare at William. He felt like an animal at a zoo.

William immediately felt uncomfortable. Not only was it an alien place, but also because everyone he'd seen inside treated him like an oddity. He tried to brush these feelings aside.

If Brock was to be believed, he was going to begin some kind of military training. He knew from past experiences that it would likely be very rough. His time in the Army Rangers and Spec Ops taught him that he would be facing rigorous physical training exercises. These would likely be followed by tactical classes, and then more training exercises. They would drill hand to hand combat, weapons, and survival tactics. He had a good idea how things were supposed to go.

It wasn't long before a man dressed head to toe in silver and blue armor approached. He was shorter than others he had seen. He had long, dark brown hair, which fell just past his shoulders. This seemed to be a popular style of haircut. Such a thing would never be found in the military on Earth.

"My name is Silvos, and I am a sentinel of Archonia. I have been tasked with overseeing your training," the man declared cordially.

"My name is William," he said, extending a hand.

Silvos looked at his proffered hand, his own hands remaining locked behind his back.

"Lord Zeus has commanded me here. I assure you, I take no pleasure in our meeting," Silvos said, the edges of his mouth turned down.

"Well then, get on with it," William responded in an equally spiteful tone.

He was so set in his ways. He tried to think of something nice to say in return, as Brock had suggested, but he came up blank. Silvos turned and began to walk. William followed silently, wondering if this was heaven at all. It sure didn't feel like it. If these were the people chosen to live in paradise, they were certainly not kind in the least.

They turned down a dark hall and, William took in the stone work around him. Expansive murals depicting great battles hung on either side. Evil looking beasts were being cut down and defeated by valiantly painted soldiers, just like the ones passing them by. William marveled at the size of their weapons. He couldn't imagine they were easy to lift, let alone wield. Even with the super strength that these men seemed to possess.

The columns supporting the walls appeared to be sculptures of different warriors. They were each magnificent in their own unique way. William ducked closer to read the inscriptions. They were written in a strange series of symbols that William had never seen before. He rubbed his eyes and looked again, and almost missed the change. What looked like gibberish before, now appeared as clear as day. The symbols popped into his head as if they had been planted there.

"Theseus of Archonia," he said softly, amazed that he was able to read it at all.

"Yes. This is the Greek wing," Silvos said, in a bored, uninterested manner. "May we continue now? We must begin. I am required to have you killing demons by nightfall."

William hurried along to catch up with Silvos, who had already rushed ahead. He looked at the other statues, excitedly reading their names. There were so many of them, but William was able to pick out a few that he recognized from stories: Perseus of Ovaria, Oedipus of Earth, Hercules of Archonia, Cadmus of Dichonia, Atalanta of Earth, Ajax of Dichonia, and Achilles of Archonia.

A bright light appeared ahead. William squinted as he passed through and found himself outside. A mass of soldiers stood before him. Some were formed in ranks, while others sparred in small groups, marched, or flew overhead as fast as jets.

William couldn't fathom the number. There must have been a million people in the field. They all wore gold and silver armor. To his immediate left, William saw men lifting stones that looked impossibly large. One man stepped forward, apparently demonstrating for a group of recruits. He held up a palm towards a massive stone, just before a blinding light shot forth. The beam instantly shattered the stone into gravel. The soldiers applauded in approval.

Silvos led William to a circular sparring ground. There was sand in the circle, and a short chain fence around it. It was obvious to William what was about to happen. Silvos leapt into the center of the circle, clearing the distance in a single bound. William figured he could probably make it over the fence, if he tried. He settled in to watch Silvos, but the short man motioned him to join him.

Son of bitch! They really don't like me at all here, William thought.

Either that or he was about to be initiated. Either way, William figured he was about to get his ass kicked. He climbed slowly over the fence, dragging his feet to his instructor.

"Let us see what the tainted one can do!" Silvos shouted so that others around could hear him.

Almost all the soldiers within earshot stopped what they were doing, and began to move towards their circle. Could word of his arrival possibly spread so fast? He tried to recount the time since his arrival, but it was fractured and jumbled.

William tried to think of what to say to diffuse the situation, but something flashed before him. Everything blurred and started to spin. He felt weightless, like he was flying, and his face hurt. William tumbled hard into the sand and skidded to a halt. Silvos stood casually where

William's face had been a moment ago, a single finger extended. Silvos had only hit him with a finger.

Through the haze of pain, William heard the gathered crowd roar with laughter. He staggered to his feet, the coppery taste of blood filling his mouth.

"Is that how you treat all new recruits?" William growled, furiously spitting out a glob of red.

"Be silent. Were you fighting your true enemy, you would already be destroyed," Silvos said seriously.

"You're a...." but again William couldn't get a word out before he was flying through the air.

This time he slammed into the fence, which shattered from the impact. His body felt wrecked, but the feeling subsided a bit as adrenaline rushed in. This time he didn't wait for Silvos to say something. He lunged up from the ground, dug his feet into the sand, and rushed at him.

The crowd burst into laughter. William must have looked like a snail running towards him, because there was more laughing. Silvos chuckled, deftly dodging an attack, before cracking him on the back of the head.

William caught a face full of sand again. Everything was blurring when he managed to lift his head. He could faintly make out a figure standing at the edge of the circle. He stood perfectly still, perhaps the one person not laughing or hollering. Then everything went dark.

* * *

William awoke, startled, and braced himself for the next blow, but it never fell. His head felt like it was in a vice, and he blubbered around a bit, pushing two fingers on each of his temples. Craning his neck slowly, he squinted his eyes looked around. He was lying on a stone slab in a room with few windows. The room's high stone walls cast long shadows, leaving the room incredibly dark. He shifted painfully, taking in the rest of the room. There was a door. Compared to everything else in Archonia, this one looked relatively normal sized for once. It was made of a light colored wood, and was no less intricate than anything else.

How many times have I been knocked unconscious lately? This can't be good for my head, he thought to himself.

"Damn it, I need to see a friggin' doctor!"

He felt a cool breeze fall upon his face and neck. The breeze fluttered through his linen clothes, sending a shiver up his spine. He stood, the stone of the floor cold against his bare feet. He pushed his hand against his chin and cracked his neck back and forth, and stretched his sore muscles.

A sudden, low growl reverberated out of the shadows, interrupting his focus. A heartbeat later the room was quiet once again. For a moment William wondered if he had simply imagined it. He held his breath and listened intently in complete silence. There was no sound, and curiosity got the better of him. After a moment he started towards the door. As he did there was a thudding on the other side, not unlike footsteps.

He paused momentarily, but then continued. He pushed, the door cracking open slowly. As it did, a wave of air rushed over him. It sounded strangely like something exhaling.

He stopped for a second, and thought to himself that this couldn't possibly be good, but nothing good had really ever happened to him. He flexed his stomach to give him courage, and gritted his teeth.

William gave the door a rough push and it swung open. The doorway opened into a large circular room, where a terrifying beast stood. It was all white and stood on four legs, each as thick as a tree trunk. Massive claws clicked against the granite floor. Two large heads sprouted from the creature's breast. They looked like the heads of dogs or lions. Armor scales circled the neck of each head like a mane. The creature snapped and snarled, baring razor sharp teeth.

William took a deep breath, and walked towards it. There were two possibilities. Either this was a test, or they had decided to execute him. Either way, he would have to fight.

The beast didn't appear to have noticed him. It seemed to be looking at something above. William craned his neck and followed its gaze. Ringed balconies lined the high walls above him, like some sort of amphitheatre. Soldiers filled each row, watching silently.

William quickened his pace, hoping to catch the creature off guard, but as he approached one of the heads snapped in his direction. Fear gripped him, and he froze. He tried to assess his options, but his train of thought was completely lost as the head facing him roared, baring an array of yellowed teeth. The hot, sickening breath washed over him.

Gabe said the laws of physics were different here. My mind determines how strong I am. He remembered the three foot thick stone wall that he had crumbled with his bare fist.

"Alright let's do this," he said to himself.

William burst forward, his bare feet finding purchase against the cool floor, and leapt. There was a rush of air and William was airborne. He closed the gap in a single bound. The creature jumped and met him in the air, teeth gnashing. William threw his shoulder into the beast, catching one of the heads in the nose. The creature howled and froze in mid-air. William bounced off, flying backwards hitting the hard granite floor and cracking a large indent into it. He turned over quickly, and sank an angry fist into the ruined floor. He pushed off, his feet digging in, further crushing the fragmented stone.

The head he had struck hung limp, evidently still stunned from the previous blow. William jumped hard into the air, dodging the snapping teeth of the other head, and locked two strong hands around its two canine teeth. With the momentum of his body, he twisted the head and the creature along with it, wrestling it to the ground. William wrapped his muscular arms around the head and twisted, yelling with all his might. There were a series of sickening cracks as the head went limp in his arms and the tongue rolled out of its mouth.

There was a howl of pain from the other head, and William cheered in silence, but his celebration was cut short. The second head ripped away from the dead one, leaving William holding a lifeless lump. The other head had separated into a completely different body. This new form turned on William and charged. Before he could react he caught a chest full of claws, the creature burying them deep into his flesh.

Searing pain came across his body as he hit the floor, digging into the magnificently detailed stone once again. He thought quickly. Years of street fighting and wrestling experience kicked in, and he crossed his arms over his face, catching the creature's mouth and blocking its deadly teeth. He quickly twisted his torso, and wrapped his legs on the inside of the creature's limb pinning him to the ground. He straightened his body with all his might, and there was another crack as the beast's leg gave way to William's strength.

The claws hurt almost as much going out as they did going in, but he felt the pressure fall away as the creature collapsed sideways. William pushed off the ground, grabbed the howling creature by the jaw and upper lip, and used its falling body to bring himself upright. With brute force he whipped the creature around in a great arc, and let it loose, sending it flying across the room. It hit one of the room's support pillars, fracturing the stone in a spray of dust and debris.

Silence fell over the room, and William fell to his knees, the pain rushing in as the adrenaline wore off. Blood seeped from the puncture wounds made by the creature's claws, staining the front of his white, linen shirt. Sweat dripped from his brow and into his eyes, blurring his vision.

He made out a figure through the haze. They landed silently in front of him.

There was a searing flash, and light poured over him like a shower. He felt it pour into his wounds, spreading like warmth through the gashes and torn flesh. Relief flooded through him as his wounds started to close. Soon the pain was gone. The light subsided, allowing his vision to return.

William looked up to find not just one figure, but twenty or more standing before him. The closest man was of average size and had short, blonde hair. He wore silver plates that protected only certain vital areas of the body. He smiled and extended a hand to him. William took it and was lifted off the floor with surprising force. He staggered back, his free hand crawling over his chest, his shirt still damp with blood.

"My chest," he said.

The man smiled, still gripping his hand.

"I have healed your wounds, son," he said, shaking William's hand vigorously. "My name is Henry. Well done, my friend."

William muttered, "Thanks," his confusion mounting.

Zeus stood amidst the group, towering over them all. Standing next to him was a relatively normal looking man. He was average height, with long blond hair, and piercing blue eyes. He wasn't smiling or laughing like the others. He stood motionless, his arms crossed, his face emotionless. He wore dull, steel armor that looked distinctively Greek. A short sword was strapped to his back. It looked miniscule compared to some of the other men's weapons.

The clamor of voices died down as Zeus raised a hand.

"So, Young Archonian, It seems you have some experience with battle," Zeus said.

William was surprised that he referred to him as an Archonian, when earlier he had called him tainted.

"I have been in a few fights before," William replied, getting up from his knees gingerly.

Zeus laughed, the noise reverberating off the walls.

"Indeed, only one other has ever defeated Henry's Chimera on their first try."

"I assume you're talking about the massive dog," William said, pointing over to the pile of rubble.

"Correct. Henry, you must be very displeased. Usually your beasts are much more formidable," Zeus said, turning towards the man that had healed William.

Henry smiled, and said, "On the contrary, sir, it was as strong as ever. It was bested fair and square by a truly powerful warrior."

"Truly powerful, indeed. He should be trained as a guardian," Zeus said.

"There is too much anger in him. He has done nothing but think of himself his entire mortal and immortal existence," the man in the dull steel armor said, cutting in sternly.

William's eyes narrowed, and took a breath to argue but Zeus spoke first.

"Oh come now, you must see a great warrior for what he is. Let him walk the path. The worst that would happen is that he would fail, and if he does, he will be trained as a Sentinel," Zeus finished in a deep voice.

The rest of the room turned to the smaller man, waiting for his response. He seemed to command great respect.

"Very well, Commander. He will report to captain Chang Fei to begin his initiation."

With that the blond-haired man and some of the others standing around him whirled around, and with unnatural speed were gone.

"Come with me, William," Henry said, putting his arm around William's back.

He followed, having to run just to keep up with Henry's swift pace.

"I'm sorry about your dog," William said, worried that he had killed the man's pet.

"Not to worry, my friend, it was only a conjuration. It had no life in it," Henry replied.

"A conjur...what?

"All Archonians have different abilities. Some are more unique than others. They are powers reflected from your life as a mortal. I was a British explorer in the year sixteen nineteen. I was very fond of animals, and came across the most incredible species on my journeys. Unfortunately it was one of the very beasts that I admired that destroyed my mortal body. I have a great connection to creatures of all kinds, and simply by seeing them I can project a sort of illusion of one, and in a way, it becomes real."

William began to wonder if he had any special powers.

William ran his hands over his chest, inspecting the torn, stained fabric. "That thing seemed real enough to me. Did you really just imagine that ugly thing?" he asked.

"I did indeed. The uglier the beast, the scarier it is for the adversary," the man said with proper English etiquette.

"The horrible breath was a particularly nice touch," William responded, rolling his eyes.

"The small details are the most important part, in my opinion," Henry said, holding a closed hand up to William.

There was a tiny flash of light, and when he opened his hand, a stunning butterfly sat on his palm. It was a brilliant aqua blue, marked with black spots. William watched as Henry let it fly into the air, before disappearing from sight.

They walked for a short while, soon coming upon a familiar face. Brock beamed at William, slapping him on the back and almost knocking him to the ground again.

"Well done, little brother!" he bellowed with a huge smile. "I have never seen anyone take down Henry's two headed dog before. I myself only got one head. Damn thing

85

split, and took me down. You are one hell of a fighter. What kind of combat did you see back on Earth?"

"Just some firefights, mostly street fighting," William responded.

"You fight with fire in your time?" Brock asked, his face crinkling in confusion.

William laughed. "No, in my time we use guns to kill each other, not swords."

"They use the expanding gas from a combustible powder to hurl projectiles at very high speeds," Henry cut in, trying to explain for Brock.

"Oh yes. I remember reading about those things one time. Those projectiles would not even tickle the weakest soldier here," Brock said, laughing.

"William, how have the weapons evolved since my time? Have they found better ways to slaughter one another?" Henry asked sarcastically.

"Well, I fired a mini gun once that fired over two thousand rounds a minute," William said with a smile.

Henry stopped walking, his mouth hanging open in shock.

"That is outrageous," Henry said after recovering.

"What exactly is a guardian, and why am I no longer going to be a sentinel?" William asked, trying to change the subject.

Brock's smile grew even wider.

"Well, there are three different branches that make up our army. The sentinels are defenders that protect the cities of Archonia, and keep the peace. Then there are the adjudicators. This section of our fighting force is made up of mostly scholars, and tacticians. They also interpret the law of the Synod. But you, my friend, are going to become a guardian. The guardians are soldiers, the elite fighting force in Archonia. They focus primarily on warfare and are purely military," Brock stated.

"We answer only to the commander of the guardians," Henry said.

"...he answers only to the Synod," Brock finished for him.

William already knew who that was.

"That man in the grey armor," he said quietly.

"Correct," Brock responded. "He is the most powerful warrior in Archonia. His name is Achilles. The only time he was ever defeated was on Earth, when an arrow shot by a lucky foe crippled him. Unfortunately that cowardly shot was all they needed to destroy his mortal body. He has otherwise never been defeated in single combat."

"So he has more influence than the Synod?" William asked.

"No, little brother. The Synod was created after the war of souls. It was modeled after the first democracies of man for it was these first societies who began to crossover into our world. Archonia was founded as a republic. Therefore, there are checks and balances that must be kept in place to ensure that no one person possesses too much power."

"What about Zeus? He seemed to defer to Achilles. In my human histories, Zeus was a god and Achilles a man," William said.

"Many humans were thought to be gods in the early days of man. I can assure you that Zeus was just a man. He was a powerful leader, and was one of the first to be taught by the Archon Kronos. Hence many people thought that he was his son. In truth he is just as much an Archonian as you or I, little brother."

"I think I understand, at least the military. Sentinels are the police. Adjudicators are the judges, and I am going to be a soldier," William said confidently.

"Not just any soldier William. If you do not fail the training, you will be among the most powerful warriors in Archonia."

CHAPTER SEVEN
A FRIEND

After his fight with Henry's two headed beast, Brock showed William to his living quarters. It was a small room on the first floor of Valhalla. Located nearest to the training grounds, the new recruit's rooms allowed the younger and slower Archonians to get to their training sessions on time.

There wasn't much to his quarters. A simple bathing tub sat in one corner, a small fountain of warm water flowing softly. There was a closet containing fresh garments as well as some training leathers. A doorway led into several smaller rooms. They contained neither beds nor storage, so he struggled to immediately identify their purpose. It was small, and simple, but without a doubt the finest lodging William had ever experienced.

William changed into some of the thick leather training gear. It was composed of a hardened chest guard that was sleeveless to keep his arms free. Next, matching leather pants, which allowed for a surprising amount of movement, and finally tall, studded leather boots. He was ready to train, but quickly learned that physical training wasn't all that awaited him. When he left the changing room he was met by a guardian who didn't speak. The man simply handed him a thick, bound stack of papers.

William crinkled his brow, but before he could thank the soldier, the man dashed off. He strolled back into the room, opening the cover and rifling through the papers. It was a book. He found a schedule outlining academic courses as well as a rigorous training regimen. Brock had told him to expect this.

Brock had also gone on to explain that he would have to complete his initiates training before continuing down the path of the guardian, and that becoming a guardian was no easy task. If he successfully completed this training he would be allowed to forge his armor. This part piqued William's interest, but when he tried to press Brock for more information, he simply said, "You will get there in due time."

Guardian training would take place over the course of two Archonian months, which equated to roughly two hundred days. By the end of that time, he hoped to be proficient in combat, written studies, and Archonian laws.

Before William knew it he was in the middle of another sparring circle. Brock stood across from him, and next to the large man was an enormous stone block. It had to be as big as a truck. It cast a shadow over William as he walked over to Brock, who stood lazily with one arm against it.

"Before you begin your training, you must first learn to forget the rules that governed your time on Earth. As Archonians, we are no longer bound by those laws. The same object here can be as heavy as an ox, or lighter than a bird."

"So, what exactly do you want me to do?" William asked.

"Lift it," Brock said, gesturing towards the massive stone.

"What!? That's impossible," William said.

Brock shook his head. Then with hardly a second look he bent down and lifted the stone straight off the ground with one hand. He lifted it high over his head, and paused at the top.

"Impossible does not exist here, little brother."

He dropped the stone to the ground. It hit with a great thud, dust kicking up all around. William stood there stunned by this feat. The stone looked to weigh tons.

"There are a stack of these on the other side of the training grounds," Brock said as he walked off. "Come find me when you've put it in its place. Then and only then can you begin your combat training."

William watched him walk off, before turning to stare at the giant block. He sighed heavily, and approached. He squatted down and tried to dig his fingers underneath it, but there wasn't even any place to grip. He would have to tip the stone a little to get his hands below it. He took a deep breath, and planted his shoulder against the rough block. He heaved with all his might, but the stone wouldn't budge. After a few more seconds of straining he gave up.

What the hell, he thought.

William knelt there for a moment, pondering his short, if not eventful immortal life. He had smashed through a brick wall with one swift blow, and had taken on a creature much larger and stronger than him. He had already done the impossible since arriving here.

This SHOULD be easy.

He got to his feet again, and crouched low. He focused his thoughts on something light. Like a box full of pillows. He imagined that the stone was just that, and lifted. There was a lot of pressure, and it definitely felt heavier than a box of pillows, but he felt it move, and when he opened his eyes the massive stone was leaning ever so slightly off the ground. A smile spread across his face, but as soon as he lost his focus the weight came back, and the stone fell to the ground.

"Well. It's a start," he said, patting the stone, and shut his eyes again.

He gazed skyward. The sun had moved a great distance, in fact, it was almost directly overhead now. It didn't feel like it, but he must have been at this for hours. He had managed to push the massive stone about two feet while it was still on the ground, but hadn't had any success in picking it up completely. He was getting nowhere. The sun's continual barrage forced him to ditch his leather chest piece. The heat then proceeded to beat down on his back, forcing him to take breaks from pure exhaustion.

More time passed. He had managed to lift one side of the stone up a few feet into the air, before his back gave out. He staggered to his feet, every muscle aching and sweat covering him in a heavy sheen. The heat only got worse, and with no discernable breeze, he didn't know how much longer he would last.

When William started his task to move the giant rock the training grounds had been bustling with life. Soldiers had been training, sparring, and marching. Now the grounds were empty. He fell to his knees, and sank a fist into the ground out of frustration. The stack of massive stones had to be miles away. He hadn't even managed to move his stone out of the circle yet.

William gasped for breath, and closed his eyes. He was never going to be good enough. Teachers told him he wasn't smart enough. Drill sergeants told him he wasn't strong enough. Hiring managers insisted he wasn't an ideal candidate. Evidently they all rang true, in life, in death, and even now.

William was filled with sadness, but also rage. He was fed up. His muscles tensed and quivered, as rage built inside. It burst forth when he couldn't contain it any longer. He yelled until his voice echoed across the empty grounds. His cry was long and loud, but it did nothing to stifle the anger.

William opened his eyes, jolted into action. He slammed his bare shoulder into the hard stone. It tipped a couple of inches, allowing him to grab the bottom of the stone, and heave again. His fingers crushed into the stone, making a place to grip. This time he didn't even think about how heavy it was. It was light in comparison to his burdens.

This gave him strength, and the stone lifted off the ground. He ran, even though he couldn't see where he was going.

He pushed forward, the awkward shape of the stone hindering him only momentarily as he sought to regain balance. Then he lifted it over his head. At that moment he saw the fence surrounding the sparring circle, and without thinking he leapt into the air. When he came down he stumbled, and it was just enough to make the stone shift out of his control. It came crashing down, and landed on its side with a thud. William fell, face-first into the sand again, but he did so with a triumphant smile. He hooted and cajoled at his victory.

This is easy, only a couple miles to go, he told himself.

After what seemed like an eternity, the sky finally began to get dark. William walked slowly with the massive stone on his back. The days were longer in this world, which was apparent. He hoped the nights would be equally long. He felt like he could sleep for an eternity.

His muscles ached before, but now they felt like they were ready to tear apart. Cramps began to bite into his coiled muscles, making his whole body shake in protest of the weight. He didn't know how he had found the strength to complete the task, but after many hours he finally managed to reach the great stack of stones. It was only then that he realized there was an empty space for his particular brick. About five stones up and three stones in.

Great, he thought to himself. *Now I simply have to toss this thing up there.*

William was a changed man. His sopping wet linens were beginning to dry in the cool evening air, and his aching muscles were past the point of pain. He was numb. He couldn't feel any of it, the pain, the anger, the rejection.

One last little toss, he thought with an exhausted laugh.

With almost zero effort, he tossed the massive stone like a shot put directly into place on the stack. William watched the rock slide into place, and collapsed onto the ground, laughing in both triumph and relief. He had spent the entire day fighting, breaking himself down, stubbornly refusing to do it any other way than his way...the hard way. Then, when he was emptied out and hollow, he found the strength he needed inside.

He stared up into the sky, gazing at the black canvas speckled with celestial bodies. It looked unreal, like something out of a dream. Large colorful planets hung unmoving in the black. Some had rings around them, like Saturn, while others appeared as multi colored balls of gas, like Jupiter. It was beautiful, just like everything he'd seen in this place.

He sighed and got up, beginning to jog. It seemed a new wave of energy had overtaken him. Even sprinting seemed to be easier. In fact, he felt light. He jumped into the air, and cried out as he flew easily twenty feet into the air and almost gapped half a football field before landing. He caught himself, and took a few more strides before jumping again, this time with more might. He rocketed into the air, letting out a cry of joy as gravity released him from a lifelong bond. The five mile hike back to Valhalla took minutes. William didn't even seem to notice.

He walked up the wide steps to the side of the building, and entered a corridor lit by what looked like lamps. They gave off a very bright, white light, and upon closer inspection they appeared to be crystals. He had expected torches or even a light bulb, but the crystals emitted a soothing white light that illuminated the white stone hallways around them.

He had taken a few steps down the hallway when he heard voices. He recognized one of them instantly. How could he forget it? Especially when the person the voice belonged to treated him like dirt when he first arrived in this new world.

He slowed as he came to a four way intersection. The voices grew louder, so he peered around the corner. Meredox stood in a pool of shadow between lamps, talking with another figure. William didn't recognize the other man's voice, and he was cloaked, so it was impossible to see his face. They whispered back and forth secretly.

"It will happen, and when it does, I need to know that I can count on you," Meredox said. His curly black hair left his face in shadows.

"You play a dangerous game, Meredox. If we are discovered..." the other man said, but was cut short by his shadowy companion.

"The Synod is blind. They have sat too long in their high chairs. There will be nothing to stop it," Meredox finished.

The voices slowly faded as the two turned and walked down the corridor. William dared not show himself. He was confident he had just overheard the two men scheming some sinister plot.

After waiting a few moments William set off again, finally reaching his barracks. It was quiet inside. He assumed that perhaps others in his unit were sleeping. He opened the door quietly to a surprising sight. Half a dozen initiates sat cross legged in a circle around a very bright light. They sat on small mats, each with their eyes closed. William didn't know what they were doing, but he also didn't want to interrupt. He crept past to look for his bed, but quickly realized that there were no beds. William looked around, turning in confusion and almost ran into Brock.

"Well hello there, little brother. Glad you could join us."

William startled, and jumped back.

"Good grief, Brock. Don't you have better things to do than scare the crap out of me?" William asked.

"Well, I wish I did, but there you have it," Brock said, chuckling, his blue eyes flickering in the lamp light.

"Well, what do you need? I was just looking for my bed," William said, hoping that Brock would inadvertently explain the apparent and odd lack of beds in his chamber.

Brock simply laughed. "We do not sleep in this world."

"What!?" William exclaimed.

"You heard me. We do not sleep here in Archonia, we have no need. Our bodies are no longer physical they need only what rest the mind can give," he said.

"I'm exhausted. I'm not sure if you noticed, but I just moved a twenty ton stone about five miles in the blistering heat, and it only took me about twenty hours, according to that crazy clock over there," William said, pointing to a clock on the wall.

"Oh come now, give yourself some credit. It was only nineteen and one half hours," Brock said mockingly. "Believe me, you will not be able to sleep a wink. What you need is to meditate. Your mind only thinks it needs rest. Do you think you actually used any muscles out there today?"

William gave Brock an incredulous look and shook his head. "Okay then. I'm gonna meditate over here in the corner."

"Very well. I will be back to fetch you in the morning."

"Oh boy. Will I get to move two rocks?" William asked sarcastically.

"I am afraid tomorrow you will start drill, and then you will really wish that you could sleep," Brock said, before disappearing out the door.

William found a couple of spare mats in the corner, and piled them up into a makeshift mattress. He relaxed for what seemed like the first time in days. In fact, he'd already lost track of how long he had been here.

Forget sleep, was he hungry? The only thing he'd eaten since arriving was that small fruit from the street vendor. He also hadn't needed to use the restroom, if there were any, which made his mind wander even more.

If I don't need to eat, then I probably don't need to piss or shit, he thought.

His heart jumped, and he checked to make sure that nobody was looking, before lifting the waistband of his linen slacks to make sure that his parts were still there. He breathed a sigh of relief and grabbed it just to be sure. He wondered why he still needed his manhood if he didn't need to use the bathroom.

He looked across the small room and his fellow initiates. They looked peaceful, sitting in a circle around the bright crystal, their eyes closed, and their breathing soft. It sure looked like they were sleeping.

His eyes felt very heavy, and he tried to focus on sleeping, but when William closed his eyes he felt uneasy. There were ten other men sitting around a strange glowing crystal, only feet away, and he didn't know any of them. His mind began to wander, and before he knew it three more hours had passed, and he hadn't fallen asleep.

William finally decided that Brock wasn't trying to lead him astray. So he decided to listen to the large man's advice. He sat up, and closed his eyes, slowing his breathing while he tried to clear his mind.

Questions flooded into his mind, but he silenced them. Instead, he focused on his task with the stone, and slowly relived every detail. His head swam and he lost all sense of time. William opened his eyes after what seemed like minutes. He was sitting in the exact same position, only now there were two massive eyes staring back at him.

"Rise and shine, little brother. It is about time you came back to us," Brock said gruffly.

William's eyes were still adjusting to the light pouring in through the windows. Brock didn't waste any time in picking William up off the floor.

"Uh... morning," he said slowly, "how long was I out?"

"Wait, how long are the days here?" he blurted suddenly, the questions flooding back in.

Brock smiled and said, "Each day is fifty hours, and each night is the same. Each hour is one hundred minutes long and there are one hundred days in a month, and ten months in our year. No seasons and only inclement weather when the keepers deem it so. You are in a new world, my young friend." He began to walk, so William followed, trying to soak it all in.

"I was out for fifty hours?" William asked.

"You needed a nice long meditation, your first day was long," Brock said, not looking back.

"Feels like I've been here for a week," William replied. "So, where do you go to meditate?"

"I do not need to meditate very much anymore. I get a few hours in every couple days," Brock said.

William wore his confusion openly, so Brock continued. "Well, do not look so shocked. Some of the older Archonians do not even need to meditate at all anymore."

"I stacked that rock about one hundred more times last night while I was meditating," William said flatly.

"Did you? Well that certainly is interesting. Everyone is different."

William remembered stumbling upon Meredox in the hallway.

"Hey Brock, I have something important to tell you," William stated seriously.

"Oh, and what might that be?"

"I saw Meredox last night,"

"Did you now?" Brock asked, seemingly indifferent.

"You are not the fondest of him are you?"

"You could say that again," William replied.

"Well, what was old Meredox doing that seemed to catch your interest?"

"He was sneaking around the corridors last night, talking with someone. They were talking about something that was going to happen, and that the Synod would be too blind to see it," William said quickly.

"Are you sure you were not imagining things? You were out in the sun for quite a long time," Brock said with a smirk.

William retorted, "I know what I saw, Brock. There is something about him that I don't like."

"William," Brock said seriously. "Meredox is the Grand Justicar. He would never do anything against either the Synod or Archonia. It is his job to see that our laws are interpreted. He is watched by the Synod, and by Achilles. He could never betray us. I'm sure that whatever you heard was nothing." Brock's tone was edged with a hint of finality.

William gritted his teeth. No one seemed to ever believe him. Why would they start now? *Fine*, he thought, *he would just have to keep an eye on Meredox himself.*

"Why does he hate me so much? If he is so omnipotent, why does he treat me like a piece of shit?" William asked.

Brock sighed heavily and spoke. "All I know is that he had a brother that he was very close to. They both lived in Archonia for many years, but his brother eventually turned to wickedness, and was banished from Archonia forever. He begged the Synod to let him have another chance, but they sent him away anyway. Now you are here, getting a second chance. You can only imagine how that would make a person feel. Regardless, this is not something you will need to worry about. You will not be seeing very much of him. Come now, there is much to be learned, little brother."

* * *

Brock informed William that he was already behind on his training schedule. He gave William an enormous map, which was almost no use at all. There were so many corridors, rooms, and nooks in the castle that he didn't see how anyone could find anything.

Eventually William gave up on using the map, and just asked people where his lectures were. Some gave him disgusted looks, while others looked annoyed, but usually pointed him in the right direction. Their frustration annoyed him, but didn't discourage him. He responded kindly and thanked them, which felt odd at first, but he could see a definite change in their mood when he did.

Kill them with kindness, he thought.

He had been placed in a group of ten recruits who, like him, had to undergo initiates training. Some had already lived in Archonia for many years, and only now had decided to join. A man, Chen Li, was a business man in his old life. Apparently there wasn't much business in Archonia, so he chose the path of the sentinel in favor of boredom.

One had to go through initiates training, regardless of their path. Yet their choice of the three branches determined the level of training they would receive in certain areas. Sentinels didn't have nearly as rigorous training as guardians. Yet, not every person made it into the Guardian's Corps if they chose it.

He met a woman named Natalia, who had long flowing red hair. She had been studying for forty years to become an Adjudicator. Only by personal invitation could someone become an Archonian Adjudicator. To be one took a keen mind, she told him.

Despite their goals, all initiates started out with the same basic studies. These days were some of the most intense William had ever experienced. His life back on Earth quickly felt like a distant vacation.

During his breaks throughout the day, he had time to ponder the purpose of life. He walked the seemingly endless corridors of Valhalla, exploring the many winding passages.

There were common areas for feasting, and sometimes parties were held for no reason at all other than to fraternize with their fellow soldiers. He attended one of these with Brock. The people were nicer if Brock introduced him. He met many soldiers that had already completed the guardian training and forged their armor. They all seemed intense and fierce in their own ways. One warrior named Benkei wore green and red armor. William thought he recognized the style from an old Japanese movie he watched. Benkei wore twenty Japanese Katanas. He counted them five times to be sure.

He sat and simply listened to their war stories for hours, feasting on course after course of the most delicious food he had ever eaten. He ate duck, pheasant, quail, wild boar, and even lion meat. There were other foods as well, many he didn't recognize. Brock told William that those were the true delicacies, because they had been fabricated by someone's mind.

William also stumbled upon places for recreation. Massive pools of water where one could swim in or simply lounge around. It seemed odd, and he wondered how anybody got anything done in this world, when they could simply sit around all day in complete comfort.

William found himself walking through the Nordic quarter one day after his studies. He looked over many of the statues, reading the names to see if he recognized any of them. He found Thor, the Norse god of thunder. His statute read "Thor of Scione". He saw many others as well – Loki, Freya, Freyr, and Heimdallr.

There were also many closed doorways in this wing. He opened a few, finding large lecture halls and study areas. One set of doors in particular caught William's attention. They were made of thick, strong wood. An inscription across them read: Only the strong may enter here.

William tried to push or pull them open, but to no avail. They would not budge. He eventually gave up, deciding it best to save his strength for the physical training.

The physical training was some of the most difficult he had ever experienced in his life. This training was guardian specific. He tried to keep telling himself that it wasn't really tiring, but it felt so real, and painful. He was assigned to a captain named Chang Fei, who in the mortal world had been revered as a god of war by the Chinese. This man was intimidating for his small size, and William had never seen a man with more discipline.

In ancient China, discipline was all that mattered, and people devoted their lives to the perfection of whatever they did. It was quite an amazing culture, which produced some of the finest soldiers that history had ever seen.

Apparently it was because he was such a good general and warrior on Earth that people had revered him as a god much like many of the other heroes from Earth like Zeus, and Achilles. He was of course killed during battle, and came here to continue doing the same thing that he had done on Earth.

He stood only four feet five inches at the most, but his gaze commanded respect. He wore very simple robes of dark blue. They hung loosely over his rather thin body. The movement they offered would help him avoid ripping his robes.

William had already shredded so many clothes in training simply because his mind was still unaccustomed to his new found strength. If he went to adjust his clothes they would rip like tissue paper. He was still having trouble finding a good balance.

Chang Fei's bald head shone in the sun. He often stroked his long stringy mustache thoughtfully as he watched the recruits struggle. He spoke very little, but when he did it was something serious.

The first lesson they had from Chang Fei was about the ancient Chinese belief in the life force or "Ch'I" as they called it, which in Archonia actually existed.

"Ch'I flows throughout your body. Surrounds us and makes us whole," the guardian captain said as the initiates sat on the ground in a cross legged fashion.

"Is that like projection?" William asked, interrupting.

"Silence!" Chang Fei shouted. "You will not speak unless spoken to!"

"Ch'I is what gives you strength and focus. You must focus on every action you make, and where the energy comes from," the Chinese warrior said. Then he walked over to a massive stone sitting off to the side. He closed his eyes, and touched a single finger to the stone.

The initiates looked at one another, and then back at their captain. With only his finger against the giant stone, it started to lift off the ground. The group gasped in awe.

It continued floating skyward. Chang Fei remained motionless, except the arm that extended along with the rock. Soon it was over his head, floating above the entire group. Some eyed the rock uneasily, standing so that they could make a fast escape. William smiled, and imagined himself doing this someday. Then to the groups surprise the stone shattered into a billowing cloud of dust with a massive crack, and sand came falling down like rain.

Some in the group applauded, while others laughed.

"Initiates, one thousand push-ups," Cheng Fei growled.

The group groaned.

"You will all focus on each push-up as if it is the only thing in your life that matters. Control your mind. Find your Ch'I," he said.

William didn't know what he meant by Ch'I, but he did know what one thousand push-ups were. He didn't focus on each one, instead gazed around the training grounds as he pumped his arms. There were many odd looking objects placed orderly around a massive circular man-made valley. The high walls of the valley were made of soil and rock.

As William struggled through the push-ups, he turned to his left and noticed a tall tower near the southern ridge of the valley. He turned to the large man next to him.

"What is that?" he asked casually, doing push-ups faster than he ever thought possible.

"The warning beacon of Helios. Should Archonia ever be under attack that bell will ring," the man said.

"How often do these attacks happen?" William asked.

"That bell has not been rung in two thousand years. Not since the twin obelisks were created," the Native American man finished.

"Then why am I doing all these push-ups?" William huffed, laughing.

There was a crack like a whip and a throbbing pain on the back of his head. William looked up, pausing the exercise. Chang Fei stood above him, his face grim.

This was to be guardian training, and it never stopped. If you quit without his word, you did more, and if you weren't doing something correctly, he would whack you on the head with a long staff. William had lived through intense physical conditions on Earth, and yet, he could barely keep up here.

The rest of the week was focused solely on this intense training and the ability to find one's Ch'I. Exercises seemed to never stop, and the limit was only what the mind could handle. They were forcing him to understand how much that truly was.

"More!" Chang Fei shouted as William counted his five hundred and sixty-fifth pull up.

These were no ordinary pull-ups either. Chains were wrapped around William's waist, holding two boulders that easily weighed a ton each. If that wasn't enough, he was dangling fifty feet in the air. The most difficult part was jumping up to the bar. William was convinced that nothing in this world was normal sized. His arms and back muscles screamed in revolt over his five hundred and sixty-seventh pull up, but he kept telling himself it wasn't real.

"When you are on crusade and you are surrounded by the enemy and they are tearing at your imaginary body with their claws and pincers, will it be made from stone, or from flesh?" Chang Fei shouted as the sweat poured like a fountain from every pore on William's body.

He thought long and hard about what a crusade would be like, if he passed his guardian training. A crusade, according to his professors, was a sacred quest that a guardian had to take once a year. These quests could be anything deemed worthy by the Guardian Corps. For the past two thousand years, however, the majority of these crusades had been back to the mortal plane where guardians would search for worthy souls and protect them from Lucifer's abominations. William pictured himself clad in his own brilliantly shining armor, cutting down seething creatures of evil on his first crusade. It turned out to be just enough to get him through his training each day.

As they were finishing their daily exercises, William looked over at a man in his group. His name was Juarez. He was small in stature and had apparently been trying to become a guardian for the past one hundred years. He could see why.

William dropped to the ground, wiping sweat from his forehead. He'd finally finished his six hundred pull-ups. He unwound the chain binding him to the massive stones, and looked himself over. The first couple of times he had done this the chains left a nasty array of bruises across his body, but now his skin was unmarred. In fact, his skin appeared thicker, stronger, and healthier than ever. His muscle mass had increased as well. He almost looked as if he was chiseled out of stone.

William looked up at Juarez, who was struggling to get his three hundred and fifth pull-up. The large stones dwarfed him in an almost comedic fashion. William seemed to normally end up the butt of torment, and rarely received help when he heeded it. He realized that this was his chance to help someone else, and be noble, where others hadn't been to him.

"You better get your ass moving, Juarez. You're over halfway done," William shouted. "Look at that fading sun. Ignore your muscles. They are lying to you!"

The others had all finished for the day, and had gone to meditate, but William stayed to encourage Juarez. He prodded and motivated him until finally, with a shout, counted six hundred and dropped to the ground with a crash. William ran over, expecting to find the smaller man hurt, instead he was laughing, and leapt from the ground, smiling and hollering with joy.

"I have never been able to do that many! Thank you, Amigo," he said with a Spanish accent.

"It's no problem."

Juarez held up a hand as if to shake, and William grasped it firmly.

"Juarez," the tiny man said

His sharp features and olive skin glowed in the fading light. He was skinny with little muscle, but what he did have was very well defined. Veins popped out all over the place.

"William," he said, smiling back.

"Thank you, William. Nobody has ever helped me before."

"Me either," William responded honestly.

At that moment, the two men decided to become training partners. William did his best to open up to Juarez, just as Brock suggested. They talked during their warm ups, which usually consisted of running around the massive valley a couple of hundred times.

If they wanted to finish in time for drill, they learned quickly that they needed to be fast. If they didn't finish before Chang Fei began training they had to run again at the end of the night. It didn't take William long to let his mind go, and become faster. He wasn't as fast as some of the more experienced recruits, but for some of them, this was their second or third attempt at gaining entry to the Guardian Corps. Chang Fei had made it very difficult to complete the warm up in time so many of the initiates, including William were forced to stay after and run again.

"How many more laps?" Juarez asked.

"Did you lose count again?" William sighed.

"Yes, I have been counting how many times that woman has passed us," he replied as they felt a rush of wind fly by.

William looked ahead and there was a blur of white racing around the field.

"She is just showing off, pal. We have twenty more laps to go, and we are home free," William said, glancing over at him.

"Did she not complete the warm up run in time?" Juarez inquired.

"Yeah she did. Like I said, showing off," William muttered.

William realized he didn't know very much about his new companion, so he decided to get to know him better.

"Tell me more about yourself, Juarez," William said casually.

There was a silence and William didn't push. Juarez looked at him.

"I come from Spain. The capitol called Madrid," he said.

"So does that mean you speak Spanish?" William asked.

"Yes of course," Juarez responded, smiling.

"Say something in Spanish!"

Juarez chuckled, "My friend, I have always spoken Spanish. Your mind simply thinks I am speaking your language."

"Oh yeah, that's right," William said, suddenly remembering.

"What made you want to be a guardian?" William asked, trying to keep the conversation going.

"I suppose so that I could protect those I care about," Juarez said seriously.

"Fair enough."

He didn't seem to want to talk on the subject further so William focused on running. They pushed themselves, William's lungs beginning to burn as they traversed the field.

"What about you, tainted one?" Juarez asked, in a slightly mocking tone.

William half-smirked, and said, "Oh you heard that, huh?"

"I did indeed, but I do not believe in such things," Juarez replied.

"Well, believe it all, because it's true."

"I know that you have done things in your life that you regret," Juarez said. "But you must not let those actions dictate your future."

"You think I should forget what I did?" William asked skeptically.

"No, amigo, those are great lessons. But you must forgive yourself," Juarez said, staring straight ahead.

William looked into the fading sunlight.

"You sound like an old priest," William chuckled.

"I was a priest," Juarez responded quickly.

William stopped running, and Juarez slowed and turned.

"Hey, let's go. If Chang Fei catches us we will have to run another hundred laps," Juarez pleaded.

William didn't say much for the rest of the evening, troubling over why a priest would want to fight. He thought about this on his way back to the barracks, but soon his thoughts strayed as he fell into his meditative state, and he was once again flooded by memories of his former life.

CHAPTER EIGHT
THE PASSING

Angelica awoke in a panic. She didn't know where she was. This had been happening for the past couple weeks. She struggled to adjust to this world. Instead of sleeping, they meditated. It seemed unnatural, and contrary to everything her mind and body were used to.

The room around her was growing lighter by the second. The large Archonian sun was already creeping into view over the horizon, starting a new day. She looked around the small room where some of her relatives sat, still in their trance. The home belonged to her grandmother, who shared the space with one of her sisters, who Angelica had never met, and a couple of her more distant relatives.

Last, but not least, was Julia. Her husband, who served as a guardian, lived with his brethren in the barracks of a castle called Valhalla, so she stayed here. The living quarters felt far too small for so many people, but she was starting to learn that they actually needed very little room to meditate, and people rarely spent much time in their living quarters. Instead, most chose to spend their time outside, exploring the world's innumerable possibilities.

With the absence of things such as movies or television, people in this world lived the experiences they only dreamed of on Earth. Angelica had already been rock climbing, white water kayaking, fishing, and sailing. Most of her days, however, were devoted to study. Julia helped her enroll with the University of Socrates. Education was free, and Angelica wanted to learn as much as she could about her new life and world. Julia, it turned out, was already well into her studies. She had recently reached maturity and wanted to pursue a life in politics.

"Are you ready to go?" Julia asked with a warm smile.

They had already become the best of friends, which filled Angelica with a joy.

"Yes cousin," she said, standing and stretching. She felt so light and full of energy every day, as if some lifelong bond had been broken.

Angelica dressed in a white, linen wrap that fell loosely over her body. She didn't like the many layered outfits her cousin favored, and despite her urges to try them on, she kindly refused. Julia was always clad in jewels, the predominant one today being rubies. They sparkled in rings, chains, and even her sandals, which wrapped around her ankles almost to her knees.

"You know, I think you look pretty without all those gemstones," Angelica said with an awkward chuckle.

Julia scowled. "Everyone here dresses like this, Angie," she said, and then stuck her tongue out at her.

Soon they were on their way. The small unit that Julia lived in was on the 43rd floor of the labyrinth-like Latin District, which was a seemingly endless array of houses stacked one on top of the other. Angelica soon realized that it was a good thing that there were so many hours in a day, otherwise people would spend much of their lives walking from place to place. Well normal people anyway. There were those, mostly the older folks, who could travel so fast that she could barely see them. She decided that she would need to learn to walk quicker. Julia wasn't pushy however, and kept pace with her cousin.

The streets weren't filled with despair, as she had come to expect in her previous life. Even this early in the morning, people were bustling about, joyfully preparing for the day. With no need for money, vendors and merchants were there simply to share their creations with the world. Nobody was rich, and nobody was poor. Angelica wasn't entirely convinced that there was no monetary system, however. She had overheard people talking of "sharing secrets" in exchange for services. This was one of the oldest forms of currency. Most of it was harmless. However, it was the harmful kind she was worried about.

Angelica accosted her cousin with questions as they made their way through the streets and gardens. Julia answered every question with a smile, and seemed to know every shortcut, and regularly got distracted by someone she knew or a piece of art that caught her eye. They passed the university. It was up on a very tall hill, accessible only by a very steep, winding path. She recognized the stone that she had read on her first day in attendance. It read: Knowledge is earned.

Earned, she thought.

Perhaps it meant the hike up the hill was a penance, or a payment to gain access to the university. They ascended the stone stair, each steps carved from the rock, and passed beneath the statue of Socrates, the founder of this university. Angelica learned early on that Socrates was one of the most influential people in this world, and moreover, sat on the great council known as the Synod.

Socrates himself and his mortal life was one of Angelica's first lessons. He had been considered an ugly man on Earth, but this didn't deter him from greatness. He had shown the world that questioning the accepted standard was a healthy practice. If people continued making the same mistakes day after day, year after year, how could they ever grow as a society?

After hours of walking, they finally made it to the university. Considered small in Archonia, in reality, the University was probably twice as large as any school on Earth. It was crafted of brilliant, white marble. It looked much like the Pantheon of ancient Athens, where Socrates himself lived and died. Vast pillars supported a hall that was perfectly geometrical and carefully proportioned. It was a masterpiece of craftsmanship that seemed almost dull against the extravagance of the rest of the city.

Angelica stopped at the doors to catch her breath. The hike had been very tiring, and yet, Julia barely seemed to have noticed. A sundial stood in the courtyard, and openly displayed that they were late for their first classes. Fortunately, Angelica was still new enough to this world that they allowed her time to adjust.

She crept into her first class quietly. It was in an open-aired courtyard full of plants Angelica couldn't recognize. This class was one about the history of Archonia which Angelica was one of four students in attendance. The class was a requirement for every young soul granted access to Archonia. It included basic history, law, physics, and the religions practiced here.

Spiritual matters were what Angelica cared most for. She had devoted nearly her entire life to the Catholic Church, and though death had brought her to this wonderful paradise, it had also torn a hole right through the middle of everything spiritual she held dear. She had chosen her next class for this very reason. It was the study of religion versus mythology, both on Earth and in Archonia. The professor was a simple woman with dark skin and a kind smile.

Her name was Shamala, and she was serving her six hundred and fifty third term as a volunteer professor. Angelica, and even some of the more experienced students, were all instantly impressed. This class was much larger than her first. The large lecture hall held nearly one hundred students, with different colored skin, and faces of all shapes and sizes. In this class, Shamala would start out each session with a significant ethnicity or culture from Earth's history, and explain their beliefs about religion and life after death. The second part of the class was discussion and questions.

"Today, young ones, we will be discussing Buddhism. It was created by a man named Siddhartha Gotama, who felt that a path to enlightenment could take the place of gods and deities. As the member of a royal family, he was showered with wealth, until he began his search for his own truth. What he discovered was what is known as the *Middle Path,* or, *The Path to Enlightenment.* A common misconception is that Buddhism is a religion, when it is more a way of life."

For the next hour Angelica sat and listened to the intricacies of Buddhism and was astonished to find that it sounded like a very appealing practice. She also agreed with what referred to as the *Four Noble Truths.* The first is that to live is suffering, and Buddhism explains how we can accept this fact and work to be happy. The second is that suffering is caused by craving, which deprives oneself of contentment. Angelica saw this as an epidemic amongst modern society on Earth. People were never satisfied with what they had. They were crippled by need. The third noble truth is that this suffering can be overcome using the fourth noble truth known as the eight fold path.

Angelica was somewhat of a quiet person and preferred to listen to others speak while she learned. When it came time to ask questions she looked at the group and waited, but nobody out of the sizable crowd wanted to speak up. Shamala appeared to sense their apprehension, so she opened the discussion.

"Angelica, I understand that you used to practice Catholicism in your previous life. How do you feel this practice of Buddhism relates to your own personal beliefs? How do you think it differs?"

Angelica was lost for words, but forced herself to speak. Her voice was weak, and her words came out a bit wobbly at first. "Many of the principals of Buddhism and its path to enlightenment seem to be similar to the laws of god. People should show compassion and not be possessive."

Another of the students, a fair-haired young woman with piercing, blue eyes, spoke.

"I see very little similarities to the two. The history of Catholicism has been written with blood. Its dominion is a decadent disgrace to the creator."

"Now Elaine, we know that you do not hold well with what happened from your time period, but there is no reason to attack anyone's personal beliefs," Shamala said. She was quickly cut off by another student.

"I think Elaine is right. The clothing that the Catholic Cardinals wear can cost twenty thousand dollars, meanwhile the Pope's robe cost anywhere from one hundred thousand to two hundred thousand dollars. There are children all over the mortal world who are starving to death. That is pretty vain," he finished.

Angelica felt her face flush hot, but she remained quiet.

Shamala didn't appear impressed. "And does your religion give more?" she asked the man.

There was no response.

"People find it easy to criticize others, but fail to criticize themselves. Elaine, you were tortured and killed by men of the church for being a witch. I can see how you would hold hostility toward Angelica's belief system, however, just because a man calls himself a man of religion does not mean that he is one. Angelica, thank you for sharing."

The class continued but Angelica tuned out most of the discussion. She began to feel sick. She had seen her beliefs dashed against the wall by people before, but something was different now that she knew her beliefs were never entirely accurate. She wasn't sure she could ever go back to that class again.

When she finally made the long trek home after her courses she found her grandmother sitting on a bench in the courtyard below their living quarters. She appeared to be waiting for someone. When Angelica approached, her grandmother smiled, and she could almost see the grey hair and soft, wrinkled face she'd always known. The beauty of her youthful form drowned out the image after a moment.

"Abuela? Who are you waiting for?"

"I am waiting for you, my child. You had a bad day."

"Grandma, how did you know I had a bad day?" Angelica asked in surprise.

"Sweet one, many people in this world have gifts. Soldiers mostly use their projection for construction or destruction, but the whole world is energy, and if you quiet your mind, you can hear each form."

"I don't understand. You can hear me?"

"No, Angie, I think of it as sense or touch. I can reach out to your soul and feel your moods," she said with a smile.

Angelica was somewhat surprised, but it made sense. In her "Study of Archonian Physics" class they had been speaking of such powers. She had even witnessed some, first at William's trial, when his life had been displayed for all to see, and again when the soldier summoned the giant feline creature before her very eyes.

"Grandma, I don't want you to worry about me. I am just having some difficulties with my personal beliefs."

"Child, everyone who comes here has these troubles, so don't fret. I am not worried. I just wanted you to know that I am here. Whether you like it or not it is still my job to love and care for you."

Angelica couldn't help but smile. She had truly been blessed with a loving family that supported one another. It put her mind at ease. She sat down next to Angelina and embraced her. They sat for many long moments simply enjoying each other's touch.

Angelica didn't really know what she was going to do with the rest of her day. There were something like seven hours left of daylight and then another fifty of night.

"Grandmother, what do you do to fill up all this time?"

"Well, like you saw we do get out for many activities. You obviously have your studies now, but everyone usually finds a couple hobbies. I had always wanted to learn how to play the violin on Earth, but there was never any money for that, so I had to set the dream aside. But in the last five years I have become quite capable with the strings. Mind you I have a long way to go before I am near good enough to perform, but it pleases me to hear the music."

"You have to play for me sometime, Abuela," Angelica insisted.

Angelina blushed and smiled, but said nothing before changing the subject. "Why don't we focus on finding you some hobbies? I know that you were a very devoted worshipper before you crossed over. Did you know that they have religions here?"

"I had heard in some of my courses that there are believers in what comes after this second life. I don't know if I am ready to start believing in something else. My faith has been really shaken."

"Angelica," her grandmother said sternly. "We believed that there was something better for us than the turmoil of the mortal life and we were right. We were good people, and our good acts have paid our way. Just because we went about it differently than some, does not make it wrong. If you took the stairs and I took an elevator we would both end up in the same place. How we got here has little relevance, but where we go from here is all that matters in the world."

She paused to give time for this to sink in, but then continued, "Your faith was a sign that you respected what came next. I have seen hundreds of people who have made it here and became lost. They believed that they would be here forever...but that is not necessarily true."

"Grandma what do you mean? I thought that the soul is immortal here in Archonia!?"

"Oh, the mind can be broken, just like on the mortal plane, my dear. If your mind is broken, how then can you exist?"

Angelica was confused. She didn't say anything for several long moments, trying to make sense of this new information.

"So, where do we go after this life?"

Her grandmother did not respond right away. Instead, she stood up and looked at the sun dial in the middle of the courtyard. "There is a celebration going on tonight. I think it would be good for you to see it. Let's walk," she said enigmatically.

Angelica followed, questions popping up and crowding her thoughts.

Why would a celebration be good for her to see?

They turned down an alley, walked a short distance, before stepping out on a large, crowded streets. Despite the size of the capitol city, and the wide street, it seemed like there was still a lack of space. With the vast stretches of untouched land she wondered why so many people would pack themselves in such a tight space. Her question was always answered the same way when she made her way through the crowds of laughing smiling people. There was a desire to be near other souls, to share your experiences with them, and to live.

An outdoor amphitheater appeared as they cleared a large building, where a concerto was in progress. Though they were at least a quarter mile off, it sounded as clear as if they stood right next to it. Large standing stones dotted the ground in the open area, standing like unrealized monuments in the green grass.

"Those stones pick up the sound waves, and deliver them back as if they came straight from the instruments. That is why the sound is carrying so far off. There is nothing like that in the physical universe," her grandmother said, winking at her.

"Abuela, is that where you want to perform someday?" she asked excitedly.

"Oh child, it would take me centuries to become that talented. That is the Helionic Harmonic Orchestra. It is comprised of musicians that have been around for hundreds, if not thousands of years."

They stopped and listened for a while. The music was so complex that it almost deterred from the sound. Nobody in a million years could have called it anything less than beautiful.

"Who do you think the man playing the grand piano is?" Angelina asked her granddaughter pointing.

"Frederic Chopin," she said with a laugh.

Angelica was bewildered. She wasn't a huge fan of classical music in life, but she had still heard of Frederic Chopin. They listened to the music until the movement ended, and Angelina set off down the lane again.

"Grandmother, don't you want to watch the rest of the show?"

"My dear, I have heard them play at least a hundred times. They perform once a week," she replied.

"I see. So, where are we off to then?"

"There is a man who has lived in Archonia a very long time, and he has decided to leave."

"Leave? Where will he go?"

"He will pass on."

"Pass on? Is someone going to kill him? Is he going to kill himself?! I do not want to see that," Angelica said, panic gripping her.

Her grandmother stopped, put a comforting hand on her shoulder, and shook her head gently. Angelica continued walking, but she became very afraid. They passed over bridges, under arches, and through all manner of courtyards, until they began to hear the sounds of celebration.

Soon they were in the midst of a sea of happy faces. People were dressed in all sorts of silks and chiffons fabrics made with actual gold strands sewed into them. Jewels caught the fading sunlight and all of it seemed of little value without a monetary system. She spied a particular girl who was wearing a diadem with a starburst shaped ruby on it that was larger than any she had ever seen. People sang and danced to the unusual music, and Angelica saw her grandmother embracing a stranger.

When she caught up with her, the two smiled kindly, and the man extended a hand from his forehead which was one of the many ways that people in Archonia greeted one another.

"Angie, this is Metriclus. He is family to the man who will be moving on this evening."

"And such a pleasure to meet you, young one. I shall insist that my great father have you as one of the nine," he said.

Angelica looked at her grandmother, who nodded eagerly. Angelica returned his smile and said, "Of course, I would be honored."

"Then it is settled. I will come find you when the ceremony begins." He bowed politely and turned to speak with some of the other people.

"Abuela, what did he mean by, one of the nine?"

"Well, it is tradition for someone who passes on to extend some of their vast knowledge to the youth of Archonia. Metriclus' great father is actually one of his ancestors, and is far too elderly to distinguish exactly how many generations stand between them. They only share a family name, which is quite a rarity when names change so often throughout the centuries."

"How old is this man?" Angelica asked.

"His name is Permesius, and he is three hundred and sixty Archonian years old."

Angelica did some quick math in her head and exclaimed, "That is over two thousand five hundred human years!"

Angelina simply nodded, and clasped her granddaughters hand as they made their way through the crowd.

"Why nine people? I imagine that he has much knowledge to share?" Angelica asked.

"One person for each of the nine Great Archons. I think nine is plenty. There is much knowledge to learn and he that passes it on does not have an eternity to teach," she said with a chuckle.

"I suppose we'd be here a long time if he was sharing his wisdom with everyone."

The sun began to dip in the sky, and people began moving over to a large stage. The platform was raised, and shone like it was made from pure silver. A solitary man stood in the center, where an ornate circular symbol was etched into the metal.

He looked unlike anyone else at the party. Not in dress, or exuberance, but because he was old. Not just in years, but in appearance. He still stood tall, his back straight, and of relatively good health, but his hair was gray and slicked back over a receding hairline. His beard was white, and greased to a point, while his face looked like it was made from wrinkled stone.

"His mind is weary. He feels old. That is why his appearance has changed. It is one of the first signs that an Archonian is becoming ready to take the next journey," her grandmother whispered.

The crowd grew silent as eight people began making their way up onto the silver platform. The silver surface was shimmering now, illuminated by crystals floating in the air above the crowd. They gave off the most pure, white light she had ever seen. Metriclus appeared from the crowd and offered his hand to Angelica. She was hesitant, but slowly placed her hand in his. He gently guided her out of the throng of people and helped her up to the platform.

The others had taken their shoes off. She saw some sandals and slippers, and without having to be told, she slid out of her sandals and took a step. The silver was cold and felt strange underfoot. She looked out amongst the crowd, their excitement evident and a little unnerving.

How could they be so happy that one of their elders was leaving this world?

She dismissed the thought. Perhaps it was something she would have to grow to understand. Permisius didn't turn around or acknowledge any one of the nine. Metriclus had receded back into the crowd. She was starting to grow uncomfortable when everyone's eyes went to the sky, where a bright light shimmered amongst darkness. Innumerable stars and planets hung overhead, looming so close that she could make out the ranges of mountains and rivers. A great yellow one with a ring of asteroids look as if it was colliding with another smaller green colored one, but they were unmoving.

Her eyes followed the rest of the people as the shining light descended upon the crowd, stinging her eyes and blinding her. The light softly hit the stage. Angelica tried to watch, but it was too intense. Then, in a blink, the light was gone, and in its place stood a man. She didn't recognize him, but like Permesius he too looked slightly older than the rest of them. His long hair was striped with gray. A long robe dangled around his body, bunching up around his feet. His bare arms were raised to the sky.

The crowd stood still, in utter silence. Even Angelica realized that she was holding her breath. Slowly, she released it, until the man spoke, and she reflexively held it again.

"Young ones, we gather here on the dusk of a man's life. This man named Permisius. He has graced us with his presence for many centuries, filling our world with joy, happiness, and a wealth of knowledge, matched only by his skills in architecture. I ask that you now honor him as he ends this stage of his journey, and begins the next."

Angelica waited, thinking that the crowd may burst into applause, but instead, thousands of hands reached toward the sky. Some people even began to ascend into the air and floated amongst the crystals. Their palms were all facing Permisius, fingers together and arms locked. No one moved. Angelica spotted her grandmother in the crowd, with eyes closed like the others. The only people not raising their arms were the eight standing on the platform next to her.

The man with the long grey hair spoke again. "It is now in the highest traditions of the passage that the journeymen pass along his wisdom to nine of our youth," he said loudly.

Without a second's hesitation, Permisius swiftly turned and was upon the first in line. He stared into her eyes for a long moment, his face unreadable as he studied her. He leaned in and whispered something into her ear. She nodded gratefully and then bowed her head, closed her eyes, and extended her palms to the sky. Angelica was on the end, and would be the last person to receive his gift. She watched anxiously as he made his way from one to the next. The crowd, still motionless, watched intently with their arms raised.

It felt like hours passed, but she knew it was actually only moments before Permisius stood in front of her. He turned his intense gaze on her. His deep coffee brown eyes made her feel as though he could see straight through her. It felt as if he was inside her head. Memories began to surface. She saw her church, and all the hours she'd spent studying the bible, and friends who were part of her faith.

The old man leaned down and gently put a hand on her face as he whispered, "Some use faith as a shield. But you, my dear Angelica, use it for nourishment. Such strong belief is not a weakness, but a gift from the creators. My wisdom to you, young one, is to hold your faith close. It is your most valuable possession."

Angelica blinked, looking into his eyes, and then he was gone. He hadn't gone far, just back into the center of the platform, where he sat cross legged with his head bowed. Angelica mindlessly put her hands in the air, but she couldn't take her eyes off of him. Too many thoughts were going through her mind and if she looked away she believed that she would miss something significant. The other old man spoke again in a voice that carried across the huge courtyard and out into the night.

"Gods, deities, and creators, we ask thee to receive thy child into your powerful embrace. Bless his passage and his renewal of life. For all his loyal millenniums of service to you, let him pass unto the next stage of being."

Angelica jumped as the crowd began to chant. It was like a low, wailing hum that was passed around in a wave. She couldn't tell what they were saying, which was unusual, because her professors told her that her mind would translate any foreign language in this world.

A swirling wind began to blow. It formed into a vortex and Angelica began to be sucked in. She screamed but the wind was drowning out all sounds. The man standing next to her grabbed her and held her to his chest. His eyes were still closed, and he continued to chant. The starry sky filled with dark, swirling clouds that form a funnel, and from the center a bright light shot forth. The pillar of light descended upon the tiny stage and everything became calm. The wind still swirled, but it was as if someone had slowed time. Her mind was working at the same pace, but her body was a prison. Like a bad dream, she struggled to move, but couldn't. She could see individual dust particles and small debris moving through the air, swirling slowly.

Everything was completely muted, at least within the light. Her head, that she couldn't move, was locked on Permisius, who stood bathed in the light, a smile upon his face, and his arms extended towards the sky. Angelica's stomach clenched as a large piece of his body broke away, and like a bit of ash, floated upwards. That part of him was only light now. The rest of him soon followed, and slowly bit by bit his broken body floated into the light above, like autumn leaves.

Just as fast as it had begun, it ended. The light receded into the sky and the clouds dissipated in a swirl of wind. The wind swept upwards, and thankfully the stranger still clutched her tight so she wouldn't get whisked away. As the light finally dissipated she closed her eyes in fear. Perhaps she thought that she would get devoured by it as well. When it was over there was complete stillness again. Opening her eyes, she confirmed that Permisius was gone. The man who had spoken for him had backed off the platform, and was standing just next to it under a starry night.

Angelica sucked in breath, and then another. In another heartbeat tears were streaming down her face. Her legs buckled, and the man holding her gently cradled her to the cold, silver surface. Metriclus was there in an instant and her grandmother as well.

"Forgive me, Angelina, I did not know this was new to her. It was never my intention to frighten her," Metriclus said urgently.

"Save your apologies, kind sir, my granddaughter is made of tougher stuff than that. She is not frightened by a little wind and a light show."

Her grandmother cupped her face in her hands and helped wipe away some of her tears. "Now you are not frightened, are you, child?" her grandmother asked.

Angelica thought for a moment. Yes, the ceremony was terrifying, but she didn't think that was why she was crying. Permisius's words had moved her down to her very core. Her faith had been her nourishment to all the atrocities of the modern society she was born into. When she crossed over, that nourishment had been stripped away, but thanks to his words, she felt like she could be whole again. She could wrap herself in faith and learn to grow in it once more.

"No Abuela, I am weeping for joy. Permisius' wisdom was exactly what I needed."

123

CHAPTER NINE
THE ARCHONS

William came out of his nightly trance later than normal the next morning, and quickly realized he was already late for his studies. For the better part of twenty hours every morning William was studying the most extraneous subjects.

There was still the lingering question on his mind of why a priest would want to become a soldier when in his previous life he had been devoted to peace. He raced up and down the corridors, trying to remember where his lectures were supposed to be, but it seemed like they were in a new room every day. When he finally found the correct room he eased open the massive doors as quietly as he could to avoid interrupting the class. But his efforts were in vain, because everyone was looking at him as he entered.

His teacher had been a historian in his previous life, and now taught not only Earth's histories, but also Archonian as well. He stared at William in silence, watching as he entered and sat in one of the padded, leather chairs.

He was a short man, with a round face and shaggy, blond hair that was never properly combed. It was as if the only thing he cared about were his history books. William liked him for that. He had something that he truly loved, and wouldn't let anything or anybody stop him from doing it. He also wore bifocals, which was odd, because in

Archonia nobody needed corrective lenses. Perhaps he wore them out of habit.

"I'm sorry I'm late, professor Echard."

Laurence Echard had been an English historian in the mid-seventeenth century. With his time on Earth and even longer time here he had become one of the most avid chroniclers in the history of Archonia. There were a few that were more knowledgeable, but they taught at the University of Socrates.

He didn't respond to William, instead, simply continued where he left off. William settled in, preparing his mind for more information that he couldn't possibly ever use. Not only were they studying Archonian philosophy, but they also studied the physics of the mortal universe as well.

William sat up, cursing the chairs and their unnecessary comfort. He was already fighting not to slip back into a meditative trance. He tried to listen intently.

"There were nine Archons in the beginning. Little more is known on the subject, because the last remaining Archon refuses to speak of it. Not even the Archons know the origin of this beautiful world, and they were born into it. What *is* known is that after many millennia they grew restless here, and began to create something entirely different. They focused their powers and together created an entirely new plane of existence. The Archon Allah created a vast void that could hold immeasurable amounts of matter. So great was this space that it would take even the Archons themselves days to travel from one end to the other.

"Matter itself was not a new concept to the Archons, but it took immense power to fill this new universe with it. Gaia, who in many Earthly histories was the mother of Earth, quite literally was the creator of all matter in the universe. This matter took on many forms: solids, liquids, and even gases. They possessed their own size, mass, and colors, combining to create anything from beautiful minerals to soft malleable soil," professor Echard stated.

William sat up, his interest piqued. He'd never thought about the creation of the physical universe. He'd always just assumed it had always been there. He listened intently.

"The matter the Archons created did nothing, however. This of course was boring to the Archons, so the Archon Ammun gave this universe energy. He gave Gaia's atoms different properties and rules, letting them to bond and react differently to one another, allowing for limitless potential energy. Unfortunately, potential and kinetic energy was very unstable, so with the help of his brother Brahma, they were able to use boundaries such as force, mass, gravity, and magnetism to give life to the universe. They spent lifetimes designing and creating, yet never imagined what it would eventually lead to," Echard said.

William and the others in the room knew exactly what it led to. The exciting question was, how?

"Naturally, the Archons grew tired of this new realm. The Archon's Othin and Kronos, who were wilder than their brethren were sparring with one another in the vast void, and by accident caused a massive explosion across the endless expanse. The balls of gas in the surrounding area ignited and sent trillions of particles flying all around the universe. Like a domino effect, the chaos that ensued was beautiful, yet unpredictable, unlike the order that they had created. Stars formed. These stars held substantial gravity, and thus were able to hold large quantities of matter in an orbit and form spheres," professor Echard continued.

William almost cursed in astonishment. Not only was religion correct to an extent, but scientists were correct as well. The big bang theory in fact had merit to it. William barely contained laughter. Scientists and religionists had wasted so much energy fighting amongst each other about the idea of creation. And in the end, they were both correct. He continued listening with enthusiasm.

"One day, while traveling through a cluster of stars, the Archons Lucifer and Prometheus discovered something wonderful. A tiny sphere held in orbit by one of the stars actually possessed the necessary conditions to form life. They found tiny, microscopic single cell beings. They were simple, but they were alive. The two brothers excitedly told the other Archons, of the miracle. They had created life. The first organic creatures, in fact. The Archons took great pleasure in watching these creatures evolve and grow.

"Many lifetimes passed, and they watched as the tiniest bacteria became amoeba, which began to grow rigid skeletons. They all started as water beings, and eventually adapted to breathe air, and moved on to land. For millions of years they eagerly watched. These creatures began to eat other living beings and then died to feed those that they ate. It was an endless circle of reproduction. The only Archons that seemed to lose interest was Lucifer. He watched the creatures live and die and became angry," the professor droned on.

Well of course even William could guess that this evolution would eventually produce mankind.

"It was Prometheus who found the first beings using tools. And, amazingly enough, they began to look like the Archons themselves. Prometheus and Gaia fell in love with them. However, Othin, and Kronos expressed their deep seeded concern. They had traveled through the rest of the universe, and nothing like this had yet happened anywhere else. Gaia took this as a sign from their creator that he had finally given them the chance to be mothers and fathers, a luxury that the Archons did not have. They could not reproduce as these creatures did, just as they could not eat, sleep, or die like these creatures did.

"It was Lucifer's envy of those very things that caused his downfall. Eventually the tool users began to stand upright, and created homes and clothing for themselves. They became smarter. They were the first in millions of years to possess more than simple instinctual thoughts. And now in a few thousand years these creatures had jumped in intellect. It was decided that each of the Archons would descend into this world, and teach the small tribes of tool users about Archonia, and where they had come from. They also taught them to follow basic rules of conduct so that they could coexist in symbiotic relationships with one another free from strife.

"It was not long, however, before the other Archons discovered that Lucifer was trying to live amongst his tribes like a king. They built massive monuments in his honor, and were sacrificing themselves to appease him. Prometheus was appalled at what Lucifer had done, and set to destroy the tribes and wipe clean his sickening corruption. Lucifer became enraged and attacked Prometheus, mortally wounding him. Prometheus barely made it back to his tribe, collapsing into the arms of a woman he had loved above all others. He used what power he had left to impregnate her with a child, so he might carry on his existence in the mortal plane. The other Archons found Prometheus' body, and cursed Lucifer.

"Kronos and Othin banished Lucifer from Archonia, telling him that he could never return. Then something incredible happened. They watched as Prometheus' son was born. He was not like the other tool users. They could see a glow within him, like the projections of the Archons. They watched him mature into a man, grow old, and eventually, die. And yet, when he died, he continued to live on. He took on a form like the Archons, and they brought him to their world to live." The ancient historian paused for a moment to take a drink of water.

It all made perfect sense. It explained why there were scientists on Earth who believed in evolution. It showed that religions were correct about some things and incorrect about others. Each Archon had been influencing different tribes, explaining the different customs, and languages. The truth of history was amazing, and William scribbled down as much as he could.

"Lucifer was banished to a realm created by his brother, Kronos. He split the land of Archonia in two, creating a lifelong prison for his treacherous brother. It was named Dichonia. And so Lucifer was forced to watch as the sons of Prometheus were born and ascended to Archonia, his former home.

"As many know the evolution of mankind was brutal. These early humans were exactly the same as any of the other creatures born to this world. They felt hunger and fear, and if threatened, they would kill each other. Lucifer liked this, and used his influence to create violent tribes of men. Their Archonian souls became darker as they were tainted by the violence and hate. They became more perverse, sacrificing themselves and laying waste to enemy tribes, all in their dark father's name.

"When they died the remaining Archons would not allow them to live amongst the pure souls of Archonia, so their tainted souls were thrown into Dichonia, where they became only more and more twisted. Soon Lucifer had amassed an army, which he used to attack the lands of Archonia. He himself could not pass the borders of his domain, but these twisted souls could," Echard said.

"Professor?" a man sitting near the front of the lecture room inquired. "Why did the Archons not simply destroy Lucifer?"

"Could you kill your own brother, young one?" the old historian asked, looking over his bifocals after readjusting them with a finger. "In fact, one of them decided to do just that. The Archonians were hopelessly outnumbered, and were nearly defeated. The Archons Othin and Kronos faced a difficult decision. Kronos finally decided that Lucifer needed to be destroyed. However, Othin thought that if they forgave Lucifer, and let him come home that he might help them destroy the very abominations that he had created.

"There was a terrible battle between the two mighty beings, and the result was devastating. When they clashed, desolation fell across both worlds, and many souls were lost. They had destroyed one another in their struggle along with one of their sisters, Allah, who had tried to break up

129

the fight," the historian said, standing before the questioning student.

The room fell silent. William finished writing, catching up with his hastily scribbled notes.

"What happened to the other Archons?" William asked, breaking the silence.

The young looking chronicler responded thoughtfully, "Ammun and Brahma gave their lives to create a barrier between our worlds to keep the twisted souls of Lucifer out, and in Dichonia,"

William counted in his head. "That leaves one. Gaia, I think," he said, staring at his notes.

The others in the class turned to look at him, their expressions hard.

"This is a history class correct?" William asked.

Laurence looked at him and nodded. "You are correct, tainted one. It is thought that the grief was too much for Gaia, seeing her brothers and sisters destroyed. She passed into Oblivion, and was never seen again."

"What is Oblivion?" William asked, before being interrupted by a familiar voice.

"Oblivion surrounds the worlds of Archonia, and Dichonia. It is an endless fog with no land above or below. Many Archonians have attempted to find their way through the fog, but it inevitably leads them back here," Juarez said.

William knew that he needed to know as much about this world as possible if he was to defend it. He smiled at Juarez, and finished his notes. He had all the Archons accounted for. The only two that remained were Lucifer, and Gabriel. He thought it very unfair that the evil of one could cause the destruction of so many and still live. He wondered why Gabriel hadn't attempted to destroy him. Perhaps he wasn't strong enough. Or maybe he couldn't bring himself to kill his brother.

The class dismissed for the day, so William jumped up and caught up with Juarez. They both wore their white linen slacks and shirts so they could head straight to the training grounds after their courses.

"Juarez," William said, matching the smaller man's stride.

"William, how are you?" his Spanish friend asked.

"I'm okay. Crazy stuff back there, huh?"

"Yes, Amigo. Those were very difficult times for everyone."

Something Juarez said the night before had been eating away at him the whole day, and he felt compelled to ask.

"Did you go through hard times back on Earth?" William asked, seriously.

This surprised Juarez, and he sort of looked away. "Yes, William. My past is a sad story," he replied.

"I killed a young boy in the line of duty on Earth, barely old enough to hold a weapon, Juarez. I doubt it could be any worse than my story," William said, pushing.

There was more silence while they walked down the vast corridors of the castle. William gave him his space. He didn't want to upset his only friend. To his surprise, Juarez spoke.

"I too killed a man on Earth. To this day I do not know how I was allowed to come to Archonia. I was a priest in the Catholic Church almost my entire life. I followed the rules and laws of God. Though there were many things I disagreed with, I always tried to obey the mandates of the church. However, my bishop was a sadistic murderer. Not only was he a glutton, but he would use the name of the Lord, and his position in the church, to lure young women to his chambers. There he would rape, and torture them to death. He was a demon, but nobody could find proof. Those that had it were paid well enough to cover it up.

I alone knew the reality, and nobody would believe or help me. The Lord had faced me against a monster to test my faith, and I failed time and time again to bring the bishop to light. One day, I learned the horrible news that my little sister had been asked to come before the bishop. He claimed that the Lord had commanded him to speak with her about becoming married to God. I knew exactly what was going to happen to her, and I asked God for forgiveness. That night, before my little Hermana was able to see the bishop, I took up the sword," Juarez said, a tear running down his smooth, dark face.

William didn't know what to say. The rest of the story didn't need to be told, as he could deduce the rest, but Juarez finished it anyway.

"They tortured me for my blasphemy, and desecrated my body. My family became outcasts. I came here and......" he tried to finish.

"I'm so sorry, Juarez. But you did the right thing. Sometimes you must do a little evil for the greater good. The man was a monster, and you did everything you could to stop him," William said, putting an arm around him.

"From then on I decided that my atonement would be devoting my life to the safety of this world," Juarez said, wiping his tear away.

"And I'm going to help you every step of the way. I've got quite a bit to atone for myself. I'm going to need your help too!" William said.

CHAPTER TEN
THE TEST

There were originally ten new guardian recruits that started with William. After two weeks there were only six. Of the five other candidates there was one, a girl named Katrina, who took a particular liking to William. She seemed to gravitate towards him every time they sparred. He couldn't tell if it was because she thought he was the toughest, or if there was attraction at work.

She was short, with cropped brown hair, and an athletic, chiseled physique. William marveled at the changes to his own body. Katrina explained it while they were sparring.

"You don't actually build muscle here. Your body simply reflects the strength of your mind," she said, striking hard. Her stature, of course mattered little here, and William was rocked by the force of the blow.

"Harder, William!" Juarez shouted cheering him on.

Katrina was the person who had been lapping him and Juarez during their runs. She was very fast, but William believed that he was stronger. He gritted his teeth, and leapt into the sky as Katrina came forward at lightning speed. He avoided her attack, but dropped so slowly that when he returned to the ground she was already waiting for him. He caught a hard fist to the jaw, and quickly found himself on the ground.

William got slowly to his feet, coughing up sand.

"Bested you again," Katrina said with a smirk.

William growled with rage, and shot forth. He caught her by surprise, grabbing either side of her head, and with all his might, flipping her into the air and smashing her against the ground. He jumped on her, and reared back to drive a fist into her face when a wooden staff swung into his throat.

"Enough!" Cheng Fei shouted.

Silence fell over the training ground, and Chang Fei tossed William aside like a rag doll.

"We do not attack out of anger," Chang Fei scolded, pointing his staff down at William "You will swallow your pride, initiate, or you shall be punished."

William stood, saluting, one hand balled up into a fist over his chest, and then bowed.

"Yes sir," he said, glancing over at Katrina, who was dusting off.

Apparently it was important not to be selfish or prideful in Archonia, but from what William had seen, everyone was a hypocrite, just like in his previous life. His words, or his actions, wouldn't change it, however. So why should he care. What was done was done, and he knew that his attitude showed it.

Chang Fei made him stay after the other recruits were done to lift the atlas. It was a stone created by a man during the time of the Greeks. He built strength by hoisting the massive stone ball for hours on end. Eventually the Greeks began worshipping him as a titan.

The stone Atlas used on Earth weighed several hundred pounds. The stone here Archonia was just plain massive. It sat in the middle of the training grounds so that everyone could see it. Most would congregate around it to poke fun at those who were forced to lift it for punishment.

William had been holding it on his back for just a few minutes when Katrina strolled up she knelt down next to him and groaned as a tremendous amount of weight lifted free.

"Why the charity?" William asked, straightening his back a little and looking up.

She was wearing linen garments like him, except she had cut off the pants, revealing her long slender legs, and instead of a shirt, a simple wrap covered her breasts. William had found that people in Archonia possessed as much modesty as he did, and apparently had most of the same rules about sexuality as they did in his former life.

"I'm bored," she responded, "and I do not think that I am ready to meditate yet."

"Well, thanks I guess. You know if Chang Fei catches you, he will probably make you hold it up by yourself after I'm done," William stated, shifting the weight.

"Let him," she said. "The old man is getting on my nerves."

She scowled when saying his name. William chuckled, finding it funny that she called him old. Chang Fei didn't look any older than she did, despite being in Archonia for a great deal longer.

"I'm sorry if I hurt you," William said.

Katrina huffed and rolled her eyes. "Please, William. I do not think that you could hurt me if you tried!"

He laughed. "Okay, then I don't feel nearly as bad."

There was a moment of silence, before she said, "I would have done the same thing. I should not have goaded you like that."

William said nothing, instead continued to stare at the distant sunset. The temperature was already dropping.

"Thanks, but Chang Fei was right. I should not have attacked you out of anger and pride," he said finally.

"Maybe not, but next time I will not turn my back on you," she said with a chuckle.

The two continued to talk for some time, sharing the burden of the atlas stone. Katrina, it turned out, was a soldier in her previous life. She had lived during a time when women weren't supposed to be soldiers, and yet she joined the revolution anyway. Her father and brothers were killed trying to bring freedom to a group of colonies in North America. In the end, she gave her life for the same cause. She lived a very good life, and only killed those who attacked the helpless. She had been selected and brought to Archonia when one of the crusading guardians decided she was worthy.

"So, Will, why exactly does everyone hate you around here?" she asked, in a slightly mocking tone.

Apparently, she was as in the dark about everything as he was. William cast her a sidelong glance, and smiled, taking in her small, mouse-like features.

"I guess I have some dirt on my record. Gabe brought me here when I wasn't supposed to come," William said casually.

"Gabe! You mean the Archon Gabriel!?" Katrina asked, her interest obviously piqued.

"Yeah, why?"

"It is just... well... he is an Archon," she blurted.

"I only knew him briefly, but now have to prove that I am worthy enough to be here. That's the only way he can come back. He traded his place here in Archonia so that I might be given a chance," William said.

"The rumors are true then. You really do have a tainted soul?" she asked, but it sounded more like a statement.

William's anger bristled. "Look, I don't know what my soul looks like, okay. I just want to live my life as best as I can."

"Good. They told me I could not be a soldier back on Earth, but I proved them wrong. I would love to help you prove them wrong as well," she responded.

William's anger melted away as quickly as it rose, replaced by a warm, tingly feeling he wasn't used to. He didn't have much experience with friendship, but was pretty sure that this was what it looked like.

"So, how did you end up kicking the can?" William asked.

"Kick what can?" Katrina asked. William squinted in annoyance but changed his tact.

"How did you end up dying?"

"Well, like I said they told me I couldn't be a soldier, but I wasn't going to have a bunch of men telling me what to do my whole life. I had taken care of my mother and my younger brothers and sister after father and some of my older brothers went to war. Apparently it was noble to die in combat for your ideals and leave your family at home defenseless.

"Well, our home was near the front and the lines broke so quickly nobody had the time to evacuate. I was only fourteen years old anyway and couldn't very well manage such a feat."

"But you *could* manage to be a soldier?" William asked skeptically.

Katrina sighed heavily in annoyance and the weight of the stone shifted slightly. "Fine William, what do you want me to say? That I was a stupid kid that thought I could hold off the entire battalion of redcoats that occupied our town?"

"Hey no worries, I'm sorry. You can be honest with me. No judgments here," William replied.

"Well, I did make some bad choices. I thought I would be the hero of the town. I took one of my father's old muskets he had left behind. I had a brilliant idea that I would sneak into the enemy camp and blow up their powder magazine. This would hopefully stunt their march and then the continental army could swoop in while they lay defenseless. Sneaking in was easy, and so was lighting up the powder, but when the chaos started the redcoats began shooting.

One stumbled in front of me while I was running away. A young boy who seemed to think I was the same. I can still see the hatred in his eyes. Then everything went dark.

"Quite a story," William said after Katrina paused. She gave him a quick look, her face a mixture of sadness and embarrassment.

"Well at least I died in one shot. That flintlock blew a gaping hole in my chest. Honestly it was better than having one of those bastards rape me and send me back home. I don't regret what I did."

William remained quiet. He didn't really know if his normal sarcastic response would be appropriate.

Just then a guardian captain arrived, releasing them from their punishment.

They walked back, and Katrina started talking about guardian training and how excited she was about the prospect of graduating and forging their own armor.

William listened, his thoughts straying a bit. He'd never been in such a long conversation before. In fact, save for Juarez, nobody had ever really taken the time to talk with him. In the military it had all just been banter and he had learned to create a wall of sarcasm to block out the seriousness of life.

"Thank you," William said, stopping and interrupting Katrina.

Katrina stopped, a confused look on her face. "What?"

"Thank you," William said again. "Nobody has ever talked with me for so long."

Katrina's mouth hung open. "I guess the people from your time are not very kind," she said slowly.

"Some were, but most just sort of avoided me," William responded honestly.

Katrina smiled. "Well, you are in a new world now, so you should have a fresh start."

The next day William roused from his meditations to find that it was the end of an Archonian month. He had been in this world for one hundred days already. At the end of each week they had a sort of weekend, but unfortunately it was only one day. This day was supposed to be for rest and recovery. But the guardian initiates had no such rest this week. Their final test was approaching. It was basically a fitness test to prove you have what it takes to be a guardian. There was a test of strength, one of endurance, one of knowledge one of martial technique, and finally one final secret test. Nobody knew what the final test was – not even Juarez, as he had never made it this far in the training. They couldn't seem to pry it out of anyone either.

If they were able to complete this test then they would be inducted into the Guardian Corps, and allowed to forge their armor, the final step in becoming one of the elite warriors.

For the next couple of days Chang Fei drilled them relentlessly for hours without breaks. William and Katrina exchanged many glances, both determined not to be the first one to drop out or fail. It was during those moments that their extra work at the atlas stone seemed to pay off.

Of the six initiates left, William hadn't gotten very close with Venice, and two men, Samuel, and Ulifrig.

Ulifrig was a beast of a man, and built much like Brock, only taller and not as bulky. He had long blond hair, and piercing blue eyes. He had lived in the age of the Vikings, and had sailed longboats across the cold waters of the north into unexplored territory, living, exploring, and raiding with his brethren.

Ulifrig seemed to be very close to the other man, Samuel, who had only been in Archonia a short time by comparison. With short brown hair and dark eyes he had lived in a time of war as well. William knew very little of the other girl, only that she had done the bare minimum to reach it this far in her training.

Juarez and William chatted while sparring, the smaller man talking animatedly about how long he had wished to be a guardian.

"Why is becoming a guardian so special?" William asked, deftly dodging a meek punch from his friend.

"William, the Guardians are the only branch of the Archonian military that sees real combat. The Crusades

139

take you face to face with the evil ones. The Sentinels may act tough, but most have never even seen a real fight. The Adjudicators squabble and delegate, and do nothing that really matters, because this world has been at peace for thousands of years. The Guardians have the chance to change the world and fight the evil that seeks to destroy it..."

"While the rest cower behind the barrier between worlds," William finished and wrapped his arms around his friend in a submission hold.

He felt the smaller man tap on his shoulder, signifying that his friend had yielded, and let go. William thought long and hard on this subject for the remainder of training. The more he thought about it, the more he realized that he wanted it too.

They got to their feet and dusted off. William shook Juarez's hand firmly. The day was winding down, and William had beaten everyone in the sparring circle. Out of the corner of his eye, he caught a blur of purple. His stomach twisted into a hard knot as he spied Meredox standing next to his captain. They were speaking in whispers, and Meredox held out a large scroll sealed with golden wax.

This event was unusual to say the least. They had never had an Adjudicator visit them in training before. William looked from Juarez to Katrina, who simply shrugged. The captain broke the seal after a serious look at Meredox, and unrolled the parchment. Meredox's gaze turned towards William. He continued to stare, standing perfectly still with his arms behind his back.

William stared back, and he thought he could see some sort of satisfaction in the man's eyes. He looked away after a moment, however, as he didn't want to waste his time worrying about the one person who'd done nothing by tear him down since he had come here. He turned and began to walk over towards Katrina.

"Initiates! At attention!" Chang Fei shouted.

The six of them all jumped quickly into line and snapped to attention. He didn't believe any of them held any delusions as to what this was about.

"William of Archonia, step forward," The captain shouted.

"Yes, Captain!" he responded loudly.

"William of Archonia, with the Synod's Approval, The Council of Justicars has decreed the following in accordance with the Commandments of the Fallen. As a tainted soul, if you do not successfully pass guardian training and become a sworn protector of the realm you shall lose citizenship in Archonia, and in so doing be deemed a threat to the peaceful peoples of Archonia. The sentence, in that case, will be obliteration!"

There were gasps behind him, but Chang Fei's eyes stifled any further noise with authority. William's heart was pounding so hard he could feel it in his head. Despite years of training and combat missions, where he'd faced death, he still felt the surge of fear. The adrenaline made his head fuzzy and everything slowed. He stared straight ahead, perfectly aware that Meredox's gaze was locked on him.

This was somehow his doing. He was the Grand Justicar, and had been fighting for this since day one. Finally, he had gotten what he wanted. The uncomfortable silence continued and William became acutely aware of his breathing, which sounded unusually loud. His head turned ever so slightly and he looked at Meredox, trying fruitlessly to wound him with his look. As of tomorrow he would be battling for his life.

He broke his gaze once more and stared off into the setting sun, before shouting with every ounce of strength in his body and lungs "Sir! Yes! Sir!

"Initiates report tomorrow for final testing. Dismissed!" Chang Fei finished and then sped away with Meredox.

"William!" Katrina gasped, already at his side. She gently placed a hand on his upper arm.

Juarez was on the other side. He didn't so much as look at any of them. He didn't want their pity. He only wanted to kill Meredox. His heart shut down, and he turned on his heel quickly and marched off.

William barely meditated that night. He secluded himself in the corner of the dimly lit meditation chamber and stared into the soft glow of the little orb in the center of the room.

He felt like he was right back in Juvi. The judge had just told him he was going to serve in the military, and he thought it was pretty much a death sentence. Tomorrow may very well be a death sentence. For a while he wondered if there was anything after this life. Then he envisioned himself beating the hell out of Meredox. He thought about fleeing in the night, but he didn't have any idea where he could flee too.

There was sorrow and rage, but that all soon turned to determination. *That greasy-haired little bastard is not going to kill me,* he thought.

* * *

William arrived first in the morning to the lecture hall. The first test was a written exam. He was worried about this test, so he sat down quickly, quietly pondering all that he had learned in his class so far. He had a book of notes which he had been studying. He hadn't had the patience to study in his former life, but there had been so many hours in a day here that he had studied more than he needed to.

Professor Echard strolled into the lecture hall, and stopped briefly, looking William over, and then looked at a clock hanging on the wall. He set a stack of parchment on his desk, and then indicated to them. William got up with his notes in hand and extended them to the historian. Professor Echard took them and handed William one of the exam packets.

"You have one hundred minutes, Initiate."

William took his seat and started in on the test. The others showed up on time and he could feel them looking at him and wondering, but he didn't look up. To his delight the test was simple. He had paid excellent attention in his classes.

He eyed the clock after he answered the final question. It had taken him just shy of 50 minutes to complete. He went back through to ensure he had completed all the questions, also double checking his answers as Juarez had recommended. He had been helping William with the academics a little, just as he had helped Juarez with the physical challenges.

He stood up and strode to the front where Professor Echard was reading a large dusty book. He looked over his bifocals at William and smiled slightly, taking the proffered exam. William turned and began to walk out.

"It will only take a moment, young one," Echard said, gently fingering through the exam.

William looked at the others, specifically Katrina and Juarez, who were still taking their tests. It was the first time he'd seen them since last night. They both looked up at him with concern. He looked away, feeling a mix of embarrassment and guilt, but then smirked at them and gave them a nod. In that short amount of time the professor completed his review, which was astounding, but not surprising. William told himself that he'd probably been grading these for decades. With that much practice, it wasn't surprising that he was incredibly fast at it.

He heard a clap as Echard pressed a stamp into his papers, and looked down to see the professor extending his papers towards him again. His heart fluttered and then a smile spread across his face as he saw "PASS" stamped in bright white ink on the paper. He snatched it triumphantly, waving it at his friends as he exited the room.

He walked around the halls for a bit, before deciding to return to the exam room, feeling every bit the excited, anxious teenager. He waited outside until Juarez emerged.

"Holy crap, Juarez, that only took you like twenty minutes," William said.

"Amigo, I have taken these courses many times. This was nothing."

Samuel and Ulifrig came out next, finishing at around fifty minutes, very close to the same time as William. The red head walked out at seventy, and finally Katrina at almost ninety minutes.

"Cutting it close there," William said.

"Stop worrying about me, William. We need to worry about getting you through these tests," she said seriously.

"Kat, don't. I'm going to be fine. Can we all just act like last night didn't happen?" he asked, looking from Juarez to Katrina.

"This isn't a joke, William," Katrina snapped.

"I know it's not a fucking joke!" William growled. Then he took a deep breathe. "Look guys, the last thing I need right now is pity. Right now I'm going to focus on doing this thing and doing it right. The best way for you to help me is to just...act normal. Now c'mon, we have to be at the second test in twenty minutes."

The group followed William to the training grounds where they found a guardian captain waiting. They had never met him before. His armor was glorious; he stood tall and broad, the silver of his armor shimmering in the morning light.

This is what I'm going to be, William thought.

"Welcome, initiates, to the test of speed. You will all have one hundred minutes to complete one hundred laps around the valley. You will stay on the ground at all times and within the boundaries of the path. Failure to meet any of these requirements will result in an immediate disqualification." A bright light flashed in his hand, forming into an hourglass. He flipped it, and the group jolted into frantic action.

William's legs swelled as he sprinted down the track. On his best day he could complete the warm up in about one hundred and forty minutes, so he knew that he had to push himself. Katrina was already half a lap ahead of the rest of them, showing off her natural speed. Her body cut through the air easily, leaving a trail of white behind her. William dug his feet into the ground hard, trying to extend his strides, and pick up the pace. His chest heaved as he fought to find his breath, but the burn was already taking hold.

You can do this...just find your stride, William told himself.

"Get your backside moving, tainted one," Kat yelled the first time she lapped him. William growled and pushed his body harder, increasing his speed. He bounded down the path, his strides twenty feet apart. He no longer marveled at the inhuman speed he had achieved. Lap ten came fast, as Kat burst by them again with a sonic boom.

"Maybe Meredox is right," her voice echoed as she disappeared.

William let go a roar. He pictured Meredox in his mind with that sleazy, victorious grin on his face. His feet thudded as they hit the ground, leaving a dent in the dirt. Laps twenty and thirty passed in a blur, and his arms and legs seared in painful revolt.

Juarez overtook William. "Come, mi amigo, we have to move faster."

"It's burning," William barely choked out."

"Nothing is burning. That is your human mind. Let go of it," he said, and then continued forward.

William moaned in pain, and yelled to relieve the wrenching in his core from the decompression of each painful breath. His legs began to feel rubbery and throbbed with pain. Laps forty and fifty went by and he fell further behind. Meredox' eyes flashed again in his head. He was going to lose and his life was going to be taken from him. His form began to waver and his legs wobbled under every footfall.

Katrina blasted by again. "Get moving, Soldier! That's an order!" she shouted, this time slowing to his pace for a moment and smacking him across the face.

The force of the strike nearly knocked William off the track, but something sparked and he caught his footing. Katrina zipped away again, her feet gliding across the dirt. William's feet sounded like thunder, and he overtook the entire group, save for Katrina in the next lap. His mind was gone. He lost count of the number of laps. He lost sight of everyone, and didn't even register that Katrina was no longer lapping him. Perhaps she had already finished.

His muscles continued to scream and his chest burned, but his mind swallowed it all and he lost all sense of time. Adrenaline alone kept him going and the fear.

He felt arms wrap around him and saw Ulifrig in front of him, blocking him. He heard muffled speech and tried to keep running, but he couldn't move, and the speech became clearer.

"William you're done! You made it," Kat said wildly.

"You ran 103 laps you fool. 87 minutes."

His legs buckled and he sprawled to the ground in complete abandon.

"Congratulations, initiates, you have all passed the test of speed. Katrina of Helios, you set a new record for the Guardian Corps. You—completed in only 66 minutes. You will all have one hour to compose yourselves for the test of strength. Report back to me in 100 minutes," the guardian said, before turning and walking away.

It took William a while to catch his breath enough to sit up. His legs felt like jelly, and his chest still ached. He spat up dirt he had inhaled, and tried to moisten his mouth.

"Well done, William," Katrina said, handing him a cup of water. He looked around for a nearby fountain but couldn't find one. She must have run clear to the other side of the field to get it.

"You too, setting records huh?"

"I didn't have any idea what the record was," she said, looking away. William could tell by her expression that she was lying.

"Frickin' show off," he mumbled, eagerly tipping the cup and feeling the fresh cool water slide down his parched throat.

"Two for two, tainted one. Only three more to go," Juarez chimed in. He wore a smile on his face that seemed brighter than the sun overhead.

"You worried about me still, little man? Isn't this the farthest you've gotten?" William shot back, smirking.

Juarez's face flushed and he shook his head.

The rest of the hour flew by, allowing William's body to recover from the run. He felt limber now, his muscles warm and stretched. He wasn't worried about the next two tests. It was the final secret test that concerned him. Soon they were all back in front of their test officer. The guardian captain smiled as they approached, the familiar challenges lined up behind him.

Six identical pillars of stone sat perfectly spaced in front of a line.

"Welcome, initiates, to the test of strength. These stones each have a corresponding position at the other end of the field. You have one hundred minutes to carry it the distance and place it into position. It must be upright and in the circle. Be sure to note the color of your circle. I wouldn't want to place it in someone else's spot."

The guardian captain wasted no more words, and flipped his ornate hourglass over once more. William rushed over to a stone, determined to make quick work of this challenge. After all, he had shown more improvement in feats of strength than any of the other initiates, and was confident he could complete this challenge with relative ease.

The pillar was easily twice the size of the stone he had moved during his first day of training. But now it felt half as heavy, although it was much taller and to carry it upright would simply be too awkward. He pushed against the stone and it tipped over. As it fell towards the ground he deftly side-stepped beneath it and caught the weight on his shoulder. He then hoisted it up, quickly finding its center of gravity so that it balanced comfortably.

He strode forth without thinking about it. The walk was strenuous, but not nearly as demanding as the run. He had to periodically pause and switch shoulders. This cost him some time, but he didn't really need the full hour. William arrived at the other side of the field and gingerly set his stone down next to his circle. Then he went to one end and hoisted it up, running toward the bottom so that the pillar tipped perfectly into place. The test officer watched him silently, before giving him a quick nod of approval. William spied the hourglass, which was now more or less halfway through.

He dusted off his hands, noting the extremely tough callouses that had accumulated in the past months. Shielding his eyes from the sun, William squinted across the field to check on his friend's progress. The large Viking Ulifrig had been a couple minutes behind William and placed his stone with ease upon his marker. He turned and stood next to William to assess the rest of the group.

Three of them came in all very close to one another. Katrina, Samuel, and then Venice. Each completed their task with time to spare. However Juarez was still a mile or so off. William glanced quickly towards the hour glass, which was quickly running dry. The rest of the group celebrated their victory, but William became frantic. He couldn't let his friend fail. Not after all the work he put into getting this far.

"Kat!" William shouted. She turned to meet his gaze, and looked as he pointed out to the field where Juarez toppled over into the dirt with his stone. Her face fell, and she shook her head in defeat, but William wasn't about to give up. The directions to this test had been extremely simple and there were very few guidelines. William nearly stumbled and fell as he jolted over towards the test captain.

"Captain, can you please repeat the guidelines of this test?"

"That is a peculiar request, initiate," the guardian replied.

"Captain, please!" William said impatiently.

"Each initiate has 100 minutes to get his or her stone across the field and place it in the designated zone."

"Nothing else?" William shot back quickly."

"No, initiate, the test is very clear and concise," the guardian said, confusion wrinkling his face.

"Kat, c'mon," William shouted, breaking into a sprint towards Juarez.

He had a good head start on Kat, but she caught up to him in no time.

"William, what in Dichonia are you doing?"

"We are helping Juarez. Nothing in the rulebook says we can't," William said, smirking triumphantly and quickening his pace.

William watched Katrina surge ahead of him. By the time he reached his two friends, Katrina already held one end of the stone and was arguing with Juarez about the rules of the test.

"Just shut the hell up you two and carry this. We can argue once we get this thing in place," William barked.

Even if the Captain decided to disqualify Juarez William wouldn't let him fail on his own. He took the center, and then shouted.

"Left! Right! Left!" William shouted, synchronizing their steps.

The remaining stretch only took a few minutes to gap, and they nearly squashed Venice, who was standing on the other side of Juarez's marker. William caught the other side and the three initiates steadied the stone as it wobbled.

Just as it settled into place they heard the test officer yell, "Time! Initiates, attention!"

They all hopped into a line and stood perfectly still.

"William of Archonia, what in the name of the creators do you think you were doing?"

"Sir, you made it very clear that each of us was to get our stone across the field. You didn't specify how, or detail any restrictions or rules pertaining to us helping one another. I was merely helping a fellow soldier."

The guardian captain looked annoyed, but didn't argue.

"Pretty clever, initiates. You are correct. I failed to specify said guidelines. Something I will surely not overlook in the next two tests." He stared at them for a few moments in silence, seemingly pondering what to say next.

William rocked on his heels, waiting to find out if they would get in trouble.

"Congratulations, initiates, you have all passed the test of strength. Juarez of Helios, you have some true friends here. Keep them close," The captain finished, and abruptly walked away.

Juarez fell to his knees, and William was right by him, patting him on the back.

"Knew you had it in ya, little guy."

The next hour passed just as quickly as the last, and William had to tell Juarez to stop thanking him numerous times. The group spotted the captain over at the sparring circles, surrounded by a growing crowd of people. They shared a look, and made their way in that direction.

"Welcome to the third test, initiates. This will gauge your martial technique. William of Archonia, why don't you go first," the captain said, ushering him into the circle.

William was confident in this test, possibly more so than the previous one. He'd learned advanced hand-to-hand combat in the U.S. military, and so far in initiate's training had been more than a match against his peers, save for Katrina, whose speed caused some serious problems.

This particular test had attracted onlookers. The other tests he had either not noticed them or they hadn't come to the training grounds that early. There were now a good fifty soldiers surrounding the pit in which they would be testing.

As he hopped in to the circle over the small fence which he had closely encountered on his first day in Valhalla, he sized up the man waiting for him in the pit. He was a smaller man dressed in the sentinel garb with a flowing blue cape. As the man's head hit the dirt the crowd surrounding the training grounds erupted into raucous cheers. A smile broke over William's face. A warmth blossomed inside him in that moment, and for the first time, he felt accepted.

I am a warrior, he thought, pounding a fist against his chest.

"Juarez did surprisingly well. William watched the smaller man dip and weave, using what looked like shaolin martial arts to block, counter, and bend around the sentinel's aggressive barrage of attacks. In a graceful move, the former spiritual leader caught the sentinel's kick with his right leg, snapped a driving punch into the man's stomach, before driving him off his feet with a snap kick to the face. William was clapping before the sentinel hit the ground."

Katrina was more of a brawler, overtaking her sparring partner with speed and brute force. She knocked the man off the ground and completed a simple, but effective submission. The test captain overseeing had to actually pull her off before she broke the man's arm.

The day wore on, the sun spanning in its relatively lazy arc across the sky. The guardian captain awaited them at the next test.

"Endurance," he said.

William followed Katrina and Juarez to the next ground, where they found tall pedestals with large round stones balanced on top of them. The trainer demonstrated this task. Evidently they would have to scale the pedestal, and maintain their balance while holding the stone above their heads for an allotted time.

"This time there will be no helping one another. Should you help a fellow initiate in any way other than verbally you will fail and so will the initiate who has breached the rules."

William laughed.

"The atlas stone is easily ten times larger than these," he whispered to Katrina.

They watched the others jump up and grip the edge of the narrow pedestals, before trying to heft the stones above their heads. The pillars looked to be about two stories high, which William could gap with relative ease. He jumped into the air, feeling the warm air rush over his skin, and grabbed the edge of the stone with one hand, while pushing the stone with the other. The stone was large and awkward, but once he found the center of gravity, it lifted easily. He slowed his breathing, finding balance and stood perfectly still, hoisting the rock above his head with a single arm.

His companions chose two arms, but this made the weight shift unevenly for most of the test. William simply switched arms when one began to burn too much, and used his free arm to maintain balance. Katrina stood on the pedestal next to him, and at about three quarters of the way through the test she began to lose control of her stone. Luckily, she began falling towards William, who quickly shifted all the weight to one foot and leaned out with his right arm and shoved the stone back up above her. She gained control quickly, steadying herself before the test officer walked by and looked up. She sighed heavily and shook her head. *That was close,* she seemed to say.

After the Captain rang the bell they got down. William turned just as Katrina ran into him, enveloping him in a strong hug. Nothing needed to be said.

The endurance test really took it out of William. And after looking around at the others, realized he wasn't alone.

They were shaking and sweaty. But there was only one test left. The secret one.

"Seek out your captain, Chang Fei. He will oversee your final test, and well done initiates you have all shown true strength and character. I hope to see you around the guardian barracks," the guardian captain stated.

They found Chang Fei not far away, on a barren part of the training ground, near a huge mound at the edge of the valley. Several large urns sat along the bottom of the mound. They looked either very old, or poorly made, crumbling to pieces, but Chang Fei gave no time to ponder what the test was going to be.

"The final test requires each of you to project your Archonian energies. Use it to destroy the three urns that are designated in your own range," he stated.

Chang Fei, as usual, was a man of few words.

William instantly felt his heart sink. Despite their extensive training, no one had taught him how to project. His speed and strength had improved, but those mattered little in this test. There was no way he was going to pass this test. His hands began to shake and he saw Meredox' face snickering in the back of his mind.

"Captain, I have never been shown how to project."

Chang Fei spoke quietly, "find your inner energy, and push it forth. He who has not destroyed his urns by the time I return tonight will be cut from the path of the guardian. You may only use your Archonian energy to destroy the urns, you may not cross the lines, and you may not help another destroy their urns."

He vanished in a cloud of dust, launching into the sky. William was beyond words, but staunched his frustration, replacing it with determination instead. He walked up to the makeshift shooting range, stopping at a line laid out in stone. He looked around, and watched as others tried futilely to push their essence forth.

Katrina had lived here quite a while, and William watched her struggle. Her best efforts were a mere shadow in comparison to the one Gabriel produced on Earth. William's confidence dwindled. Even Samuel, and Ulifrig, who had been in guardian training before, struggled. They at least showed signs of projection, although it lacked shape and substance. The two men shouted and strained, holding faint glowing auras that shot off waves of heat in every direction.

William focused. He looked down range, staring at his three urns. They were a reddish brown, and although they looked fragile and crumbling before, now they seemed all but indestructible. William focused. He tried to feel what Chang Fei had described as his inner energy.

Before William could begin to unravel what that meant, there was a shrill sound and light erupted next to him, demolishing a giant urn down range. They all turned, startled to see Juarez standing, his palm extended. He felt his eyes go wide as two more brilliant balls of light shoot from his hand, and blow two more urns to dust. Katrina howled with joy.

"Juarez, you have been holding out on us!" she shouted, running over and embracing him.

"Well, I have been at this for a long time," he responded with a small smile.

"You have to teach us!" she exclaimed.

He smiled and said, "It seems so simple now. I don't know where to begin. I have never made it this far in the guardian training. Chang Fei is right. You must learn to feel the energy inside you. Your Archonian essence is an almost unlimited pool of energy. You simply need to learn how to tap into it, push it out, and use it to create or destroy."

Juarez proceeded to work with all of them, helping each student to produce small projections. Katrina even managed to knock one of her urns over. William, however, stared at his urns, and every so often he felt a twinge in his body. When he did, he would grunt and strain to push it forth, but nothing would happen.

The first hour passed and William was positive he was done for. The words kept echoing in his mind about him being obliterated. But Chang Fei didn't return.

Night began to fall. Nobody seemed to be able to tell William when this test would end or when Chang Fei would return, which drove him and everyone else to work desperately at the task. Venice became so angry that she couldn't project that she picked up a stone and hurled it at one of her pots with such a force that the pottery exploded, showering everyone in sand and jagged shards.

"NO!" Juarez shouted, but it was too late.

"There. I have destroyed one," she said triumphantly.

A blinding flash split the air and the pieces of the broken pot shot back together again. They all looked up to where the blinding light had come from, and found Chang Fei floating in the air a couple hundred yards above their heads. Venice cursed under her breath, a look of dread in her eyes. The captain descended, landing slowly in front of her, and simply pointed towards the castle. Venice scowled, and limped slowly away, making her solemn walk of shame into the night.

And then there were five.

Juarez stood with Chang Fei a few meters away, talking and gesturing animatedly. They spoke briefly, and then the Chinese warlord took off into the sky again. Juarez strolled back to the group, his eyes pointed at the ground.

"We have until morning to complete the task," he said sullenly.

"How long till sunrise?" Katrina asked.

Samuel said, "Ten more hours."

They all went back to work with renewed vigor. William watched Chang Fei float above the group. He hung in the night sky, like a black speck against an impossibly large, orange planet.

Juarez hovered near William, while the rest of the group were able to damage or destroy their targets in relatively short order. Samuel projected in a wide bubble, which Juarez stated was a shield. He expanded the bubble until it knocked over his three pots, shattering them.

"Focus," Juarez said softly, jarring William's attention back to his own urns.

"I am focusing," William said gruffly. "I have been for the past day and night."

William hadn't even managed to project a single wisp of smoke. His frustration had grown beyond simple anger, and simmered on the verge of rage. He looked between his urns, which were still intact, and the rest down the line. Every single one was broken, save for his. Just like life. It always came easier for some. Privilege, wealth, or opportunity. It never came down to skill. His rage festered, feeding itself.

He started to shake, feeling something build along with the anger inside of him. But it wasn't where he expected. It was in his head. There was a pulse thrumming somewhere beyond his thoughts.

His desperate hope told him that this was the energy he was looking for. Juarez was the only one still standing by, remaining behind to encourage him as William had done for him so many times before. Katrina couldn't face the thought of him being destroyed and took off as tears formed in her eyes. He figured the others had returned to meditate, but even they came back just before the sun broke over the mound, the first light of day breaking William slumped to the ground as Chang Fei descended from his perch in the clouds.

He spoke quietly, but sternly. "Those of you who completed this task, I congratulate. All of your discipline has become fruitful. I hereby declare you to be guardian recruits."

Samuel and Ulifrig rejoiced, but Katrina and Juarez remained silent. They looked at William with somber faces. The captain continued.

"You will report to the Hall of the Guardians immediately to prepare yourselves for your new life. The tempering process will begin in the morning.

"William you will remain here to be taken into custody," Chang Fei stated.

"This is a pile of horses shit!" Katrina shouted flailing her arms in the air. Juarez grabbed her quickly and tried to contain the outburst.

"Recruits! Dismissed!" Chang Fei growled.

William's new friends retreated slowly in defeat. There was nothing more they could do.

With an entire day of trying to focus his inner energy, which he swore wasn't there, he found that he didn't even have the energy to shout, or even get upset, so he simply sat and watched the sunrise.

He thought about everything he had gone through to get to this point in his training. Hadn't he worked every bit as hard as the others? He had outshone many of them in the training. He felt betrayed.

I overcame more than anyone, he thought.

He deserved to pass. He thought about the pots, and felt the pulse build inside his head again. He startled, and took a breath.

He looked down the range at the pots looming in the fading light. This bane wouldn't stand in his way. He wouldn't simply give up like he had in his previous life. Even if it was too late and they planned on executing him, he would overcome this obstacle. He crouched into a fighting stance, and focused on that small pulse buzzing in his head. It grew as he closed his eyes, his rage building. Then he could feel it in his chest. He pictured Chang Fei's face as he disregarded his many weeks of training, all over a simple test.

William let loose a roar more terrifying than he had ever heard. He felt this anger rip forth out of his chest in a wave of energy. It was hot like fire, but didn't burn. It felt invigorating, and enlivening. A wave of light burst from his body, so broad that it not only consumed the three urns, but it plowed a massive ravine into the mound of sand behind.

Sand, dust, and rock exploded in a violent shower. When it subsided, William stood breathing heavily, smoke rising off of his body. The sand from the mound glowed in the fading light, the blast melting it instantly into glass.

"There is your stupid test, Chang," he said angrily.

Just then there were bright flashes around him and he felt strong hands force his arms behind his back. He jerked in response to the abrupt restraint, but couldn't break free. Two much older Adjudicators forced him to his knees. William looked up and locked eyes with Meredox.

"William of Archonia, you are under arrest for your crimes on the mortal plane. You are hereby sentenced to an immediate obliteration."

"Burn in Hell, you bastard," William said, spitting on the ground at Meredox' feet.

"We don't know what comes after this life, tainted one, but for you it will surely be damnation," Meredox replied acidly.

"I passed all the stupid tests. I outshone most of the other recruits. I'm more committed than any of them. So go ahead and kill me. My conscience is clean."

Meredox's face twitched in annoyance, but then he pulled a long, slender sword from a loop at his side.

"You have been judged. Let the execution commence!"

CHAPTER ELEVEN
THE GARDEN

William wasn't scared. He stared straight at his executioner as the sword slowly rose. He breathed evenly, willing his body still. He had already died once.

How hard could it be to do it again?

He had always thought his life was supposed to flash before his eyes at the time of death, but his hadn't either time. He began to wonder what the next life would hold as he waited for the blow to be struck. A thundering crack issued through the sky at that moment and William looked up to see Meredox staring over top of him at someone else.

"Commander Achilles, have you come to watch the execution?" Meredox asked, lowering his sword slightly.

William craned his neck, trying to catch a glimpse of the great warrior.

"I am afraid there will be no execution today, Grand Justicar."

Meredox nodded to one of his adjudicators, who immediately released William, while the other took hold of both of his arms. The soldier quickly produced a scroll, likely the same scroll they had shown Chang Fei the day before.

"I have here a decree..."

"I am aware of your feeble paper, Grand Justicar, but this initiate has not failed the tests. He *will* be a guardian."

"My adjudicators were just informed that this tainted soul has failed the final test," Meredox said calmly and evenly.

"I will keep my own council on who has passed or failed the initiates test," Achilles stated flatly."

William's entire body shook, either from joy or relief, he wasn't sure. He glanced up at Meredox, who was now scowling. Meredox said nothing so Achilles spoke again.

"Release my recruit, or would you like me to provide you with a paper first?"

Meredox scoffed at the obvious mockery. "Nay, your word is law in the Guardian Corps, Commander. Justicars release this man, you are dismissed."

William's arms were released, hand prints smashed into his skin where they had been gripping him so fiercely. The three Adjudicators departed without another word. William quietly wondered if they would appeal to the Synod again, or whether they had finally given up trying to kill him. He rubbed his arms, and stood up, slowly turning.

"Commander!" William said, snapping him a salute.

Achilles touched his chest lightly, acknowledging the salute, and spoke.

"The Archon believes there is something special inside of you, tainted one, but I am troubled by the way in which you completed the last test," Achilles said, pointing to the hole William's wave of energy made. "I will only allow you to become a guardian if you can project once more tonight. Follow me, I have something to show you," he said, lifting off from the ground and soaring through the air.

William's mind went mad with joy and confusion, but Achilles had already taken off, flying low and fast to the north, so William took off, trying to keep up. He was getting faster, but he was still relatively slow. He strained, using every ounce of his remaining will to keep up, and after many miles, Achilles finally stopped in front of a beautiful stone archway that stood in a large stone wall. William was gasping for air and his muscles screamed by the time he reached the arch. Achilles looked calm and collected. He hadn't even broken a sweat.

"This is the Garden of Medina. I come here to think sometimes," Achilles said, floating slowly through the archway. William followed, still catching his breath.

"Now, can you tell me how you destroyed those ceramic pots?" Achilles asked.

"I projected. I thought you saw it?" William responded flatly.

"Yes. But how did you project? You failed to do it for an entire day, and night," Achilles said.

William knew the answer, but he didn't say it right away. Achilles turned, his feet kissing the ground softly as he landed. William looked around, mesmerized by the wildlife growing around him. He turned back suddenly, the guardian commander's gaze piercing through him.

"I got angry," William said finally.

"Correct, and you must never do it again," Achilles cautioned with finality. "Your soul is teetering on the edge of a sword."

William remained silent.

"Do you remember what color the Archon's aura was when he first found you on Earth?" The commander asked softly.

"It was the most brilliant light I have ever seen. It drowned out all others," William replied.

"Quite amazing, was it not?" Achilles asked, with a wry grin.

"Do you know what color yours is?"

William was caught off guard, and he thought back to a few minutes ago when he obliterated the firing range. He realized he didn't know, so he simply shook his head.

"Find out what color your aura is, and you may join the guardians. You will report to the guardian's barracks tomorrow morning after your meditation if you can do this," Achilles stated, and then vanished in a flash of light.

William looked around. He was in a small courtyard. He'd never been overly fond of plants, but he had to admit the garden was gorgeous.

As if anything in this world could be ugly, he thought sarcastically.

There were sculptures so intricate that it looked as if they could come alive at any moment. Trellises made of stone arched throughout the tiny square, with plants growing around them, twisting and turning through the hard stone. These were some of the first plants William had seen here, besides the long, white grass outside the city. He bent down, astounded at their surreal color and alien appearance. He didn't recognize a single one, although they were all similar to the plants he had seen before.

William walked for a few more moments, before finding a nice spot to sit down. He settled down cross-legged on a patch of grass just off one of the pathways. The sky spanned expansively above him, allowing him to see the massive celestial bodies hovering throughout the sky. He sighed, and held up his hand palm up, and focused.

Hours passed and his palm remained empty, but he refused to break his focus. On several occasions a spark flared, and one time he even sent a small shockwave out from his body, singeing the grass he was sitting in. He was more curious now than angry, and he continued to search for the answer to Achilles' question.

What color was his soul?

William faded off for a while, drifting into deep thought. It felt similar to his meditations. He came to, his palm still held in the air, but now he could feel the tingle inside him. The same feeling when the urns shattered. He knew now what he had to do. He took the tingle, and moved it. Concentrating and shifting it from the center of his body, up his arm, and out to his palm. Then he let it leak out. He opened his eyes, and to his amazement found a stream of vapor escaping from his hand. He pushed a little harder with his mind and the vapor became more energized. He formed it into a ball. As it took shape, his heart sank.

Hovering in his hand was a tiny crystal ball. It wasn't white and full of light like other projections he had seen. It wasn't even clear. The energy appeared opaque, or cloudy It pulsed with energy like Gabe's had done, and it was very warm.

What did this mean?

William thought to himself, and then he felt sick. He had done things in his life, bad things. He was no angel. Not like the others here. Not like Gabe. His light had been so bright and strong when he saved Angelica that it almost blinded him. Now William understood why people here hated him.

They had earned the right to live in this paradise, and now the Synod had let him, a tainted being, live amongst them. William didn't know whether to be angry at himself, or the new world around him. He broke down, struggling as the visions of his past life poured out like a waterfall. Tears streamed down his face, and he wept all alone under a sky bright with large, shining stars.

After a while the tears subsided, and William's back started to itch. He had the sudden feeling that he was being watched.

He jumped to his feet, and called out, "who's there?"

Only silence greeted him. He waited for a moment longer then shouted again.

"I can hear you," he bluffed.

This seemed to work because there was a rustling in front of him and a woman stepped out of the bushes.

"Angelica!?" William gasped.

Embarrassment washed over him, and he quickly wiped away the moisture around his eyes.

"It's okay. I'm sorry I startled you. I just saw you enter the garden with that man, and I thought I would say hello. But you looked like you didn't want to talk," she said sheepishly.

"And so you thought you would..." William started, pointing to the bushes.

"Oh, I'm so sorry," she said, putting her hands to her head, and turning to leave.

"Wait, no," William said, taking a few steps and reaching for her. "It's okay. No harm done. I was just having a little pity party, but I'm done now, so..." he trailed off.

"Did you just project?" she asked slowly, batting her big brown eyes.

William felt his throat go dry.

"You saw that?" William asked, his gaze dropping to the ground.

"Yes, that was very beautiful," she said, smiling. "From what I understand, this entire garden was created from people's projections."

It made perfect sense, as none of it seemed real. He refocused his thoughts, and said, "Not many people would think that my projection is beautiful."

"William," she replied, shaking her head and stepping closer, "back on Earth, that night before we came here, I saw a man mistreated by the world. And it crushed me."

William's eyes went wide, and locked onto hers.

"You have the choice, William. You can let it get you down, or you can stay positive, and make what you can of your situation," she said.

William felt more tears bubbling in his eyes, but he forced them back.

"You're right," he said, turning away. He could still feel her close behind him.

"They are beautiful, aren't they?" Angelica asked, pointing towards a cluster of flowers on a bush. They were glowing brightly in the light of the different colored planets and moons. She walked up beside him.

"Yes. Beautiful," he replied, but he wasn't looking at the plants. He was looking at her.

Her long brown hair was braided loosely, and fell down her back, which was draped with white cloth much like a toga. Her dark, smooth skin reflected as much light as the flowers. She turned to him, and he snapped his head forward, looking at the flowers once more.

His face flushed, and he knew he'd been caught, but she was kind enough not to say anything. There was a long moment of silence, and then she turned, looking at the large spheres in the sky.

"Do you miss it?" she asked.

William knew she was talking about Earth.

"I don't," he said truthfully, staring upwards next to her.

"I had a little sister back home."

William looked at her again this time with empathy.

"I'm sorry," he said, but she just shook her head.

"My family, they will mourn for me, but it does me good to know that we will see each other again." Angelica turned, looking into William's eyes.

William was rendered breathless. He didn't know what to say. He had been in the middle of firefights, with bullets whizzing and snapping around him, and yet, he had never felt these paralyzing affects before. In that moment the plants all around began to glow bright purple. They looked around, as the soft hum of the insects transformed into a melody. The unnatural luminescent glow from the plants seemed to catch the tension in the air.

They walked for a while, soaking in the splendor of it, and finally sat down next to a tree. William had never been one for small talk, so silence quickly overtook the pair. Angelica broke the silence first.

"So, what are some of your favorite things?"

William was dumbfounded. Nobody had ever asked him such a simple yet personal question before. He stumbled over words in his head until finally coming up with something.

"Chocolate," he sputtered awkwardly.

Angelica burst into laughter and began rolling around in the grass.

"What?" William demanded. "What is so funny?"

"You are," she replied, continuing to laugh.

"Well, what do you like then?" he asked, scowling and turning away, but Angelica quickly grabbed him by the arm, wrapping his bicep in a hug and pressing her warm skin against his.

"Oh come on, don't be such a grump!" She tried to make eye contact with him for a few moments before finally sighing.

"I like new born baby kittens, and the feel of sun on my skin. I like my grandmother's empanadas, and fresh cut pineapples," she said, smiling warmly. It was the same smile that made him stop that fateful night back on Earth.

"What the heck are empanadas?" William asked with a furrowed brow.

"You have never had them?" she asked in shock. "You'll have to come to my home sometime and we will have some. My grandmother still makes the best ones I've ever had."

"Wait. Your grandmother is here?"

"Yes! She found me the day that I was brought here. She helped get me cleaned up before the trial. I have been living with her," she said excitedly. "What about you? Do you have any family here?"

William scoffed. "Hell no. The people in my family were horrible," he said, trailing off.

"I can't imagine they were that bad. What were your parents like?" she asked.

William frowned. Angelica had come from a loving family and clearly didn't understand. He breathed out slowly. It didn't hurt him to talk about it anymore, especially because he was too young to remember most of it. But it was still a part of his past he was ashamed of.

"My father was a drunk. And he liked to beat my mother. One night he beat her so hard she didn't get back up. He got away with it. When I was older, I read through the case. He pled self defense, saying that she had attacked him with a knife. He must have inflicted the wounds himself because I didn't see it happen that way," William said quietly.

Angelica listened, her eyes sad and mouth open.

"I am so sorry, William. Nobody should have to go through that."

"It only got worse after that. Without my mom to hit, he had to find someone else. I was the only other one around. But what doesn't kill you makes you stronger, I guess," William said.

Tears formed in Angelica's eyes and her face flushed even darker.

"No. No. No. Please don't cry," William said, holding up his hands as if a torrent of water was going to come rushing out of her at any moment. "I don't need pity."

"I'm sorry it is just so sad," she responded, as tears rolled down her soft cheeks.

William couldn't help himself. He reached out and wiped them away. It was an innate reaction that surprised him more than Angelica. He stared into her caramel eyes again, totally mesmerized. He didn't know why she put him in such a stupor. Now would have been the perfect time to lean forward and kiss her, but after a few moments he cleared his throat and turned, looking back out at the glowing purple plant life around them.

The creatures of the night began to play an enchanting melody again as Angelica laid her head on William's chest. He wrapped his arm around her, taking solace in her company and the shared silence. They sat together for the rest of the night, listening to the lullaby of the garden's invisible creatures.

CHAPTER TWELVE
FAITH

The air was thick with the smell of smoky meats and spicy curry. Those aromas, mixed with heavy incense made it difficult for Angelica to breathe in the small, cramped tent. The structure was made of stitched together canvas and animal hides, propped up by tall stilts of rich, dark mahogany. Angelica noticed how similar it looked to the teepees some nomadic Native American tribes used.

A column of smoke rose from the center of the tent, where the night's meal cooked on the small fire. Part of her found it odd that the Archonian people still regularly cooked. But then she came to realize that it was the comfort in the idea of cooking and eating, if not just for the wonderful taste, but more for the excuse to socialize. People were laughing, singing, and conversing all around her.

Angelica quietly studied the people in her pilgrimage. There were many young women, like her, but children as well. There were very few men however. She wondered why fewer men found the need for faith in this second life.

After the passing ceremony, Angelica decided to learn and practice Crequoatl, the primary religion practiced in Archonia. According to Julia, the word itself meant "the spiritual study of oneself". Much like Autology, or the scientific study of oneself.

As in Buddhism, a person essentially tries to find happiness, before spreading it to others. Unlike Catholism, one of the cardinal rules of Creqouatl is that a person doesn't witness to other people. In fact, one doesn't speak of the personal, introspective search at all. And if somebody asks about it, a person invites them to a sermon, and that is the end of it. This is because Creqouatl isn't a religion designed to push itself upon others, nor does it expect any reciprocation. The gift for practicing is personal enlightenment, and perhaps a small measure of advice on how to live kindly and spread joy.

After only a few days of learning, Angelica was invited on a pilgrimage to one of the many way shrines of Cre, or "the path". She'd been so excited to go that she turned in her application for religious leave to the university the very same day. A few days later she joined up with a group of about five hundred of the most eccentric people she had ever seen.

Julia's husband had recently departed on a crusade to the mortal plane, and would likely be gone a full Archonian month. Angelica saw the strain it put on her cousin, and insisted she come along. Julia, it turned out, had been practicing Creqouatl for several years, but hadn't started her Cre, so it afforded them the opportunity to bond in friendship and faith together.

"Julia, you knew that this was part of his life when you married him," Angelica said, noting her cousin's sad, watery eyes.

She was sympathetic to her cousin's plight, but was quickly moving past the point of comforting her. The tears were, after all, getting a little out of hand. She couldn't flat out chastise her for her behavior though, because Angelica had probably cried more in the first few days of this new life than Julia had all week.

"Ninety percent of the guardians that go on crusades return. It's not completely without danger, but that is the point. He puts himself in the way of the danger to protect the pure souls of Earth," Angelica said, trying to bring her cousin out of her stupor.

William was training to become a guardian as well, a thought that made her more than a little anxious. It had been weeks since they had held each other in the garden. Her mind instantly wandered back to his short crop of hair, his muscular body pressed up against hers, and the scratch of his scruffy chin. He'd looked like a mess when she found him on the streets, but he cleaned up well. There was a good man buried inside of him. No one else seemed to want to see it, but she knew it was there.

Her face flushed red when she remembered standing over him that morning, wondering whether she should shake him out of his trance to say goodbye. She'd wanted to, but ultimately decided against it. The flush of heat from her face quickly moved downwards as she roamed over his body in her mind again.

She shook loose from the memory when she heard Julia sob loudly. She put her arm around her cousin in a loving embrace and stared into the fire.

"Rona, how are your feet today?"

"Oh, much better. Thank you, Angelica. It is such a blessing having someone with your healing skills on this pilgrimage."

Angelica watched the woman walked away, a rising sense of fulfillment warming her inside. She suddenly stopped regretting those years spent changing bedpans and bandages at the memorial hospital.

The haze from the feasting had died away, and the morning warmth filled the tent. She rose and walked outside to find the blazing sun hovering over the horizon. The grime from the previous night coated her skin, helping her decide to stop by the bathing tents. Some in Archonia had taught their mind to prevent dirt from accumulating on their skin, while others could clean themselves with their own energy. Unfortunately, Angelica had to resort to the old fashioned method, for now.

The steaming hot bath felt amazing, and the soaps smelled divine. After her bath she made her way to the breakfast tent. This caravan was no small affair. Five hundred people all practicing to give of themselves was quite a sight to see. With her mind not strong enough to help erect tents, or carry the heavy supply loads, Angelica had been assigned wash and laundry duties.

She sat down and was served a cup of spiced cider, banana berry crepes, and oats with grape jelly and honey. She enjoyed a few bites, chewing and savoring the flavors of each, struggling with the idea the food was simply an illusion. She still felt human, and understood that it would be a slow progression from that to Archonian. Or, so she had been told.

After her breakfast she found her way to the laundry tent, where they already had the steaming baths of water churning the innumerable linen garments in the sudsy detergents. It smelled of lilac and lemons, two of Angelica's favorites. They put her to work, folding freshly laundered clothing. A woman stood nearby, drying them. Angelica watched her, enthralled. Her energy slowly flowed out of her hands and washed over the cloth, separating the water from the fibers. It took them several hours to complete the laundering, and by the time she exited the tent it was already being taken down around her. The rest of the camp had disappeared and was all loaded onto the many wagons and carts.

Some of the carts were pulled by great beasts of burden. They were twice the size of any oxen and had thick armored hides that were marbled with a rainbow of colors. Other carts were powered by engines. It was rare to see, but people still created machines. It was rare because for the most part they weren't needed. Most things could be done using the mind, if a person was practiced enough.

She found Julia trying to reign in a group of children, struggling to guide them to the wayshrine and back, as she had been directed. The first day, one of the children had projected a giant spider, which chased Julia off. The next they had filled her shoes with porridge from the meal tent.

Today it was a swarm of flies buzzing around her head. She was in tears once again. Angelica couldn't suppress a snort as she watched her helpless cousin. After a few moments she approached the young boy she knew had instigated the situation, and grabbed him firmly by the arm.

"Derek, would you like to walk alone behind the caravan today?" she asked him. The boy put his eyes to the ground and the flies disappeared into shimmering flecks of light.

"Thank you. Now, if I see you torturing Lady Julia again you will all get baths tonight."

For Archonian children this was the worst of punishments. Most children here knew nothing of the mortal world. Their souls were collected before they had experienced anything of life. So, most of them were quick studies, and had already learned to project, fly, and keep themselves clean without bathing. With that threat looming, Angelica knew she could count on their best behavior.

"I had it under control, Angie."

Angelica laughed and replied, "The fact that you think so makes me think you might need a Lady watching over you as well."

"Ladies watch over children, Angie. I am not a..." Julia replied with a huff, but stopped and seemed to finally understand, and made an angry, pouty face.

They began the day's march, watching the children play amongst the carts and people. They had what seemed to be limitless energy.

"So, someone briefly mentioned what this *wayshrine* was going to be like, but they didn't give much detail," Angelica said casually.

"It is the water shrine. It sits in the middle of a vast lake, and we have to swim to reach it," Julia said.

"Why not take a boat?"

"Because that would defeat the purpose of the trial, Angie."

"Okay... how far do we have to swim?"

"Uh...I think only like thirty miles."

Angelica felt her mouth fall open. "Only thirty miles? Jules, I don't think I've ever swam further than a two hundred meter."

"Oh don't worry about it so much. You never get tired here in Archonia so you shouldn't have a problem."

"That's easy for you to say, you grew up here, Julia. I just got here. My mind isn't strong enough yet. I can't do the things you do yet, I'm not ready!" Angelica responded.

"Then I suppose you shouldn't try the swim."

Angelica's heart dropped. Had she come all this way for nothing?

"You said the manner in which one reaches the shrine doesn't matter, correct?" she asked.

"No, as long as you're in the water it really doesn't matter. Some fly but they have to be really strong, I guess. There is high gravity around the lake. Some old Archonian priest made it that way so it was more difficult to reach for people who fly. The true test is getting there on your own through the water."

Angelica sighed heavily and resigned herself to trying the swim, but held little hope that she would succeed.

Angelica turned away from Julia and spied a man she had helped on the second day of their journey. His name was Jonas, and was in charge of one of the tent carts. It was a large cart, the beasts pulling it bigger than elephants. When securing the tents onto the back, the beasts had jerked the cart and sent him sprawling from the top. He plummeted from the twenty foot drop and landed awkwardly, breaking his leg. Angelica set the bone, while another woman gave him a tonic for the pain. They asked everyone, hoping someone could mend his leg with energy, but nobody knew how. Jonas remained very calm through it all, and thanked Angelica.

With Julia's children back under control, she decided to see how his leg was doing.

"Jonas. How is that leg?" she asked, the man coming into view as she walked around the cart.

He was hobbling along on a makeshift crutch fashioned out of a stout tree branch. He had to continue on his pilgrimage, even with the broken leg.

"Splendid! I have been medicating myself with hot mulled wine," he laughed.

Jonas was a tall man. He was rather thin, despite the strength he showcased regularly, reigning in the large beasts pulling his cart. His face was long, and his jaw strong, a splashing of freckles covering his cheeks. His nose was long and a tad crooked, and he had a penchant for blowing his nose regularly. Julia chastised Angelica for paying him so much attention while tending to his leg, referring to him as the "homely" or "unsightly" wagon hand. Angelica didn't agree, however. She quickly discovered that Jonas had a warm, kind smile, and an even kinder heart.

"Just don't drink too much. You're going to want to keep hydrated with water," Angelica said, her medical training kicking in.

"My lady, you do know that one can't become dehydrated here, correct?" Jonas asked with a small laugh.

Angelica felt a little embarrassed, but she was able to work her way out of it.

"Your mind may make it so. Just don't drink too much wine. Too much of a good thing can be bad," she replied.

"Too true, my good lady. As for my leg, it is nearly healed. I can feel it growing stronger every day."

Angelica spied the splint she had made from a wooden steak and tightly wound linen. It was in a raggedy condition from all the hiking, but it still looked tight and effective.

"You broke your tibia. A break like that could take a good month or longer to heal," she said.

"Perhaps in the mortal world, my lady. But here, my mind is making faster progress than my body would."

Angelica shook her head and continued to walk. She spun, her smile turning to a grimace as someone shrieked. She ran, moving along the line of pilgrims, trying to see what was going on. She stumbled through a group of people, coming upon an unpleasant sight. A woman lay on the ground, her face twisted in agony. Angelica could see serious burns covering her arms and hands. The massing group of pilgrims turned and looked at her.

Her medical training kicked in and she set to work. This wasn't going to be pleasant.

"What is your name?" Angelica asked, the woman's eyes flooding with tears.

Then she turned and whispered to someone nearby. "Bring me iced water as much as you can." Then towards another girl, "I need fresh linen cloths, bring as many as you can carry."

Why won't they send someone back to the city for a healer? she wondered.

"I have salve," a woman shouted over the crowd. Angelica nodded in approval, shaken from her thoughts, and the woman scurried off.

"What is your name?" Angelica asked again.

"T-t-trisha," she managed to say.

"Okay, Trisha everything is going to be okay. Can you tell me what happened?"

"She was put in charge of one of those machines," a man said, pointing to one of the carts that had an exposed combustion engine on the back.

Angelica put two and two together. She must have touched the engine while it was running.

"Okay someone needs to explain to everyone that these engines can be hot."

Someone brought half a wooden barrel filled with ice water.

Angelica helped Trisha up and said, "Okay we need to stop the

175

burn." She forced the woman's arms into the ice bath, holding her as she cringed and shook in pain.

"We need to soak your arms for a couple of minutes. This will stop the burn from further damaging the cells. By the time Angelica was satisfied that she had soaked long enough the women with the bandages and salve had returned. However, before they could wrap the wounds the dead flesh would have to be removed. Angelica hadn't debrided a burn wound since nursing school.

"Give me a clean cloth, please."

The girl did so with a smile. The smile quickly faded to horror when Angelica began scrubbing the burnt flesh off of Trisha's arms. Her screams and wails were so loud it halted the whole of the caravan. It took four women to hold her down, and all Angelica could do was say she was sorry. It wasn't her fault that nobody had thought to bring a healer.

"Why haven't we sent someone back for a healer?" Angelica whispered angrily to one of the women holding Trisha down.

"We cannot. Once the pilgrimage is started, we cannot go back, or have any contact with the city until we have prayed at the shrine," the woman responded shakily.

Angelic growled and resumed her work. It seemed an eternity before she was finally able to apply the salve and then wrap her arms. Trisha had calmed down, whether from relief or shock Angelica didn't know. The mass of people standing around them gave her fearful looks. They clearly didn't understand burns, and she realized that it must have looked like she was torturing the poor woman.

Angelica got out of the way as people helped Trisha off the ground. A few of them thanked her, but the majority avoided her. Soon the caravan was underway again. Some of Trisha's friends made a stretcher from wood and fabric and were carrying her along. They were forbidden from placing her on the carts.

That night Angelica didn't join in any of the celebrations, but instead found a nice quiet spot in the open field. She looked out over the sea of grass and found some small measure of peace in the quiet. The thick, white stalks looked so much like wheat as they swayed in the evening breeze. When she sat down the grass reached above her head, and created a little room for her to lose herself in. She sprawled out, the soft blades cushioning her like a feather bed. She drifted off into her trance, her mind seeking rest and renewal for the day to come. She continued to hear the woman screaming and writhing in agony while in the trance, and found she couldn't escape it. It seemed only when the screams had died down that she finally came around. She looked up to find the sun already blazing in the sky.

* * *

The next week proved to be no easier. It seemed a new ailment befell someone each day. It grew so bad that they allowed her to forego her laundry duties in exchange for her healing skills. She had already re-wrapped Trisha's arms twice, and now she was caring for a child who had been bitten by another child's projection. Jonas' leg was nearly healed, but at least three people had succumbed to heat exhaustion. Angelica began to wonder if this really was heaven, or just another life she would have to suffer through like everyone else.

On the fortieth day of their journey they crested a hill, and she saw the lake. To say it was large would be an understatement. Julia hadn't exaggerated. Angelica shielded her eyes and spotted a little spec of land far out in the middle of the water.

That must be the wayshrine.

The water of the lake was a greenish blue, broken by small, lively waves. The coastline was smooth, making it look almost unnatural, but the trees and the brush dotting its periphery gave it a beauty Angelica would never forget. The trees were exotic looking palms with an array of peculiar fruit dangling from the branches. Pulverized sand covered the shore, so fine that it felt as though you were walking on cotton.

It took them the remainder of the morning and into the afternoon to close the remaining distance. People rejoiced when they reached the water, the children running headlong into it, splashing each other and laughing. Everyone else moved to set up camp. Angelica stopped to watch the children playing. It appeared to be relatively shallow where they were, the water only knee high. She saw their hair and their clothes weighted down by what must have been the intense gravity fashioned by the creators of the pilgrimage. Children threw handfuls of water and sand into the air only to watch it fall back heavily into the greenish spray of the lake water.

She watched Julia cross the threshold of the gravitational field and stumble under the weight of her own body. Angelica chuckled nervously, realizing that if someone stronger and more experienced like Julia struggled so mightily, then she likely had no chance. The realization that she couldn't complete the journey to the island made her insides sink. With her heart pained by this prospect, Angelica decided to help the others set up camp.

The fortieth night came upon them much as the last thirty nine had, with the exception of a gentle breeze and a cool spray from the nearby water. The fragrance of salt and palm trees took Angelica back to the Gulf of Mexico, where she had vacationed as a child.

The camp became boisterous again, the merriment of her fellow pilgrims extending out over the emptiness of the lake. Angelica chose to seclude herself yet again. Julia had already gone to her tent to meditate, no doubt exhausted from the children. For once Angelica didn't feel the need to worry about her. It was unusual, worrying about Julia, when she had been in this world longer and knew much more about it. In many ways, Julia was still the little girl she had known back on Earth.

Angelica looked out into the brightly lit planets above and let her mind relax. Her linen clothing let in the refreshing breeze. It kissed her face and neck while gently moving her hair. They had yet to complete their journey, but she couldn't help but feel as though she'd accomplished something already. She had made it this far without injury, unlike many of the others. But more importantly, she had been able to help those who were injured. If Creqouatl was truly a religion of enlightenment, then she hoped they wouldn't look down on her for not completing the journey, but instead reward her personal discoveries.

I have to try, she thought, fighting against the small voice in her head telling her that she couldn't swim the lake.

She roused herself from the grass and when she rose she found that her legs had stiffened. She did a little stretch, shaking and limbering up her legs to get the blood flowing. Then she walked right up to where the sand was being wetted by the gentle waves rolling in on the tide. She wondered briefly what force had been fabricated to create the illusion of a tide. That mattered less than the abrupt pull as her first leg crossed into the field. She gasped, her skin sagging from the force. She struggled to draw breath, the great weight like a heavy, lead vest.

Angelica breathed deeply, steadying herself and took a few steps forward. It was a mighty struggle, but soon realized that although the majority of her body felt staggeringly heavy, her feet actually felt light in the water. In fact, she could move her toes normally. The water rose up to her knees and would remain that way for at least fifty yards, as she had seen earlier that day.

The water felt soothing, her clothes barely weighing her down as she dropped to her knees, letting the wake splash against her chest. She could already feel the weight lifting away. She plunged headfirst into the water, completely submerging her body and releasing the remaining weight. She turned over onto her back and floated, lightly kicking. She could taste the salt, her eyes and a few scrapes she had accumulated stinging as well. But it wasn't so bad she couldn't ignore it. Plus, the water was refreshing, making her feel alive.

Optimism swept over her as she paddled further out into the dark. Soon however, her muscles began to tire, and she brought her body upright to tread water. It was now too deep for her to touch the bottom.

Angelica cried out in alarm as the gravity pushed her head down, forcing her to swallow a large gulp of salty water. She struggled to maintain her composure. She turned her body around, but panic was already taking hold. She couldn't get her entire head above the water to breathe, no matter how hard she tried. The invisible force was pushing right up to the liquid's surface, with seemingly no gap in between.

Doing the only thing she could, Angelica dove under. The pressure stopped pushing and she held her breath, forcing her mind to calm. Then she swam slowly back up to the surface on her back, and kicked until the water grew shallow once again. With her backside in the sand, she sat up, feeling the weight smash down on her once her head broke the surface. She fought against the weight, her head down, and back slumping. But she could breathe.

Angelica had been a strong swimmer on Earth, but she knew that what she did was stupid to swim at night, not knowing the limits of her body or the artificial gravity. She slapped the water in anger, and then crawled back to the beach where she sprawled out in the sand. She didn't care that it clung to her wet skin.

The next morning was a crisp, sunny morning, like seemingly every day in Archonia. The crowd was gathering around the beach, as pilgrims began preparing for the small ceremony before the swim.

Angelica hoped it was less frightening than the passing ceremony, but she never did know what to expect in

Archonia. She had donned her linens much the same as everyone else, though many now wore darker fabrics to afford more privacy once wet. Julia appeared from the crowd, grabbed and hugged her arm, surprising her.

"Today is the day! Are you ready?" she asked

"Jules, I can't hope to make that swim. I can't even see the island anymore."

It was true. Without the aid of elevation, it had been swallowed by the waves. Though considered a lake, it seemed more like a sea. Especially when considering the salt water and tropical setting.

"You have to try, Angie. I can help you some of the way, if you need me too. I can swim really far."

"Julia, I am not going to risk your safety. There is no point. I have made the journey on the road, and I have learned so much about myself. It was a good experience...but it ends here."

Julia looked sad, like she wanted to continue to argue, but also knew that Angelica was right. Jonas walked up beside them suddenly.

"Good morning, Angelica. Miss..." he said, motioning towards Julia.

"Hello, Jonas. This is my cousin, Julia," Angelica said, slightly startled

"How do you do, miss? Jonas, at your service," he replied in his very old fashioned manner.
Angelica noticed that he was walking normally now, with no trace of a limp, crutch, or cast. "Jonas, your leg!"

"I daresay it is as good as when the creators saw fit to give it to me," he said, flashing a brilliantly white smile.

"I'm so glad that you will be able to make the swim."

"And what was this I was hearing about you not being able to accompany us?" he asked, eyebrows raised.

"Jonas, I am too new to this world. I could never swim that far. I tried last night and the weight above the water nearly drowned me."

Jonas laughed out loud. It almost sounded mocking, but his smile told her it was in good fun.

"Oh, young Angelica, you do not have to swim alone. Your lovely cousin here offered to assist you. And how could I not lend you my aid when you so graciously came to mine own?"

"Uh... for the record, I am married," Julia said, flashing a silver band on her finger.

Jonas didn't seem to take notice, but looked between them as if waiting for a response.

His straightforwardness took her aback, and at first she couldn't respond. When she finally unscrambled the words in her head all she came up with was, "Ok."

"Then it is settled. Julia will help you with the first stretch. I will help you with the second stretch, and hmmm, I think someone might be able to help you with the last part," he said, pointing towards the crowd still gathering.

Angelica noticed Trisha right away. Her arms were no longer bandaged. Angelica hadn't changed the dressing for a week, but it looked like they weren't necessary any longer. The woman outstretched her arms. Angelica could see faint scars, but other than that should see any other indications the woman was ever burned. Such a wound should have left a person disfigured for the rest of their life.

She embraced Trisha warmly, who acted as if Angelica was a long lost sister.

"I never got to thank you. They always seemed to have me doped up on that good wine," Trisha said.

"There is no need to thank me. I was just sorry that we didn't have the proper equipment on hand. I thought it was atrocious that they didn't send us a healer along."

"Well, whether you want my thanks or not, you have it. And I am a very strong swimmer. I have made the trip to this wayshrine three times before."

"I really don't want to put anyone at risk," Angelica said.

"Oh, Angie just shut up and take the help," Julia said rolling her eyes.

A smile broke out across Angelica's face and she nodded. Trisha and Jonas cheered and the little group made their way into the crowd to watch the ceremony.

A man known simply as priest shushed the crowd. He wore a simple dark brown robe, tied with braided hemp rope. He had shaved his head, which set him apart from almost everyone else in Archonia. There was, after all, almost no baldness here. The crowd quieted as he began to speak.

"Children of the Creators, You have come many leagues, seeking the discovery of self. Whether through the mind, the body, or both you have been tested already in many ways," he said, his voice higher in pitch than Angelica expected.

His words struck Angelica. Perhaps her trials were on the road. Perhaps she had already been faced with her lesson.

"Whatever you have discovered, know that it is for you, and you alone. Each of you is unique, made from an entirely different mold, and shaped by different hands. No matter how much you try to be alike in social culture...you...are...all...different!"

Small murmurs of approval rippled through the crowd. Angelica looked at her friends, who stood quietly and listened.

"At the same time, each of us shares a fundamentally identical feature. We are all human. Whether it be the color of our skin and eyes, or the shape and size of our body. We were all human. And as humans, we were bound to water upon the mortal plane - a nourishing substance that made up a majority of our flesh. Though life giving, it could also be treacherous. In accordance with the Creqouatl, I wish you all a safe journey through the waters. When we all meet upon the other shore we will celebrate what we have learned. Thank you my friends," he said, finishing with a humble bow.

As soon as the speech ended people began to walk to the water. Most had wrapped linens tightly around their private areas, crafting crude swimwear. Angelica spotted a few younger people wearing their own swimwear, which looked more modern and almost out of place. Angelica, who had resigned herself to not participate, had donned a long, flowing gown of bleached white cotton for the ceremony. She turned to her cousin, hoping for some advice or assistance.

Julia grabbed her by the hand and marched her over to the garment tent. There she stripped off Angelica's gown quickly, making her jump with fright and cover herself.

"Oh relax! They are all probably a mile out in the water already."

"What about the people who are packing up the camp?" Angelica snapped.

"Do not worry about it!"

She started twirling Angelica at frightening speed, winding strips of linen around her body. She wrapped her breasts so tight that she could hardly breathe. Then she covered her hips, forming a rather tight undergarment.

"You should be a fashion designer," Angelica said, sarcastically.

Julian didn't respond. Instead, she simply dragged her back out onto the beach where Trisha and Jonas were waiting.

"Ready?" Julia asked. The two nodded and turned towards the water, where many people were saying silent prayers on the sandy beach, or just wading out through the shallows.

"A mile out in the water, huh?" Angelica said, throwing her cousin a little attitude. Julia simply shrugged her shoulders and rolled her eyes.

They stepped into the water as a group and felt the weight.

"Okay. I can help you the first part of the swim," said Jonas, breathing heavily under the crushing pull.

"I will help you along the middle part," Trisha said.

"I suppose that means I have to drag your butt the last part," Julia said with a smirk.

"Okay, but I am not completely helpless. I can swim too. I will go until I get tired."

Soon they were in knee deep water, and Angelica dove headfirst under the cool, refreshing water. It was the perfect temperature, neither too cold nor too warm. While submerged she twisted her body so that she came up on her back and began to kick. The others jumped in too, though not as gracefully. She was clearly the better swimmer, but endurance was all that mattered here.

Angelica relaxed her body, save her arms and legs, and fell into a comfortable scissor kick. It was a slow stroke, but the easiest to do while keeping her head level with the water. Whenever she tried to lift it up it felt like an invisible hand was forcing it back down again, so naturally she felt at home under the water. Occasionally she would dive and open her eyes. The bottom of the lake was no less spectacular than the rest of Archonia. There were endless reefs, teeming with exotic life forms, just beyond her arm's reach.

Angelica felt an urge to linger and explore the aquatic wonders, but knew that it would be wasted energy. Instead, she vowed to herself that she would return one day with more time and practice. Perhaps she could stay under for hours at a time. Who knew?

When she surfaced she was momentarily blinded by the salt and light in her eyes. When her vision finally cleared she was astonished to find feet resting on the surface of the water next to her. She spotted toes sticking out from under a long, dark robe, and when she looked up she found the priest smiling down at her. She blinked again to confirm she wasn't seeing things. He strode swiftly across the water, as confidently as if he walked on dry land. She craned her neck, straining to watch him until he was out of sight.

"Did everyone just see that?" she asked

Laughter spilled out over the water.

"Yes, Angelica, he has done this many times," Jonas replied. "Are you getting tired yet?"

She was getting tired, but she didn't want to give up yet.

"How far have we swum? It feels like a couple of miles at least."

"Wow, you're out of shape. We aren't even out of sight of the shore yet."

Angelica made a point to kick towards Julia a little harder than normal, which only caused her cousin to laugh. Jonas was behind her and he swam up very quickly and grabbed both of Angelica's arms and put them over his shoulders. Before she knew it they were flying through the water.

She held on for dear life, as the water flowed forcefully around her, trying to pull her free.

"This is a little fast!" she shrieked, her grip starting to slip almost immediately. He slowed up and allowed her to better position herself.

"Sorry. Hold on tight!" he said.

Even Julia was keeping the crazy pace. She had seen displays of the strength and speed of an Archonian mind, but it was still breathtaking to behold. They must have been going crazy trying to hold back while she slowly swam. They had easily gone five times the distance in a fraction of the time.

Jonas was incredibly strong. His skin felt supple and soft, while forming perfectly over his muscles. She tried not to fixate on it, but that was difficult while draped over his shoulders He smelled good, even in the salty water. She could make out the faint musk of pine, and something else, but couldn't quite put her finger on it. He plowed through the waves in a front crawl. His form didn't look too bad, except for the fact that he had his head above the water the whole time.

What must have been ten miles or more passed in a heartbeat. Soon, Trisha swam over and Angelica exchanged places. When Trisha's arms wrapped around her and began to kick she felt very humbled, but also overcome with happiness. A few good deeds had made her some very loyal friends.

Angelica wondered if this was the lesson she was meant to learn. It was something fundamental she learned when she was very young. But somehow, a refresher felt like just what she needed.

Do unto others as you would have them do unto you.

The people she helped hadn't asked for it. She had given it freely. In return, she hadn't asked for theirs, yet they helped her all the same. Complete strangers that could have simply thanked her and went about their business. She wished so deeply that she had seen more of this on Earth. People in that world were so selfish. Anger was a virus that seemingly plagued the whole population. If someone cut you off in traffic they were automatically a horrible person. If a stranger came up to talk to you it was suspicious.

The feelings that she'd experienced on the road about the suffering in this world were washed away. Pain was a part of life, but anger and hatred were true suffering. She couldn't help but feel that she finally knew the difference between them.

CHAPTER THIRTEEN
THE SWORD

Morning came, and William awoke on a soft bed of grass. He rubbed his eyes and looked around. Angelica was nowhere in sight. She must have gone when he had fallen into his meditative state.

Jumping to his feet, William began to stretch. He felt a renewed sense of purpose, and not from rage, but from determination.

Gabe believes in me, Katrina believes in me, and so does Brock, he thought to himself.

It was time that he started believing in himself. No more feeling sorry. No more despising other people for his misfortunes. He would do this. He would prove to everyone that he belonged in Archonia. That he could become a strong guardian.

With otherworldly speed, William ran out of the garden. The sun was already rising on the horizon, which meant that he was late. It wouldn't stop him, however. He wouldn't let anyone stop him this time. The garden of Medina was a good distance from Valhalla, so he would have to push his body to the limits.

As he made his way across the open plains of Archonia he set his eyes on the large castle. It jutted out from the city, seemingly swallowed by its shadow. A horrible thought struck William, and he realized that he had no idea where the guardian's barracks was. They had never mentioned it during his training.

Shoot, he thought. *Think!*

Where could it be located? He considered the various places in the castle that he had been. None of those places seemed likely. He had seen most of it. Then it clicked.

The door with the inscription! The wooden door that stood all alone in that lonely corridor in the Nordic wing. It was perhaps the one place he had yet to explore.

William didn't second guess himself. That had to be where it was. He quickened his already fast pace, but then his stomach lurched. What if he couldn't open it still? He ran into some soldiers on their way out for morning watch, and apologized without looking back, before skidding to a halt in front of the massive, wooden doors. They loomed above him and he suddenly became more than little nervous. The inscription stared back at him, his breathing hard in the quiet corridor.

William read it out loud, "Only the strong may enter here."

Well here goes nothing, he thought, and walked up, giving the doors a push.

To his amazement the door swung lightly open and standing before him was a sight that filled him with happiness.

"William!" Katrina shouted jumping at him and wrapping him in a hug.

Juarez stood watching, his arms crossed, a huge smile spread over his face.

"Brock only just told us," Juarez said

"I can't believe you actually destroyed the pots. I knew Chang Fei hadn't given you enough time. So I went to Brock. I knew they could not cut you. I just knew it," Katrina said, finally releasing him from her bear hug.

"Thank you, guys, I wouldn't be here without you," William said, finally breathing again.

"No, amigo," Juarez said, his Spanish accent thick, "It is I who would not be here without you. You were the only person to believe in me. Everyone else has always just overlooked me."

William knew exactly how it felt to be overlooked, and ignored. He simply nodded in understanding. Then Katrina grabbed William by the arm.

"Come on, we are already late. Chang Fei was angry that we waited for you."

"Wait," William said slowly. "Are we forging our armor?

"Yes, William," Juarez said chuckling. "Do you think you will be going into battle in those?" he said, gesturing to William's tattered training garbs.

"I guess not," William smirked.

"Juarez," Katrina said, "we do not know what we are going to be doing."

"What else could we possibly be doing today?" he asked.

"I'm just saying, let's not get our hopes up," Katrina said, punching him in the arm.

They ran down the long entrance hall to the guardian's barracks, William looking around in wonder. Massive statues stood between thick pillars. They spanned high overhead. They all wore different armor and weapons, giving them a distinctly unique appearance. William guessed that they had been very powerful guardians.

The hall opened into a large circular room with many sofas and chairs. It seemed to be a common area, where people could interact and socialize. Portraits hung on the walls, as did a vast array of weaponry. Brock stood next to Chang Fei in the middle of the room.

The small Chinese warlord stood motionless, his face as grim as ever. William spotted the two other recruits, Ulifrig and Samuel. They both wore their training robes, but each had a weapon strapped to their back. Samuel had a long, decorative pike with an elaborate blade at the end, while Ulifrig had chosen a massive battle axe that looked like it should take two men to wield.

William quickly connected the dots, and looked around the room in wonder. He snapped back to find Brock standing right in front of him. He hadn't seen or heard approach.

"Well done, William," he said, his voice booming. Then he slapped William on the shoulder, flattening him to the ground.

"Ugh," he groaned getting up. "Brock, I'm still not as strong as you are. Could you lighten up, please?"

Brock laughed and said, "What doesn't kill you makes you stronger. Besides, if you wish to be a guardian, you must be tough."

"Ok. I'll keep working on that," William said, rubbing his shoulder.

He noticed that Brock wasn't wearing armor. Instead, he wore the same robes as the initiates.

"So, what's next?" William asked, peering around Brock's massive body.

"Now you're a recruit, but not a guardian yet. Trials still lie before you. The first of which is selecting a suitable weapon with which to defend your life," Brock said, waving his arm to the walls. "Pick one."

William's eyes wandered over the wall, his excitement building. He was a grown man, but this felt like a Christmas he had only dreamed of – he'd never been able to pick or choose what he wanted before. He'd simply gotten by on what he needed. His eyes went wide, and an uncharacteristically greedy urge blossomed inside. He wanted all of them. He exchanged glances with his friends. They looked as excited as he did.

"You can only choose one," Brock said, smiling like he knew exactly what William was thinking.

He smiled back, looking at him out of the corner of his eye. Then a glimmer caught his attention. It was a sword, hanging almost inconspicuously amongst the massive assortment of weaponry. It was a human sized claymore that could fit both of his hands on the hilt. Compared to the other weapons however it was small. Many of them were twice the width and length, but they all seemed dull to William.

Katrina deftly jumped into the air with a grace befitting her petite size, and gripped the wall high above. She grabbed a large, golden bow and descended to the ground.

William watched her play with it. There was no quiver, or arrows, and William wondered how and where she would get some, but his question was answered straight away. When she drew back the string a blaze of white light flashed brightly and in the notch sat a glowing arrow. She relaxed the string, and the arrow disappeared.

"Not in here!" Chang Fei said sternly, and she quickly apologized.

William continued searching the walls. There were spears, pikes, and tridents. But he also saw swords, Claymores, daggers, maces hammers, and axes of all shapes and sizes. And yet, his eyes were continuously drawn back to the simple sword.

He approached it to study its intricacies. The hilt was blued steel, and the handle wrapped in black leather. It looked old, like an antique. There was very little inscription upon it. Only some symbols near the cross-guard. Compared to the other weapons, it was nothing flashy, yet it shone brighter than any other. He slowly reached up, his palm hovering just above the metal to grab it. He could feel energy pulsing off of it.

His hand flinched, and he paused momentarily, but then reached out and grabbed it. It was metal, but the surface didn't feel cold. He lifted it carefully from the hooks, and almost dropped it. He took a breath and regained his hold. It was very heavy...much too heavy for its size. He lifted it to study the blade, just as Brock spoke.

"That is a puny little sword," the large man said.

William felt a pang of anger and looked up just in time to see Brock swing a massive hammer above his head. It looked like a wrecking ball attached to a twig. William only had time for a single, basic reaction, so he hoisted the sword above his head in an overhead parry.

There was a bone shaking boom, an explosion, and a burst of energy. William fell to a knee under the force of the blow, while Brock was thrown backwards by the blast. He hit the floor with a crash, his eyes wide.

"What the?" Brock growled in surprise.

William stood up in shocked silence.

"I guess it isn't as small as it looks," Brock said huffing as he got to his feet slowly.

The others watched the little encounter wide-eyed, chuckling nervously.

"Enough!" Cheng Fei shouted. "Recruits, by choosing your weapons you have taken your first step towards becoming a true guardian. *They* have chosen *you* just as much as *you* chose *them*. They will be your life, so trust in them, and they will protect you."

The group looked at one another. William spotted Juarez with a long elegant rapier. It suited him. He looked at Brock who handed him a leather covered scabbard. Apparently it went to William's sword, because it fit perfectly inside. Brock helped him get the scabbard slung over his shoulder. Though Brock thought the sword was small it was still too long to dangle at his waist. The others worked likewise to sling and fit their weapons.

"Now, some of my finest students have agreed to help you train with these weapons," Chang Fei said gruffly. "Do not disappoint me. I do not want my old students thinking that I have become soft. The first one to embarrass me will hold the atlas ball all night long."

William exchanged looks with Juarez and Katrina, who both rolled their eyes. Chang Fei turned and departed in a blur, leaving William and the others scrambling to catch up. Before they knew it, they were on the training grounds, surrounded by five fully-armored guardian soldiers.

"William watched the group around him. They all eyed the group of warriors, the envy painted clearly on their faces.

Each of the warriors armor was different, most likely a reflection of the individuality of their own soul, just as no two faces are alike. A very tall man, donned in white, leather armor stepped towards Katrina, before directing her over to an archery range.

Juarez squared his shoulders as another man stepped forward, brandishing a cutlass not dissimilar from his rapier. Samuel and Ulifrig stepped aside next as they were claimed by their chosen trainer.

The last, remaining guardian stepped slowly up to William. He was of average build, but carried his weight confidently. He wore plate armor over shiny chain mail. A mail coif covered most of his head, leaving only his face exposed. He drew a sword out of a scabbard at his side. The blade was at least a foot wide, and looked lopsided considering the much smaller hilt. Still the man hoisted it as easily if it were a feather.

"Hello. My name is William," he said introducing himself to the stranger.

"I am well aware of who you are, tainted one. Believe me, I am only here on orders from my superiors," the man stated.

William scowled. *What a jerk*, he thought to himself.

"Where I'm from, if someone introduces themselves it is polite to return the favor," William said more than a little annoyed.

The guardian studied him for a moment, and then spat, "Draw your sword, filth."

By now, William was used to people treating him like garbage. Although, it had been a while, thanks to the seclusion of initiate training. But now he was back in the thick of it.

William rolled his eyes, and gripped his sword. He slowly slid it out of its scabbard. God, it weighed a ton. The blade glimmered in the morning light, and William smiled a bit. Then out of the corner of his eye he saw a flash of steel, and his trainer's sword cut in. William flexed with all his might to wield his sword, and was just able to block the incoming attack. There was a crash as the two metal blades collided. He felt the force vibrate through his arms as the connection was made. Then a crack issue forth and William's sword struck back against the enemy blade of its own accord and knocked the enemy blade backwards.

The guardian looked shocked, his focus lost for a moment. William took this opportunity to whip his sword around, and nail the man in the head with the flat of his blade. He was knocked to the ground, kicking up dirt. Rolling out of the fall, he hopped back up into a defensive stance almost immediately. He eyed William, his posture relaxing, and his eyes wide.

"The blade of Othin all father," he stated.

"Uh. Yeah. Sure," William said sarcastically.

"That is Gungnir," the man said, pointing at it like it was on fire.

"I thought Othin wielded a spear?" William asked, inspecting the sword.

"It must take the form of whatever weapon you wish, but I recognize these inscriptions," his trainer said. "This weapon has chosen you? The tainted one?" he said with obvious disgust.

William didn't have a response, so he stood there for a few, long moments, glancing from the guardian to the sword in his hand. A sudden and undeniable wave of pride swept over him.

"My name is Alacron. Please forgive my earlier rudeness," the man said, walking forward and extending a hand.

William looked at him skeptically, expecting him to pull it away at the last second, but eventually put his hand up slowly. Alacron took it and gave it one firm shake.

"I have only ever heard tales and read stories of this weapon. I never saw this hanging in the Barracks," he said looking it over.

William almost laughed, and asked, "You want to touch it?"

Alacron snapped his head up at William, and shook his head, "You would let me?"

William smiled, and held it out. "C'mon."

Alacron sheathed his sword, and whipped his shield deftly onto his back. William held the sword by the flat of the blade, so he could take it by the handle. Once resting in Alacron's hands he let it go and was shocked when his trainer cried in surprise and hit the ground. Alacron roared in pain, the sword pinning his hands to the dirt. Everyone stopped sparring, and huddled in to watch the exchange.

"Oh crap," William said, grabbing the sword and lifting it back up. Alacron sprung to his feet, rubbing his hands together and cursing.

"It is quite alright. It seems only the one the weapon owes allegiance to can wield it."

William laughed, "That is awesome. I am going to have to use that one on Brock."

"First you will need to know how to use it in combat," Alacron said, now smiling. "I will teach you, and you will listen." He drew his own sword back out.

The rest of the day William worked with Alacron, learning simple ways of using the weight of his sword to his benefit, until he became stronger. They went through different stances and parries. They took occasional breaks, because the sword tired him quickly. He used that down time to watch Katrina work with her bow. She was a natural. By the end of the day she was grouping arrows right around the bull's eye.

Juarez already had some skill with a blade apparently, and remained busy dueling with his trainer all afternoon. Their swords were like lighting, flashing and clashing at every speed and angle.

William was at a disadvantage. He was a very good shot with a rifle, but what good was marksmanship if there were no firearms in this world.

William wondered how effective Katrina's arrows would be in battle, considering their lower velocity. His question was soon answered as he watched one of her projected arrows impact the target which exploded with energy. He suddenly felt very bad for anyone caught in her bow sights.

At the end of a long and rigorous day the group retired to the barracks, and were able to explore it for the first time. There was a men's and a women's wing for obvious reasons. The bathing facilities were much nicer than the ones at the recruit's barracks as well. Water flowed like a waterfall from ducts on the walls into wide pools scented with jasmine, lilac, and other aromas William didn't recognize. The bath water was hot, motivating William and Juarez to linger and soak in it.

William carried his sword with him everywhere, refusing to let it out of his sight. Juarez decided to leave his in the meditation chamber on a weapon rack next to the fresh linen closet. William grabbed his sword, and swung it around as they walked down the hallway.

The group met again in the common area where they found Katrina seated down at a piano. She was playing a soothing melody. Her speed on the piano keys matched her speed on the training grounds, and sound filled the room. There were other guardians around, listening intently and applauded her when she finished playing the very somber piece.

"When did you learn to play like that?" William asked.

"I'm two hundred and fifty two human years old," Katrina said, smiling. "I have been in this world for a long time. I got bored." She looked up at William, starting another tune without looking at her hands.

"I guess I keep forgetting how long you all have been here," William admitted. "Why did you choose to become a soldier again? Wasn't dying in battle once enough?"

Katrina looked at him and then back at the keys, evidently trying to decide whether she was going to answer.

"I guess I have just been having some bad dreams during my meditation in the past year or so. I felt like it was a good idea to join," she said finally, casually shrugging her shoulders without missing a beat in the tune.

Her song evolved, and William looked over at Juarez, who sat reading a book.

"How old are you, priest?" William said, plopping down on a sofa across from him. Juarez looked over his book, and smiled.

"Had my four hundred and twenty sixth birthday a few weeks ago. Of course that would be in human years," he said, before going back to his book.

"Yeah, time here is a little weird," William said. "Let me see if I got this right. Fifty seconds in a minute. One hundred minutes in an hour. One hundred hours in a day. One hundred days in a month, and ten months in a year."

"That seems so artificial."

Just then Samuel entered the room, and chimed in. "Well time doesn't really pass here though, does it? So essentially it is artificial."

"Hey, Sam. Getting settled in?" William asked.

Samuel nodded, and continued, "What I want to know is, who made the sun set exactly fifty hours every day?"

Juarez looked up from his book again. "It would have to have been the Archons, correct?" he asked.

"No, there are men called the keepers. They control the details of the world and make it seem more like Earth," Ulifrig offered.

The conversation continued like this for a while until Samuel finally looked at William, who was balancing his sword on two fingers.

"The sword of Othin all father," Samuel said, slowly eyeing the weapon.

William let the sword tip sideways and caught it very carefully, before looking at Samuel.

"That's what I was told."

"Supposedly the spear Gungnir was lost in the war of souls when the two Archons destroyed one another. I can see why people must have thought it lost if it turned into a sword," Samuel said in wonder.

"So it is true then? This book says that Gungnir can change into whatever form you want it to." Juarez said.

In fact, the whole group watched William, anticipating his response.

"Look. I don't really know how it works, okay? I just got it today," William said.

"Well, go on try to change its shape," Katrina retorted playfully.

Great, William thought to himself. He looked around, growing more uncomfortable as the group continued to watch him closely. He gripped the blade, and looked at it. It shimmered in the light of the torches and candles lighting the room, but otherwise didn't move or change.

"Go, go, gadget spear!" William shouted, bursting into laughter.

His joke was wasted. The others stared, eyebrows raised, or mouths open. None in the group could have possibly known that the joke pertained to a cartoon television show that he had watched as a kid. He sighed, and focused. The blade was shimmering, and when William looked closer, it looked as if it was actually moving, as though the blade was made from flowing water.

His eyes widened, and he felt the handle of the blade become soft and malleable. It felt like it was going to slip through his fingers, but he had a clear picture in his mind, and held it there. It was the spear that had been pointed at him so many times during his first few hours in Archonia.

He clearly saw the long golden tip serrated on one side, and bound with golden rings for strength. Its long pole shone of silver and white, the runes etched into its length gleaming.

Katrina shouted, interrupting his thoughts, "Now look at you! The one with the tainted soul is chosen to carry the blade of an Archon."

William looked back at his hands, taking in the magnificent spear that had previously been his sword. It was roughly the same color and weight of his sword, but looked far more impressive.

"That was easy," William said, swinging the spear around. As he did, he accidentally hit a vase that was on a table nearby, shattering it to pieces.

"Maybe you should learn to use a spear before you go swinging it around, Amigo," Juarez said, laughing with the others.

William joined in on the laughter, but noticed that Ulifrig wasn't laughing. He caught Samuel's attention and motioned towards Ulifrig, who seemed very distant as he thumbed through a stack of parchment.

"Ulifrig, is everything ok?" Samuel asked, sitting down next to him and placing a hand gently on his upper arm. The room grew quiet.

"Have you all heard about the strange disappearances and rumors of beast sightings?" he asked everyone.

They all looked to one another, most simply shrugging or looking confused. William, however, remembered something Angelica had mentioned to him briefly.

"I heard someone talk about it, but I kind of dismissed it. There has been peace in this world for thousands of years, right? This is probably just people trying to get a rise out of the crowd," William replied tentatively.

"I have kin that live up north in the wetlands. I received word today that my great, great grandniece has gone missing."

"Ulifrig, I'm sure she is okay. She is probably just branching out on her own. Archonia is a vast place to explore," Katrina said.

"But without telling anyone? And so suddenly? My kin are very close. This would not have happened without anyone's knowledge. I'm sorry Katrina," Ulifrig said darkly.

"I wonder if the military has gotten involved," William said.

"They dispatched two measly sentinels to aid in the search. They could not even spare an oracle or adjudicator. Like there is anything else for them to do in this day and age," Ulifrig said, rising from his cushy seat and crumpling the parchment into a tiny ball and hurling it at the wall.

Samuel continued to comfort the large man as they both exited the room.

"Well that kind of sucks," William said.

"We have to keep our ears closer to the ground," Juarez stated.

William and his friends spent the rest of the evening watching William transform his sword into all sorts of different weapons.

* * *

The new recruits spent the rest of the month honing their skills with their own unique weapons. The trainers worked rigorously with them, providing new challenges each day. Katrina worked on firing while running, which she wasn't nearly as good at. The trainers told her to slow down, but William doubted that slow was in her vocabulary.

Juarez was busy learning to deflect projectiles with his rapier. A group of trainers threw stones at him, some moving faster than bullets. This was a hard and painful lesson, especially if he wasn't able to deflect the stones.

William was getting the raw end of the deal. He had four trainers now, each of them wielding a different weapon. One had a bow, one a sword and shield, another had a hammer, and the last one a spear.

They went slowly so as not to overwhelm him, but their attacks were still very fast, and it was all he could do to defend himself. He was still not proficient with shape shifting his weapon, especially on the fly, but this was his greatest trick, and obviously one that the trainers were pushing him to learn.

The man with the hammer attacked, and William's sword turned into a shield, which he held above his head. The hammer recoiled as it hit Gungnir, the weapon fighting back on its own. This allowed him time to turn it into a mace, and bash the trainer in the stomach. Seamlessly the weapon transformed back into a shield, deflecting an arrow shot by another trainer.

William jumped to the side to avoid a jab from a large spear, and transformed his weapon into a chain and wrapped it around the weapon, taking control of it, and its holder. He landed a high kick to his trainer's face, and sent him flying across the ground. Finally, Gungnir snapped back into a blade, allowing him to parry blows from Alacron, who attacked with enthusiasm and vigor.

Sweat dripped from his face as he staved off the attacks of the veteran guardian.

"Well done, young one," Alacron praised.

William nodded, wiping the sweat from his brow. His hair had now grown out several inches, and did little to keep the sweat from his eyes.

"Do not forget that you possess other weapons in your arsenal," Alacron said. "I have yet to see you project a single time today in training."

It was true, William had become so focused on honing his skills with a blade that he had completely forgotten that he was still fairly inept at projecting.

"Your assignment for this evening will be to project at least twenty times," Alacron said.

It had already been a long day. They still had morning drills with Chang Fei, and then studies. After that they worked with their trainers until evening, when they were supposed to have some free time before meditation. William's mind felt stretched, but he nodded.

"Okay I will," he said, sighing.

Everyone began to disperse, but Juarez, and Katrina stayed behind.

"We thought we would practice with you, Amigo," Juarez said.

"I'd welcome the company," he responded, sheathing his sword across his back.

"Your trainer is really tough on you," Katrina said.

"*Your* trainer just knows that you can't hack it, Kat," William snapped back with a smirk.

"What did you just call me!?" she shouted, flying at him. William deftly dodged her attack, and sent her face first into the short cropped grass of the training ground.

"I kind of like that. Kat," William said, egging her on a little more.

She got up quickly, her face creased with a scowl. "Whatever you say, tainted one." Her scowl morphed to a lopsided grin.

The group walked to the firing range, where there were still some pots standing from the day's training. Katrina took a piece of broken pot and flung it into the air. Juarez extended his palm, and a ball of light shot out, striking the fragment, and turning it do dust.

"Quit showing off, Juarez. We get enough of that when Katrina laps us every morning in drill," William said, just as another fragment of pot hit him in the back of the head.

He didn't turn. He enjoyed picking on Katrina. She was tough enough to handle it, and she knew he was only joking. His friends continued their game of skeet, while

William turned towards the hill and focused. He lifted his palm, and aimed it towards his target.

After a couple of hours he managed to blast apart three pots, and put a few small craters in the hillside. William glanced up across the training field at the bell tower, which stood like a spike in the sky. Underneath the massive warning bell there was a clock face that looked very peculiar with ten hours instead of twelve, and five large lines indicating the tenth hour in every rotation. It was the forty eighth hour in the day, and the light was fading quickly. William felt exhausted, but he kept pushing himself.

Katrina and Juarez rooted him on for a while, but even they ended up saying goodnight. He stood alone in the dark, trying to find the will to project. He kept telling himself that he didn't need to get angry to accomplish his task. Then an idea hit him. Alacron said that he needed to project twenty times. The manner in which he projected wasn't discussed, and William turned north and began to sprint. He remembered exactly how he had gotten there, and soon came upon the Garden of Medina.

He slowed to a normal pace once he passed the threshold. The luscious greenery hit him like a splash of water on a hot day, and he smelled all the flowers and plants. He breathed a sigh of relief. There was something very relaxing about this place. He looked around for a patch of dirt that was perhaps untouched, and found a small meadow about half a mile into the treeline.

William sat down, which felt like bliss. He had been on his feet almost the entire day, and the human part of his mind made the pain very real. He breathed out and relaxed for a moment, then sat cross-legged and looked around. He had all sorts of inspiration, but he didn't immediately know how to complete his task.

He wanted to create something with his projections, instead of destroying. He started simply, just as he did the first night he had visited the garden. He held out his upturned hand, and pushed his energy forth. It was delicate and responded to his slightest urge. It bubbled out of his palm, forming a vapor, before transforming into a ball with his mind.

He molded it again into a long strand, like piano wire. He strained his mind to change its shape. The energy felt oddly similar to the way his sword changed shape, and the vapor began to get clearer. As it did the picture in William's mind became real, and he was left holding a rose. It wasn't soft, like a real rose, but very hard. Upon closer inspection, William found that it felt like it was made out of plastic or wood. He snapped it in half like a twig, and tossed it aside.

Great artists have to start somewhere, I guess.

"That wasn't too bad," a voice said.

William shot up so fast that he left the ground, and turned quickly to find Angelica. He let out his breath.

"Are you stalking me?" he asked with a joking grin.

"Excuse me, William, but I have been coming here every night since my very first day in Archonia," she said with a touch of attitude.

"Oh. Sorry. You just startled me," William said, easing back against the tree. "It's been like a month since I've seen you. Where have you been?" he asked as she sat down next to him.

"I've been on pilgrimage with friends," she said, putting her hand in the air and watching an insect land on it. William nodded his head in approval.

"That sounds like a good fit for you," he said trying to focus on projecting again.

"Isn't it funny? We died, and it feels like we just picked up and kept on going," Angelica said.

William snapped out of his trance, and looked at her.

"Yeah. I guess you're right. Personally I like this place a lot better. Don't have to worry about food, rent, or owning a car. It's like freedom," he said.

"It is still lonely though," Angelica replied turning away.

"Lonely? There are like a billion people living in the city. Haven't you met any friends at the university?" he asked.

"That's not what I meant," she said, shaking her head.

William had to think for a second, and then it hit him like Brock's massive hammer, and his stomach lurched. He forced himself to be calm.

"Nobody special back on Earth?" he inquired, trying to sound as nonchalant as possible.

Angelica didn't respond, so William went back to trying to create a rose again. He must have looked funny in his concentration, because Angelica laughed.

"You need to be more delicate. Imagine what the flower looks like, but also imagine how it feels. The way it smells. How light and delicate it is," she said, holding her hands out. As she did a light bluish light issued forth from her palms, and after a moment she was holding a red rose, shining brilliantly in the starlight. William caught himself staring into Angelica's eyes again, and dropped his gaze quickly to his hands.

She giggled, and turned. His face flushed hot, and he held both his hands up again, cupping them like he was holding something fragile. Angelica rolled over, laughing at this, and William got annoyed.

"What is so funny?" he asked.

"Oh nothing, you big strong warrior," she said mockingly. William grabbed her rose and crushed it in his iron grip, before tossing it away.

They talked the rest of the night. Angelica helped William finish his assignment, and by morning they had created a whole meadow full of different colored roses. They all smelled like something different too.

Angelica said goodbye to William when she had to leave for class, and he made his way back to the guardian's barracks. He walked through the giant wooden doors, and down into the common area of the barracks, nearly running into Brock. The big man had his arms crossed, and a grimace on his face.

"You're late, recruit," he growled.

CHAPTER FOURTEEN
THE FORGE

William tried to swallow, but his mouth was dry.

"What am I late for?" he asked, trying hard to think of anything that he had this morning besides drill.

A smile broke across Brock's large face.

"You're late for the most important task yet. Today you will be forging your armor!"

William tried to return the smile, but he was exhausted. He hadn't meditated in over a day. William followed Brock the rest of the way down the hall where the new recruits all stood in fresh linens, and ready for drill. Chang Fei stood at the head of the group.

"As you know the next step in becoming a guardian is to forge armor," Chang Fei said evenly.

"Why do we need armor?" William asked, raising his arm and falling into line with the others.

Samuel and Ulifrig snickered.

"Ok," William responded irritably, staring back at the two "for those of us who have only been in Archonia for a couple of months. Why do we need this armor?"

Brock walked over next to Chang Fei. He noticed that the large man was only wearing sparring linens as well. He couldn't remember ever seeing the large man out of his armor before.

The big man smiled, and said, "Hit me."

William looked at him wildly. "What? Why?"

"Just hit me, little brother," Brock repeated, puffing his chest out. "Right here," he said, pointing to his broad pectoral region.

William looked to the others, who all watched with great interest.

"You asked for it," William said, dropping into a fighting stance.

He took a deep, steadying breath for courage, and then charged, slamming Brock in the chest with all his might.

The big man grunted and stumbled back, rubbing his chest.

"Well there, young one, you're getting a bit stronger. You might be as strong as me someday," Brock grunted with a grin.

William smirked, feeling some satisfaction that he had actually moved Brock's massive body.

"Ok so what was the point of...?" William tried to ask, but before he could finish, there was a flash of light and wind swept outward from his large friend's body.

Massive plates materialized, locking to his body. William's eyes grew wide. Brock now stood clad head to toe in his usual armor with thick plates made of steel, and leather all brown, and silver.

"Now. Hit me again," Brock said, his eyes narrowing.

William scrunched his face in determination. He tightened his stance once more. This time he focused all his energy.

It is just metal, he thought. *Mind over matter. The laws of physics as I knew them no longer apply.*

With a roar, William charged. Brock didn't flinch, and William threw his fist into the large bald man with everything that he had.

William howled in agony, punctuated by a sickening crack and a wave of pain that shot through his arm. He might as well have just hit a brick wall. His knuckles were broken and crimson blood flowed down his arm. The other initiates burst into laughter as William clutched at his ruined arm, forcing hot tears back. He knew he broke knuckles, but he probably also broke his hand too. He couldn't move his fingers either. Brock wrapped a large hand around William's forearm as he fell to his knees, gasping in pain. A blinding light surrounded his hand and wrist, warmth seeping into his skin and muscles, spreading up his arm. The pain subsided, when the light died away, and the blood disappeared.

William looked up at Brock and winced, "...so, that's why I need armor."

Brock grabbed him by the other hand and lifted him bodily off the ground.

"Your armor is not just metal and buckles. It is a projection hardened by your mind, and you make it as strong as you will it to be," Chang Fei said, addressing everyone.

* * *

A short time later, they were dashing across the rich plains of Archonia. Chang Fei flew overhead, followed closely by Samuel. Like Juarez, Samuel had some hidden talents. William took note of this for later. The rest of the initiates were on the ground with Brock. Brock insisted on keeping his feet on the ground, with the others. Although William had rarely seen the large man fly, and was starting to wonder if he didn't like to, or wasn't good at it.

"Where are we going?" Katrina asked Brock, as they plowed through fields of long, white grass.

"The Greige Forge," Brock bellowed over the rushing wind.

William didn't really know what or where that was, but he followed along, sharing in the excitement. The fields were mundane, but the creatures around captured his attention. Herds of beasts grazed standing as tall as dinosaurs covered in a mix of feathers and fur. They shimmered silver ad white in the sunlight.

With his attention on their surroundings, William followed the others into a large body of water. His feet, which were light as a feather, skimmed right across the surface. A smile spread over his face, and he gave out a hoot. Katrina and Juarez joined in.

Strange aquatic creatures jumped out of the water, following them. This was like something out of a dream. William turned, watching them. They resembled dolphins but had glimmering coats of scales that shined in every color of the rainbow.

It took the group most of the day to travel the vast expanse of Archonia, even running at great speeds. Thirty hours passed in no time. They stopped several times along the way, resting briefly and taking water from crystal clear streams.

The sun began to sink, and as it did the mountains became silhouetted.

"Where do we forge our armor?" William said sprinting in close to Brock.

"At the northern most point in Archonia on the highest peak of the great mountain called Olympus."

"And that is where this Greige forge is?"

"Indeed, little brother. And just you wait. If you think I'm big. You will be dumbfounded by the size of Vulcanus"

William had learned of Vulcanus in his introductory academic courses. He was once a man, like Zeus, whom many mortals believed was more than a man. The Romans had worshipped him as the patron deity of fire and forges. He was one of the first humans to become an Archonian, and helped the Archons teach men the art of molding metal. It was inevitable that men would then use this gift to create weapons to destroy one another.

Finally Chang Fei came to a stop and lightly floated to the ground. He turned and waited, giving everyone time to catch up. William was exhausted from the run, unlike

Juarez, who seemed to have a knack for distance running. Brock looked unaffected.

"How many miles have we traveled today?" William asked sucking in air.

"Oh, I think from Valhalla it is around seven thousand kilometers," Brock said.

Incredible.

The massive mountain loomed overhead, throwing them all in shadow.

Chang Fei motioned to it and said, "Mount Olympus."

William chuckled when he had first read that the fabled mountain from Greek mythology actually existed here. So many things from history keep popping up, that he wasn't exactly surprised anymore.

I wonder if Zeus is up there, William thought with amusement.

"You must now climb to the top," Cheng Fei said, his face severe.

Ulifrig gasped and protested, his Nordic accent thick, "We are exhausted!"

His long blond hair was sopping wet with sweat. William too had been sweating. His short crop of hair was moist and beads of sweat dripped down into his eyes, but to a lesser degree than his Scandinavian counterpart.

"You're guardians now, and you will never be tired," Chang Fei said rigidly, before tossing something at Ulifrig. It hit the blond-haired man, knocking him to the ground. William looked just in time to see something flying at him. He caught it, and staggered back. It was a vest, but it was very heavy. Chang Fei projected, and another flew out.

"These are projections?" William asked.

"Yes," Brock said. "That is why they feel so heavy. They are made from Chang Fei's energy. Projections in this world can have any property the creator wants."

William had just become accustomed to his new found strength, and now it seemed finite again. He slipped on the heavy vest, and felt it tug him towards the ground.

"Climb," Chang Fei shouted, his words clipped and harsh Then he and Brock took off into the dark sky. The group moaned, complaining to one another, strapping on their vests, and began to climb.

This mountain wasn't ordinary. William expected a gradual ascension in the foothills, but it rose from the ground at an extreme angle. He and the other initiates walked on their hands and knees up its steep slope. One by one they had all tried taking their vests off, but once on, they had clamped down around their skin. Even Samuel, who had flown most of the way here, was simply too heavy to leave the ground.

The cliff face was covered in scrub and tufts of grass, casting shadows on the rocks. William spotted caves burrowing into the sheer stone. He exchanged glances with Katrina and Juarez, glancing back at the caves warily. Hours passed, and William's muscles screamed in protest to the weight of the vest, but he'd gone too far to turn back.

Juarez fell behind the others, and more than once William grabbed him, and pulled him up. Even Samuel and Ulifrig, who hadn't been very close to the rest of their guardian recruits, began helping Katrina. Loyalties were forming amongst them. True fellowships, the kind he'd gained thanks to the military. Trust the man at your side, and he you.

"Samuel," William said as they stopped on a precipice to rest. "Where are you from?"

Samuel looked at him, and began, "I'm from Georgia...born on a plantation in the Great South. My family grew cotton, and was a very prosperous bunch, but as you probably know, William, it wasn't to last. A civil war broke our country apart, and I, being a fool, enlisted in the Confederate Army. I didn't even make it through my first battle. I lacked the nerve to kill, and died in a pile of bloody bodies, crying for my mother. A guardian came and picked me up. I have been striving to make up for that lack of courage ever sense."

William nodded in approval. "You're doing good, Sam."

He looked at Ulifrig, who must have been expecting it, because he sighed and said, "I was a warrior in the northlands long ago. I never wanted to fight, and every chance I got I would flee from battle. I pretended to survive them, and came back a great hero, but when I needed to defend my village, I couldn't run any longer. I let down my people, and died. I too was brought here by a guardian. I vowed to him that I would become a truly great warrior." He turned to Samuel, who patted him on the shoulder.

"We will help you, amigo," Juarez said with earnest. There was a moment of silence as the group sat in darkness.

"And you, William, what happened to you?" Ulifrig asked, solemnly.

William's gut clenched up.

"I made some bad decisions and I'm here to fix those mistakes as best I can," he sighed.

Katrina looked at him skeptically, but didn't push it. Ulifrig nodded understanding. Juarez began to speak, but before he could tell his story a low rumble shook the rocks around the small group.

William and the others looked around in surprise, small bits of stone and dust rattling down around them. Juarez turned slowly towards the face of a cliff, drawn by the source of the noise. It was so dark that they hadn't noticed the fissure in the cliff it was the opening to a cavern. William and the others stood uneasily.

Katrina muttered, "What in the world..." but was interrupted again by a long and guttural growl.

"Katrina. Get out your bow," William said slowly. Katrina nodded and William unsheathed his sword.

Rocks crumbled all around they had been so distracted with the growling noise that they hadn't noticed a large group of figures approaching from all sides.

Juarez let out a cry, lifted his hand in the air. Juarez projected a blazing light towards the approaching figures. It cascaded around the Cliffside blanketing everything in light.

"Bears!" Ulifrig shouted.

"No, wolves," Samuel responded.

They stood on all fours, and did indeed resemble a mixture of wolf and bear. They looked large and strong their mouths full of razor sharp teeth. William didn't take the time to think about what they looked like for very long.

"Kill em!" he shouted, and lunged forward, bearing his sword with ferocity.

The creatures recoiled in reaction to his charge, snarling, their teeth bared. Katrina drew her bow, a bolt of energy appearing instantly, and with a determined face she let it fly. The bolt hit its target, a brilliant explosion of light filling the darkness. Sparks flew, and the creature hit the ground hard. The other creatures closed the gap almost instantly, making her bow useless.

William arched his sword, catching one of the unlucky creatures in its face, splitting it open. It recoiled from the strike, yelping and tearing William's sword out of his hands as it fell to the ground, dead.

William didn't try to go after the sword. Instead, he spun and sidestepped an incoming lunge from another beast, and caught it by the back of the neck. He yanked the creature back towards him, taking it by the inside of the mouth and ripping. Its upper jaw gave way, and cracked under his strength. With a roar it went limp. He saw Katrina pinned to the ground, and gave a cry.

He focused and held his hands, pointing his palms forward. He pushed forth his inner energy, and with a tremendous effort projected a wave of gray light. It caught two of the beasts, sending them flying over the edge of the cliff top and into the black abyss. William saw Juarez blast three more with small balls of light, and the remaining creatures dispersed.

"What in the hell were those things?" Samuel asked, gasping for breath.

"Creatures in Archonia are supposed to be peaceful. There are no predators," Juarez said.

William held up his hand, igniting it in a ball of light, just as Juarez had done. He scoured the small precipice for the creatures he had felled, but they were nowhere to be found.

"Where are they?" William asked through gritted teeth.

"I sense the work of a conjurer here," Samuel said.

"A conjurer?" William asked.

"Those were projections," Juarez stated.

William immediately thought of that day when he had battled Henry's massive two headed beast. *Of course.*

"Someone is testing us again," Katrina surmised, her expression sour.

"Then let's keep moving," William offered, "before we get any more surprises."

He walked over to where he had felled the first creature to find his sword lying in the dirt. The creature had vanished. He picked up his weapon, and slung it over his back.

The group gathered themselves, and headed towards the cliff face. It was a sheer climb from here. William found some good hand grabs and footholds, and started to climb. They climbed slowly for another couple of hours, the wind whipping them ferociously. William discovered quite by accident that he could dig his hands into the stone, making his own handgrips if he couldn't find his own.

The others adopted this technique quickly, approving of his good idea. Samuel discovered that if he projected like he was flying, he could burst forth at short intervals. He moved ahead of the group, scouting the rock face for them.

William lifted his head, noticing a light ahead of them. It was orange like fire, at the top of the peak. He sped up in excitement, but as he did, something hit him. It beat against him rapidly, gusting strokes pounding the air. He spun, clutching the stone to see a giant winged creature with white eyes screeching wildly. William's own eyes went wide and he heard Ulifrig yell loudly. He looked, finding his fellow initiates under attack as well.

Lunging out, William managed to grab the creature by its skinny throat. It was hideous. Thick leathery wings spanning a good six feet in length beat ferociously against his grip and nearly caused him to lose his grip on the cliff face.

A hissing issued from the gaping mouth that was filled with needle like teeth. It was black with tufts of fur and patches of scales. William growled, realizing painfully the creature had long arms and razor sharp talons. With a click the claws ripped at William's hand, helping it break free of his grasp. William hollered and punched his hands into the cliff.

He climbed as fast as he could upwards, more of the terrible creatures swarming him. Juarez let fly a salvo of energy, but the creatures were so fast that he missed most of them. When he managed to hit one they burst into light embers burning their outlines in the night sky. William tried projecting as well, but couldn't concentrate.

He found a new footing, and whipped around with a large stone in his hand dug straight from the cliff. He twisted his arm, grunted as he hurled the stone at a group of the bat-like creatures. It caught one square in the chest, scattering the group and sending them screeching in a panic.

Just when it appeared that the battle had turned in their favor Ulifrig gave another cry. One was beating against him as he dangled from one hand. His hand slipped from the cliff wall. Ulifrig fell, scrabbling against the wall, falling in a slow, desperate battle he appeared helpless to stop.

"No!" Katrina shrieked.

William looked up at Samuel, who had only just made it back down to the rest of the group.

"Samuel!" William shouted. "You have to get him!"

Samuel shook his head, "I can't fly with this vest on."

"You have to!" William shouted quickly.

Samuel's bright energy encompassed his body. He yelled a long and loud battle cry, and then he pushed off, diving like a swimmer into the void.

A blast split the air, rocks flying as he kicked off from the rock face. Golden energy streamed behind him. He plummeted catching up to his friend in seconds. William followed their descent, visible now as only a tiny light fading in the distance. The sight of Samuel's selfless bravery invigorated William, and he successfully projected several blasts of energy towards the flying creatures. The balls of light clipped some of the beasts, burning their wings to ash. Unable to fly, the injured beasts plummeted out of the sky, screeching in terror. The remaining creatures, witnessing their defeated, flew away, squawking loudly.

William looked down in despair. Katrina pounded the cliff face, cursing loudly.

"Could they die from the fall?" William asked.

No one answered. They just stared dejectedly down into the darkness. He decided that it may have been possible despite their strength their minds were still fragile, and the two might not have been able to survive the fall.

William could see Samuel's ball of light in the distance, and it appeared to still be fading. He turned his head in dismay, but when he looked again the light appeared to be stronger. *Could it be?*

"Look!" Juarez shouted, almost jarring him from his roost on the cliff.

The light was definitely getting stronger. A huge wave of wind shook them, almost breaking their grips on the stone. The light shot past them, and William hooted, before starting to jump up the side of the mountain.

After a short, labored climb, they reached the peak. The cliff flattened out to a plateau at the very top, and as William's vision broke the plane he caught sight of source of the orange, fiery glow. Flames burst forth from a massive stone sculpture, licking the sky in angry torrents. Two figures, completely in shadow, stood between them and the statue. He knew it was Samuel and Ulifrig before he could see their faces. Steam rolled off of Samuel's body as he pressed his forehead against Ulifrig's. Katrina ran and wrapped them in a hug.

William looked around, his gaze settling on the peculiar statue bathed in flame. It was a dragon, the carving was spectacularly detailed. Individual scales of the dragon's armor glistened in the blinding light of the flames against the dark night. William's legs started to cramp. The climb had really taken it out of him. Not to mention that he hadn't meditated in two days.

He undid the clasps holding his vests in place, and let it fall off and hit the ground with a thud. The others follow suit, before leaning, or settling onto the ground for a rest. As they did Chang Fei emerged from the shadows, flanked by Brock, and Henry.

"Well done, recruits," Brock offered.

"How faired your climb?" Henry asked. The other initiates scowled in response to his question. The beasts suddenly made sense to William. Henry had summoned the vicious beasts.

"It was pretty uneventful," William said, sarcastically.

"Those wolves were pretty meek," Katrina said, looking towards Henry.

"I didn't like the bats though," Samuel added, still gasping for air.

"Bats?" Henry asked, jerking his head toward him.

Brock turned a concerned gaze his way. William took a breath to speak, but was interrupted by an intense pain shooting through his leg. The cramps worsened, and he flopped to the ground, clutching his legs.

"Come now, William, was it really that bad?" Brock asked, skeptically.

"...You're very welcome to try it," William growled through gritted teeth.

Brock laughed uncomfortably, their small conversation interrupted by the flames bathing the large statue. They rose and flared brighter for a moment, the heat intensifying. William watched as a figure emerged, striding straight from the fire.

It was a man, standing at least nine feet tall. He wore a long, well-groomed beard. He didn't look old physically, but his eyes spoke to extensive experience. A tattered loin cloth hung from his waist. The rest of his body was covered in soot, and ash. William exchanged glances with his friends.

This must be Vulcanus. What an intimidating figure, he thought.

With a few massive strides, the large man closed the gap between them.

"Welcome, young guardians. My name is Vulcanus," he said, his tone husky, but surprisingly docile.

"Hello, brother, how have you been?" Brock asked, embracing the large man in a half hug.

"It has been a great while since you last brought me a group of new recruits, Brock," Vulcanus responded.

"They are as fresh as they come. They are ready to be fit with armor." Brock said.

"I have not been asked to forge steel for a tainted soul in many centuries," Vulcanus said, looking William over.

"Do it for Gabriel," Brock said softly.

Vulcanus looked at Brock, and then at Chang Fei. Chang Fei simply grunted and nodded his head. Then Vulcanus turned and headed back into the flames.

"We will begin in the morning. Get some rest, young ones," he said, and disappeared into the flames. The fire dissipated almost as soon as he disappeared. Darkness fell over the mountaintop.

It took a moment for William's eyes to adjust to the lack of light. He didn't move, even when he heard everybody else begin to. Vulcanus' words had cut deep...deeper than he ever believed possible. Had rumor of his taint spread so far, and so fast, to reach even this remote place? Or was his taint so very obvious to everyone? William shook the thoughts away and turned to see the others huddling around a large flame. It floated in midair, projecting warmth to the small group. Katrina shivered and moved in closer to the flame. The night had become cold at the peak of the world.

Samuel and Ulifrig moved into the darkness to meditate. Juarez and Katrina sat with William by the fire. It crackled, and burned slowly. Brock and Henry remained with them for the evening, but despite their presence, William caught himself flinching, his eyes searching the shadows.

Chang Fei remained for a short time, but eventually pulled Brock aside, and whispered something in the big man's ear. Judging from Brock's expression, he was told something he didn't like, but William didn't want to push the issue, and he had been used to compartmentalization in the military. If he needed to know they would tell him.

"Brock, come and join us. Sit. You're making me nervous," William said, shortly after Chang Fei left.

Brock jumped and spun, startled by his words.

"My apologies, little brother, it is just such an exciting time for you young ones. To forge your armor is a major step in your journey. I...I can't seem to find rest."

"So, how does it work?" William asked, glancing over at the forge, where the flames had burned so brightly before.

"Henry, perhaps you can tell the story. You know it better than I," Brock said, his eyes only half-focused.

"Indeed," Henry said, sighing. "The Greige Forge has been around as long as the Archonians have. During the War of Souls over six thousand years ago, when the first Archonians went into battle against the demons of Lucifer their bodies and armor was no match for his evil power. The

221

man you saw earlier, Vulcanus, was a master of metallurgy in his previous life, and instantly knew what needed to be done. In our previous world, metal was the strongest material, yet it could still be molded," Henry said, pausing to see if everyone was paying attention. They all appeared to him to be enthralled by the explanation. Henry chuckled and continued, "Vulcanus is very clever. Knowing only metal in his previous life, he asked himself what the strongest thing in Archonia was."

"Projected energy," Katrina interrupted quickly. Henry nodded appreciatively.

"Correct. Our inner energy is what this world revolves around. We can use it not only to destroy, but to create. Vulcanus was one of the first Archonians to begin molding his inner energy. As you can imagine, his reputation grew, and was commissioned to create armor for one of the mightiest warriors ever to come from Earth. Thor, who was so great in battle in both worlds that he was thought to be the son of the Archon, Othin. No demon could stand against him, and he single-handedly turned the tide of the war," Henry finished.

"So how does he make the armor? How did Brock summon it from...well, nowhere?" William asked.

"Vulcanus delves into your mind, and helps you mold your inner energy. But ultimately you must be the one to create it. Vulcanus has found a way to make the process a necessity in order to speed it up. The "tempering process" is needed to make the armor as strong as possible. You will find out all about it tomorrow, my friends. For now you should all meditate. You have all had a long day," Henry said, resting his hands on his knees and pushing off to stand.

William couldn't disagree. He felt like he had been pushed to the limit, plus he had seen his first real combat in a long time. He stared into the flames, wondering if the fire was real. According to everything he'd learned, everything was in his mind. He pondered this as Katrina started singing softly to herself. She had a beautiful voice, and William quickly became lost in her song.

Images of the past day flew through his mind. *Flash:* William was running across the great plains of Archonia. *Flash:* he was climbing the massive mountain. William had been in Archonia here for many months now, yet he was still not used to the meditation process.

His eyes fluttered open, and he was sitting in front his friends, the sun now burning bright in the sky. His fellow initiates were all still deep in their meditations. Some of them sat with eyes open. Others closed. All sat motionless. William felt a pang of uneasiness, like he was being watched.

William stood, scouring the cliff top. Nothing appeared out of place or amiss, but he held his breath, listening for anything and everything. He heard nothing.

My mind must be playing tricks on me, he thought, breathing out a slow sigh of relief, and as he did, a low voice cut the silence.

"Tainted one."

William jumped, and spun around to find Vulcanus looming over him. His eyes appeared thoughtful. His body relaxed.

"Why do you come here?" the large man asked.

William was taken aback by the question.

Because my superior officers told me to come, he thought to himself. However, he knew that this wasn't the real reason why he had come. William spoke, truth ringing in every word.

"I wish to defend those who are unable to defend themselves. To prove to this world that I am more than a tainted soul," he said.

There was a long silence before Vulcanus responded softly. "This is the truth. Follow me." He turned and walked towards the great dragon statue, once again enshrouded in flames.

223

Vulcanus walked into the inferno, but William stopped upon the threshold. He looked at the very real looking flames. He thought back to the fire they had huddled around the previous night.

Was it real? Is this? The heat emanating off the blaze felt real enough. He reached out and slowly let his hand sink into the wall of fire. He smiled for a split second, until a fierce pain shot up his arm, and blinded him. He fell backwards, clutching his hand. The flesh was bright red, and burned so badly that he could think of nothing else.

William breathed through clenched teeth as he focused. He had seen people heal each other many times. He let his energy flow to his hand, wrapping it around the burn, and slowly the red subsided. After a moment he looked down. The faint glow of his aura encompassed his arm. His focus broke, and the glow subsided. He was staring at his hand, which was no longer red or hurt. He flexed his hand, wincing as it throbbed, a bit.

Not a professional job, he thought to himself, *but it will have to do.*

He stood up again, gritting his teeth. He peered into the waves of red and orange fire, and could see Vulcanus standing with his arms crossed, completely still amidst the chaos of fire.

This must be what Henry meant by the tempering process?

William let out a breath.

This is mad, he thought, before forcing his energy out and letting it surround him. It flowed over his skin, encasing him completely in a dull gray glow. He undoubtedly would be ashamed of the dull energy if anyone else was watching. He hadn't told anyone what color his projection was, and the others had been too busy to see it during the climb.

At this point, color didn't matter. He put his glowing hand into the flames once again. He felt the heat. He felt it burn, but it was tolerable now. He flexed his body, telling his mind that the pain wasn't real. William fought with every ounce of strength, and then stepped into the flames.

The fire pushed at him as he marched slowly towards Vulcanus, cringing in pain. His skin screamed in agony. His garments blackened and melted away, until he was completely exposed. After what seemed like the longest walk in his life he stood in front of Vulcanus. He could go no further, so he stood before the large man, growling to help with the pain. His eyes met the giant Archonian's stone cold gaze. Then Vulcanus spoke.

"Now you have endured what those poor souls experience every day in the deepest places of Dichonia." Vulcanus whispered through the flames.

William's mind registered his words, but he couldn't didn't think on it further. He needed all of his focus on keeping the pain at bay. It was staggering, and blinding, almost more than he could handle.

His mind worked to block out the heat and pain, denying that it was happening. William had been punched, stabbed, and shot in his life time, those pains now miniscule in comparison. It felt like his skin was being scraped off with a knife, and he dared not look, or he might lose his focus and make that horrible possibility real. It was red, yes, but real flames would have turned the skin black, and made it melt away. He told himself that it was just an illusion.

Vulcanus stood in nothing but a loin cloth, surround by this inferno, but apparently not affected by it. He was definitely not projecting. Everything told William that he had to be in worse pain than him, yet he showed no signs of it. Perhaps his garment was a projection, or he was the one projecting the flames.

"I can grant you the means to defend yourself, William," the ancient man said.

"Please," William pleaded, finally falling to his knees in agony. Then William heard a voice inside his head.

Picture your armor, young Archonian. See the plates of metal, and imagine the strength within them. They cover your body, protecting you from all evil. Feel the strength within your soul, tainted one. Use the energy within to form them. Mold them with your mind.

Vulcanus began to chant. It was an unrecognizable mantra that grew in volume.

William could barely focus on anything now. It felt like his body was being incinerated over and over again. He looked up at Vulcanus, who shouted in the strange language. William roared defiantly, and burst to his feet. A wave of energy rolled over him, and started to take shape. He saw his armor clearly in his mind. He saw himself standing tall and strong, clad head to toe in metal. It wasn't what he expected, however. It wasn't the silver and gold he had seen his fellow Archonians wearing. His armor was dull gray, like iron, and didn't shine.

William's cloudy energy blew back the flames, his deafening cry shaking the cliff top. He held out his arms as if to pull something in, and grey steel plates appeared out of thin air. He could see them clearly in his mind now, and before him. The perpetual agony had made it so.

The energy upon his skin expanded outward wrapping him in thick quilted fabric and a clinking sound resonated as chainmail flowed like water from his shoulders down. Finally the plates clasped to his body roughly shaking him with each impact, they molded to his body like a second skin. It was only a moment before the whole process was complete.

A rush of relief filled him. The flames collapsed back onto him, but they lacked the searing bite. They were cool now, like he had just jumped into a pool of water on a hot day. He closed his eyes, and basked in the sensation.

When William focused, he realized the only audible sound was the whipping of the flames as they washed over him. He looked up at Vulcanus who quietly watched him. William inspected the metal plates adorning his body. They

226

were simply stunning. Their solid and geometrical form was covered in tiny etchings, made up of many intricate details.

He had thick black leather gloves on and a flowing cape draping over one of his shoulders. He shifted and moved trying to get the feel of it. There were many layers underneath the plate which made for a lot of bulk, but he wasn't heavy in the slightest.

Did my mind really create this? he wondered.

"Thank you, old man," William said, glancing up at Vulcanus once again.

Vulcanus didn't respond right away. His stare was long, and penetrating.

"Every tainted soul that I have forged armor for has fallen to darkness, save for one. I struggle to believe that it will be any different now. Prove me wrong," he said darkly.

William nodded, and said, "I will." Then he turned and walked out of the flames.

CHAPTER FIFTEEN
THE PLOT

William's eyes adjusted to the light of the bright sun, to find that he was standing face to face with his fellow initiates. They looked astonished. Samuel eyed William's armor, his jaw dropping open.

"William, we heard you screaming. We were terrified," Katrina said.

"All part of the process, I guess," William said, chuckling. "Do you want a closer look? I can take it off so you can crawl inside. Or, maybe take a photo."

"What is a photo?" Katrina asked, her face scrunching up.

"Oh, right. You guys wouldn't know what that is," he said dryly.

"It doesn't matter," Juarez said. "Look at you, a true guardian," he said tugging on the armor.

William moved, noticing that the heavy armor didn't encumber him, in fact, they felt as light as a feather.

"That is an interesting color," Katrina said. "All the armor I've seen has been silver and gold."

William tried to change the subject.

"I think Vulcanus is waiting for you guys," he said, motioning with a thumb towards the fire behind him.

The group's eyes went wide, and Samuel actually took a step back. "Does it hurt?" he asked, staring warily at the surging inferno.

"Yes," William said bluntly, "it hurts like a son of a bitch."

"What is a son of a bitch?" Ulifrig asked.

"Just go," William said, annoyed that his modern colloquialisms continued to go over his counterpart's heads.

The excitement on Juarez's face was apparent, as he broke into a run towards the flames.

"Juarez!" William yelled before his friend dove in. "Shield yourself!"

Juarez considered him for a moment, and then a golden wave passed over his skin.

"Thanks for the tip," he said, flashing a quick smile, before disappearing into the flames.

Katrina took a deep breath. Juarez screamed from within the flames, roaring in defiance of the pain. Samuel looked hesitant, but Ulifrig grabbed him by the arm and pulled him to the edge of the flames.

"We didn't come this far to be cowards," he said.

Slowly, one by one, his fellow initiates entered the inferno. William let out a slow breath. Ever since exiting the fire with his armor he had felt an unusual surge of energy, which gradually grew as he tried to remain calm.

He had just faced pain beyond anything he previously thought possible, thanks to the forge. Everything now seemed a little less scary. Such a release of inhibition must have increased his power. Whether it came from his armor, or somewhere inside of him, he didn't know. All he knew in that moment was that he could no longer contain it.

The peak wasn't a very large plateau, and he had passed the edge in an instant.

Without thought he burst from the ground and was airborne. The peak passed in a blur as he soared out into open air, moving like a bullet. William felt himself slowly start to descend, his momentum faltering. Panic and doubt blossomed inside, but he pushed them away. He had just survived the forge. His inner energy was no longer hidden from him.

With a shout, William pushed it forth, fighting against the gravity trying desperately to bring him to the ground. It was almost effortless, and suddenly William could feel his body lift. He laughed, and began spinning, letting the wind whip his face. It was bliss...perhaps the first real freedom he'd felt in a long time.

William was free. Not even gravity could hold him back any longer. The chains of his former life whisked away in a moment. As he broke the cloud line he came to an abrupt halt. The sun shone brightly, splashing warmth upon his face. He hovered and soaked it in. He had finally found a place that he could live in happiness.

* * *

The excess energy flowing through William's body burned off after flying around for a few minutes, so he decided to turn and head back to the mountain top. It took him the span of a few seconds to find his way back, and when he landed the force of his impact formed a small crater in the hard stone.

I will have to work on a softer landing, he thought to himself.

William went over to the edge of the fire, where he could hear his friends crying in agony, and winced. They would have to endure this, as he did, and there was nothing he could do to help.

So, that is the point of this trial? To endure pain so intense that a person never fears pain again.

After pacing for what seemed like hours, the other recruits began to emerge one by one. Ulifrig emerged first.

"Awesome," William whispered when he saw Ulifrig's armor.

Thick white leather covered chain mail which shined gold in the daylight. Two large horns curved around in front of his helmet and his axe strapped to the back of it made him look like a mythical warrior. *Though technically I am now*, William thought to himself.

Juarez appeared next, beaming with excitement in his eyes. Apparently the pain had not even fazed him. William thought immediately of the musketeers from Juarez's era, but with more armor. There was an excess of white and gold cloth that bloomed out from under silver plates that were engraved with flowers and thorns. Upon his head a flamboyant white hat pinned up on one side with a golden feather that hung lazily behind him.

"Good job, buddy, you look dapper," William said with a grin.

Katrina was next, and she surprised everyone. Her armor looked very delicate. She wore a breast plate, but the rest of her body was covered in a flowing tunic over shiny chain mail. She wore no helmet, only a diadem of bright silver with many jewels encrusted upon it.

Samuel rocketed out of the flames last, a look of utter relief plastered on his face. He stopped and spun circles in the sun, taking in his new appointments. His armor was shiny silver plate, etched with scrolling gold filigree. Hardened mail gleamed from underneath, tied into place with corded leather. Beneath that, William could see an intricately quilted jerkin, his movements hinting at gold rose-gold colored thread.

"What now?" Samuel asked, finally finished examining his armor.

"Follow me!" William said with a wink, and dove off the edge of the cliff.

He couldn't see their reactions, but he knew what they were feeling in their new armor. Naturally, Samuel caught up with him first. He already had some skill with flying after all. Juarez followed closely behind, and Katrina and Ulifrig after that. They wove in and out of the sky, making great patterns in the clouds, enjoying the welcomed reprieve from training.

"William!" Katrina shouted. He looked back to find her beaming. "I. Am. Flying!" she hollered happily.

William nodded his head, and took off above the clouds again. The others whooped and hollered excitedly, defying the clinging bonds of gravity for the first time as they too slipped the bonds of gravity for the first time. Their trip back to Valhalla took half the time, and felt less like a journey.

* * *

The group's visit to the Greige Forge symbolized the end of their recruitment training. The only thing standing between themselves and guardian status was a ceremony inducting them into the order. An induction into the Order of Guardians was for life.

Not an oath to be taken lightly, William told himself over and over.

He had heard of the oath many times, and had been studying it since the night Achilles approached him on the training grounds. Yet it was only now that its significance was truly sinking in. He went over the words he had learned in his mind:

I guard the innocent
I guard the light
I will not feign at evil's might

I speak the truth when faced with death
And strive for honor with every breath

I don my armor and now crusade
To see laws of gods and men obeyed

From now 'til death I solemnly swear
To Guard against darkness everywhere

William thought that it sounded ridiculous at first. After all, rhymed and sounded cheesy, like something out of a superhero comic book. But it didn't feel like a joke now. The reality of it filled him with anxiety and pride. Soon the words would mean much more than he could ever truly fathom.

Until death is a long time in Archonia, he thought.

William also knew that not every guardian returned from their crusades in the mortal world, and that it was an honor to die while aiding the cause. William felt the fear of dying on many occasions and wasn't in a hurry to experience it again any time soon.

He wouldn't have to worry about crusades for a while however, as Chang Fei assured them they were still far from being combat ready. The trip to the forge had unofficially made them guardians, but while the preparations of the ceremony took place. Their intense training continued. Their Armor had unlocked significant power within the recruits, but they had only begun to discover their true potential. Samuel developed the ability to create powerful shields to protect himself as well as others. Katrina was becoming even faster. She could now overtake some of the more experienced soldiers.

Juarez discovered that he had a knack for healing. More than once William overworked himself in training, and his own healing skills weren't strong enough. Huge gashes and bruises would cover his body at the end of a training day, and although William could make the pain subside, Juarez could make wounds disappear.

William's projections became the talk of the entire barracks as soon as they returned from the Greige Forge. Rumors spread of their unique color. Some feared William for it, while others were intrigued.

His fellow guardians had remained steadfast by his side. This new feeling of brotherhood had helped him focus on his training and less on what people thought of him. He was one of the stronger soldiers, though he didn't possess any extraordinary gifts, he could unleash vicious waves of energy that would flatten most anything. In fact William was excelling in all areas of combat, and it seemed that he wouldn't be stopped until he fought Achilles himself.

William found himself holding the Atlas ball, inspired by his cocky attitude during his earlier sparring session. He held the atlas ball for what seemed like the entire day before Change Fei appeared and ended his punishment. He set it down, and headed back towards the barracks.

William enjoyed the darkness, especially now, since he didn't want to be noticed. Though he stayed incredibly busy with his training regimen, he started devoting a large portion of his extra time at night patrolling the halls, hoping he would catch sight of Meredox.

The light crystals shimmered down the castle halls, leaving large pools of inky shadow between them. It was a nice contrast to the overly bright days in Archonia. He also could have projected to give himself more light, but was comforted by the shadows.

He turned left and stepped into the hall of the samurai, glancing at some of the plaques detailing the ancient heroes of feudal japan when he heard low voices in the dark. He picked up his pace, keeping his footsteps light to muffle the sound. He moved slowly, peering around each corner carefully. The voices grew louder. He crept down another corridor and peered around the edge. A bright light glowed down the next passage.

He moved slowly forward, until he reached the orange glow coming from a doorway. William's heart leapt up into his throat as an adjudicator suddenly strode into the hall. With his new reflexes, he leapt straight into the air and grappled onto a sculpture near the ceiling. He held his breath, waiting for the soldier to pass, but the man was fiddling with a piece of parchment filled with some sort of dried plant, or herb, and walked right on by.

William couldn't help but feel that something was amiss. He didn't dare try to float to the ground, or summon his armor for fear of making too much noise. Instead, he clung to the wall and crawled bug-like sideways until he was above the lit doorway.

The soldier below had lit his cigarette, the potent smoke wafting past William. It was like nothing he smelled before. It already made his head buzz and his vision blur. He crawled slowly down the wall, and peeked his head past the top of the arched doorway, gripping the raised stone edge for support. Once settled he noticed a group of figures in the room. A few paced back and forth, others lounged in large cushy chairs.

"Why do you think that I chose to have this conversation away from the Adjudicator's wing?" Meredox spat, his voice instantly recognizable.

"Surely this is not possible," he heard another man say. Their voice was raspy, and William didn't recognize them.

"Achilles' new recruits destroyed a pack of them on the climb to the Greige Forge," another said.

"I will need more proof than the word of a tainted Justicar for me to commit to this secret, Meredox," the man with the raspy voice said.

"Then you shall have it, Benjamin," Meredox replied.

William peered around the corner of the statue, making certain that he wouldn't be seen. He saw Meredox, and the man he called Benjamin. It was dark, and hard to see, but Meredox held something out to him. It glowed with a dull orange fire.

William focused hard, trying to discern what it was, but the two were inadvertently shielding it with their bodies. Another spoke up.

"Meredox, if we decided to help, you must know what it will mean for all of us, should your plan fail."

"I believe everyone in this room is aware of the consequences."

William couldn't believe what he was hearing. He was sure that they were about to get to the point, when the soldier coughed below. William looked down involuntarily, finding the Adjudicator staring back at him.

His heart stopped, the deeply embedded spec ops training kicking in. William released his grip from the sculpture and plummeted. The soldier choked on his cigarette, and couldn't croak out a warning in time. He froze too, most likely because this world had been at peace for thousands of years. Real life combat situations rarely occurred.

William wrapped his thick arms around the man's neck, sliding into a powerful, rear naked choke. The soldier was strong, and for a moment William feared that he would throw him off. But to his relief, after a few moments of struggle, he felt the soldier go limp in his arms.

He set the body down gently, but he could already hear the people in the room moving towards the hallway. His commotion had alerted them. William drove his foot into the ground and jetted off down the corridor, running as swiftly and quietly as he could, hoping beyond hope that the soldier hadn't recognized him. He knew if he'd been caught the punishment would be swift and severe. He would instantly be dismissed from the Guardian Corps and banished to Dichonia. This was the fate he'd been reminded of constantly by other soldiers as they looked down on him.

But now he had a name, but more, he had the proof he needed. He just needed to get his hands on it. He knew something was being plotted, it wasn't just his paranoia. Now he needed to find out what they were actually planning.

William entered the barracks common area, and flopped down on a lounge chair. He shut his eyes for a minute to ponder what Meredox was up to. His thoughts circled around and around, until he finally decided he needed to tell his friends. William leapt out of his chair and swept into the meditation chamber. It was a large, circular room, built up in many tiers, all leading to the center, where a massive crystal sat. It emanated heat and a gentle glow, casting long shadows over the hundreds of guardians now deep in meditative states.

"Wake up!" William shouted, shaking Juarez vigorously, filling the noiseless room with his echoing voice.

He looked around at the other guardians, who all sat motionless. Juarez grunted and fell off of his small meditation pad. Juarez was startled, and jumped to his feet, instantly ready for a fight.

"Calm down, it is just me," William said, whispering.

"William, what are you doing...what's wrong?" Juarez asked, his brow furrowing.

"I need to tell you something. We need to go wake Katrina," he said.

The women's barracks was in the opposite side of the wing. William found it ironic that even in the afterlife there was gender separation.

"Go wake her," William said sharply, peering towards the meditation chamber.

"Why me?" Juarez asked, scowling.

"Alright," William said, nodding.

"Together," they agreed.

They crept into the women's meditation chamber, which was smaller, and rectangular in shape with no tiers. Rows of female guardians sat facing the middle, where a similar crystal glowed faintly in the darkness. They whisked down the rows, until finally coming to a halt in front of familiar face.

Katrina sat, donned in her usual linens. William approached slowly, and put a hand on her shoulder. An iron grip fell over his wrist and twisted his arm, jerking him straight to the ground.

"You're not supposed to be in here," Katrina said, wrenching William's arm behind his back.

"Damn it, Katrina, let me go. We *need* to talk." She let his arm go, as Juarez chuckled quietly to himself.

"Are you always so hostile?" William asked, glancing around to see if she had disturbed anyone.

"Hostile? I'm hostile, but you're the one creeping around the women's wing in the middle of the night. You know that it is forbidden," she said, whispering harshly.

"Sorry, but we need to speak with you. Or...William needs to speak with you," Juarez said, ducking in to calm her.

"What is it? I was having a good dream," she growled loudly.

"Keep your voice down," William hissed.

"Why? They are out cold," she said, pushing her finger against the side of a woman's head.

William rolled his eyes, before standing and walking out of the door.

They met up in the common area, glancing around to make sure that they weren't going to be overheard.

"So, what is so important, William, that you had to disturb our meditation time?" Katrina asked, turning to a window filled with stars and usual cosmic colors.

"Do you all know who Meredox is?" William asked lowly. They looked at one another, and then back at him.

Juarez said, "He is the Grand Justicars. He leads the Adjudicators."

"I have now seen him twice meeting with shadowy figures after dark, first near the training grounds, and again tonight in a study in the hall of samurai. They were discussing something that is coming, and he said the Synod won't be able to stop it. They also mentioned those creatures we fought on the cliffs at Olympus. Do you remember the bat-like creatures?" William asked.

"Yes, Katrina said those were Henry's projections," Juarez responded.

"I don't think they were," William said, shaking his head slowly. "Remember back to our studies of the ancient wars here in Archonia. The way the tomes described the creatures that Lucifer commanded. It almost perfectly describes the creatures we fought on the cliffs. When Samuel mentioned the bats, Henry and Brock looked concerned. Now I hear Meredox talking about it in the middle of the night," William finished.

"What are you getting at, amigo?" Juarez asked, sighing.

"Why does Archonia have such a large army? Besides the crusades, there is no reason to have a standing army," William continued. "I think that the Synod is afraid of something. I think that those were demons we fought on the cliffs of Olympus. I think that Meredox is the one who found a way to get them into Archonia, and I am going to find out how."

Katrina and Juarez looked at him, their eyes wide with shock.

"That is crazy. The Archons gave their power to create the obelisks to keep the demons where they belong. In hell," Katrina said firmly.

William growled in response, almost shouting. "Meredox has found a way to get past them, and we need to find out how!"

"William, Meredox is not only a Justicar but he is the highest ranking kind. Their training basically erases their opinions, and purges them of selfishness. He has been a Justicar for over a thousand years, and his record is flawless," Juarez said in a soft tone.

"You're right, but something must have set him off...maybe me being allowed in Archonia pushed him over the edge. Brock told me he had a brother. His brother ended up in Dichonia. The Synod ordered Meredox himself to cast him out. That's when he chose the path of the Adjudicator. In my opinion this is a long time coming. Meredox has been waiting for revenge," he said, his conviction firming with every word.

William stood, looking back and forth between his two friends.

"Now I can't do this alone. Are you with me?"

Juarez looked at Katrina, and she him.

Juarez sighed, and said, "I hope you're wrong, my friend, but in case you're not, I am with you." He stepped forward and patted William on the shoulder.

Katrina scoffed, and said, "You're crazy boys. But you know I'll support you.

Finally, in agreement, they all went back to the meditation room for the evening.

CHAPTER SIXTEEN
THE CEREMONY

The sounds of birds chirping and bells ringing filled the air outside the window. Someone's foot thumped against the stone floor to her left. Behind Angelica, two students were engrossed in a lively, whispered discussion, adding to the buzz of noise and annoying her down to the core.

Beyond all that, she was struggling to listen to a very old professor's lecture about the Archon Ammun. This was apparently not his first time giving the lecture, because he looked bored and his voice fell to a numbing, monotone that threatened to put her to sleep.

She didn't realize how annoying it would be to not have a clock to look at. So far, the only clock she'd found was on a great bell tower in the Plaza del Sol in the Latin district.

I need a watch.

She knew it would do little good for her to watch a clock all day, but there was something comforting about the action, therapeutic even. Nothing could make the time pass by faster, but she could at least occupy her mind to better fill it.

It wasn't that the course wasn't interesting, it was because of something far more personal. Today was the day new guardian recruits would swear their oaths before all of

Archonia. According to her family, it was a ceremony that should not be missed.

She had first learned about the ceremony on her return trip from the water shrine. And she could think of little else since.

Angelica hadn't noticed that the professor stopped talking. She had been tapping an ivory fountain pen against the table, her thoughts drifting off to seeing William again.

"Young one, I can see your mind is elsewhere. If it is too difficult to focus, you may leave. I would prefer that you not interrupt the other students," the professor said.

Angelica felt her cheeks flush, and then dropped her pen, as she stumbled to get up from the table.

"I am so sorry," she said loudly, and managed to gather up her papers and leave. In truth she wasn't really sorry. She did want to leave, after all, and even with ten hours to the ceremony she realized there were a million things she could be doing, and sitting nervously behind a desk wasn't one of them.

She nimbly strode down the large hill, butterflies fluttering in her stomach. She stopped at a small shop in the Aromatise market where a woman crafted the loveliest fragrances. She picked out a perfume that smelled of fresh, sea air, with hints of coconut and mango. A tropical blend that smelled even sweeter in the heat of the day.

Her next stop was the most important. First she rushed home, to pick up her grandmother's famous empanadas, to offer as a gift. The pan was very hot, so she wrapped it in a woolen blanket, and placed them in a basket so they were easier to carry.

"Thank you, Abuela!" she said, hugging and kissing her grandmother, before running back out the door.

"Tell them they can keep the blanket and basket if they want, or just return it to me as it pleases them," she called after her.

Angelica walked to the Islamic district, which was only a few miles from the Latin district. She reveled in the magnificence of the couturier's shop, her gaze drifting over the spectacle. The windows glass, much like a modern day store, allowing passerby's on the street to see the quality of her goods.

Angelica watched actual people standing in the window, turning and modeling the garments. There seemed to be new people every day, as well as new styles. She saw gowns, wraps, and some sort of toga, the kind of fashion that used large amounts of fabric, unusual angles, and extravagant decorations. The owner was Nephthys, an Egyptian woman, and from what Angelica learned, one of the most popular fashion designers in Archonia, at least right now. Her grandmother told her that it was very difficult to even get an appointment with her. Angelica actually put in for one a month prior for good measure.

She entered the shop to the sound of harps, twinkling a luxurious melody. A citrus perfume drifted on the air, instantly relaxing her mind and body. The Egyptian architecture and decoration was distinct, highlighting the space in white stucco, glimmering blue mosaics, and some familiar Egyptian god-theme statues. Despite the windows, the lighting was very dim. She approached a page greeting patrons at the door. He wasn't an overly large man, and held up his head with an obvious aire of importance.

"I will take your gifts for my mistress, and be sure that she receives them," he said.

She felt awkward handing the basket over to him.

"My grandmother said that you can keep the basket if you wish, otherwise you may return it at your leisure."

The man gave a single, snobbish chuckle. "That is so cute," he responded dryly.

"Come with me, I will take you to the waiting room. Please feel free to help yourself to any refreshments. I do need to go over some of the basic rules of my mistress's house. If your name is called and you're not there you, will lose your appointment. If the mistress desires a break you will lose your appointment. If you displease the mistress in any way, you lose your appointment. If you lose your appointment you will be asked to leave the premises immediately. You may only have one appointment in your lifetime."

When he finally finished, Angelica was at a loss for words. This place wasn't what she thought it was, and her impulse was to turn and leave. And yet, she really wanted to look her best tonight. Her thoughts went to William, the strange man she was slowly getting to know. He was so different from almost everyone she'd met in Archonia. He seemed honest, willing to show his true face, while everyone else hid behind a mask. Every time she thought of him her stomach twisted, and her heart fluttered.

Lost in her thoughts, Angelica realized two hours had already passed. She couldn't believe it, as there wasn't anyone else in the waiting room with her. Looking at the wall clock, she noticed that it was now well past her appointment time. She left the waiting room and asked the page if she had missed it. He assured her that his mistress ran behind schedule regularly, without even so much as looking up from his date book.

Without the poisonous effects on the body, alcohol took on different properties here. It still warmed her body, but in large enough quantities, could induce visions, and make the drinker hallucinate. Or, so she'd been told. After only a single glass, Angelica found her head spinning, so she quickly switched to cold water.

Finally, after considering leaving, she heard someone call her name.

"Angelica," said a tiny, female voice. It was so soft and small that she immediately questioned if she'd heard her own name.

"Yes, that's me."

"Please follow me, young one. The mistress will see you now."

Angelica followed the woman through a curtained off corridor, which felt as if it was made for someone far smaller than her. They passed into a small room, the air hazy with incense. Draperies and carpets hung on the walls and covered the floor, making the room feel very small and hot.

A mirror sat on the back wall, twice as tall as any person. Great, round lights stood around it, shining back onto an elevated pedestal in the center of the room, casting the rest of the room in deep shadow. Angelica noticed another woman standing near the mirror, a large smile creasing her face. She almost missed her completely, if it weren't for the gleam off her white teeth. Angelica's eyes started to adjust and she saw there was another figure in the corner, working where the great puffs of steam were billowing in the back corner.

"Oh, my lady! Thank you from the bottom of my heart. The elegance that you have graced me with is beyond words," the smiling woman said.

The gown hugging her frame was beyond extravagant. In fact, Angelica struggled to sum up words befitting such a magnificent garment. The sheer size and volume of the gown made Angelica wonder how the woman could move, but she didn't seem to be encumbered by it. She paraded back and forth in front of the mirror to look again, the colors striking the lights. Angelica saw deep, rich jade fabric, shifting to a blue, accented with a vibrant orange. Pure gold links and brooches fastened the fabric at key points, to make it drape in many directions. A train hung over her arm, to prevent it from tangling upon the floor.

"Your appointment is over. The mistress wishes you a fine day, and thanks you for coming," the girl with the squeaky voice said.

The woman stopped smiling, a worried look settling on her face.

"Y-yes of course," she replied and exited, rushing past Angelica.

To Angelica's surprise, the mousy, squeaky woman grabbed her by the arm, and pulled her toward the center of the room.

"If you would please stand upon the pedestal and try to hold completely still. I need to take your measurements for the mistress. Then she will begin her work. You will be asked to remain still, and quiet, until she is completed."

Angelica nodded, her insides winding into a surprising ball of nerves. What a ridiculous façade. She recognized the whole thoroughly practiced charade, meant to belittle and discomfort her. She took a steadying breath, resolving herself to see it through. She'd already come this far, after all.

The mousy girl was rough with her, using a measuring tape to expertly take a series of measurements - some of which left Angelica feeling violated.

"Thank you for your patience. The mistress will be with you shortly," the girl said when she was done. She walked over to the figure standing in the shadows, handed them the measurements, and then swiftly disappeared.

It was obvious that the figure in the shadows was Nephthys. Angelica wasn't coy. She looked over at her expectantly, waiting while the woman sucked on a hookah. Such vices were generally looked down upon in Archonia, but even that didn't dissuade her, or, evidently diminish her reputation.

Finally, after Angelica's feet started to tingle, Nephthys approached. It looked like she floated, rather than walked, and when the light struck her face, Angelica cringed. She'd seen some truly outlandish things since arriving in Archonia, but this woman was in a league of her own. Heavy makeup was spackled onto her face, highlighting her features in almost clown-like contrast. Her eyebrows were so long they almost looked alien. Nephthys appeared young, like most in Archonia, but Angelica struggled to consider her beautiful. More than odd, but strange. She scolded herself for the uncharacteristic judgment.

Angelica didn't speak as the woman approached. Her voice was very sharp and her tone businesslike.

"Your name?"

"Angelica."

"How old are you?"

"Thirty one."

The woman stopped and looked at her, as if something she'd said offended her. Angelica involuntarily furrowed her brow in response. Then the questions continued.

"Favorite color?"

"Purple."

"Oh, I hate purple. Pick another color," Nephthys replied.

Before Angelica could respond the woman continued, "Look at these measurements," she shook her head. "It is because you're still so young. You must be imaging yourself the way you looked before. You should come back in twenty years, or so. Hmmm, too bad I don't make second appointments." She promptly started circling, and looking at Angelica from all angles.

The shock and dismay hit Angelica hard. She was no longer nervous, but annoyed. She suddenly remembered stories William told her, about the way people were mistreating him because of the life he lived on Earth.

People here claim to be different, but Angelica realized that these so called pure-souled individuals struggled with just as much selfishness and bigotry as those people they looked down upon.

"Remain still. No, I am not seeing it. I just don't know," Nephthys said, talking to herself. Angelica was fed up

"Thank you for your time. I'm leaving now," she said, stepping off the pedestal.

"Leaving! You won't leave while I am working."

"I will leave, ma'am, we are finished here," Angelica responded assertively.

"What is, ma'am!? No *I* am finished with you! Get out of my studio, and never return," Nephthys said harshly.

She didn't have to ask her twice.

Angelica stormed back through the waiting room, where she saw her grandmother's empanadas laid out on the refreshment table. A page was eating one. Of course she would reuse a gift for appearances sake. She thought it was tacky that they didn't have the decency to at least wait until she left to repurpose her gift.

At least Abuela's food will be enjoyed by others, she thought to herself.

Angelica huffed out onto the street, deciding that she would look for a small clothier, perhaps one that wasn't nearly as renowned. There, she would commission a simpler garment. More than likely that is all she could get on such short notice now anyway. She was passing through the Greek district when she came across a small shop. The only indication that it was a clothing store was from a small, wooden sign hanging above the door, picturing a thread and needle.

She didn't think twice. Angelica pushed through the door, a bell chiming above her heard. A woman stood behind a counter, a wide smile splaying across her face.

"Welcome to my home. My name is Adonia," she said.

"Hello, I'm Angelica. This is your home?" Angelica asked in surprise.

"Of course. Can I offer you something to eat or drink?"

"No. But thank you for offering."

She nodded politely. "Is there some special occasion I can help you prepare for?"

"Well...actually yes. I am going to the Guardian's induction ceremony tonight."

"Say no more, say no more," she said, coming around and taking Angelica by the hand.

Adonia led her over to a set of three mirrors. Two were at a forty five degree angle to the center, so you could see every angle of yourself at once. There was no platform or special lighting.

Adonia waved her hand, casting a bright light that floated above their heads. Angelica watched the pulsing light in wonder, but startled when an unexpected weight fell over her body. With another flash the clothier projected a rippling length of white cotton. It fell against her skin, the knit tightly woven but undeniably soft.

"So tell me, will you be going to the ceremony alone? Or, are you going to see someone?" Adonia asked.

"I am going with my grandmother. And I am going to see the young guardian, William."

"The tainted one? Oh my goodness! Wait, are you the one he helped save? Yes, I see it now!"

Adonia's reaction made Angelica a little uncomfortable. It was a peculiar notion that her name would be known to strangers, especially with over one hundred billion souls living in Archonia. Was her and William's story that unique? Had word spread that quickly?

"Please don't call him that," Angelica said, quietly but assertively.

"My apologies, my dear. One can get caught up in the gossip a bit too easily. I have only the utmost respect for those safeguarding our world. Please forgive me."

"Of course," Angelica said, relieved by Adonia's honest remorse

"My dear, do you like gold, silver, or platinum?"

"Actually, I really like obsidian," Angelica replied.

"Ah...the lava rock. Polished down, correct? Yes, we will make it look very nice."

After working for just a short time, Adonia stepped back and had Angelica turn before the mirrors. She couldn't believe her eyes. The white cotton draped on two shoulders, hanging down past her feet, where it bunched up slightly on the ground. Obsidian adorned the fabric, but also hung around her neck as a necklace, cut into the shape of tiny suns, linked together with black gold. A matching bracelet and earrings materialized in place with a wave of Adonia's hand. Next, she jerked and wove her hands in the air, Angelica's hair twisting into a bun, held in place with a long curved piece of obsidian.

Adonia took a step back.

"Do you like?" she asked.

"Yes...more than anything!" Angelica shouted and started giggling, grabbing the woman in a hug. Adonia hugged her back, and then took her by the cheeks.

"You come back anytime you need to look beautiful for this William," she said, smiling wide.

Angelica blushed. "I definitely won't be going back to Nephthys," Angelica replied sarcastically.

"Oh, that woman," Adonia said, with a barely stifled laugh. "Do you know why she is so popular?"

Angelica shook her head.

"She can look into the mind, and use a person's hopes, dreams, and desires to craft the perfect garment."

Angelica snorted, warmth blossoming on her neck and cheeks. She disliked how the woman acted, and her presumptions about almost everything else. But she disliked the idea of someone digging around in her head even more...even if it was to tailor the perfect dress. She suddenly felt vindicated by her decision to walk out on Nephythys.

"Thank you for your honesty, Adonia. I needed it more than you know. I'm only sorry that I didn't bring a gift for you. I took..." Angelica said, but the Greek woman clasped a hand over her arm, and cut in warmly.

"Not to worry, my dear. You smile is thanks enough!"

Angelica jumped, grabbing her in another furious hug.

"Thank you so much. I really must go, but please come have dinner with me and my family sometime."

"Ok, young one, that sounds very nice. Please come see Adonia anytime. Just don't tell too many people or I will become snobby like Egyptian woman," she said with a chuckle.

With that Angelica rushed out. Though her trip to Adonia's shop was fast, she had wasted almost six hours at Nephthys' boutique. And she still had to get home, before making her way across the city to the ceremony. Angelica was terrified that she was going to be late.

Thankfully, her new, beautiful garb was loose and fluid, making it possible to move quickly. She ran nearly the whole way home. When she arrived back in her family's courtyard her grandmother was waiting on the same bench that she had before.

"Oh, Abuela, I am so sorry. I had a very difficult time."

"Not to worry, my dear. I could sense your feelings. Tell me, did Nephthys make your dreams come true?"

"No, grandmother, she was an awful, old woman. I'm so sorry they took your empanadas," she said, scowling.

They were interrupted by the soft jingle of little bells and the clattering of hooves. A carriage made from gold and crystal suddenly rolled into the courtyard. It was drawn by creatures that looked much like pure white, hairless horses. Massive, curving golden horns sprouted from their head, gleaming in the sunlight. She could see no driver, and the seat only looked large enough for two people.

"I figured we could treat ourselves, and travel a little more luxuriously this evening," Angelina said, rising from her seat.

She approached the front of the cart as it turned and leaned in towards one of the creatures, gently stroking its head. She whispered into the creature's ear, and it whinnied in response. Angelica could have sworn she saw it nod as well.

"Come, child, we really must be going."

Without a second thought they boarded the magnificent carriage and it lurched forward. Soon they were making their way through the throngs of people in the streets, moving at a surprisingly fast pace. People got out of the way quickly, too.

Angelica found the seat of the cart quite comfortable, the cushioned seat molding to her backside. The car didn't rock or jostle, which she found surprising, considering the wooden wheels rolling across stone roads.

After a half hour they reached the outskirts of the Latin district, and started seeing other carriages and carts merging onto the main road. Some were small rickshaw carts pulled by men, just like the ones she saw while on a mission trip to China. Others were larger and held large groups of people. They puffed along, powered by some sort of engine. Angelica even spotted a group of people floating by on a large carpet. Angelica giggled in excitement as it went by, pointing it out to her grandmother.

"Is there anything that isn't possible in this world, grandma?" she asked.

"There are only a few things, child," she replied, but Angelica was looking around in wonderment, and didn't hear her.

It took another hour before they came to the Norse district, wherein lay the stronghold of Valhalla. Angelica had seen it before from afar, but it was breathtaking to behold up close. Most of the buildings in this world were large, but this one made her feel very small.

The carriage circled around a large turnaround in front of the main gates. They patiently waited until it was their turn, before getting down from the cart. Angelina produced two apples from a bag around her shoulder, and held them up to their drivers, who quickly snatched them up. She hugged both of them, whispering something into each of their ears. They were still chewing on their treats as they plodded off.

Angelica looked down, realizing she was standing on a long, plush purple carpet. Men at arms stood at attention on either side of the carpet, clad head to toe in matching silver armor. They wore the blue capes of the Sentinel.

"Grandma, have you ever been here before?"

"No, child. They don't have a Guardian induction ceremony very often. Most of the applicants don't pass the training. According to Julia, this is the biggest class they have had in many years."

"Where is Julia?"

"She came ahead of time. Her husband Edmund returned from his crusade for the ceremony and she wanted to see him right away."

Angelica trudged up the stairs after passing through the main gate, her breathing becoming labored. She struggled, even with her newfound endurance from climbing the hill to the university. She counted perhaps two hundred steps already, and on each stood a Sentinel, standing as quietly as stone statues.

The massive front doors stood open, ushering them into the entrance hall. Thousands of people were already gathered, talking and milling about. Their voices combined into a roar that echoed throughout the chamber.

"There is Julia," her grandmother said, pointing. She and Edmund were talking to some people near a column larger around than a redwood tree. "Right where she said she would be."

Edmund saw them first, and gestured them over "Lady Angelica, Lady Angelina. Welcome to Valhalla. I am so glad that you could attend the ceremony this evening," the large guardian said.

"I am glad I could come," Angelica replied.

Julia stared at Angelica, despite an elbow from her husband.

"Angie, Nephthys did amazing!" she exclaimed finally, her eyes wide.

"Actually a Greek clothier named Adonia made it for me. Nephthys and I had...differing opinions," Angelica said, delicately, after all, Julia had referred her to the woman.

253

"Cousin! Did you miss your appointment?" Julia asked.

"No, I didn't miss anything. Nephthys was a self-centered, egotistical old witch," Angelica snapped.

She even surprised herself, and slapped a hand to her mouth. Everyone else just watched her cautiously.

"I'm sorry. I meant she wasn't very nice," she finished.

"Well, I think this dress suits you much better than anything that old hag has ever made," someone said from behind them.

They turned to find a short but regal figure. His curly, black hair fell over his purple cape.

"Grand Justicar," Edmund exclaimed, bowing his head and crossing a closed fist over his chest.

"Edmund, it's always a pleasure to see you. How faired your crusade?" the Adjudicator asked.

Angelica realized who he was. She saw him at the trial. He was the one who spoke out against William. She'd formed an immediate dislike for him after that. He stood now, pompous, with his chest puffed out, his armor considerably lighter than the other men. An entourage of purple-caped Adjudicators stood behind him.

"It was not without success. I managed to save two souls from annihilation, and another from infestation. Nothing for the history books, but a necessary deed nonetheless," Edmund replied.

"Good on you, my young friend. I wish they would let me return from time to time, and root out some of the evil plaguing the mortal plane. Unfortunately, this office requires much of my time," Meredox said.

Then he turned to Angelica and her grandmother.

"My ladies, I am afraid that I haven't had the pleasure. My name is Meredox, son of Vaxus, Adjudicator of Archonia, and Grand Justicar of Helios," he said taking Angelica's grandmother's hand in his own and lightly pecking it with his lips. Angelica saw her grandma blush slightly, which only made her angrier.

"We have met before. At a trial held before the great Synod, many months ago. You spoke against my friend William," she said, crossing her arms over her chest as he reached out to her.

Meredox's right eye twitched and he stood up a little straighter.

"The tainted one? Ah...yes. I do recognize you. You look a right, proper Archonian now," he offered with a formal kindness.

"Don't you think you should stop calling him the tainted one now that he is to become a protector of the realm?" Angelica asked.

The whole group shrunk away from her, except Julia, who tried to grab her arm. The Grand Justicar looked her up and down appraisingly, a wry grin pulling up one side of his mouth.

"You're bold, my dear. I fear that you still have much to learn of our ways. Your William will have his chance at redemption, but until he proves his worth to me he will remain a tainted soul. As the Grand Justicar it is my job to see that justice is done. As he has done no wrong within these borders I am obliged to let him don his armor and gallivant around, calling himself a guardian. For this you should be happy. Were it my way, I would see him exiled from this land...or worse."

Angelica's anger turned to fury, but there was little it could do for her. She bit her lip and remained quiet. She didn't want to be the cause of further confrontation, or worse, problems for William. She already regretted saying anything to him to begin with.

"Edmund, it was a pleasure as always," Meredox said, nodding and sweeping his cape out of the way as he took his leave.

Angelica's eyes lingered on the Grand Justicar for a few moments, before turning back to her grandmother and cousin. She could see her own embarrassment and rage in their expressions. She wasn't about to let this ruin her

255

evening, so without a word she walked away from everyone. She didn't know where she was going, only that she didn't want to be near them anymore. She pushed through the crowd, not paying attention to where she was going.

Abruptly, she ran into what she thought was surely a wall. Angelica landed hard on her back, her breath nearly knocked from her, strong hands reached down and plucked her off the ground. It wasn't a wall that she ran into at all, but Brock.

"Hello there, little sister," he said.

She took in his large, hairless face and toothy grin, and couldn't help but smile.

"Brock! Hello. How are you?"

"I am well, young one. Have you come to see our William fight for glory?" he asked.

"Fight? I was under the impression that he would be swearing an oath," Angelica responded.

"Of course he will swear an oath, but the people will expect to see their newest guardian's showcase their prowess in battle. It is common for new guardians to face live enemies."

Angelica hadn't heard of this part of the ceremony and was more than a little disturbed. She didn't say anything, but her face must have betrayed her, because Brock spoke quickly.

"Young one, there will be no killing today. The creatures they face will be false predators made from the minds of the best conjurers in the Guardian Corps. There won't even be any blood. People need to be inspired, and know that they are protected," he said gently, reassuring her.

"It sounds barbaric to me," Angelica replied.

She was starting to regret coming to the ceremony at all. "I thought that I was coming to a world without conflict. But it seems the minds of men are plagued with the need for killing and destruction."

The large man furrowed his brow, and with a heavy sigh, said, "Someday you may be thankful that these men exist. A soldier's duty is to do those things that no other man will. You must trust me when I say that none of us relish the thought of death and destruction, but we must always be prepared."

Angelica found his little speech somewhat comforting, but a lingering doubt remained. She nodded and looked down, realizing everyone was moving around them, flowing like a river towards another corridor.

"The ceremony begins, come, Angelica. I will get you a close spot."

Angelica yelped slightly when Brock hefted her into his arms, and again when they took off from the ground. Her hands looked tiny as they desperately clung to the giant's shoulders. They flew over thousands of people, and she was momentarily blinded when they found themselves outside.

"These are the training grounds," Brock said, casually.

They descended into an open area of the field, where an amphitheater had been constructed. A large semicircle of bleacher style seating made up one half of the field. Thousands were already seated and many more thousands were standing in the field in front of it. She definitely underestimated just how big a deal this ceremony was.

"Brock, all of these people came to see this?"

"This is a tremendous accomplishment. The mantle of Guardian is no easy thing to attain. The training far exceeds that of normal soldiers. Seldom are there ever multiple oaths taken at a time, but tonight there will be five. It is a happening that has not been seen for many decades," he replied.

"Five? Who are they?"

Just as she asked there was a mighty roar from the crowd. Brock had landed close. They were perhaps only fifty yards from a raised mound of dirt in front of the seats.

257

Between them and the mound stood a large roped off circle of sand, forming what looked like an arena. The majority of the crowd around them was made up of soldiers.

"There they are now, little sister."

Angelica looked up to the mound, where a line of men stood, expressionless with their arms behind their backs. They wore the white capes of the Guardian, forcing Angelica to guess that they were important officers. There was no sign of William however, so she looked back to Brock. His eyes were raised to the sky, so she followed his gaze.

As she looked up into the clouds a crash like thunder split the air, and five shapes appeared, hurtling towards them like meteors. A shrill sound followed as they approached, not unlike jets that roared over Angelica's apartment growing up. When they struck the ground the crowd roared with such ferocity that Angelica thought that she would go deaf. She covered her ears and tried to glimpse the mound through the people jumping and flailing their arms in the air.

When the crowd began to settle she saw him, her breath catching in her throat. He'd changed so much that she barely recognized him. The last time she saw him his hair had been buzzed down to the scalp. It had grown out since, which she thought was a welcomed change. Light stubble covered his cheeks and chin, making him look older. But it was his gleaming steel armor that marked the biggest change. It was darker than the armor of those around him, its sharp edges looking far different from that of the other recruits. There was a certain ferocity to it. A large sword was strapped onto his back, matching the business-like expression on his face.

He was the only one who didn't wave. The other four, made up of three men and a smaller woman, couldn't seem to get enough of the crowd. Angelica's stomach twisted when she saw the woman grab William by the arm, and give him a smile. Then she stood on a tiptoe and whispered something into his ear.

Who is this woman, Angelica wondered, forcing down a jolt of jealousy. She barely even noticed that Brock was still next to her.

"That big one is Ulifrig, and the small one next to him is Samuel. The really skinny one is the Spaniard, Juarez, and the woman is Katrina. She is a feisty one. And of course we both know William," Brock said, clapping along with the crowd.

"Katrina, huh?" Angelica repeated her name aloud, but was drowned out by the applause.

Soon the guardian standing in the middle of the mound raised a hand, all of the crowd almost instantly falling silent. The man's voice boomed across the open field, as if he spoke through an invisible megaphone.

"Citizens of Helios. We are gathered here on the eve of Sunday, on the third week of Sedetoch, to bear witness to five young souls swear oaths to the land and people of Archonia. I ask that you remain silent as the words are spoken. Once complete our warriors will prove their strength and valor in the arena. Their words will be sealed in the fire of combat, and their loyalty to the safety of the realm displayed for all to see."

His voice faded off and, and the grounds fell silent. Five small orbs appeared before the new guardians, and they all knelt before them. Their voices carried over the distance, ringing loud and clear. And in unison, their words rang:

I guard the innocent
I guard the light
I will not feign at evil's might

I speak the truth when faced with death
And strive for honor with every breath

I don my armor and now crusade
To see laws of gods and men obeyed

From now 'til death I solemnly swear
To guard against darkness everywhere.

A chill ran down Angelica's spine as the last word of the oath continued to reverberate across the valley.

She suddenly longed to speak with him alone, and congratulate him in private. But her thoughts were interrupted by a terrifying sound. A tremble started in the ground, and then the very dirt beneath them began to quake. Soon the screams followed, and the only other thing that Angelica saw was the gleam of William's sword as it left its sheath.

Fire and debris rained upon the crowd, just as Brock Scooped Angelica up in his arms, and they were in the air. Her insides squished to the bottom of her body, and she shrieked. She had never felt the effects of flying in a space shuttle before but if she had to imagine how it would feel it felt like this. When Brock gently set her down she collapsed to her knees and promptly vomited.

"Oh dear, little sister, I'm sorry. I wanted to make sure you were safe. Those foolish conjurers and their ridiculous beasts. They need to learn to keep them under control."

"Its fine," she said, getting to her feet and trying to brush the dirt and soot off her dress. "Angie, oh my goodness, are you okay?" her grandmother asked, rushing over.

"Yes, Abuela, I'm fine."

"You don't look fine!" Angelina said, scowling.

Her grandmother waved her hand over Angelica's dress, and the soot and dust disappeared.

"Abuela, this is Brock, he is a guardian I met on my first day here. He looked after me."

"What were you thinking? How dare you take my granddaughter so close to that...to that," her grandmother stammered, a red flush covering her cheeks. She was interrupted by a dreadful shriek, followed by a roar of the crowd. They watched from a distance as the massive beast collapsed.

Cheers erupted from the remaining crowd, and then a voice boomed above the roar, amplified by some unknown means. "The guardians are victorious!"

"Such savagery," Angelica said again.

"What's savage? asked an all too familiar voice.

"Angelica and her grandmother jumped in response, but Brock smiled.

"William of Archonia, Guardian of the realm. Well done, little brother!" Brock said.

"William!" Angelica shouted, jumping up and grabbing him in a hug. It was difficult to hold onto him with his bulky armor, but he held her up a moment then set her down, as if her weight hardly bothered him.

"How did you get over here so fast? Angelica asked.

"I've gotten quicker. How was the show?" he asked.

"That was what I was referring to as savage," she replied, her tone a little drier than she intended.

"Well, sometimes a little savagery is needed," William replied with a wink.

And then Angelica noticed it, the biggest change in him. He was happy. He was confident. Gone was the beaten down, broken husk. He was a completely new man.

"Congratulations, young Guardian," Angelina said, walking up to him and giving him a hug.

Angelica caught William staring at her in confusion. He pointed from her to her grandmother, as if to ask a question.

"Abuela, this is William. William this is my grandmother, Angelina."

"Silly girl, I know who he is. You saved my granddaughter from a fate worse than death. I will forever be in your debt," she said with candor.

"To be honest, your granddaughter saved me too. But thank you, I'm glad I could help," William said, beaming.

"Shall we all go enjoy the night's festivities? I have heard the cuisine in Valhalla is divine," Angelina offered.

"That sounds fantastic. I have the rest of the night off," William said.

Angelica walked close to William, who seemed to want to move far too fast for her. He continuously apologized, telling her that he was used to moving fast now. They all eventually made it back to the party which was far more involved and spectacular than anything she'd ever seen before. Tables were spread across the hall, while magnificently dressed chefs stood behind them, projecting delectable dishes as fast as people could eat. William filled Angelica a plate of food, for fear of letting her get too close to the hungry soldiers.

She was driven by the urge to stay so close to him, even going so far as to wrap her arms around one of his. He didn't seem to mind. William spent most of the evening accepting congratulatory salutes or handshakes. She finally got him alone for a moment when a magnificent show began. Nearly one hundred trapeze artists and acrobats descended from the ceiling. Each wore colorful garb, wowing the crowd with unique talents. A juggler tossed twenty balls into the air, while a man zoomed around, doing acrobatics with a flying carpet. A woman danced by Angelica, projecting wonderful creatures that zipped around the room. They watched for a bit before Angelica pulled William aside.

"Hey, I'm sorry I've been so distracted. Thank you so much for coming," he said.

"You're welcome! I wanted to be here for you, this is a very big deal."

"I mean my life kind of depended on it." William said, letting out a tense breath.

"I'm very proud of you."

"That means a lot. I pretty much owe all of this to you though. I wouldn't be here without you," William said.

He stared deeply into her eyes, her face suddenly growing hot.

"...I just feel bad that it has been so hard for you here."

"Don't worry about it. Now that I am a sworn guardian things should get easier. People will quit harassing me."

"Just watch out for that creep in the purple cape...Meredox. I saw him earlier tonight and he didn't have anything nice to say about you. I tried to defend you, but I may have just made things worse. I don't know."

"You spoke to Meredox? Where is he?" William asked, his eyes narrowing.

Before Angelica could say anything William was off through the crowd. She immediately regretted bring Meredox up at all.

She followed after him, pushing her way through the crowds as fast as she could. But she was too late. She could hear yelling before she was anywhere close.

"How do you like me now, you purple-caped prick!?" William shouted above the crowd.

"Stand down, Guardian," another voice shouted in response. This one she didn't recognize. Finally she pushed her way to the front of the scene.

Two men held William back, as he struggled to get to Meredox. The Adjudicator stood a few paces away, his arms crossed over his chest and a smirk on his face.

"See here, good people of Archonia! Look how quickly this tainted soul rushes to anger. Do you really want him guarding the realm? This whole ceremony is a farce," Meredox spat.

"You're the fucking farce, Meredox! Don't stain my name with your tongue...just stay away from me, understand?" William roared.

Angelica tried to run to William, but was blocked by a wall of shiny metal armor.

"William!" she shouted.

"Stay back please, miss, this guardian is being taken into custody.

CHAPTER SEVENTEEN
THE GUARDIAN

Dust motes flew through the air, made visible by rays from the intense, Archonian sun. A full day had passed since their initiation ceremony, and William and his friends had fought valiantly in the arena.

Katrina agreed that the spectacle put too many people in danger. The conjurers summoned three beasts that ripped forth from the ground. Easily fifty feet tall, they were black as coal, with large, boney wings and horns protruding from their heads. They appeared more than a little demon-like in nature.

In their yearning for spectacle, the Conjurers hadn't stopped to consider the crowd, most specifically those closest to the arena. Those unfortunates were showered with fiery debris, causing a fair amount of injuries, and ultimately sent the crowds fleeing. In the end, not many people actually bore witness to the young guardian's stunning victory.

"You're free to go soldier, no more outbursts like that or next time we will leave you to the Adjudicators justice," said a guardian lieutenant.

William tossed the atlas ball on the ground, and tried to get up, but felt frozen in place. His mouth was parched and his entire body was numb. He considered the punishment worthwhile. After all, he'd finally been able to tell that overstuffed peacock Meredox, how he really felt. He did regret not being able to see Angelica, but there would be time for that moving forward.

After a few tries he got up and worked the ache out of his legs, wincing with the first few steps. Eventually he made it back to the guardian barracks, where he doubled over into a meditation mat and almost instantly fell into a trance.

* * *

William thought that everything would change after they had said their words, but in fact very little did. Their training picked up where it left off, battering them day and night with sparring drills, the elements, or their captain.

At the week's end all of Archonia celebrated a day referred to as Dua Da Medatante, which translated roughly into *day of rest*. This was the one day that afforded guardian's unrestricted liberties.

William spent much of his time in extra training, or exploring Valhalla. Recently, he and his friends decided to explore the library for information supporting William's theory, and devise a plan to expose the truth about Meredox and the obelisks.

William pored over a book about the War of Souls. It was a historical record, but read more like an adventure, and William found it difficult to stop reading. The narrator explained that the war broke out, with Ares and Hades allied against Thor and Anubis. The Archons fought to maintain peace, condemning both sides, but after witnessing the slaughter they had no choice but to step in and end the conflict Prometheus and Lucifer started. It ultimately ended with the Archon's destruction and the creation of the twin obelisks, separating the two worlds. William was so engrossed in the story that he was startled when Katrina spoke.

"That's it, William," she said, slamming a book on the table.

"There is absolutely nothing in the Archonian histories that suggest the obelisks could be at risk. Look it says right here: For the Archons were twins, and shared one heart, only their power together could create a power great enough. And so it was that Brahma and Ammun brother and sister transformed, and a bright light spread over all of Archonia. This light would ward those who were not fit to dwell amongst the pure kin of Prometheus."

"But..." William tried to counter, but Katrina cut back in.

"The two Archon's power created an impenetrable shield against corrupted souls."

"...Gabriel brought me in," William finally managed to say, cutting in.

"Yes, William but you're not corrupted. Your soul is gray, not black. Gabriel bringing you here proved that you have the right to live here," she said.

"Or, it proves that there are ways around the shield," William retorted.

"Either way, William, we need proof," Juarez offered.

Katrina nodded in approval.

"Okay. Well let's get some proof," William shot back, rubbing his hands together.

"What do you have in mind?" Katrina asked, skeptically.

"The other night when I woke you two, I saw Meredox handing something to his partner. We need to break into Meredox's private quarters and find out what it is," he said.

Juarez chuckled nervously. "You must be joking, William. That is against the law."

"But, what if it is to serve the greater good?" William asked, pleading. "I believe sometimes good people are forced do a little evil to serve that greater good."

William waited for a response or rebuttal, but none came.

He sighed, "Okay. I won't ask you to break any laws, but I will need your help."

Juarez nodded, Katrina following suit.

"I need a distraction," William said with a grin.

"What kind of distraction?" Katrina asked.

"I need one of you to ring the warning bell."

"It is forbidden to ring the bell, William. That would be breaking the law as well," Katrina offered flatly.

William shook his head, and set a book on the table in front of them. Then he put his finger on an excerpt and read. "The warning bell of Valhalla is one of four identical bells created to call the armies of Archonia to arms during the War of Souls. Any Archonian can ring the bell if Archonia is in need.

"Interesting wording, William," Juarez smiled. "I will do this for you."

William shook his head. "I need Katrina to do this for me. She will be the only one fast enough to get away unseen after the bell is rung. Even if Archonia is in need there are those who would probably not agree. Juarez, I need you to tail Meredox and see where he goes after the warning goes off. If he thinks something is coming we need to know where it will be from, and I have a feeling he will lead you to it," he said.

Juarez nodded.

"During the commotion I will slip into the Adjudicator wing, and find the proof I need," William finished, triumphantly.

"This is a risky plan, William," Katrina said. "I will have to run clear around the castle and come back to make it look like I am being called to arms as well."

"You're fast enough," William offered confidently

Katrina nodded, apprehension pulling her face tight

"What if Meredox realizes I am following him?" Juarez asked.

"Don't say anything. If you remain silent, then you won't be lying, and you won't give me away," William responded quickly.

"Okay, when do we act?" Juarez asked.

"Next week. On our day of rest. People will be at their most relaxed, and there should be fewer sentinels on duty, because of their day of rest rotation. But first, we need to do a little recon," William said excitedly.

"What is recon?" Katrina asked.

"Uh... scouting," William corrected. "Juarez I can understand you speaking Spanish but you guys don't get when I use some words. What gives?" William asked.

"Did every English speaking person from Earth understand your way of speaking all the time?" Juarez asked.

No, most of the British sounded like crazy people.

"Yeah, William, if recon is short for reconnaissance then I get it," Katrina said.

"Ugh," William replied.

"Amigo, it will take some years, but eventually you will start speaking so that everyone can understand. It will happen naturally," Juarez said.

"Okay fine, back to the task at hand. First, we need to find out everything we can about Benjamin, and what his relationship is with Meredox. They are consorting about something, and we need to find out what his role is in all of this," William said to his two friends.

After they smoothed out some of the finer details and separated tasks to one another they headed back to the barracks.

William settled in to meditate, but found that he was far too anxious about Meredox and their secret missions to uncover his plot. So he settled in and continued to read a lengthy tome that he had borrowed from the library. It was titled "The war of souls". The details of the battles and the tactics were certainly useful information, beyond the historical significance, along with whatever information he could gleam as to Meredox's motivations. Beyond all that, he was genuinely interested in the story.

Anubis had not been the mightiest of warriors, but he possessed defensive prowess, especially for creating shields.

When he focused he could shield several thousand soldiers at the same time Next, his troops formed an impenetrable phalanx formation, locking shield and spear, cutting through wave after wave of desecrated souls. His techniques were so effective that they turned the tide of the war, but only for a time. On the opposing side, Ares proved to be no novice to military strategy. He commissioned his followers to create massive creatures called wyrms, and used them to smash through Anubis' defensive formations.

William continued to read with such enthusiasm that someone cleared their throat, and startled him. Brock walked up and plopped down on one of the sofas across from him in the common room.

"Awfully late, little brother. That must be some tale."

"Yeah, it's about the War of Souls."

"Well, no wonder. Those were glorious days," he said, sprawling out on the sofa, which looked far too small for his sizable frame.

"Hundreds of thousands of souls were obliterated. You call that glorious?" William asked darkly.

"Forgive me, young one. We come from different times. I know that one should not relish the thought of such bloodshed, but many times I wish that I had been there. I believe I could have made a real difference."

This made William smile. "Yeah, me too."

"Instead, I crusade once a year, rarely meeting the enemy in combat," Brock replied callously.

"How do you go back?"

"Not easily. The realm between worlds is a dark place...ripe with terror around every corner."

"Does anyone ever take their crusade to Dichonia?" William asked, trying not to sound too interested.

Brock looked him over incredulously. "William, no. That is a place of pure evil, far more dangerous than any place imaginable. Only one soul has ever gone there, and returned."

William didn't press the subject further. He could tell that it bothered his large friend. Instead, he asked a question that had been nagging at him since he had formulated his little plan.

"Brock...If you knew in your heart that something had to be done, even if you were to be persecuted for it, would you do it?" William sat up, and put the book down.

To his surprise, Brock chuckled heartily. "Little brother, that is the very essence of being a guardian. Putting the good of the collective before yourself."

This was all the reassurance that William needed. Though he was confident that his friend had no idea of his intentions were with Meredox. The two remained in silence for a time, until Brock rubbed his face and announced that he needed to leave.

William watched him walk out, wondering what the elder guardian did in his free time. Brock barely meditated anymore. He could only imagine that filling the time must be difficult. As for his own meditation, William soon drifted off, the War of Souls repeating over and over again.

For the next week William and his friends did everything they could do to prepare for their mission. Katrina watched the sentinels who guarded the bell tower, and learned that only one guard stood post on the day of rest. Those guards changed only once during the evening hours, always on the top of the fortieth hour. She would swoop in and hit the bell during their change.

Meanwhile, Juarez watched Meredox every night while the others meditated. This assignment suited him, as he had been in Archonia longer, and needed the least meditation. Katrina nosed around, carefully listening and asking questions, and learned that Benjamin was another high level Justicar, ironically enough, whom Meredox had mentored. The two became extraordinarily close as master and pupil, and from what she heard, thought of each other as brothers.

271

William spent his time scouring the castle for clues, searching for Meredox's private quarters. Some of the higher level officers were given their own quarters in the castle. He finally had to ask a sentinel if he knew where the Grand Justicar's private quarters were. The sentinel told him.

"He resides in the Adjudicators wing, of course."

To his dismay, William was also told that guardians weren't allowed in the Adjudicator's wing. Primarily because Adjudicator initiates resided within, and were undergoing a ritual they referred to as "The Purge".

William asked Juarez, who defined the process as brainwashing and reprogramming someone, in order to be perfect machines of the law.

"They purge them of opinion, and make them completely selfless, so the law might be upheld perfectly. Outside interference was not allowed. Apparently the process takes years, which is why the path of the Adjudicator is so difficult," Juarez had told him.

After learning about the purge, William was very happy that the Synod hadn't seen fit to send him down that path.

"Meredox's private quarters are in the Adjudicators wing as we have feared," William said, once their laborious Windday drills had finally ended.

"Then there is no way we are getting in, not even with a distraction," Katrina half-yelled.

"We can't give up now. Look, I've devised a little plan that I think will gain me access to the Adjudicator's library."

He had been daydreaming in one of his lectures, when his plan started to come together. He would ask Chang Fei for permission to study in the Hall of the Adjudicators library, to learn more about Archonian laws. He quickly explained the plan to his friends. Juarez gave a little half-smile, while Katrina scoffed.

"Do you guys have your part of the plan figured out?" William asked, ignoring their lack of support.

"Yeah, William, I know the guard changes like the back of my hand," Katrina said dismissively.

"Affirmative, amigo. I have been working on trailing people at a distance. I am confident he won't notice me for a while... unless we get out in the open."

William's confidence sored. His part of the plan was going to be the flimsiest, so he knew he had to utilize just the right approach. The following day he carefully approached Chang Fei.

"Why do you need access to the Library?" Chang Fei asked, his face a stern mask.

The two walked out of the castle, headed to the fields for drill.

"In my special forces unit we were taught that, in order to achieve victory, we needed to know our enemies as well as we know ourselves. How can I know my enemies, if I don't know what my allies are capable of?" William asked.

Chang Fei stared off into the distance, before turning his piercing gaze on William.

"Come with me," he said, swiftly taking off down the corridor.

William followed the captain, his newly acquired speed helping him keep pace. The two flew past the first two floors of the castle devoted to housing. Here, the majority of the sentinels, the largest branch of the military, lived. They flew past the guardian's barracks on the fourth floor, past Adjudicator's wing on the fifth, before moving past two floors William had never been to. Finally when it seemed they were at the pinnacle of the castle, they came upon a single, broad door. It was smooth, dark mahogany with a symbol carved in it. One that William didn't recognize.

Chang Fei approached the door, and with a steady fist, knocked an unusual series of beats. A slot appeared in the door at eye level. A face peered out at them at them for a moment. The slot shut quickly, and the door swung open. Chang Fei walked inside, and William followed.

"Where are we?" William asked.

"Achilles private quarters," Chang Fei said.

William's heart skipped a beat.

Oh crap, I'm screwed.

He followed Chang Fei, who was now escorted down a short hall by a heavily armored guard. William started to regret his request, his heartrate increasing to an uncomfortable level. They entered another room, where two stone-faced guards swung open the doors anticipation of their entry.

William walked into a space he didn't entirely expect. At first he thought they would be entering an office, but instead the space looked more like a training room. There were weapon racks and weights against the wall, and the floor was covered with mats. Men wrestled and sparred. These men looked tougher than any soldiers he had yet encountered.

William spotted Achilles in the center of five men, whom were all attempting to attack him. William's eyes could barely track the lightning movements. Achilles' fluid motions were graceful and brutal at the same time, flattening the five men assaulting him in an instant.

After a moment's pause the ancient warrior stood up in a relaxed position and looked over at William and Chang Fei. Then he motioned with two fingers that they should approach.

"What is it?" Achilles asked after Chang Fei bowed.

William followed suit, but it was delayed and more than a little awkward.

"This recruit has requested entry to the Library of the Adjudicator, to become better acquainted with his allies," the Chinese warlord stated.

Achilles looked William over.

"So, it seems there is more to you than simply rage," he said.

William nodded.

"I would like to see your armor," Achilles said, his voice soft but strong.

William looked around. The men stopped sparring, and looked at him. He felt the blood rush to his head, but he did his best to stifle his embarrassment.

He flexed, and felt the energy within flow freely. Then he thrust his arms out, and felt the satisfying rush as the solid metal materialized out of thin air, and clung to his body. His sword appeared, the familiar weight falling on his back. The etchings inset in his armor and sword glowed briefly, like they were alive with a dancing inner fire.

"Well done, young one," Achilles said, a slight smile breaking across his face.

William stood awkwardly, fully armored, in full plate and mail while the rest of the group stared in silence. Chang Fei approached Achilles, and whispered something in his ear. Achilles' eyes never left William, and his emotion never changed. Chang Fei turned and addressed William.

"Report for drills when you have concluded your business with the commander," he said, disappearing into the passage in a blur of color. Achilles turned and began walking and talking. William jumped into motion, quickly following after him.

"Your captain tells me that you wish to study in the hall of the Adjudicator, to learn your allies, to know yourself, so that your enemies may not have an edge against you," Achilles said, his piercing blue eyes studying him.

William looked around at the other men, who had returned to their sparring without a word. Achilles followed his gaze.

"They train for their crusades. My myrmidons go on two crusades a year, instead of the traditional one. I demand my men be the best in every aspect."

"They seem tough," William said casually.

Achilles smiled.

"Leave us," The ancient Greek warrior said, and almost immediately everyone in the room disappeared in a flash.

A long, uncomfortable moment of silence stretched between them. William struggled, trying to decide what to say.

"I am a warrior, young Guardian, but do not think me a fool. You seek more in the Adjudicator's wing than the library," Achilles said, finally breaking the silence.

William stammered, his mind running in circles, trying to decide on a lie or the truth. He finally gave up, and decided to tell the truth.

"My lord, there is a plot that threatens our world, and nobody believes me. It is my intention to discover the truth for myself," William said, staring straight ahead and avoided the guardian master's gaze. William was surprised at the confidence ringing in his voice, especially with his heart pumping so fast. He was afraid that Achilles would shut his plan down, and worse...

"You're full of surprises, William of Archonia. I was ready to bet all the gold in Archonia that you were going to lie to me, as you did your captain," Achilles said.

"I didn't lie to the captain, my lord. In this case, knowing my ally better would directly help me know my enemy better. It is coincidental that our ally is also the enemy," William offered.

"It seems you have a silver tongue, young one. I respect the cleverness of your ploy," he said, before walking slowly into the next room and motioning William to follow.

The next room was small and held a desk and a large chair. Achilles walked behind it, took a piece of parchment and a pen, and began to write.

"I wish to know more of your plan, but I am afraid that it will fail...in which case I would be assisting a traitor to Archonia. I feel I must warn you of the obvious. Meddling like this will lead to conflict," Achilles said, finishing his writing.

He held up the parchment, extending it towards William. He took it and scanned over the writing quickly. It was a writ of passage into the Adjudicator's wing, to study in the library. A wave of excitement blossomed inside William, and as he looked at the commander he barely stifled a smiled. Achilles' face remained stiff, and William quickly looked away.

"My lord, something is coming and I have to find out what it is. I think that conflict will be inevitable, and that it will be more than anyone is prepared for," William said.

Achilles nodded, and William turned to leave. As he did, Achilles spoke.

"Only the very wise may enter the hall of the Adjudicator."

William didn't turn back, but only paused, and then walked out.

***

Brock entered the room after watching William leave. He strode over to Achilles desk and waited for his commander to acknowledge his entrance.

"Captain," Achilles said, not looking up.

"Commander, do you think it wise to let the young guardian risk so much?"

"I figured you would be glad that someone is following up on your concerns. You and Captain Fei seemed convinced that your recruits fought and destroyed Tera-spawn on their climb to the Greige Forge."

Brock paused, studying the commander's nearly unreadable expression. He thought on his words carefully.

"Commander, I could have been wrong. Their description of the beasts seemed so accurate. They were waylaid much longer than expected on the climb. I...I don't know," Brock said, his brow furrowed in fear and confusion.

"Captain you have a keen instinct. We must get to the bottom of this, even if it is conjecture. I will not let any threat to the realm go uninvestigated. For now the tainted soul is doing the dirty work. He knows the rules and still seeks to willingly break them. His actions will circumvent days of official inquiry in which evidence of any treachery could be destroyed."

"You would use this young soul who is seeking to find his way?" Brock asked, incredulously.

He holds the Archon's favor. I have a feeling things will turn out fine for our new soldier. You are dismissed, Captain."

Brock saluted and backed out of the room. His flight back the mead hall was fraught with concern. Just before he passed into the hall where he could already hear the merriment commencing, he silently promised himself that he would keep a closer eye on William.

CHAPTER EIGHTEEN
THE TRAITOR

A bead of sweat trickled down William's face. Whether it was from the heat of the sun or his anxiety, he didn't know. He had been granted leave to study in the library of the Adjudicator, but he still needed to prepare his mind for the greater task at hand.

His mind swirled with the possibilities. What exactly would he be looking for? Would there be any evidence at all? Was he just chasing shadows? He sat in the Hall of Heroes, contemplating what he needed to do and trying to work it into a series of tasks he could understand.

The hall spanned above and around him, larger than almost every other single chamber in Valhalla. It was a place of feasting and celebration, where depictions of Archonia's mightiest heroes adorned the walls. The space made him feel horribly small, and with the monumental task of investigating Meredox's corruption looming like a mountain of stone above him, that wasn't a good thing.

Samuel and Ulifrig sat on either side of him, eating their breakfast. William barely touched his food. Most of it was far too rich for a simple breakfast. He looked over the many platters laid out on the hall's table. It was covered in herb-butter marinated swan, suckling pig broiled with garlic cloves, crepes stuffed with fresh fruit and butter and sugar glazed pastries of every kind. He would have given anything for a simple sausage biscuit. Instead, he listlessly picked over some of the entrees, before finally getting up and leaving.

Juarez and Katrina were lost in the newfound glory and daily tasks of being guardians, and for the most part, avoided William and his mission. He wondered if they thought he would pursue it, find no evidence, and hopefully, move on. This thought annoyed him, and instead of driving himself to anger, he decided not to now dwell on it. He needed to act.

William politely took his leave from the hall and made his way towards the Adjudicator's wing. It was effectively cut off from the rest of the castle, accessible by a single door on the fourth floor.

"What knowledge do you seek in the hall of the Adjudicator?" asked a man, standing before the massive set of double doors.

The doors were clad in gold with detailed, purple engravings spanning their impressive height - above the man stood an inscription, similar to the one on the guardian's door. It read: Only the wise may enter.

William spoke with confidence. "I am here to study the laws of Archonia. I have a writ of passage from Achilles himself, stating that I may do so with an escort, so I don't disturb the initiates in training."

The Adjudicator took the writ, and smiled.

"Very well, tainted one. You may enter," he said, before floating out of the way and gesturing towards the door.

A hiccup marred William's step. Perhaps this door was like the guardian's door. Powerful forces had barred him entry until he'd passed his initiation.

Only the wise, William thought, and pushed on the doors.

Thankfully, the doors swung open easily He turned and smiled at the guard, who threw him a scowl.

"It appears you're worthy, tainted one. I shall send for an escort," he spat, before lifting a hand and releasing a beam of light down the long hall. A woman appeared a few moments later, wearing very simple robes of green and gold. Her hair was a nest of tangles and she had a crazy look in her violet eyes.

"Hello, tainted one. May I have your writ of passage?" she asked, politely.

"I have a name," William said as he handed her the scroll. Their refusal to use his name was seriously starting to aggravate him.

"Forgive me, William," she said, looking over the writ. "I have heard only rumors about you, and was under the impression that is what they refer to you as. I am Sylvia." She gave William a genuine smile and curtseyed.

She led William down a hall and into a very large room filled with more books than William had ever seen. Stone shelves two stories high lined the walls, holding what he believed to be millions of books. Fresh new murals covered the walls, while statues of famous Adjudicators bracketed each groups of the shelving. An aisle separated the sides of the room from the rows of tables, where many people were already hard at work poring over mounds of books and scrolls. Most stopped, turning to look at him in wonder.

I must look like some kind of freak to them, he thought.

"Do I have something on my face?" William asked a man nearby, who openly stared at him with no discretion.

The man flinched, looked embarrassed, and went back to his studies.

"What is it that you wish to study, Guardian?" Sylvia asked.

"Well, Sylvia," William began, slowly, "I think, and lord Achilles agreed, that the Guardians need to learn more about their jurisdiction when it comes to protecting Archonia."

"Of course, dear William," she said as she swept over to a book case. "This section is devoted to jurisdictional grievances brought before the Synod throughout Archonian history. It is quite a fascinating subject."

"I'm sure it is," William responded, sarcastically.

"I will leave you to your studies then. I do advise that you to stay in the library wing. The rest of the hall is forbidden to you," she said, her voice small and squeaky.

William's eyes got very wide in disbelief as she explained the obvious.

"Thank you, Sylvia," he said as if speaking to a young child.

William spent his entire day perusing books written by Meredox himself. Evidently he had served as a Grand Justicar for four hundred and fifty years, before that a Justicar for three hundred, and also a judge. And most judges of the age had never seen any real combat since the obelisks had been created. William continued reading engrossed in the tales about Meredox. He found a memo amongst the pages written by none other than his history professor Laurence Echard.

A bill came before the Synod to invade hell and bring a group of fallen Archonians to justice. Before he had become an Adjudicator, Meredox and his brother had lived in Archonia in peace. This was at a time before the rigid rules quit letting every soul pass into this land. You see, not all people who are welcomed here stay. Some went bad. Perhaps they got bored or tired, but they fell into darkness, and brought sorrow to many.

One of these was Meredox's brother Luxor. Meredox vowed he would bring his brother to justice, and so took the path of the soldier. The Synod saw fit to send Meredox, and a group of the finest warriors to hell to destroy these fallen Archonians. The warriors were obliterated. Only Meredox made it back, barely alive. To this day the Grand Justicar would not say what they had faced in Dichonia. He only saw fit to propose the creation of the Guardian Corps to create a more fearsome soldier to battle the forces of hell should they ever break through.

Laurence Echard of Helios

That treacherous bastard, William thought to himself, slamming his fist on the table and leaving a crater in the stone tabletop. Clearly Meredox had led his fellow Archonian soldiers into a trap. *There is no way he would kill his own brother.*

Some adjudicators looked at him in surprise and annoyance, and he slowly covered the dent in the table with a book. William could no longer focus on the books, so he got up, and decided to look around the hall he put his books away, before heading towards an exit as casually as he could. He thought he was home free when he had passed out of the hall, but his hope died away quickly as he rounded a corner

"Tainted one," Meredox said his voice smooth and quiet. "What in the name of the gods are you doing here?"

"My lord," William said, bowing low, and saluting with one fist over his chest. He knew that he had to treat his superiors with the utmost respect, especially after his outburst at the ceremony. "I have a writ of passage to study in the Adjudicator's library."

"Yes, Sylvia told me, however, the library is not here," Meredox said, his face not betraying any emotion.

"My lord I..." William began, but Meredox cut him off.

"Curiosity is not a sin, tainted one. Come with me," he said, walking past him.

William followed the Grand Justicar warily. He knew he was in no place to refuse.

"How fares your training, young Guardian?" Meredox asked calmly.

He caught William off guard, who simply said, "fine my lord," and paused.

"It's very interesting...the words you speak, and the way you say them," Meredox said, walking steadily down winding halls.

William was trying to memorize every passage, but there were so many, and they all looked so similar.

"The era from which you hail must be very interesting as well," Meredox continued.

"No one should ever have to live where I'm from," William replied bitterly, shaking his head.

"Yes, I saw a glimpse of this life at the trial, all those many months ago. We all saw the suffering you endured," the Grand Justicar said, not flinching.

They came to a stop in front of a small set of doors. He opened them, light flooding the already lit hallway.

"These are my private quarters," Meredox said. "Please come in."

William struggled to hide his shock, but also his nervousness.

That was easy, he thought. *I found his private quarters.*

The rooms appeared to be very decadently appointed. Rich tapestry hung from the walls, while bookshelves lined with trinkets and treasures took up the remaining space. It felt very warm and inviting compared to the vast, dark halls of Valhalla.

"These are fine quarters, sir," William said.

"Thank you. Perhaps one day you will have your own quarters," Meredox said, turning to a bookshelf. "But I didn't bring you here for idle chatter, tainted one. I would like you to answer my original question. Why are you here? What are you seeking in the library of the Adjudicators?" he asked, not looking at William.

A long moment of silence passed, and Meredox began looking for something on his shelves.

"I wanted to learn more about Archonia, specifically the Adjudicators," William said, skirting the truth but avoiding an outright lie.

"Do you know that I have a gift, young one?" Meredox asked, casually.

"No," William said slowly.

"Yes. It is rather useful. You see, I can tell if someone is lying. I have had centuries of practice. All the human signs, the *tells*, are on your body right now. You still lack the discipline to mask them. The tension that is in your body shows in your muscles, while the sudden flush of blood in your face betrays you. Even if they weren't so painstakingly represented, I can see inside you. I can see your soul, and do you know what I see?" he asked.

William fought the urge to turn and flee, keeping his face emotionless and resisting the impulse to make eye contact with Meredox, even when the man got right in his face. The tension was staggering, and William's heart could barely handle it. His thoughts screamed move! Act! But he used every ounce of determination to resist.

"I came here to learn more about *you*," William said, letting his gaze slide up to Meredox's eyes. Meredox smiled and stepped back.

"I do not trust you, tainted one. Twice today you have been very close to lying to me. Do you know the punishment for lying?" he asked.

William shrugged. As he did, Meredox produced a long metal object from a case.

"We mark you as a liar," the Justicar said, brandishing the metal rod in the air, before pressing it into his own skin. He screwed up his face in mock pain.

So, it's a branding iron.

William didn't flinch, nor would he speak and incriminate himself. Meredox studied him closely, waiting for a reaction. Finally, he took a step back and continued.

"You're doing well, tainted one, but know this. If you ever even think about breaking our laws, I will be there, and rain down swift retribution. Now go," he said, turning and placing the iron back in its case.

William saluted, bowed, and exited the chambers. Sylvia appeared out of thin air as soon as he stepped into the hall. She quietly escorted him to the entrance of the hall.

* * *

The whole encounter had left William exhausted. Yet he was eager to tell his friends the news. He raced outside to the training grounds, where he knew Katrina and Juarez would be. They were sparring, and from the looks of it Katrina was winning.

"I have you again," she said triumphantly, pinning Juarez to the ground.

"Guys!" William shouted.

The two turned, looking at him in surprise.

"I have news." He then proceeded to tell them all that had occurred in the hall of the Adjudicators.

"I can't believe it. I didn't know anyone could even pass through the barrier between Archonia and Dichonia," Juarez said in disbelief.

"Apparently anyone pure enough to live in Archonia can pass in or out through that door. I think that is why Gabe is fighting for more people to come live here," William reasoned.

"I think I finally believe you, William," Katrina said. "I have been reading about the creatures that dwell in Dichonia. I do not think that anybody could have survived there. Even Meredox," she stated.

"There are only a few days until the day of rest. We must be prepared," William said.

The group spent the next few days going through the motions of training, but they held back, conserving strength and energy. Meditation on the eve of the day of rest was difficult, as they struggled to relax and clarify their thoughts. When meditation failed them, William, Katrina, and Juarez fell back into familiar hobbies. Juarez had a knack for painting, and Katrina had her piano. William had his as well, but didn't do it in the daylight hours. When he could get away, he would visit the Garden of Medina, and work on projecting plants as life-like as he possibly could. He had been meeting Angelica there regularly now. William descended from the sky, spotting her instantly.

"Angelica. How are you?" he asked.

She smiled and said, "I'm great. Look at you, flying through the sky."

William smirked and felt his face flush hot. "That's not the half of it," he said. He looked around, to make sure there wasn't anyone watching.

William held his hand out to Angelica. His gray light shot forth, slowly molding into a simple, beautiful flower. He picked it up and handed it to Angelica.

"You like showing off?" she asked, smelling it.

"Only if it works," William said, lightly.

He had made the flower smell like a salty ocean breeze one of his favorite memories of his time abroad in the military.

"...what have you been up to?" he asked casually as they walked towards the open sky. Despite his strength and prowess, he found the idea of talking to Angelica nerve wracking, like he was an awkward teenager again.

"Hmm. I have been attending classes, as you know," she said.

"This world is still not what you were expecting?" William asked, as soon as her voice trailed off.

"Most definitely not. I think that it's wonderful, but I couldn't believe that I had it so wrong...well, you know," she said, sighing.

"Come on. You weren't that far off. You believed in a life after death. I think that you had it pretty close. All religions on Earth do. They all agree that you should be a good person and give of yourself. They all believe in a life after death. They just have some of the details mixed up. I mean with so many different religions, some were bound to

287

mess up the details here and there," William said, comfortingly.

"Yes, you're right," she said, softly.

They continued to talk for hours. Angelica had been as busy as William, though her path was considerably more peaceful. In addition to her classes, she attended religious studies and groups.

"Do you know that religions here believe that after this life you will be united with the creators, as they called them? I've gone on three pilgrimages already, and visited nearly all the great cities of Archonia. It's so wonderful, William. I wish that you could see it too!" Angelica said, excitedly.

William watched her walk, taking in her enthusiasm and energy. He'd only read about most of what she'd seen and done. For example, the city of Ionia, which lay on the farthest eastern boundaries of the world, at the borders of Oblivion, was home to one of the obelisks. Then to the west it's twin city, Ovaria. To the south was the city of Scione, where a great wall was erected along the borders of Archonia and Dichonia. There, sentinels tirelessly watched to ensure the forces of hell didn't somehow break into their world. Each of these great cities held a shrine to the creators. Angelica had already paid homage to them all.

William listened as she went on and on, enthralled with her stories of the great forests and wide plains of Archonia. They found a place to sit next to a beautiful lake, where they continued to talk.

Exotic trees clustered around the water's edge, their roots jutting out of the ground and rolling down into the water to drink. Strange song birds filled the branches. Their song was so pleasant that William almost fell into a meditative state. Angelica's voice enthralled him, and he didn't realize the time. The sun was dipping in the sky, forcing William's heart to skip a beat, as he realized he had completely forgotten his task.

William interrupted her.

"Angelica, I have to go," he said, solemnly.

"Oh, I'm sorry, have I kept you from your duties?" she asked.

"No...no, but there is something I must do tonight, for all of Archonia," he said, softly.

"What is it?" she asked, a glint of fear in her eyes.

"I'm sorry, but I can't tell you, Angelica," he said, his face tight and insides clenching up. "Let me carry you back to the city."

"I'll be fine, William. We are in no danger here," she laughed. "Go!"

He turned to go, and she hollered after him.

"Be careful, William!" He faced her again and smiled, then took off into the dwindling light.

* * *

"Where have you been?!" Katrina shouted at William. "The guards are about ready to change. We almost missed our chance!"

"I'm so sorry, guys. Juarez let's go," William said, racing towards the Adjudicator's wing. "We'll wait for the signal, Katrina."

Katrina veered off down another hallway.

It was a few, tense moments before the two were at the entrance to the wing, the halls already filling with darkness. The bright crystals lighting the hallway could not reach the full height of the ceiling, so William and Juarez climbed the wall and moved from statue to statue, careful to move as quietly as possible.

"Okay," William said to Juarez. "This is it. Just remember, don't say anything to anyone, and the worst you can be accused of is not reporting to your designated ranks. At most, you might get a night under the atlas ball."

Juarez nodded. "You just make sure to get in and out quick, amigo," Juarez said.

They floated in complete silence, waiting for the bell. When it sounded, it rolled over them like a wave, a ghastly tremor that filled the halls and shook William to his core. A feeling of dread washed over him, and then the action began. The doors to the wing flew open, and hundreds of bodies shot out like bolts of lightning. The commotion was staggering, and Juarez disappeared in an instant.

Alright, he saw Meredox, and is following him, William thought. *Ok this is it.*

He shot forth from the wall once the hallway was empty He didn't waste any time, utilizing his memory well. He found Meredox's private quarters right away. He opened the doors, and crept in. It was so silent in the room that he could hear his soft footfalls. He looked around the room at all the artifacts lining the walls, the hair on his neck and arms standing on end. He was being watched.

In the darkness the room didn't feel as homely as it had previously. It actually put William more on edge. The silence was suddenly split by a whizzing sound. William looked up at a book shelf, where an object was flashing brightly, and making a very loud noise.

Oh no, he thought with dread.

He must have triggered some sort of alarm. He was already in too deep. If he was ever going to get out of this, he needed to secure proof, and fast.

His gaze snapped around the room as he tried to decide where to look first. He saw Meredox's desk at one end of the room, and rifled through papers as fast as he could.

It didn't take William long to find what he was looking for, as it stood out rather boldly. It was a single piece of parchment as black as coal. The edges were burnt, and the script was glowing red like flame. William picked it up, and it was hot to the touch. He held it as if it would fall apart at any moment, and read.

My Dearest Meredox,

The time of my coming is nigh. I pray you will be by my side. I have found a way past the Obelisks. Together we can rule Archonia, and make things the way we always wanted. Look for my coming at Last Light on the first day of Antioch. We shall be united once more.

L

William's throat went dry, and he swallowed hard. He had to get this letter to Brock, or the Synod, or somebody. Panic struck him. He knew that he was right about a plot, but he simply didn't know how serious it was. He moved quickly back towards the door, but a force hit him like a wall, and scattering the letter out of his hand. The force took him through the wall of Meredox's chambers, and out into the hall. A man walked through the hole after him. It was the same man William had seen Meredox conversing with in the middle of the night.

"Thief!" he shouted.

"Traitor!" William growled back, and wrenched himself from the ground.

Blazing light filled the hallway as William projected, his armor appearing out of thin air and securing itself to his body. Benjamin's armor appeared as well, and wasted no time in his second strike. This time William was ready, and using his experience in jujitsu, used the weight of his attacker to toss him into the wall.

The wall crumbled, as Benjamin continued to bowl through several more layers of wall. William shot after him through the tunnel of holes, eventually stepping into the library. Books and pages flew everywhere, and the man came shooting back at him. William caught his wild haymaker with a strong arm, and cracked him on the head with an armored elbow. Benjamin smashed into the stone

291

floor with a crunch, forming a small crater, and went still. William turned him over, to find that he was unconscious.

He didn't realize just how strong he had become. He was able to take on an experienced judge. Though their main focus wasn't combat, he thought that the man would have provided a little more fight. His thought was cut short as bright flashes filled the room, and four men fell over him, restraining him. William struggled, but couldn't break free. They turned him around, and he came face to face with Meredox.

"Tainted one!" Meredox's face was filled with rage.

"Traitor!" William shouted.

Meredox and his men burst into laughter.

"Ironic that you deem me a traitor, yet I am not the one sneaking about in places where I should not be," Meredox said, before stepping aside to reveal Juarez on his knees.

"This one was following me. I thought it amiss that a guardian would be amongst our ranks. He refuses to speak, even under the threat of punishment. And I wonder who it was that rang the bell?" he asked, probing.

William didn't speak. He wouldn't give the vile traitor the honor of his voice.

"It matters little. You have all broken the law and shall be punished," Meredox spat.

"He has broken no law," William said, defiantly, looking at Juarez. "It is not a crime to follow someone."

"The filth is not as dumb as he looks. You are correct, escort him out," Meredox said, motioning towards his men.

"William, no!" Juarez shouted as they began to drag him out. Meredox held up a hand for them to stop.

"Have you something to say" the Grand Justicar asked.

William locked eyes with his friend, and shook his head. Juarez went silent, a single tear dripping down his face. Meredox motioned for them to drag him away.

"Very well. He was not in ranks when he was supposed to be however, so I imagine his commander will be none too pleased," Meredox said casually. "Very noble of you to bear the blame for this little endeavor."

"I would risk everything to save this world," William growled, and was struck in the face with a hard fist as he struggled.

"And what exactly will you be saving it from?" Meredox inquired.

William spit blood onto the floor at Meredox's feet.

"I think you know. I saw the note he wrote to you. You're in league with Lucifer, and he is planning an invasion," William spat.

"Lucifer?" Meredox and his men laughed again. "Lucifer has been banished to the underworld for all eternity!"

"I will stop you, Meredox," William said solemnly, still struggling against the strength of the men holding him.

"You will stop nothing," Meredox said, his tone almost bored. "You will be punished for your crimes, tainted one. I am the law. And before the creators and all the eyes of Archonia you shall be branded a liar, a thief, and a traitor for attacking one of your brothers." He motioned towards Benjamin, who was now sitting up, holding his head while one of the guards attended to him.

"With any luck that fool Achilles will finally see fit to strip you of your rank as Guardian. Maybe he will finally see reason, and allow me to punish you appropriately," Meredox said, practically glowing at the thought.

"You bastard!" William roared, and strained with all his might.

"You do not think this fair, tainted one? Were it up to me, I would have you destroyed or banished to hell, where you could rot away in flame and sorrow for all eternity." Meredox stared down on him, a triumphant gleam in his eyes, and then abruptly turned away.

"Like your brother?" William asked, slowly.

293

Meredox spun and raised his hand as if to strike. William didn't flinch, and Meredox didn't follow through. "Take this filth from my sight."

CHAPTER NINETEEN
LAST LIGHT

William opened his eyes, and took in the room around him. It was a miniscule space, with no window, and metal bars for a door. He sat on a small stool in the center of the room, facing the door. Chains bound his hands, feet, and neck. Waist projections created by a group the sentinels that had escorted and bound him in place. They were strong, but William could break them, if he wanted to.

William quietly pondered his options. He could break free of the feeble prison, and perhaps avoid pursuit. He was much faster now, but he didn't know where he would go if he was able to escape. He could break free and attempt to find the letter he discovered in Meredox's office, although the deceiver had most likely already destroyed any evidence that could jeopardize his position. William's heart began to stray. There was an alternative to all of this. He could side with Meredox, and try to gain favor and power when the attack came.

"NO!" he shouted, and stamped his feet on the ground, causing the room to shake. "Get those thoughts out of your head, William. You're better than that," he said to himself.

Many hours passed, and finally a visitor arrived to see him. Brock, his face sullen, slowly opened the cell door. He knew Katrina and Juarez wouldn't come. They would only be incriminating themselves.

"I didn't expect this of you, William," Brock said, sadly.

"Brock," William said, his voice quiet and tense. "It had to be done. I found evidence that Meredox *is* a traitor."

"Yes, William, your friends came to me, and asked for my help. Meredox has been confronted, and his quarters searched. There is no such letter to be found," Brock replied.

William's heart sank.

"He destroyed it then," William sighed.

"My friend, I want to believe you, but Meredox is a hero. He defeated the fallen Archonians so they would never threaten Archonia ever again," Brock said, moving towards him, only to falter and step away.

"Then you have fallen for his ruse," William said, spitefully. "Weird that only he survived, don't you think?" William asked.

Brock turned away slowly.

"I can't tell you if you're correct," Brock said. "The only thing we can do is let these events unfold."

"My friend Juarez, who spoke to you," William said.

"The Spaniard?" Brock asked.

"Yes. Did he tell you where Meredox went when the bell rang?" William asked, desperately.

Brock looked at him, seemingly weighing his options, debating if he should speak further.

"He headed north, towards Mount Olympus," the large guardian muttered and turned to leave.

"Wait, Brock. What is Antioch?" William asked.

Brock turned and squinted at him.

"That is a very odd question," Brock said, slowly.

"Please, Brock," William pleaded. "Look, I will take this punishment. I broke the law. I will pay for what I have done, but you must believe me!"

There was a long silence, where William wondered if his large friend would speak again.

"Antioch is the name of a month, William," Brock said softly at long last. "One of the ten in the year."

"And when does Antioch start?" William asked, focusing.

"Uh," Brock said looking at the ceiling and thinking. "Today, little brother. The first day is today," he said confused. "Why is this important?"

William felt a shiver run down his spine, and a bead of sweat ran down his face.

"The letter, Brock. It said look for my coming on the first day of Antioch. Lucifer is coming," William gasped.

His large counterpart's face grew very serious now.

"Who is coming?" Brock asked, his tone very guttural tone.

"The letter...it was signed 'L'. It must be Lucifer the Archon, right?" William said. "You must take the Guardians to Mount Olympus immediately!" William could hear his own voice, and knew he sounded half-crazed.

"William, I..." but William wouldn't let him finish.

"This is what we are trained for! You must do your duty! To Archonia!" William shouted so loudly that even the experienced guardian recoiled.

"William I can't just go flying off to the edge of the world with the Guardians because you claimed you saw a letter from Lucifer. Do you know how crazy you sound?" Brock asked, shaking his head.

"Then take your squad," William retorted. "And if I'm wrong, no harm done. Everyone gets to see the tainted one branded and beaten, and everyone will have a merry old time," William said, sarcastically.

There was a momentary pause and William could see the cogs turning in his friends head.

"Brock, think about the reports of strange disappearances. The bat-like creatures that we fought below the forge. I could tell you have been worrying over

297

something. What if Meredox has been testing the barrier for a weakness, and succeeded at getting demons through." William said exasperation.

"Alright, little brother," Brock said, holding his hands up, trying to calm him down.

Just then there was a commotion outside the door, and it swung open. Ten armed guards flowed in through the passage, instantly making the tiny room very claustrophobic. They unbound William from the walls, and each grabbed a chain to restrain him. As they escorted him out William looked over his shoulder at Brock.

"Take Katrina with you to ring the warning beacon. She is the fastest guardian," William said, struggling to meet Brock's gaze. The old warrior stood in the corner, watching him speechless.

The guards led William to the training grounds, where two massive stone pillars had been erected upon a stage overlooking the grounds. William sized up the massive constructs, wondering if he could break them, if the need arise.

A vast sea of people covered the training ground beyond the stage, lined up in endless rows. It appeared the entire Archonian military was in attendance. He didn't see the gleam of armor, instead the crowd appeared to be in formal dress. They were going to make his discipline into a public spectacle. Not just shame him, and try to break him, but do it in front of everyone. William felt a flush of anger warm his insides, fueled by his indignation.

Yes, I tried to serve Archonia. Punish me...makes sense. This world is just like the last one, he thought, eying the crowd, and suddenly realizing that there appeared to be no civilians in attendance. *Good, at least Angelica won't have to watch. I only hope she will talk to me again.*

The guards pulled him into place on the stage and chained William to the ground. Next they bound his wrists with massive manacles. When the guards let go William's arms sagged. They felt as though they weighed a ton each.

He tugged at them, and they didn't break. Apparently they didn't trust him to take his punishment honestly.

The chains binding him drew backwards towards the pillars, pulling William's arms out wide, stealing almost all of his strength. With his arms pulled back, his chest was exposed. The guards ripped his shirt off, leaving him completely bare. The crowd remained still, and silent. William half-expected them to cheer, to take pleasure in the savage spectacle. That he could've handled, but the silence was worse. It was unnerving.

Drums suddenly split the still air, and a man stepped forth, clad in the armor and purple of an Adjudicator. He wore a large cowl over his face, so William couldn't immediately identify him. He was too tall to be Meredox. That much he did know.

He produced a scroll, unrolled it, and with a loud voice started reading it aloud.

"William of Archonia...you have knowingly, and willingly, broken the laws of the Synod, and of our people. As punishment for your crimes...you shall be branded a liar, a thief, and a traitor to this world," the adjudicator paused for effect, and this time a ripple of motion and noise rose up from the audience. "In addition, you shall be stripped of all rank, your title as Guardian, and be henceforth exiled from the great hall of Valhalla!"

The light dwindled, the shadows growing longer, reaching out to him like dark, sinister fingers.

"Do you wish to speak?" the Adjudicator asked.

William scoured the crowd, looking for Brock, Katrina, or Juarez, but couldn't pick them out of the sea of faces. His panic quickly turned to hope. Perhaps Brock listened after all, or, maybe his friends were loyal, and refused to watch him be tortured.

Of course Meredox was absent. If William was right, then he would be elsewhere, preparing for the attack. William's last hope would be that someone would see the invasion coming before it was too late, and ring the nearest beacon. He struggled with doubt. There was no telling exactly where the attack would come from, or how Lucifer would be getting past the power of the obelisks. He looked out at the fading light, and took a steadying breath.

"I have nothing to say. Let's get this over with," William said, grinding his teeth.

The Adjudicator nodded, and motioned towards a man in thick armor, a metallic mask covering his face, save for his eyes.

"Hey, ugly," William smirked. "Afraid to show me your face?"

He came forward, holding up a branding iron. It was round, featuring an intricate Chinese seal. Light shot forth from the large man's hand, heating the metal. William swallowed hard, his nerve and strength wavering.

Then the crowd began to chant. "Liar! Liar! Liar," over and over again, rising in a deafening crescendo.

William saw the red-hot iron moving towards his chest. He breathed in slowly and focused his mind. The metal touched his skin, and for a brief moment it felt cold. Then the pain shot forth, scrambling his thoughts. His body shook, rattling the chains loudly.

William winced but then remembered the fire of the forge, and managed to gain control. Compared to that, this pain seemed like nothing. He began to chuckle. The second iron came quickly, preceded by more chanting by the crowd. "Thief, thief, theif!"

William took quick breaths to help numb his mind.

"Is that all you've got?!" William shouted at the brander, his flesh melting against the hot metal, and the pain filling his head.

The third iron came, and William remained silent. The crowd chanted, but William blocked them out, instead focusing on the man holding the steel.

"I may be a liar and a thief, but I am no traitor," William growled, staring straight through the mask at the man's brown eyes.

With that the man shoved the fiery steel into William's face. He roared, squeezing his eyes closed as the fire ripped through his nerves. But the fire and pain abruptly stopped, and William heard metal hit the ground. The last light had faded from the sky, leaving the training grounds in the half-dark of dusk, just before the deep, dark of night fell. William felt something reverberate in the air.

A deep tone cut through the still air, vibrating and filling William with dread, and echoing off the stone walls of Valhalla. The warning beacon had been rung.

"The forces of Dichonia are attacking!" a voice boomed out across the vast expanse of the training grounds, projected by some unseen guardian.

It wasn't Katrina. That much he knew.

"Fly to the aid of your brothers. To mount Olympus!" the voice boomed again.

There was a moment of pause, as people seemed to take in the news and decide how to react. Then flashes of light split the darkness amongst the crowd, blinking like fireflies as soldiers began to summon their armor. Captains shouted commands, and bodies shot off into the darkness.

Everyone was moving now, asking for direction or giving orders, and everyone forgot about William.

"Hey! Cut me loose, I can help!" William shouted frantically, but he was drowned out by the clamor of armor, and swords.

He tugged at his bindings, but they were very strong projections, made by a higher ranking Adjudicator. They held him firmly. William gasped for breath and tried again. They wouldn't budge. Feeling cornered and desperate, William let out a frustrated bellow, and began thrashing wildly. But the chains held. They were simply too strong. He tried to catch the attention of someone, anyone. He shouted at the top of his lungs until his voice cracked and broke, the pain from the brandings now forgotten.

William stopped. The grounds had fallen quiet. They had all gone, moving to the north. He could see flashes of light off in the distance. It looked just like every other battle scene he had ever seen, flashes of violence. There were probably screams of pain and terror, too, but he was too far away to hear them. He was powerless to stop any of it.

Readjusting himself so that he could gain some leverage with his legs, William pulled against just one side of his bindings. He strained until his muscles quivered and failed, and he slumped in the chains, black spots swimming across his vision.

"Come on!" he shouted, refusing to give in. To accept the weakness and frailty of his past existence.

A good hour passed before he stopped to rest and looked out across the horizon. Darkness had fallen over the training grounds. The guards that usually attended to this were now many miles from here facing lord only knows what, he thought to himself.

Why had Katrina not rung the warning bell? Was she stopped, or did someone get there first. Was she in danger? Had Juarez gone with Brock as well? Questions flooded his mind, and he fought off a wave of nausea. Not only did he not know if his friends were in danger, but he could do nothing to help them.

He hung his head in defeat. William felt a tear run down his cheek. How had this gone so very wrong? Why did nobody believe him?

He couldn't decide if he wanted to cry or yell in anger, but as his mind tried to decide he heard an enchanting voice.

"Fear not my friend," someone said suddenly.

Startled, William looked up to find a figure wreathed in light standing before him.

"G...Gabe?" William asked, squinting against the light.

"Yes, my friend it is I," Gabriel said, his voice echoing from far off.

"Thank god you're here! Free me!" William said, relief pouring into him like icy water. "Everyone is in danger. Archonia is under attack."

"Yes, I know. I tried to warn the Synod many times of this danger, but it fell on deaf ears. I do not know if they were trying to deny it from themselves, or simply trying to avoid panic," Gabe said.

"None of that matters anymore! We must help the others! Free me!" William yelled, desperation gnawing at his insides.

"I cannot, my friend," Gabe said, passing a glowing hand through one of the massive chains restraining William.

"I don't understand?" William said. "Are you not real?"

"I am still on Earth, William. I am speaking to you through your mind," Gabe said, his ghostly image smiling.

"My mind? Is that possible?"

"Unless you have gone mad, William, we have been speaking for about a minute now," Gabe said, chuckling. William's face flushed. *"I joke, William. I have been around for a long time, and have learned a good many things along the way,"* the Archon said serenely.

"I need your help Gabe," William pleaded. "You have to come back," he said, hanging his head.

"I cannot return. I still have business here on Earth. And you think too little of yourself, young William. I saw you break through stronger chains than these on Earth. Surely these bonds cannot hold you down. Now go help your friends," Gabe finished.

"If you can't help me, why come?" William asked, desperately.

"Sometimes, William, all the help we need is a simple reminder that we are strong. Break free, William," Gabe said in a whisper, and then was gone.

***

Brock stared, dumbfounded by the scene stretched out before him. Against his better judgement he had taken his unit north to investigate William's claims. He had dispatched his scout when he saw the dark cloud hovering just above the ground in front of the mountain range.

The plot was real. And Brock now stared at a force of twisted demonic souls that had somehow circumvented the power of the barrier. His heart pounded and the thrill he felt before a fight was pushing outward against his very skin.

Brock's unit remained at a distance. He could hear the beacons ringing across the land. Quelling the urge to attack, he ordered his men to wait until the army arrived. For as long as he could remember, he had wished to find glory in the wars of old. With this force set before him, regret lingered on the edge of his mind.

Massive beasts writhed and roared, slithering across the plains below. Flocks of demons blotted out the skyline too numerous to count. They radiated from a single point at the base of the mountain which glowed blue.

The wait seemed an eternity and with each passing moment the enemies grew in number. Finally, Brock heard the horns blowing. He turned finding the banners of all three Archonian Corps glimmering on their approach. He cringed at the disorganization.

Hundreds of years of training and preparation for just such an event and nobody could remember their duties. Brock watched helplessly as the ranks formed. The majority of the sentinels were on the ground dropped in by those who could fly. Their undisciplined lines looked feeble.

The Guardians flew headlong into the advancing force with sheer abandoned, each eager to show their strength. Brock shook his head and shouted.

"Follow me men!"

Swiftly he flew up to meet the Guardian Corps. He spotted Achilles at the head of his Myrmidon squadron.

"Commander! Pull them back! They will be separated and scattered to the wind!" Brock bellowed, pointing at his comrades already engulfed in waves of enemy wings.

"Get in line Captain. I will worry about the rest of them," Achilles replied not looking at him. Then, he proceeded to bark orders to his officers.

Brock watched in horror at the ground below. Huge Wryms crashed through the sentinel line battering it to pieces in a matter of seconds. His Guardian brothers were specks of gold and silver amongst the black curtain on twisted souls. One by one they were disappearing.

Suddenly he heard the shouts of retreat. After less than a minute of combat, the fear had set in and soldiers began to flee south. Brock intercepted a rogue soldier and grabbed him by the collar.

"Form up, soldier!" he cried.

Then, Brock swooped into the fray, his men close behind him.

CHAPTER TWENTY
THE BREACH

William flexed his arms, and roared. His cry echoed across the now empty field. Light erupted from his body, and the ground trembled around him. His armor clamped down upon his arms and legs, His vision clouded by a gray light. The massive stones and chains that bound him crumbled under his returned strength.

In seconds, William was airborne. Breathing through his teeth, he barreled through the sky towards Olympus. It was no longer fear that gripped him, but a raw determination to face whatever was coming. His face and chest still burned where he had been branded, but it was motivation. He would not forget that pain.

The world around him blurred as he picked up speed, and a trip that should've taken him the better part of a day would only take him a small fraction of that time. He was already so far behind, but he couldn't change that now. All he could do was help.

His rage slowly subsided as he flew further, until he could finally see the peak far off in the distance, riddled with fire and explosions, heralding a fierce battle. He spotted tiny dots coming towards him. When they got closer he could see that they were soldiers, retreating from the battle.

He didn't think twice, moving to intercept them. William's leather clad hand landed firmly against the chest of a Sentinel. The soldier's armor was in shambles, and his eyes wild. A group of other soldiers following the frightened man came to an abrupt halt at the sight of the two.

"Soldier, where are you going?" William asked eyes narrowed.

"The battle is lost, the forces of the fallen are too numerous! We must flee!" the soldier gasped.

Other frightened soldiers slowed to listen in on their conversation.

"And where will you flee to?!" William shouted, addressing the entire group. "This force isn't here to claim territories or land. This evil is here to take your souls!" No one spoke. "You all took oaths to defend the people of this world from the very evil threatening it right now!"

"What do you know of oaths, traitor?" a nearby Adjudicator asked.

"You all eagerly branded me a liar and traitor for trying to warn the people about what's happening right now! I'm moving towards the danger, while you run from it. I think you're a traitor."

"Nothing can stand against this force, William."

He recognized the voice, and turned quickly to see Samuel. His armor was in shambles, and he was covered in black soot.

"That is what they said about me, Samuel. They said a tainted soul could never live in this world. They said that I would fail, but here I stand, ready and willing to face evil," William snapped back.

"You have not seen this enemy," Samuel responded.

"I don't need to. I know why it frightens you, Samuel," William said, looking around.

The number of soldiers floating around him was growing larger.

"I lived hell in my previous life I didn't learn soon enough that you can't do everything alone. Flee and you may live, but our lines will break, and then you will be alone, isolated when this evil comes for you. You can watch it destroy everything you have in this life, and all the innocents that will die with it. You can let this evil come into your world, and take it from you. Or, you can stand together, and show these demons why you were chosen to live in Archonia!"

This was the first time that William had ever given a speech, and surprisingly, it felt good. The soldiers roared in approval, and as William took off they all followed him. He led a force of almost seventy soldiers. Samuel floated up next to him.

"You're crazy, William, you know that?" Samuel whispered.

"It's amazing how people tend to follow crazy," William said with smirk. "Now I need you to surround this whole group in one of your shields. Don't focus on anything else."

He didn't have to ask twice, for a sphere of light expanded around Samuel. It bubbled out, engulfing the entire group. A rumble of excited approval swept across the group.

The sounds of battle in the distance drew nearer, the shrieks and cries of beasts rising above the din.

William shouted, "I need any archers or projectors to the rear of the shield, if anything flanks us kill it! Fighters to the front. Work together as a team! Fly in and out of the bubble, and make your kills count!"

"We should keep the bubble high, so that the wyrms can't consume us all," said the Sentinel that William had first stopped.

"I don't know what the hell those are, but sounds good," William said. "What else can we expect?"

"Tera-spawn up high," the man shot back quickly. William shook his head, feeling more than a little confused and unprepared for what lay ahead.

"The bats," Samuel said, after noticing his confusion.

"Right," William responded. He remembered his encounter with them on the cliff well enough. Perhaps the flock he fought on the cliff was a recon force, testing their path in Archonia.

"There might also be dredgers on the ground, and demon kin footmen."

"Your name, Sentinel?" William asked.

"We have met once before, tainted one. I am Silvos. I was not so courteous to you in our first encounter," he said.

William finally put it together, and married the man's familiar face to that early, painful lesson. He had never really given a second thought to the thrashing he took that day. After all, he'd been through so much that first day in Archonia. William met his gaze, the man's eyes seemingly begging for William's pardon.

"You're forgiven, brother," William said, nodding.

Silvos smiled. "Thank you...William," he said, using his name for the first time.

William nodded, struggling to force down a smile, and continued.

"You must lead these men to victory, Silvos," William said.

"Where will you go?" Samuel asked.

"I have to find my friends," William replied, a determined edge to his voice. "Gather as many men as you can for the counter attack. Take it slow, and stay with the shield. Find more shield bearers and more archers. Contain them as best you can. If we can provide our men order and discipline...that is the first battle to win. Win that, and maybe we survive this conflict."

William pushed forward out of the protective bubble. He crested a hill, finally allowing him a view of the battlefield. The sight before him stilled the beating of his heart. Screams and shouts filled the air, punctuated by the angry bellows of fearsome beasts. Beams of bright light and fiery explosions pitted the darkness at the foot of the great mountain. The air grew black with soot, moving like living smog. Millions of demon spawn covered the vast expanse as far as he could see. From his perch in the sky it looked as if the ground was squirming...and bleeding.

Flashes of gold glinted amidst the sea of writhing bodies, like distant, sparkling flecks. The defending army's line hadn't just been broken, but worse, scattered. Each of the Archonian protectors were now struggling just to stay alive. They were completely unprepared for an attack like this.

William swallowed hard, and tried to make sense of the chaotic battlefield. He knew that he had to bring them together if they were to have a chance. He had to rally them somehow. Lightning bolts and energy blasts rained down suddenly from the top of the mountain. He tracked the bright flashes, guessing that Zeus and his Sentinels were making a stand on the high ground.

Zeus's flash of light pulsed against the ground. William realized what it was. A beacon. The tiny specs of gold started to move, gravitating towards the flashing strobe.

Good, William thought. *Zeus is trying to rally them together.*

Bolstered by the sight of the Archonian's coming together, William took a deep breath and shot down from the sky, his energy building and engulfing him. He roared a mighty battle cry, unsheathing his sword. The weapon transformed into a spear as he held it out before him, its handle buzzing with violent purpose in his palm. He plummeted from the sky, falling like a glowing, terrible meteor.

William approached the field, squirming demons blocking any view of the ground beneath them. A sudden pressure formed inside him, pushing against his fall, and right before he landed, he spun and flexed with all his force, projecting a violent wave of energy before him. The wave struck the ground, exploding in a shower of dirt, rocks, and demonic bodies, instantly clearing everything in his path.

William landed, and they were on him again. Demons, bats, creatures of every shape and size were screeching and clawing at him. He arched his weapon back and forth, morphing it back into a sword, and slashing again, and again, cutting through bodies like butter. He parried a crooked blade wielded by a larger demon. He cleaved it in half, felling it like wheat at the harvest. Waves of energy spouted from his hand, knocking back hundreds of enemies. Even more swarmed over their bodies and continued to attack.

Their strategy isn't power, or technique, but sheer numbers, he realized.

William fought fear with rage, roaring and bursting through a cloud of the vicious spawn whose gnashing teeth ripped at him. The energy surrounding his body disintegrated their flesh, leaving a trail of falling maimed demons behind him. He couldn't keep up such energy output indefinitely. He had to change his strategy.

He decided that he needed to gather as many forces as he could, and send them to the shield. He spotted a group of guardians through the chaos. Their white armor gleamed against the red and black masses.

The cut off group were mounting a futile defense many hundreds of meters below him. Gungnir formed into a spear and he dove headfirst towards the ground. His shoulders strained with every hit as he impaled demon after demon. The spear struck the ground and cratered the dirt beneath and ten or more demon carcasses squished to the ground around it.

One Hell of a Shish Kabob.

He hefted the spear and pirouetted flinging the bodies off the end of the spear. Gungnir abruptly turned into a gleaming Scythe and continuing his spin the blade cut through a score of demons who had closed in around him again. Their screeches and gurgles of agony filled his ears as they flopped to the ground in multiple pieces.

He had reached the soldiers. They faced outwards in a tight circle, their backs to one another. Mounds of bloody, hewn body parts and demon carcasses were piled around them. Their faces were ashen, smeared, and weary. A score of Archonian soldiers lay behind them in their circle, motionless. Another wave of demons pushed in at the circle of battered soldiers, driving their defensive formation back and threatening to break their lines.

William formed Gungnir into a massive hammer. He forced his energy into the weapon, before leaping forward and driving it into the ground. The hammer connected with the ground, exploding with a blinding flash. The energy rippled out, fracturing the ground and passing harmlessly into the beleaguered soldier's formation. The demons scattered, the violent energy striking them with incredible force.

William looked up, his eyes meeting a familiar face. He moved to greet Ulifrig, but the wall of demons was already reforming and collapsing upon them again.

"Ulifrig! Get your ass up to Samuel," he said, pointing wildly at the glowing shield, which was now twice the size.

There were more tiny specs of gold flitting their way towards it, and new bubbles starting to form, connecting to the larger one. Ulifrig simply nodded, and with a burst of light the group of soldiers shot off into the sky.

William took off as well, splitting Gungnir into two axes.

Time to do some more damage, he thought.

The two small war axes became like ripping saw blades, spinning them in his hands, dicing any enemies before him into pieces. The demon's blood was like sticky tar, flinging from torn and ruined bodies, and covering William from head to toe.

William had just finished decapitating a particularly large demon whose eyes had somehow been sewn shut and seemed to be sewn together itself from the parts of many different bodies. He was blindsided by a sword. It drove hard into his armor, but didn't get through. William staggered and turned, finding a large human-shaped demon, floating in the air. He wore very thick armor, and bore a large shield. His white skin made him look like a corpse and it didn't have any whites in its eyes they were merely black voids.

William slapped the two small axes together, forming them into one large axe, the blade the size of his own body. The axe fell, sinking into the shield, but not rending it as he had expected.

Oh shit.

This enemy was more powerful. William had just left himself completely open to a counter attack. He heard the crunch and felt something dig its way into his left side. He looked down. The demon's blade hadn't pierced through his armor, completely. A crack resounded as the demon thrust, and pain shot through his insides, taking his breath away.

He fell towards the ground and just managed to catch his focus before he crashed into the dirt. He stumbled, but caught himself just in time to parry another blow from the black-eyed demon.

He loosed a barrage of energy from his offhand in two or three spurts, pressing his sword arm into his injured side. Black eyes held his shield up and crouched. The first two blasts missed, but the third found its mark and the energy exploded, ripping apart the enemy's shield and melting away a large portion of his armor.

Black eyes didn't waste any time in his counter attack, and charged in close. William was having trouble lifting his sword hand, due to the pain in his side, and barely managed to parry the first strike. Pain shot through his body. He knew he had to try his offhand.

He William would have little to no technique with his right, so Gungnir formed into a wicked cudgel, and he switched hands as he ducked an angular strike from above. The next strike came straight across his torso, and he spun and put all his weight into the strike, knocking the enemy blade away with Gungnir. He spun again in the same direction keeping his momentum going, and the cudgel put a large dent into Black eyes exposed shoulder.

The enemy's blade fell from his grasp as he hollered in agony, but was cut short as the cudgel battered him again in the face, caving in his skull. William yelled in a battle frenzy and delivered a couple more unnecessary blows to the dead demon's head.

He was babying his left side, and trying to breathe as evenly as he could. The other demons seemed to have been giving the two a wide berth, but now they converged on him once again. The cudgel turned into a flail, and he spun it ferociously above his head, knocking back enemies, but they were beginning to overwhelm him.

He spun and lashed in desperation, but soon he heard claws scrapping his armor, and a weight bearing down upon him as the decrepit and twisted creatures piled on him. He was tripped up by one that had latched onto his legs, and he fell over, hitting the ground on his bad side. Claws raked his face which was already caked in blood and sinew. The fresh blood from his own body along with that of his enemy's blood seeped down into his eyes.

Before his sight was completely blurred he caught a glint of gold through the pile of demons trying to rip him apart. He grunted and burst from the ground towards the glint.

"Man Down!"

"Get those things off of him,"

There was a sickening sound of flesh tearing and ripping and William no longer felt anything struggling to kill him at the moment. He smeared the blood around on his face, trying get it out of his eyes, which stung horribly.

"Where are you hit? the voice asked.

"Broken rib, can't see a damn thing," William stammered.

A cold splash of liquid caused him to jerk in surprise, but he was able to blink and then eventually his eyes focused, finding a guardian standing over him.

"Did you just project water?" William asked.

"Hold still, Guardian, I'll get you back in the fight."

He was blind again, but this time from the light emanated from the guardian's hand, which he had wrapped forcefully onto William's face. Burning pain from the claw marks was replaced with heavenly warmth he also felt his rib snap back into place and he took a huge breathe of relief. In moments he was sitting up catching his bearings.

"The tainted one, he brought this on us, kill him!" he heard a soldier say.

"Nay, he warned you all of this attack, you fools. Stay back or I won't heal another one of you." He heard a familiar voice say.

"There is no time to argue, he was killing demons by the hundreds I saw him. We need every sword we can get." An officer barked.

William quickly scoured the circle, and settled upon a familiar, small form. Juarez bent over a figure, cradling him, his hands glowing over a number of grievous wounds on vital spots. After a few moments he set the wounded soldier to the ground. And struck the ground in anger, beside the now motionless body.

"Juarez!" William shouted, whisking over to him.

"Bastardos!" Juarez shouted. "They just won't quit!"

William grabbed Juarez, and shook him. "Where is Katrina?" he asked, but Juarez was out of it, and William had to shake him again to get anything out of him. "Juarez I need you to focus. Where is Katrina?"

"I do not know. I think she went to the peak," the Spaniard said.

"Oh shit," William said, looking up at the top of the mountain, which looked like a volcano in mid-eruption. Flashes of light snaked, glowing eerily within the swirling clouds of ashy cloud. He could see the mass of bodies

315

surging up the cliffs, swarming to join the battle at the mountain top.

"Okay, Juarez, I need you to pull it together. These men still need your healing gifts," he said, watching as more and more fell from the formation covered in blood and screaming.

Juarez slowly got up, and nodded.

"Juarez, listen to me. Get as many men healed as you can, and you get to that," William yelled, pointing to Samuel's sphere of light floating in the sky. Juarez nodded gain, and William patted him hard on the shoulder.

William spotted a man barking orders and walked over to him. He was an Adjudicator of considerable rank, but William didn't have time to consider the hierarchy.

"Soldier, do you have any shield bearers among you?" he asked.

The man looked William up and down, evidently realizing who he was, and said, "I have none to spare."

"We need to get to the peak. We have men cut off," William growled, desperation driving his purpose.

"Be silent, tainted one," the Adjudicator spat. "Such a mission is folly."

"I don't know what folly means," William snarled back in anger. "But we need to get up there!"

"Know your place, traitor. You should be fed to these creatures," the Adjudicator said, squaring off against him.

Just then there were flashes of light and several booms behind the Adjudicator. Achilles appeared through the throng of demons, moving at an incredible speed. Behind him were twenty or more men, brutalizing their opposition in a magnificent display or power.

It was one of the few times that William had ever seen him in his full armor. William was surprised by how much it looked like his own, not bright and gleaming, but dull in color

"I agree with the young guardian," the ancient warrior said, his piercing gaze bearing down on the Adjudicator, whom cowered before the commander.

"My lord! Of course, as you wish," he said, bowing low.

"I have a shield bearer awaiting your orders," the Adjudicator said, motioning towards a man healing a nearby soldier. "This is Pious, he will help you."

William looked him over, and asked, "Can you make a strong shield?" Pious looked up from his charge, and nodded. William pointed to the sky. "Like that?" he asked.

Pious chuckled, but there was no mirth in the sound.

"Stronger," he said, nodding.

"Good," William replied, before turn his gaze to Achilles.

"We will punch a hole for you, young Guardian," Achilles said.

William looked over the elite soldiers flanking him, their strength bolstering his own. The soldiers watched him, fear and uncertainty surprisingly missing from their faces.

Achilles turned to the Adjudicator and said, "Get your healers to the shield, and tell everyone to assemble there for the counter attack."

The Adjudicator nodded and Achilles took off into the sky with his Myrmidons close at heal.

William and Pious took off after him, pushing hard to keep up. Achilles shouted something that he couldn't quite make out through the chaos and his guard shouted a response in unison as they formed a cone-like formation, and hit the oncoming wall of enemies like a bullet, disappearing into the cloud of spawn. A blinding flash of light, followed by an explosion, left the sky alight with the burning bodies of demons. Even the clouds peeled back from the energy pulse, briefly revealing the stars.

William and Pious rocketed through the hole. William could make out the forms of his fellow guardians with his peripheral vision, moving with confident, fluid strokes, dealing death with frightening efficiency. The hole Achilles and his men created finally collapsed, as a horde of shadowy demons beset William and Pious. The gaseous, demonic forms moaned, and grabbed at their heels. William and Pious fired blasts of energy back into the wave, but there were too many of them. They were still overtaking them.

"Guardian!" Pious yelled, William turning to see him engulfed by shadows.

William let a flurry of beams fly, the energy striking the creatures and sending them burning to the ground. Shadows fell over him, just as he unsheathed his sword. His sword rang out, the twang of steel filling his ears as he cut the beasts down. Their teeth and claws raked against him, tearing at his armor and slipping through the crease to his skin. William felt the heat, and smelled his blood. Hope fled William's mind as he struggled against the sheer weight and numbers of the creatures.

I just need a little...help, he thought.

Then as if an answer to his prayer, streaks of light rained down from the sky, the creatures surrounding him instantly turned to ash. William fell away, and as energy bolts passed through his own body his numerous wounds closed slightly. The brief reprieve gave him just enough wiggle room to break free.

Without wasting any time he grabbed Pious by the pauldron, and heaved him towards the peak. They were greeted by a welcome sight as they crested the top of the mountain. A man, standing nine feet tall, the length of his frame covered with soot and scars, bellowed in laughter that shook the peak. His thick, leather armor had been torn, and left to hang around his waist. He hurled massive energy beams down into the fray, while the archers flanking him loosed flecks of light into the horde below. William and Pious landed within the ring of allies.

Smoke rose from Pious' armor, so William patted him down to make sure he wasn't on fire.

Pious grabbed William by the shoulder, and pulled him so close that William thought he might kiss him, "Thank you."

William nodded, relieved once the man finally released his grip. He tried to respond, but a mighty voice bellowed.

"Well, if it is not the tainted guardian," Zeus bellowed.

"I have a name, old man," William smirked.

"Indeed you do, William, and shall have an even greater one after this battle is lost," Zeus said, waving to indicate the field.

"I'm not planning on losing," William responded.

"Enlighten me, young Archonian. How is it that you will achieve victory?" the god of lightning asked.

William slammed Pious on the shoulder, and said, "Everyone needs to assemble on this Sentinel. My fellow guardian has erected a shield on the far side. By now our forces are rallied to him. Once we join him we set up a defense, and take things slow. Chip away at them, and use our range and speed to achieve victory!"

"You make it sound so easy, young one, but for all your tact I fear there is a problem within your plan," Zeus said, hurling an energy beam down the mountain.

"Tell me," William demanded. The massive man made his way through the crowd of soldiers to the edge of the peak. William followed, and looked down. Zeus pointed a large finger towards the base of the mountain. A pulsing, blue light stood in the very center of the enemy forces.

"That is where they come from," Zeus said fiercely, "a portal between Archonia and Dichonia."

"Only someone of this world could have opened that portal, correct?" William asked.

"Yes," he said, and spat at the ground.

William knew exactly who let them all in. He knew exactly who betrayed them, and more, he knew exactly what he had to do.

"I'll take care of it. I suggest you get to the main force assembling on the other side of the field, my lord."

"And what? Do you think you will be closing that portal all on your own?"

"I have to try," William said through gritted teeth, but stopped when he heard a shout.

"William!" Katrina yelled, and ran into William, embracing him. "You came!"

"I would never leave my friends behind," William said, breaking free of her bear hug.

"Juarez?" she asked, her eyes wide.

William pointed to the massive ball of light across the darkness. She smiled and gripped him in another hug.

"How many demons have you destroyed?" Katrina asked.

"Not enough," William said, just as light shot out, engulfing everyone in a protective shield.

"You brought us a shield!"

"Yeah, you're getting out of here," he responded quickly.

"What do you mean, *you're*?" Katrina asked, skeptically.

"There is something I have to do, Kat." William broke eye contact, and looked down at the portal. She shook her head violently. "William. No. That is suicide!"

"I have to do it," William argued. "I have to redeem myself."

"William, we will regroup with the others and assemble a strike force to destroy it."

"There is no time. More and more demons pour through every second, and we are already overwhelmed," he said as Katrina put a hand up to his face.

It still burned from the hot iron that had scorched it marking him as a traitor. "William you don't have to prove anything to anybody. You were right. They all know it now! What you did was for the good of our world. They will reverse your punishment... you have been vindicated," Katrina said.

"I'm not doing this to redeem myself for anything I have done in this life, Katrina. It is for what I did in the last one. I followed the easy paths, and led a life that was full of regret. I thought the world was unfair to me, that I didn't have any power to change it all. But I realize now that I was wrong... we always have a choice. I could've chosen to disobey my orders so many years ago, and not kill that innocent woman, or that little boy. But I didn't, and I did kill them...to my everlasting shame. Now I have the strength to do what is right, and I will be damned if I make the same mistake twice," he said fiercely, energy building deep inside and buzzing behind his eyes.

Katrina's eyes welled up with tears, as the protective bubble from Pious swept over them.

"I'm coming with you," she said, wiping her face.

"No, you're not, Katrina. You get to Juarez, and you destroy these things. I'm the only one that is going to be throwing away their life today. I'm a soldier, and I was born to do this," he said, turning.

"You can't stop me from coming, William," she said defiantly, wiping her eyes, trying to remain tough.

"I don't want to have to stop you. I'm asking you to let me do this. I already have too many people's deaths on my conscience. I don't want yours too," he said, staring deeply into her emerald eyes.

"William is right, young one. There is no need to throw your life away. This is a one man mission," Zeus stated.

"Then order William not to go, my lord. He doesn't need to die needlessly either!" she shouted.

"I would, Guardian, but I believe that this is why Gabriel brought him here. I think this is his chance at Redemption," he said.

She stared back at him, but finally nodded reluctantly and embraced him in a hug, pressing her cheek against his breastplate.

"Come, Young Guardian, we must go."

William looked up. Lightning bolts spread across the darkness, forking in all directions, the massive bubble now engulfing the troops lifted into the sky. Only one person remained with him on the mountaintop. William could feel their eyes on him. He turned to find Vulcanus standing in front of his forge. The fire was extinguished, and the massive statue torn to rubble.

"Vulcanus," William said, walking towards him. Even as he did the hell spawn circled in, recovering from Zeus' mighty attack. "Why do you not flee with the others?"

"I do not fight in such wars, William."

"You create weapons of war, but you do not use them?" William asked, looking around as the screeches grew louder around.

"You're mistaken, William of Archonia. I only create that which protects. Never once have I forged a blade."

William failed to hide his shock.

"Well good luck, old man," William said.

"Do not worry about me tainted one," Vulcanus stated.

William turned, but the massive smith spoke up.

"William. Take this," Vulcanus said a large metal object appearing out of thin air. It was a shield, simple in design and perfectly round, with some engravings on the front. It floated towards William, and he plucked it from the air.

"One of my favorites," Vulcanus offered as William nodded, marveling at the craftsmanship.

"Oh and, young one...you have proven me wrong," the giant man said, before disappearing in a burst of flame.

William smiled, and whirled around coming face to face with a howling demon. He held up the shield feeling a slight pressure, and a loud clang as the enemy blade hit. He unsheathed his own blade, and spun, cutting the creature from shoulder to crotch. Bolstered by the shield's addition, William loosed a wave of energy, and with an explosion the enemies were back off the mountaintop.

He took off into the sky, cutting through any enemy foolish enough to linger before him. The shield was light, and strong, and he found that it helped immensely. It was much like Gungnir, for when an enemy hit the shield, it hit back. The wings and bodies of the spawn pounded William as he flew, but he didn't let up or let them stop him. Some of the human demon hybrids that he faced were a bit more challenging, with their skinny skeletal looking limbs, and their beady red eyes. However all in all his opposition was small. The bulk of the enemy force now converged on the wall of light at the other end of the field.

Somehow he had managed to pull the forces together, and mount a serviceable defense. There were now three massive bubble shields, floating side by side, protecting the armored Archonians inside.

A bat crashed into William's new shield, exploding into a cloud of light and body parts. His blade cut the air, felling another beast, but the horde looked to have no end. He put up his shield, and transformed Gungnir into a spiked ball flail again, which he spun before him, cutting the air and beast alike with equal regard.

Using the spiked ball flail, William navigated his way towards the ground. Fewer demons blocked his path, thanks to the Archonian counter attack drawing most of the demon's attention. No one seemed to notice him approaching the portal from above. It was massive, and black, wreathed in clouds of brilliant blue. It looked eerily similar to Gabe's portal used during his ascent to Archonia.

It's just a projection, William thought to himself.

It could be destroyed, but that would prove useless unless he could find the conjurer. They would simply open another. William scanned the area, before spotting his target. The dark creatures flooding out of the portal gave the man a wide berth.

Meredox wasn't wearing his normal regalia. His armor had changed. It was now black, trimmed in gold, adorned with twisted looking spikes. A long cape flowed from his back, and he wore no helm, his dark hair and features terrifying, as if the life and color had been drained from him. Meredox stood with his hands high, energy pouring out of them to keep the massive portal open.

He was facing away, so he couldn't see William. An enormous slithering creature with huge scales, and a horned head rolled out past the traitorous man.

A wyrm, William thought, connecting the beast to its name. He dropped down behind Meredox, hitting the ground without opposition. He caught leverage in the stone and leapt forth, kicking Meredox in the back, sending him flying towards the portal. William gathered his energy, gave a mighty battle cry, and sent a massive energy blast at the black light of the portal. The beam struck the portal which momentarily bubbled like glass, before shattering into a million pieces. The wyrm, having only made it halfway through, was cut in two, a horrifying screech splitting the air before it flopped lifeless to the ground.

William smiled with satisfaction, but it was short lived as demons howled and rushed toward him. He stood his ground, but these were no ordinary spawn. They were hybrids. Half-Archonian, half-demon, they were very strong. Such a creature hadn't been completely mutilated or reincorporated into a new form in Dichonia. They were able to be strong like an Archonian and looked for the most part human.

Equipped with Vulcanus' shield, and Gungnir, the blade of an Archon, William burst forward, coming inside of the first demon's wild swing, and sinking his blade all the way to the hilt into its stomach. He tossed the creature off and spun to parry another attack, but was met with a large starburst mace to the chest. His armor cracked, and he flew back skidding awkwardly along the ground.

Another hammer strike came towards him while he was still prone on the ground, but he held up his shield, and as the hammer struck it threw the weapon high into the air, and blinded the demon attacking. William swung his blade, cutting the creature's legs out from under it, and then exploded from the ground as several more weapons struck at him.

William twisted in the air, and loosed a flurry of energy balls towards the ground engulfing the group of demons in fiery light but something struck him hard, sending him flying back to the ground. Pain shot through his back as he hit, kicking up a massive plume of dust. He looked around quickly, trying to find an incoming attack, but there was a space between him, and the encroaching lines of demons. He painfully rose to his knees, and waited. It appeared they were waiting for something.

"Another tainted soul," he heard a familiar voice say.

William got to his feet, and turned, coming face to face with Meredox. He had changed considerably. His normally curly, shimmering hair was wild, and his face much paler than usual, the veins showing dark from under his skint. He actually looked like a warrior now, his body heavily armored by rigid, spiked-plates.

"You will pay for this, traitor!" William shouted.

Meredox looked at him, a quizzical almost bored look on his face.

"It looks as though you're the traitor," he replied, indicating the burn upon William's face.

"Your lies will be brought to light," William said through gritted teeth.

"I assure you, Archonian, that I have no idea what you're talking about," Meredox said, dismissing William's accusation with a wave. "But you can see that there is no way that you will be getting out of this alive." Meredox

325

gestured to the hordes around him, the creatures snapping and barking at the chance to rip William to pieces.

"Unless...why not join us?" he asked, smiling, and standing with open arms.

William was taken aback for a moment. But his resolve was stronger now than it had ever been.

"You'll have to kill me," he said defiantly.

"Well that is unfortunate," the fallen Archonian said. "You know in the underworld we Archonians live as gods amongst the damned and decrepit!"

William wouldn't waste another moment listening to the deceiver's words. He charged suddenly, decisively arching his sword above his head, and bringing it down hard. His strike stopped mid-swing, his shoulders straining against the recoil as Meredox caught the blade. The ghostly, dark-haired adjudicator stood clutching the sword, barley exerting any effort.

William swung his shield arm around, catching Meredox in the side. It hit his armor with a single, anticlimactic ding, but Meredox didn't even move. He looked down at the shield, and grabbed it, twisting William's arm and wrenching it free from his grasp, before sending it spinning off into the distance. The shield hit a demon, crushing it. Meredox snapped forward, sinking a fist into William's face, the cold, metal of his gauntlet rupturing his skin.

William lost all sense of direction as he felt himself skip violently across the ground, each bump jarring him viciously.

"Oh god," William sputtered in agony. His eye was already swelling shut, and his mouth and nose were bleeding. He moaned gurgling on blood. He was face down in the dirt and struggled to his hands and knees where he hacked blood out onto the compacted soil below. Through his un-swelled eye he saw some of his teeth in the spit. He shook his head back and forth in determination and began to slowly get up, rasping a painful breath as Meredox applauded.

"Oh, young one, you do put on a good show," he almost sang.

William's anger bubbled to the surface, and he growled, sending a flurry of energy beams flying. Explosions consumed Meredox in a bright, fiery ball of light. William staggered back, smiling hopefully, but disappointment swept over him as the fire subsided and Meredox emerged unscathed, an aura of black energy subsiding around him.

"Pitiful," Meredox hissed, and disappeared in a blur.

William spun on the spot. He felt Meredox behind too late, and turned, just as a ball of energy flashed towards him. The blast was scorching hot, and William screamed, his armor taking the brunt of the force. He landed in a smoking heap, the armor on one side of his body blackened and ruined. He barely managed to stand this time the line of demons watching the fight clawing and whipping at the air, trying to tear loose a chunk of his flesh.

William gripped his burnt arm to his body, silently wishing he had a sling to immobilize it. He needed to buy his friends as much time as he could, so they could gain the edge, and survive. There would be no getting out of this for him. Although he knew that going in.

He glanced back to the mighty golden shield that his friends fought behind.

He coughed up more of his own blood, and thought briefly of Angelica. I wish I could see your face one more time, he thought to himself. He collapsed to his knees, and looked back at Meredox, who stood above him, waiting for something.

William smiled, a tooth falling out of his mouth. He could lay down and die, fail quietly and move on, but that just wasn't William's style. He had one last chance to be a smart ass.

"Is that all you've got, you greasy backstabbing piece of..." William started to say, but a crushing flurry of fists rained down, pounding him into the ground.

William became numb to the pain. He'd felt this before. It almost felt like falling asleep. Dying, he'd discovered, was actually quite easy. Living was the hard part.

Would there be another life after this one? he wondered, drifting off into darkness.

William's heart shuddered in his chest, failing him, as his muscles relaxed. His vision tunneled, narrowing down around him, a distant flicker of silver the last thing he saw.

***

Meredox swooped in viciously catching his twin in the chin with his knee as he pounded iron-clad fists into the tainted one. Luxor skittered across the ground for a moment until he regained his composure from the strike and righted himself.

"Brother! It has been so long!" Luxor said, spitting a bit of blood out on the ground.

"Leave this place, Luxor. Achilles will soon be here." Meredox said.

"I do not fear him. I've come home!" Luxor said, rising and reveling in the destruction about.

"Don't make me rectify my mistake, brother. You told me you would never return." Meredox said, evenly.

"You left me to rot in the underworld!" Luxor spat, his demeanor changing from calm to crazed.

"I let you live! It was the only thing I could do!" Meredox replied sadly.

"After you let them throw me from my home? And why? Because I have a tainted soul? What about him? You protect this tainted soul? They let him in to the land of light?" Luxor yelled.

"I tried to stop them, Brother. I loved you."

"Save your hollow apologies, filth." Luxor said, charging wildly.

Meredox grabbed William from the small carter he lay motionless in and leapt into the air. Luxor missed his mark and slid past harmlessly. Suddenly the fallen Archonian looked to the sky where the bubble shield had advance quickly.

Spotting the familiar formation of Achilles and his men, Meredox made for them. Glancing behind he spotted his brother jumping through a small bluish black portal.

CHAPTER TWENTY ONE
VINDICATION

A familiar, desperate voice rang out, far off in the distance. "WILLIAM!"

"He will be fine, young Guardian," another voice chimed in.

"How do you know?" the first voice, definitely a woman, responded.

"Some of the wounds are not healing like normal," Katrina shouted. Yes, it was Katrina. He recognized her voice.

"Because he knows I am as stubborn as he is," William said, groggily, his eyes fluttering open.

Katrina, Brock, and Juarez stood over him. William felt a warm touch as Juarez pushed his healing powers into him once again. The Spaniard apparently had been working hard to restore his mangled body, and with just a quick glance, William realized that a lot of work still lay ahead of him.

"William!" Katrina cried, wrapping her arms around him.

"Katrina, please settle down, I need to finish," Juarez said, impatiently trying to brush her aside.

"What happened?" William asked, sputtering blood. "Where am I?"

"You took one hell of a beating, little brother. We thought we lost you, but Juarez here would not give up he said he felt you still nearby." Brock said, with a reserved chuckle.

"It felt like someone dropping a mountain on top of me. I honestly didn't expect to open my eyes ever again." William mumbled, pushing up painfully onto his elbows and looking around. He saw familiar carvings, and murals.

I must be back in the castle, he reasoned, *and turned back to Brock.*

"What about the battle. If I'm alive we must have won."

"Yes, young Guardian, we were victorious," Achilles said, appearing between Brock and Katrina.

William considered the commander, who stood tall and strong, flanked by his guards. Another man stepped up next to him, and William's blood ran cold. Standing on the other side of Achilles was Meredox.

"Bastard!" William shouted, and lunged for the man, who was once again clad in his Archonian clothing. Katrina and Brock came forward and caught him, helping him back down onto the bed.

"Little brother, calm down. He is on our side," Brock said, holding William, half-crazed, down.

"That son of a bitch opened the portal! He is the one..."

"...that saved your life," Achilles finished his sentence for him. Then he stepped forward and put a hand on William's chest. The commander's fierce, piercing gaze calmed him.

"He opened the portal, lord Achilles, you must believe me!" he reiterated, his tone soft but direct.

"Achilles, it is time they learned the truth," Meredox said, loudly cutting into the conversation.

Achilles nodded and turned, stepping to the side so that William could see him. William struggled against Brock and Katrina, but they refused to loosen their grip.

"William, let me be the first to apologize," Meredox said slowly. "You were right all along about the threat to Archonia."

"There, he admits it," William growled through gritted teeth.

Meredox held up his hands. "Please, let me finish. Long ago I was assigned with the task of bringing a group of fallen Archonians to justice. I took a group of the finest soldiers into the depths of hell, wading through the filth and flame to hunt them all down. And yet, when it came to the last one, I faltered," he said.

There was a long pause, where Meredox seemed to struggle with the next part.

"I couldn't kill him, not even as he ripped my fellow Archonians to pieces. You did not fight me at Mount Olympus, but my Brother," Meredox said, his head hanging low.

William was dumbstruck.

"A twin brother," William said, the truth dawning on him finally.

"Yes, young Guardian, to my everlasting shame," Meredox replied, pulling down a portion of his toga, to expose a black ring burned into his flesh. It was identical to the one on William's chest, marking him as a liar.

A dull roar filled the room as people muttered amongst each other.

"I marked myself when I returned home from my journey, only after I lied to the Synod. I told them that my task was completed. That he was dead," the Adjudicator said.

William relaxed his aching body now. The surprise and anger subsiding as he listened to the story.

"I have hidden this secret for fifteen hundred years. It was not until recently that I received correspondence from my brother, Luxor, who told me he was coming. I had to keep it a secret, so I convened with my closest friends and allies and informed them of my brother, my lie, and his letter. We believed we could end this threat alone, without hassle to the people, or risking anyone else's life. Simple, and quiet...the way dirty secrets should remain. But William, I'm glad that you were there," Meredox said, his brown eyes meeting William's.

William didn't say anything. He didn't know how to respond.

"You were right, William. You don't deserve this," the disgraced Adjudicator said, closing the gap between them and placing a hand on his face. A dull, burning pain seeped into his skin from the touch, but it quickly subsided.

"This man is no traitor," Meredox said aloud.

William felt his face where he had been branded and the skin was fresh and new. Meredox moved to touch his chest, and William recoiled

"Leave them," he said, and Meredox looked at him in confusion. "I was a liar and a thief. I need that as a reminder."

Meredox nodded.

"Please forgive me, William," Meredox said, searching his eyes.

"We have all made mistakes," William responded, somewhat apprehensive.

William held out his hand, which Meredox grasped in his own. The gesture was simple, and heartfelt. It wouldn't wash away all the lies and hatred between them, but it was a good start.

"Thank you, William of Archonia," Meredox said, reverentially. "Without you, my home would have been lost."

William nodded.

"What happened in the battle? How did we win?" William asked, looking at Achilles.

"You won the day, little brother!" Brock bellowed. "Your shield wall worked. After the portal was closed we were able to manage the numbers, and drove them back."

"How am I alive?" William asked, turning back to Meredox.

"I gave my brother a welcome home present," Meredox said, smugly. "Achilles and his Myrmidons helped me punch through, and when he realized that the battle had turned, Luxor ran scared through another portal. The coward didn't even bother waiting for his fellow soldiers. With their reinforcements cut off, the enemy was no match for the combined forces of Archonia."

The crowd around his bed applauded, and smiled, but all of them jumped at the chance to shake William's hand. He'd never been treated like a hero before, and he found it all a bit overwhelming.

"Against an unknown enemy, and impossible odds, you rallied our forces, and in the end, led Archonia to victory. Amazing what a simple act of courage can accomplish," Achilles offered, and then turned and began to walk away. "Your prowess grows, William of Archonia. I will have need of you in the future," he said loudly, before disappearing from the room.

The rest of the onlookers left as well, leaving William with Brock, Katrina, and Juarez. His friends helped him out of bed, down the stairs, and out into the flowing fields of Archonia. The sun was dipping low in the sky, casting the long grasses in a radiant, strawberry hue.

They looked at each other and sighed.

"Are you feeling better?" Katrina asked.

"I think so...Juarez works wonders. I'm just a little stiff."

"Good," Katrina said slugging him in the arm.

"Ow what was that for?"

"That was for leaving me to go on that suicide mission."

"Kat I really didn't think I was going to make it out of that. I wasn't lying to you."

"I know, I'm just upset at myself most. Friends protect one another, they don't sacrifice alone, William. I was ready to give my life alongside you, to save Archonia," Katrina said, her eyes glassy with the promise of tears.

"I'm sorry, Katrina. I didn't want you to throw away your life," William said, sincerely.

"Yes, you saved us all, amigo," Juarez said. "But next time, you're bringing us along!"

William put a hand on his shoulder, and smiled.

"Deal!"

William held up his other arm to Katrina, who still scowled. Finally, after a few moments, she threw her arms around them both, and pulled them into a hug.

* * *

During the next few days Helios held large funeral services. Many soldiers fell during battle, passing on to the next life. The city glowed with pyres as the bodies were burned like, honoring the old-world traditions of Earth. William attended as many as he could.

One of the evenings he was asked to light a pyre for a warrior of particular renown. This lone warrior had been one of the first on the scene of the attack. He was a part of Brock's regiment, and when William saw him his heart sank. It was Alacron, the man who had taught him the ways of the blade.

His heart ached as he watched his friends light another fire later that night. Samuel and Juarez lit the pyre under Ulifrig. The guardian had only just forged his armor, and was already gone.

For the first time in his life, William prayed. He asked that his fallen friends find the next world, and peace. He didn't know who he was praying to. But he hoped they got the message.

Brock stood next to William, his large hand resting comfortably on his shoulder, lending him a bit of strength. They watched Samuel and Juarez set torches into the high pile of wood, before floating down to join them. Meredox appeared out of the crowd and stood beside William.

"How was he able to create a portal between worlds?" William asked solemnly. There was a pause before Meredox responded.

"The twin heart," he said.

William didn't know what that meant, but didn't trust his voice to ask. The flames spread over the pyre, engulfing Ulifrig's body.

"Twins share a soul," Meredox continued, sparing William the effort of asking. "It is often why they appear identical, but it is also why they share deeper, stronger bonds. As long as we each live, we share each other's power."

"Then he will return," William said.

"Yes, he will return," Meredox responded, sighing.

"Unless he is stopped," William said, his eyes narrowing.

Meredox didn't respond, his silence all the acknowledgment William needed. They stood together and watched as a fellow warrior made the journey to the next life. The flames danced into the night sky, eventually William's thoughts settling on only one thing. After the ceremony he headed towards the Garden of Medina.

The aftermath of the battle was visible even there. Many of the beautiful things, columns, flowers, and vines created by his fellow Archonians were gone, leaving empty patches in the elegant designs. They, like those that projected them, were gone forever.

I...we, will rebuild it, little by little, he thought to himself. Everyone would.

He burst forward, driven by what he wanted for once, and not what he needed. As if his wish had been answered he saw Angelica. He floated up behind her, stopping a few feet away. She wore a beautiful blue gown, embroidered with silver that shimmered in the starlight. She turned to him.

They looked into each other's eyes, and then as if drawn together, embraced. William took her chin in his hand and pressed his lips against hers. They kissed, William feeling as if the stars were exploding around them.

"I didn't think I would ever get to see you again," he said softly when they finally pulled apart.

"You still don't believe in yourself, do you, William?" she said, smiling, her arms around his neck. "From the very first moment I saw you, I knew there was more to you than people realized."

"Thank you for believing in me. Thank you for everything, Angelica," he said, kissing her softly, again and again. They sat together for a long time, with the light of the cosmos, and the strange plants in the garden, watching over them.

"What will happen now?" she asked.

William didn't know how to answer, so he simply shook his head.

"Are we safe?"

He didn't have the heart to tell her the truth, nor was he entirely sure he was allowed to, so he wrapped his arms around her, pulling her close. He would protect her from whatever was coming...somehow.

EPILOGUE

"My lords, the commander has not been seen since the battle, and no remains have been found," a man with dark skin said.

He watched the Synod members, who besides himself were the only ones in the chamber.

"Where was he last seen, Mikael?" Ibrahim asked, adjusting the sash on his black mourning robes.

"He and a group of his finest Sentinels broke off from the main force near the end of the conflict. They sought out a group of rogue demons that had strayed from the battlefield. He suspected their target may have been the obelisk at Iona," Mikael said.

"And who commands the Sentinels now?" Isaiah asked, his freshly shaved head gleaming in the light.

"Commander of the Guardians has assumed control during this transitional period," Mikael said, slowly and carefully. "I am ready to take command of them, should this great council wish it." He bowed, keeping his eyes upon the group.

The Synod members looked to each other briefly, whispering back and forth, and then the man in the center seat spoke.

"You will take command of the Sentinels, Mikael, but be warned. The council has not forgotten your past."

Mikael bowed so low his face almost touched his knees, and promptly took his leave.

* * *

"Do we think it wise to promote Mikael once more?" Athena asked the other Synod members, once the man had left.

"We have little choice. He is a strong leader, and one who has the most military experience. He will train, and

338

lead our forces well in the coming days," Socrates said, from the head of the table.

"Do we know who might have been behind Commander Zeus' disappearance?" Ibrahim inquired.

No one spoke.

"The loss of the commander is devastating, but we must deal with the real problem...the tainted Adjudicator, Meredox. Due to his actions, or lack thereof, Archonia's borders have been opened to the atrocities of war. We should make an example of him," Anubis said, fiercely.

Socrates held up his hands, and the others fell silent.

"Dark hours approach. It is important that we not fight amongst ourselves. We must provide our people with hope, or they will falter," he said.

"What hope?" Athena asked

"One soul saved our world from total destruction. Once again, Gabriel has led us to salvation. We must stand behind this tainted soul. His courage will be our beacon of hope," Socrates finished.

"And when he is destroyed?" Lar asked.

"We must weather this storm, my brethren. For now he will suffice."

Read next

WILLIAM OF ARCHONIA

RETALIATION

ARCHONIAN CALENDAR

Days of the week:
1. Sunday   day of the sun
2. Moonday day of the moon
3. Archday   day of the Archonia
4. Dichday   day of Dichonia
5. Earthday day of earth
6. Windday day of wind
7. Waterday day of water
8. Fireday day of fire
9. Sabbaday day of the Sabbath
10. Mediday day of rest

Months of the year:
1. Benetoch Brahma
2. Militoch   Othin
3. Sedetoch Gaia
4. Antioch   Ammun
5. Protioch   Prometheus
6. Valetoch Allah
7. Lucetoch Lucifer
8. Gabioch   Gabriel
9. Kronioch Kronos
10. Helitoch Creators

Archonian clock:
50 seconds – 1 minute
50 minutes – 1 hour
100 hours – 1 day
10 days – 1 week
10 weeks – 1 month
10 months - year

ARCHONIAN MILITARY

THE GUARDIAN CORPS:

Commander: 1
Generals: 10
Lieutenants: 100
Captains: 1000
Warriors: 100,000
Recruits: as many as needed

THE ADJUDICATOR CORPS:

Grand Justicars: 10
Justicars: 100
Judges: 1000
Arbitrators: 10,000
The Purge: as many as selected

THE SENTINEL CORPS:

Commander: 1
Chiefs: 100
Officers: 10,000
Captains: 1,000,000
Peacekeepers: 1,000,000,000+

LOCATIONS:

Earth: The mortal plane of existence bearing physical boundaries of a massive universe.

Limbo: The spirit world between the mortal and immortal worlds. Archonian essences that have not been chosen to live in Archonia linger here until they are either taken to Dichonia by demons known as reapers or are destroyed.

Archonia: The immortal world outside of the physical boundaries of the universe. It was created by the Archons as a place for mankind's souls to dwell after their mortal life.

Helios: The city of light where the majority of untainted Archonian souls dwell in peace. It is the home of the great Synod and the location of Valhalla the center of military forces of Archonia.

Ionia: Another city that dwells within the light. It is the location of one of the obelisks of protection created by the life force of the Archon Brahma.

Ovaria: Another city that dwells within the light. It is the location of another obelisk of protection created by the life force of the Archon Ammun.

Dichonia: The immortal world that was created by the Archon's Kronos and Othin on the same plane of existence as Archonia, made as a prison for their Brother Lucifer who betrayed them all.

Greige forge: Where Archonian warriors go to create their armor. Found at the peak of Mt. Olympus. This is the final trial to become an Archonian soldier.

Scione: pronounced (zion); a great city that houses the soldiers that guard the white ward, a great wall of stone separating the light and shadow. Enchanted with the power of the two obelisks of protection it is the barrier that keeps the evil of Dichonia at bay.

Oblivion: beyond the great mountains surrounding Archonia there lays an endless fog. Space where time has no meaning and even the immortal souls of Archonia can't exist. Perhaps a way to contain the power of the Archons set down by the creators. Little is understood about this place.

The Garden of Medina: a place of life, and great beauty in Archonia. Every plant in it was created by an Archonian's projection

The Signets of Hangaku Gozen:

The Signet of Wrath
(William)

The Signet of Jealousy
(Angelica)

www.ingramcontent.com/pod-product-compliance
Lightning Source LLC
Chambersburg PA
CBHW071155100726
47908CB00002B/384